ROSETTA ALLAN is a writer of prose and poetry. Her work is widely anthologised, and she has published two volumes of poetry, *Little Rock* (2007) and *Over Lunch* (2010). Her first novel, *Purgatory*, was published by Penguin in 2014 and was selected by Apple Books as one of the best reads of that year. Rosetta has received the Kathleen Grattan Poetry Award, the Metonymy Best Poem Award, a South Pacific Pictures Emerging Writers' Lab internship, a Sir James Wallace Master of Creative Writing Scholarship, and a Michael King Writers Centre Emerging Writers Residency, and is the 2019 University of Waikato & Creative New Zealand Writer in Residence. In 2016, she was the first New Zealander to take up the St Petersburg Art Residency, located within the Museum of Nonconformist Art in Russia where she spent time researching *The Unreliable People*.

THE UNRELIABLE PEOPLE

ROSETTA ALLAN

PENGUIN BOOKS

PENGUIN

UK | USA | Canada | Ireland | Australia
India | New Zealand | South Africa | China

Penguin is an imprint of the Penguin Random House group of companies,
whose addresses can be found at global.penguinrandomhouse.com.

Penguin
Random House
New Zealand

First published by Penguin Random House New Zealand, 2019

1 3 5 7 9 10 8 6 4 2

Cover design by James Allan © Penguin Random House New Zealand
Text design by Rachel Clark © Penguin Random House New Zealand
Cover photograph by Creative Exchange NZ Ltd.
Author photograph by Colleen Maria Lenihan
Prepress by Image Centre Group
Printed and bound in Australia by Griffin Press,
an Accredited ISO AS/NZS 14001 Environmental Management Systems Printer

A catalogue record for this book is available from
the National Library of New Zealand.

ISBN 978-0-14-377356-6
eISBN 978-0-14-377357-3

The assistance of Creative New Zealand towards the production
of this book is gratefully acknowledged by the publisher.

ARTS COUNCIL OF NEW ZEALAND TOI AOTEAROA

penguin.co.nz

MIX
Paper from
responsible sources
FSC™ C009448

For Uncle John,
my hero

*If you but knew the flames that burn in me which
I attempt to beat down with my reason.*
Alexander Pushkin

RED LEATHER GLOVES
ALMA-ATA, KAZAKHSTAN, USSR — 1974

Katerina arrived on a flight from Vladivostok in the early after-noon, the plan already devised for the abduction of the Sharm child. There was no baggage to collect — a single shoulder bag contained all she needed, including a child's Siberian sheepskin coat and a pair of size four, blue rubber boots. Katerina marched through the station to the cubical outside the main entrance to catch a bus, hoping to beat the crowds, but the queue outside was already well established, commuters layered front to back with hands thrust deep into pockets, shoulders hunched against the cold. She stopped short of the line, wincing at the length of it, raised her shawl over her head and waited for another option to present itself, illegal as it would be, but she was no stranger to acting illicitly when she needed to.

A young Russian man leaned against a concrete pillar to her right. She could feel him sizing her up and returned a slanted, collusive stare, then turned away and waited as he sauntered over.

I can get you to the city in quick time, he whispered in her ear.

Ten roubles. Katerina spoke into her open handbag, pretending to look for a handkerchief.

Twenty, he said.

She shut her handbag with a snap of the metal clasp and offered sixteen and no more. Cowboy cab rates, and they both knew it. He hesitated, so she stepped towards the end of the queue. When he tapped her arm, she knew the deal was done and changed course, following the track of his footsteps through the dirty slush and on to the clean snow across the road.

The car, an old-style ZAZ, was parked at an awkward angle in the sparsely populated car park. Its compact size made the height of the cabin look out of proportion to its length. Like an insect, Katerina thought, with its rounded edges and large globular windows. Hardly luxurious, but owning such a thing was a privilege, and given the age of the driver, this one most probably belonged to an older relative.

Katerina shuffled onto the backseat, filling it with a flurry of snow. The moment she settled in, the tingle started inside her gloves on a couple of her fingertips — one tiny, itchy, pinprick at first, one single bead of blood forming, then another, and another, spreading through the notched rings of her fingerprints. She brought her hands to rest in her lap, palms up, in the hope that the bleeding would stop once the car started and her mind tuned in elsewhere.

Your father must be an important man to own such a car, she said.

So-so, the young man said, and he switched the radio on loud, beating out the rhythm of a song with his thumbs on the steering wheel.

The car pulled onto the main highway, wipers working double-time, scratching the dry-frosted windscreen that was in need of a good scrape. Condensation was doing its work on the inside as well, exposing the pattern of an earlier wipe from either a cloth or a sleeve. The car must have been sitting idle for a good while, she realised. She was most likely his only customer of the day. Should have bartered harder.

The young man turned the fan on high, creating two rounded hills stretching up the foggy front window. Katerina unhooked her bag from her shoulder, relaxed the scarf knot beneath her chin, and tucked herself in behind the driver's seat, where the rear-vision mirror couldn't reach. There, she was free to watch the landscape go by in private and relive the sadness of her time spent in that region, as a young woman, alone in a *kolkhoz* not far away in Ushtobe. Every time she returned it was the same — the memories danced before her with a haunting accuracy that refused to fade over time the way sad dreams ought to.

Fields of white-coated scrubland sped past the window like a faded old movie. Icicled sagebrush was soon replaced with thin tree trunks that flickered black and white, a pretty sight that would usually bring pleasure, but in her state of unease Katerina did not register the beauty. Instead, she looked for the ghosts of the old people from Ushtobe; only there was no one there, or at least no one who wanted to make themselves known to Katerina.

Barbed-wired-enclosed factories soon gave way to apartment blocks and stores, cable cars and buses, squares with statues of Soviet heroes. By the time they neared the inner city, the pearls of blood had seeped into the lining of Katerina's gloves. She squeezed the tops of her thighs, feeling the warm squelch of blood in the cushioned softness of the fine woven wool.

When the car pulled into the kerb to let her out, Katerina removed one of her gloves. The blood from her fingers smeared across the face of Lenin on the ten-rouble note. It didn't matter — the young man couldn't see it. No one could. The smudged red prints were her own personal horror — evidence of the malignant guilt mercilessly haunting her since being severed from her child and her husband. Trauma that seeped from her fingertips whenever the past and the present crossed each other like a large red X— and in the centre of that X was her Nikolai.

Katerina found a store that sold fizzy water and syrup for three *kopeks*. Without her own jar to pour the fizz into, a screw-top bottle cost her another three *kopeks*. She slipped a paper cup into her bag, determined not to have to pay for that as well. Katerina then pointed at an assortment of packaged snacks and waited at the till. The money she dropped onto the counter beside the items to be sure that her hand would not be touched.

Vodka? the shop assistant offered in a flat, emotionless voice, crystal-blue eyes stark against the forest green of her starched service tunic.

Cigarettes?

Not today, Katerina motioned with a shake of her head and waited for her change.

The attendant dropped Katerina's coins one by one on the counter by way of protest for not having the right change. With everyone needing small change for quick transactions, Katerina wasn't going to leave hers behind. As there wasn't a change dish, Katerina was forced to drag the coins across the Formica top and drop them into her cupped palm, careful not to show the difficulty of such a small task.

An old gypsy sat outside on a square of matting, and when Katerina came through the doors the old woman bowed over on her knees, face hidden under a shawl, arms stretched out in front with shaking red hands cupped and ungloved in the cold.

Prayer for a coin, the gypsy offered.

Katerina dropped a coin in the woman's palm and walked on without waiting. She did not need someone else's prayers, but the last old gypsy she'd shunned at a bus station followed her to a café and glared murderously through the glass, jinxing Katerina, she was sure of it. With every spoonful of soup, Katerina had felt more and more damned. They were everywhere, and Katerina dared not tempt their resolve today.

The Sharm child's apartment was just a short walk away. The greater part of the Koryo-saram community had moved from Ushtobe into the city of Alma-Ata when Stalin died, when they were at last free to travel — at least within Kazakhstan. Most took residence near the city centre within the blocks of repetitious medium-rise buildings that stood solemn and gloomy from neglect, rust weeping down from the gutters. All of these buildings looked the same, but Katerina knew the path to the apartment with the child. Years earlier she had searched, and although there were many Koryo-saram residing in the city at the time, there weren't many with the last name Sharm, so the mother hadn't been difficult to find.

Initially, Katerina watched the child from a distance, but twice before she had made her way to the apartment.

There she had waited until the streets quietened, the curtains in the buildings were closed, and the children were put to bed early enough for mothers to get some peace. That's when Katerina dared to tap on the bedroom window. She never gave the child anything that would leave evidence of her visit. Just small chocolates or candies that could be devoured quickly — the wrappers hidden away inside Katerina's bag. Once she was bold enough to visit the kindergarten at the ceramic factory where the mother worked. The kindergarten was so understaffed that she was able to push the child on a swing in the playground for half an hour without anyone bothering to ask who she was.

—

From the back of the apartment building Katerina had a clear view of the windows that housed the Sharm woman and her child. The apartment was located on the ground floor, with easy access to a spacious courtyard with trees that were no doubt pretty in the spring. But it was not spring. The trees were barren, and against the snow-powdered tiers of apartment floors their branches looked like black fleshless limbs — more dead than alive in the velvety darkness of advancing night. Most of the windows were curtained in respectful, neutral tones, the light shining through in amber gleams, but a few burst with the colours of the times, including the child's curtains: a clash of purple, red, pink, and white, with geometric patterns that could be flowers or kidneys, or kissing creatures.

The trees lined a walkway to the back of the building, where gas pipes ran above ground and met other pipes possessing pressure valves that looked like steering wheels on tractors. Here Katerina was, for the most part, left on her own. Still, she knew it would be smart to be quick when the time came. She twisted the top of the bottle and the fizz sprayed like a sprinkler through the sides of the lid. Katerina held the bottle away from herself and opened it quickly to allow the excess foam to dribble into the snow where it left a soiled brown indent.

A small paper bag contained the sleeping herbs she'd prepared before leaving Vladivostok. Half a teaspoon, she estimated, would do. She tapped the side of the bag, and when it looked as though enough had fallen into the paper cup, she gave the mixture a gentle swirl. Tiny fireworks spat from the cup before it ran out of fury and settled down.

Katerina had never given the sleeping herbs to a child before, and for a moment she worried about the side-effects. When she took the herbs herself, she usually woke with a stomach-ache that took a few hours to disappear. A child might vomit; surely though, that would be the worst of it.

Her heart thumped and she felt a sudden rush of anxiety. She loosened her shawl from her mouth and tucked it under her chin, drew in a deep breath to calm herself, the cold air raking the insides of her throat.

She waited long enough for the mother to deliver a bedtime story and a kiss. When the overhead light went out, and only a dim light tinted the corner of the curtain, she placed two empty crates onto the snow and stepped up to tap the glass of the window.

Kanaiji oneora, she said, with just enough energy to carry through the glass so only the child would hear.

At first, the side of the curtain opened a fraction, so a

slit of gentle light slanted across the corner of Katerina's chest, then the curtain was thrown back, and the little face was there, beaming, with the same chestnut eyes that once belonged to her Nikolai.

Shhh, Katerina said pressing a finger to her lips, wide-eyed and mischievous as if it were part of a game.

The child unfastened the window latch to the inner window, then the outer, and sat back, waiting, with eager expectation in the openness of her smile. The head of her bed was nestled against the outer wall, just beneath the ledge of the window. A bed too big for only one body. Katerina leaned over the sill to touch the cheek of the child, but the pillows caused her to draw back. Mud-markers. It made her want to laugh. All four corners of the pillow slips were smudged with thumbprints of mud — such an old and tragic superstition.

Katerina guided the cup of fizz to the child's mouth. Drink, she whispered, and the girl took hold of the cup and tipped it too quickly, causing a little stream that slipped down her chin and soaked into the smocking of her nightdress before Katerina could readjust the angle. Enough now, Katerina said and took hold of the cup, but the child was reluctant to let go and stood as the cup was being taken away, her feet padding the mattress, making it squeak like a hungry mouse. Shhh, Katerina said again, and they both froze. Katerina listened for the sound of the mother's feet in the hall, ready to run if need be.

But the mother didn't come. The muted clap of dish against dish continued undisturbed in the room next door — a mother busy inside the details of her domestic chores, braiding strands of a song Katerina recognised from the days of her own innocence. A lullaby. A song of love. A blessing that had no power to keep her child from being taken away, just as it had been for Katerina's baby.

Good girl, Katerina said. She shook the last of the foam from the cup then covered the evidence with a fresh layer of snow. The cup she tucked away inside her bag with the bottle.

Mud markers. Katerina leaned in, wondering at their worth. She dared to touch the pillow on the side where the mother must sleep, unsure what she expected to feel, but there was no energy there — nothing to catch her conscience by the tail. She tugged at the fingers of a glove and pressed her naked hand into the curve of the pillow to see if that made any difference. There was no warmth there — no connection or snare of guilt to change Katerina's mind. A bad place to dream, Katerina clicked her tongue and stretched her hand to fill every crevice of the glove again, pleased with the five bloody fingerprints she had left behind in an almost-circle. The shape of a head, perhaps. A halo of sorts. A bad place to sleep — beside a window, where the moon shines down and robs all the energy. If this woman were her daughter, she would know this.

Come, little puppy, Katerina said.

The child shifted to the window ledge so Katerina could lift her down onto the crates. She quickly dressed the child in the Siberian coat and blue boots before they set off. The coat was lovely the way it splayed below the burnt orange sash; only it was too big. The girl was smaller than Katerina expected. Rolling the sleeves over and folding pleats of fabric beneath the sash was as much as she could do. The coat covered almost everything, including a great deal of the child's face. One tiny blue boot nipped out in front of the fur trim, disappearing as the other one jutted forward. Just like the characters in the wooden weather-house Katerina remembered from her childhood home. Perhaps she could buy one for the child when they reached her city?

On board the trolley-bus, the little one yawned and yawned.

Babulya, she murmured and nestled onto Katerina's lap, her arms around Katerina's neck, at first firm, then wilting.

Katerina held the child to her chest and rocked as she hummed, thinking about that wooden weather-house that hung on the wall beside the front door of her parents' home. The night the first knock came, the weatherman in the blue shorts and suspenders was out. The night her father and brother were taken for questioning by the secret militia, no neighbours came out of their houses. No one dared even to turn on a light. They all hid like the woman with the flower basket in her yellow dress, fearful of the black raven parked in the street. The little wooden man was out though — the charm of his innocent smile much more menacing than it had ever appeared before. Perhaps there are weather-houses that have animals instead of humans, or two women, or two children. Any of those options would be better than the man in blue shorts and the coward woman with the flower basket.

The top of the child's head was as warm and soft as a kitten. Katerina rested her cheek there and watched the people on the pavements as the trolley-bus passed them by, unafraid of who might see her by this point. Her large shawl draped down the sides of her face and around her neck, hiding most of the details of her face anyway. The face of anonymity. The look of any one of the babushkas on the street in their thick winter coats, shawls and rubber boots, face down, praying that no spears of icicles would fall from the guttering above to kill them in the street.

By the time they reached their stop, the child was droopy, but not yet asleep, so Katerina carried her into the station. Katerina's legs were strong and reliable from years of dancing, but the hip, it wasn't happy, and it ground in the socket each time her left leg swung forward with its load. She crouched to catch her breath, the child leaning into the fur of Katerina's collar, fingers of one hand hooked into her mouth.

Look at that, Katerina said and pointed up at the mural that spread across the wall above the ticket booths. The mural had seen better days. It reflected the celebration of music and dance that represented the mix of cultures in Kazakhstan. Produced in the robust styling of Soviet art, it was still lovely. Towards the front was the Koryo-saram dancer with the open fan that Katerina had modelled for when she was new to the travelling Korean theatre. Such an honour it was to be chosen. Seeing it again after such a long time was bittersweet. As if it were the crumbling façade of her own beauty or the lost honour that once belonged to the Koryo-saram. They were always such a peaceable people. Gullible perhaps. Stalin had promised them liberation and land, a joyful life as a Soviet, when what he really wanted was slaves. But what could they do?

The voices of travellers sounded hard and cold bouncing off the marble walls of the railway station. The overhead speaker crackled and hissed with the command for final boarding. Katerina had hardly recovered, but she scooped the child up onto her complaining hip and made her way to platform two.

Outside, the white lights on tall poles took on a spectral air as the mist of early evening drifted in to cover the city for the night. The teal colour of the train's carriages felt chilly in contrast to the golden light spilling from windows across the concrete. Diesel fumes smelt like a traveller's welcome. Katerina drew them deep into her lungs and pushed herself on to find their carriage. With just a few minutes to spare, they boarded the train — the child getting heavier and heavier as Katerina scanned the numbers down the aisle in search of their hideaway. The sounds of passengers settling in for the overnight trip seeped through open compartment doors — the murmured excitement of voices tucking themselves away inside closed compartments, the shuffle of claiming beds and stowing belongings. First-class meant Katerina didn't have to share an open space with them, and when they were inside the cabin, she laid the sleepy child down on one of the bench seats, locked the door and drew the curtains shut.

One bench seat ran the length of each side of the cabin with a small table in between. The bench seats were made up into two tidy beds with the pillows at the window end of the cabin. It was tricky manoeuvring around the table that poked out from the wall. The chipped corners snagged the edges of Katerina's clothes, but she managed to switch the bedding around so the moonlight wouldn't touch their faces as they slept. She removed the child's boots and coat and tucked her in tight, facing the wall, then sat opposite to wait for their departure.

The whistle shriek outside their carriage made Katerina jump and the child stir. For a moment Katerina expected the militia to belt through the door, and drag her off to a black raven in the car park to take her away. Only when her body jerked forward from the motion of the train shunting into action could she sit back and relax. First-class was not what

Katerina had expected. The cabin was damp from the sweat of pickled-cabbage eaters, the curtains bleached and brittle from too much sunlight, and only one of the light bulbs worked. She lifted a pillow to her nose and sniffed. At least the stiff cotton slip smelt fresh.

Out in the passage, the drone of the conductor's voice grew louder and more urgent, coming closer with the dull thud of each cabin door shutting behind him. When he arrived at her door he didn't have to knock, Katerina was waiting, tickets in hand, with two fake internal passports that named them Alina and Valentina Mun. Lina, she would call the child, which was close enough to Nina. Lina Mun. The conductor clipped the tickets; Lina grizzled and released her arms from the confining blanket. Her cheeks were still flushed from the cold air. She groaned again, her eyes flickering in the drugged stupor.

Chickenpox, Katerina whispered behind a cupped hand, and the conductor backed out of the cabin with a scarcely concealed urgency that pleased her very much.

The next morning, the child was up long enough to play a few games, to eat and toilet and wash before Katerina planted more sleeping herbs into her drink. It was not ideal to keep a young one sedated, but it was easiest to keep the child in bed and out of sight, especially when she grizzled for her mama.

Read me a story? the girl murmured when Katerina checked to see whether she had drifted off.

A story. If there was one thing Katerina was good at, it was telling stories. She had spent a great portion of her adult life doing that very thing in the travelling Korean theatre.

What story would you like?

The child pulled the blankets up, so the silk-trimmed edge draped across her nose.

The rice farmer's wife, she said, the blankets stiff despite the movement of her chin.

You mean the crow king, don't you?

The little head nodded, and the blankets buckled beneath her chin to reveal a sleepy smile. The crow king was an old story that mothers told and retold their children generation after generation, and it pleased Katerina to know this tradition was being kept alive.

Tell me your name, Katerina said, as if she didn't already know. Then I'll tell you the story of the crow king.

Nina, the child said.

Is Nina short for something?

Antonina Sharm, she said.

Good girl, said Katerina. However I think you look like a Mun. What if we called you Lina Mun? Would that suit you? It will be our very own make-believe name for the story.

The child didn't respond, but she also didn't object, so Katerina started the story.

A long time ago, in the land of the crows, there lived a king who ruled with terror. He would take anyone he liked, and no one could stop him. One day, a rice farmer and his wife were at home asleep in bed when the crow king's secret militia came banging on their door. In one giant swoop, the militia grabbed the woman's father, then her mother, then her husband, and flew away with them to the deep dark bowels of the Gulag from where no human had ever returned alive.

That's not the right story, Lina complained. Mama reads from the book.

A book. Katerina was unaware the crow king had been published. That's no way to tell a story. The blankets had been pulled up onto the bridge of Lina's nose again, and this time there was a squeeze of mistrust in her eyes.

Have you not heard this one? Katerina altered her poise to the dancer mode she once inhabited when telling stories to the farmers of the collectives. She touched her cheek to accentuate the gesture of puzzled innocence.

Lina shook her head.

Well, this one is even better than . . . She hesitated and decided it was best not to mention the mama word again. This one is much better than a book. Let me show you. Once upon a time, she began again.

Katerina stood between the two beds and moved with as much grace as the limited space allowed, enacting the steps of the crow king story with dance. Lina lay still, eyes wide with wonder, drawing in all the details of the tale while concentrating on the rolling rhythm of Katerina's hands, the puppetry of her movements, the exaggeration of her expressions.

In the Korean fable, the crow creature was half-man, half-bird, with an army of crows, each one as large as a human. Most people told a simple story of a woman being abducted by the king and her husband battling to get her back, but Katerina liked to infuse the retelling with the details of her own story. A real story.

In her tale, the crow king sent an entire community into exile, including the rice farmer's wife. However, her rice farmer was left behind, and, like the husband in the tale, he swore that he would find his wife again, even though the way was rough and gloomy, and he could barely see through the white mist. Twelve doors he had to open, and at each entry, the crow king's men kept watch, waiting to kill him. However, he knew that no matter what happened, the crow king was evil, and evil always had an end. The rice farmer eventually defied the odds and battled not only the crow king's men but the crow king himself. The rice farmer drank some magic water, so he had the spirit of the dragon within him, then used a giant sword to cut off the crow king's arms. Only the arms grew back. He cut off the king's legs, and they grew back too. The wings were the same. No new head could be so evil, the rice farmer thought, and when he cut off the crow king's head the fight was finally won. No new head grew in its place. For once, there was silence everywhere. The rice farmer was finally reunited with his wife, and as they left for home, they prayed that a new, gentler king would be found.

By the time Katerina came to the end of the story, Lina had fallen asleep. She lay on her side, face relaxed on the pillow facing away from Katerina, so the plump youth of her cheek created a little mound that hid her nose. Her chest moved with long rises and falls that were mesmerising to watch. Katerina lay on her bed, comforted by the rhythmic clack of the train. The abduction had gone well. Much easier than expected. Deep, satisfying tiredness pressed her body into the softness of the blanket beneath her. She was pleased with the natural connection she had with the child. She had no idea what she would have done if there had been a fuss. It was an option too hard to fathom — an option she hadn't planned for, and one she was glad she didn't have to deal with.

Katerina closed her eyes and drifted away to the place where she dreamed of the child's mother when she opened the bedroom door to the empty room, where the drawn curtains swelled in the breeze. The mother hesitated before them, frightened by what horror she might see outside the window. A dead husband with a bullet in his head. A stone-cold baby wrapped in silk shawls. But those were Katerina's fears. The mother saw what she most dreaded — the track of footsteps in the ankle-deep snow that led across the courtyard, past the trees, the gas pipes, and the rubbish bins. The pain was the same for all mothers who lost their children. The wound for Katerina was universal, powerful and tormenting. She had seen too many die in the fields of Ushtobe to be sensitive to this one woman's loss. And even before Ushtobe, there was the train. The ghost train, they called it.

—

The child's mother felt the chill the moment she opened the bedroom door. Her stomach plummeted, pulling her heart down with the weight of the unbearable truth that her baby was no longer in the room. The absence propelled her forward, to whatever terrible truth lay beyond the open window. She climbed out into the snow in her slippers, to follow the footsteps all the way to the kerb of the street, where the track mixed with the treads of other boots.

Antonina! she cried in a bellow so violent and primal that her child should have heard it.

No sound came back to her. She ran to the corner, where nothing but fear faced her. Nothing but disbelief. Behind her, fresh snowfall was already filling in the evidence of the footprints. The bedroom curtain flapped in the open window, pink and purple — red hearts split in two.

By mid-afternoon, the train charged closer to the bridge that crossed the Irtysh River — the last bastion before the station of Semipalatinsk. Lina had been up for two hours, and Katerina used the time to teach the dance that called up the ancestors, just as the *mudang* had shown her. It could have waited until they reached Vladivostok, but the anticipation of passing through Semipalatinsk was too great. Katerina needed to know whether her rice farmer would come and find her after all these years, the child with the blood of Nikolai's sister in her veins being the connector Katerina needed.

But the Sharm child wouldn't complete the dance. My name is Moon she kept saying, mispronouncing the Mun of Katerina's family name so often that it sounded deliberate. And as much as Katerina tried to coax Lina on, she remained miserable and teary-eyed. Her cheeks were still as flushed as when they had started the journey, her temperature was up, but she hadn't vomited, and she had eaten some of the snacks, so the herbs weren't making her unreasonably ill. Her temper, on the other hand, her silent little glare when she didn't want to dance — that was a difficulty Katerina found she lacked the skill to push beyond.

Soon nothing Katerina could do would settle Lina. Not the suggestion of a new story. Not a game of I-spy. Not a hug. Not even a gentle chide. In the end, Katerina gave up and loaded a swill of sweetened tea with even more sedative. When Lina refused to drink, Katerina forced the child's mouth open and spooned as much as possible through the stubborn lips. Lina pulled away and sulked beneath the table. A little while later she was subdued again, and guilt at the brutality of what she had done caught up with Katerina. It hurt to think that motherhood hadn't come as naturally as it could have, and the realisation that she should have left the child alone was starting to gnaw at the edges of Katerina's conscience. She knew the *mudang* did not intend for a child to do the dance, but if Nikolai had been expecting a child to be part of Katerina's life, surely he would be drawn to his bloodline through this one.

Lina was still awake, but droopy. Not happy, but manageable. She came back to sit on Katerina's knee, making them both hotter than they needed to be, her snotty nose pressed against Katerina's chest, leaving tracks on her dress like a snail. Katerina extracted a handkerchief from her pocket to wipe the small face, and the medal that once belonged to her husband's father fell onto the seat. The red ribbon rose that her mother-in-law had sewn around the outside was now faded, but the red banner was as bright as new, with the words *Proletarians of the World, Unite!* still legible above the red star with the hammer and sickle. The child flicked her fingers, demanding the little trinket, so Katerina showed her how to make the catch on the back squeak by turning the little lever to and fro. A few small hiccups of amused laughter escaped Lina's lips. The simple unexpected joy pacified them both, so Katerina allowed the girl to keep hold of the medal. Just for a while. She would take it back soon.

Lina sat in Katerina's lap turning the lever so it sounded like the chirp of a baby bird, cheerful and mild — an idea the child liked when Katerina mentioned it. Katerina rested her head back against the wall, resolving not to think any more of her Nikolai for the rest of the journey. To think of him was like pressing an old wound. The desire never did die.

The view passing by the train window could have been the same expanse they had passed through an hour earlier, two hours earlier, half a day earlier. All the steppes looked the same — miles of windswept snow, here and there a ramshackle farm, then nothing but flat scrubland with power-poles following the train tracks with a road running parallel.

After a while, the lever on the back of the medal stopped chirping, and the farms gave way to the pine forests just outside of Semipalatinsk. White birch trees and black firs raced past the window like chequered flags. Soon they would come to the Irtysh River, then the city where Katerina would need to disembark to buy supplies. She had not brought many provisions on board as most travellers did. No wheels of cheese in string bags. No pot-bellied jars of mayonnaise, pickles, cooked chickens, or bologna. Katerina had depended on the packaged snacks she'd bought earlier, and the nibble-sized packets of salted nuts that were available for purchase on board the train, and they had left her thirsty and unsatisfied. Now she longed for a slice of black bread, tomatoes, some boiled eggs or sausages. Simple food. Good food.

Semipalatinsk. They would be out of Kazakhstan by midnight and into the vast expanse of Siberia. But first, there was Semipalatinsk — a turbulent district that marked the place of her baby's death. Since then, Katerina had been through the city a few times in the days of the travelling Korean theatre, though never by train. It had been over three decades since she crossed the bridge outside the city, but she recognised the hideous sound of it as they approached.

As far as Katerina knew, the screaming bridge was a myth, but nevertheless she thought it wise to fear it. During her years as a dancer, she had learnt that the simplest of fables could be grounded in the skeletons of truth, and if anyone was susceptible to stories of the living dead, it was those who had lost the most. To the Koryo-saram, the shrill cry of the train rushing through the arched metal framework was not the wind, as mothers often told their children it was. It was the ghosts of those who had died during the deportations; restless spirits cursed to roam the length of the railway track for eternity in search of their loved ones, unable to return home to Vladivostok, to the arms of their ancestors, or those who grieved their loss. Abandoned — *Arirang, Arirang* — said the popular song of the Korean theatre, although Katerina refused to sing it.

She held the small, warm head of the child firmly against her chest. They moved together with the rhythm of the train, the child's hands resting in her lap, the little medal almost falling from her loose fingers. Katerina lingered on the memory of her dead baby wrapped in his silk cocoon, nestled inside the arms of Nikolai's father — the dead within the dead. She could have lain down in the snow and let herself pass away as well, but there was the hope of her Nikolai. He would come for her, he had said. How could either of them know that their child would not survive? And if the curse of the screaming bridge were real, then he still wouldn't know. A cruel thought.

The chain of carriages stretched out ahead of Katerina's window. She watched as they took the curve of the track, the nose of the engine out front leaving the land for the steel bridge where the souls of the doomed had gathered. Shadows crossed the grey metal struts like clouds, which Katerina soon realised were the restless spirits of her people, just as the myth described. A phenomenon she had never experienced before. The dance must have opened the door. There was no other explanation. Dabbling in shamanism was dangerous, and wrong. She knew that now, but it was too late. The number of shadows was significant, and there was nothing she could do but watch the nightmare approach.

The winding silver braids of the river looked pretty in the afternoon light, but Katerina could smell the rotting carcass of its muddy banks — or was that the bile rising in her throat? In the next cabin, voices lifted in mock howling sounds, preparing for the crossing in their own way. A song came to mind, but it was best not to open her mouth in case one of the cursed tried to steal her teeth. She hummed instead — the sound snagging in her throat as if caught by fish bones. The train charged across the bridge, and the fingers of the cursed reached through the glass window. She hummed louder as she searched for her husband in the blur of metal and eyes passing by. She listened for him in the wind-rushing screams, but he was not there. Of course he wouldn't be there, she scolded herself — he didn't die on the train. He had been left behind in Vladivostok — his spirit would have a greater distance to cross to find her. He wouldn't give up the search though, would he?

Children skittered by in the passageway outside the cabin door. A man's voice ordered them to stop and walk, and they did, but only briefly. Lina stirred in Katerina's lap with a whimper, her tiny hands clamped shut and shaking, her face tucked into the middle of Katerina's breasts.

Can you see them, too? Katerina wanted to ask, but instead she hummed and patted the child's back, keeping her lips clenched. The shadows on the railing grew larger and seemed to recognise her. Some of them entered the space of the cabin bearing questions — so many of them tangled together that it was difficult to decipher what they were saying. They surrounded her, and yes, they said, they remembered. They didn't mention the word, but the accusation of betrayal prickled Katerina's flesh, and she wondered whether it was these shadows that blocked her husband's way to find her.

Arirang, Arirang, the shadows chanted in unison. They circled over and around her, like eels. *Dear one who abandoned us here*, they sang, *shall not walk even ten ri before her feet will hurt. Arirang, Arirang* . . .

The train's rocking did not comfort her anymore. It was not me who left you here, Katerina wanted to say, but that wasn't entirely true. Lina squirmed away under the table, the soft pat of her feet heading for the bed. Katerina dared not move. Dared not speak, nor intervene, but she prayed. Prayed the shadows would not poison the young mind of a child. Prayed for forgiveness for visiting the *mudang* priest. Promised she wouldn't do it again.

Once upon a time, there was a princess.

One of the shadows was entering Lina with a story. The wrong story. Katerina wanted to tell her to cover her ears, tell her to hum, and close her mouth. The shadows plucked at the chords of Katerina's spine as if they were the strings of an instrument. They asked for favours, for messages, for love. Yes, yes, she nodded just to quieten their grief. All the while she tried to hear the rest of the story being told to the child, but only fragments reached through the noise.

The rice farmer locked his wife in the highest room of the house, but the rice farmer's wife knew how to bewitch his sister, and soon the door was unlocked. The rice farmer's wife escaped

into the night to trade secrets and lies with the crow king's men,
and as she did, her fingertips burned to coal.

A bad story. The wrong story. Why were the cursed ones telling the wrong story?

One by one the shadows retreated. Crossing the river lasted just a few minutes, but by the time the train had left the bridge, Katerina's back ached from their pinching. In that short time she was weakened and damaged. Only when the train had passed through the industrial outskirts of Semipalatinsk did Katerina feel safe enough to speak without fear. She smoothed down the sides of her hair with the flat of her palms, expecting to find some dishevelment as if she'd been caught in a gust of wind, but the French twist was as tidy as ever.

Are you all right, little puppy? she said.

Lina turned over in her bed and scrunched the blanket under her chin, her expression all flint and flower petals. She opened her mouth with the kind of silent, agonised, pitiful bawl that would never save anyone lost in the woods. A string of drool stretched from lip to lip, and tears slipped across her temple. Katerina swept back the hair that had stuck to the small, sweaty forehead, the leather of her gloves failing to transfer the warmth and care she wanted to convey.

Hush, little puppy, she said. I promise we'll be there soon. And it was true. The journey that had taken about five weeks in 1937, to travel all the way from Vladivostok to Ushtobe, now lasted less than a week.

When the sound did find its way into the child's throat, all she could manage was a drawn-out, heart-wrenching cry for her mama that shocked Katerina to the core.

The train reduced speed as it rumbled through the suburbs, then deeper into the heart of the city, and the child's bawling settled into the occasional convulsing gasp of breath. When they drew into the station the brakes ground, metal on metal, and the clacking rock of the cabin calmed to a gentle sway. A line of vendors stood along the platform with goods for sale in baskets on blankets or foldout tables. Something was cooking on an open grill, and smoke billowed with the pleasing aroma of pancakes, and even through the closed window Katerina could smell they were good. There would be plenty of time to reach them when the child was asleep. Only she was still not sleeping.

It appeared Lina had grown stronger, and more resilient to the sedative. Katerina would have to try something else to get her to sleep. It had been a long time, but there was another trick she knew. During the first years of the Korean theatre, she was responsible for the chores, the cooking, the washing, and the putting of babies to sleep while the performers were busy with distinguished visitors. It was then that she learnt how to apply the sleep massage that quietened the babies. Katerina wasn't sure whether it would work on a child of four, but thankfully, Lina was already partway there, her eyes half-closed as if watching fairies in the air just beyond the tip of her nose.

Katerina removed a glove. The fingertips didn't bleed, which surprised her after the ordeal of the bridge. There wasn't even a tingle — a good sign. She waited for one of Lina's lazy blinks, as if catching a wave, before she stroked the top of the child's head. When the eyes remained closed, Katarina dared to circle the tiny face, her cheeks, her ears, and around her temples.

Shhhh, Katerina said over and over with a looping rhythm. Shhhh, until the child no longer stirred.

The moment Katerina stepped down from the train the cold air took hold of the insides of her nose. She wrapped her shawl around the lower part of her face and covered her mouth with the extra padding of her hand, eager not to think of the baby she had left there over thirty years earlier. Anxious to get back to the Sharm child as quickly as possible, to the security of their cabin, she approached the first vendor she came to with the intention of paying whatever was asked, no negotiation needed. Some raisin-studded pound cakes and a jar of fresh milk caught her eye. She handed over her money and looked up only when her change was given.

Katerina clasped the coins and recoiled, her hand held to her chest. The vendor stared back with reptilian green eyes, blinking casually, unresponsive to Katerina's reaction. The eyes were so far apart that they almost rounded the side of the woman's temples. The rise of her forehead extended like a misshapen melon, slightly dented on the side, the largeness of her disfigured head clearly apparent beneath the cover of her woollen hat.

Katerina studied the full platform to see if anyone else had seen the strangeness of her vendor. But all she noticed were the other unfortunates. A man with skin folded over his eyes so he couldn't see. Flaps of excess skin covering his entire face. Children with cleft lips and missing limbs. A woman with melting features and a bottom lip that drooped like a pannier over the back wheel of a pushbike. Semipalatinsk was a city of monsters like she had never seen. They were everywhere, families of them lining up for photographs with train passengers. Smile, they said, but what grotesque stretches of the mouth they were, all of them, the passengers too. How could they pay for such a thing?

Katerina was gathering herself to take another look at her own wide-eyed vendor when the ground rumbled, and the windows of the station rattled against their frames. Some of the fruit tumbled from their neat mounds in small avalanches across the tables that were caught by the vendors before they fell to the ground. Katerina reached for something to hold and found an arm, a sturdy arm. Then, just as quickly as it started, the rumble subsided.

It's all right, the crocodile woman said. It's just the bombs. The nuclear bombs. They're detonated over in Kurchatov. You're safe here. They can't reach us.

The Polygon. Katerina had heard of it, but it wasn't a nuclear detonation that was making her feel sick. She caught sight of a militiaman stepping out of the station door. He glanced their way, then headed towards the engine. Katerina let go of the crocodile woman's arm and crouched between vendors as if to examine the fabric of a souvenir tea towel, keeping an eye on the militiaman until he stepped into the first carriage of the train. She clenched her teeth and nipped the edge of her tongue.

What had she been thinking? This was all too much. Too overwhelming. She had only just survived the last time the world set itself against her. She was a young woman then, and here she was, middle-aged and doing it again. Who was she to steal a child for her own selfish needs, anyway?

Katerina stood, and this time she saw only kindness in the poor vendor's face. Her fingers squelched inside her gloves, and the blood in her mouth tasted metallic. The handkerchief she padded her damp lips with came away smeared and she stared at it as if trying to interpret the shape of something to foretell her future. You are not the beautiful person your husband once thought you were, she told herself. Or, at least, who you once were before the government ruined everything. But that gave her no excuse for what she had done.

You dropped your milk, the crocodile said, and she was right — the jar lay broken at Katerina's feet, the milk splattered up her pantyhose. Would you like another?

No, Katerina said, and she bent to pick up the shards of broken glass, but the woman told her to leave it.

You should lie down, the woman said with pity in her voice, and she handed Katerina another jar of milk from her basket.

Katerina felt as if her features were distorting in the reflection of the woman's kindness. Her own face mutating into the monster hidden within. She pushed her change into her coat pocket with the chink of brass hitting brass. It was time to go, but instead of heading straight back to the train, Katerina went into the station and bought a new train ticket. One-way back to Alma-Ata.

In the semi-darkened cabin, Lina's breathing was slow and quiet, her elbows up next to her ears on the pillow like a baby. She wasn't too disturbed when Katerina wrapped her in the blanket and carried her across the tracks to board the southbound train. Inside the new cabin, Katerina tucked Lina into bed and closed the curtains. The raisin cakes were placed on the table, and under the edge of the jar of milk, she slid a cardboard label with the name Antonina Sharm and the mother's address.

Go well, little puppy, she whispered, and she sent a small prayer towards the sky so the child would reach the safety of her mother without harm. Perhaps the mud markers had worked, after all, she thought as she pressed her cheek against the softness of Lina's hands.

I'm sorry, she said. I would have liked to know you better.

And then she left.

Katerina couldn't watch as the child's train pulled out, but she felt it leave — a quick amputation, but an amputation nonetheless. Her own train was still headed for the north. The curtains closed off the outside world, the room no longer smelling of cabbage, but of the child and the sweet sweat Katerina's herbs had caused. Unbearable. As soon as the train was in motion, Katerina opened the window and left to tuck herself into the toilet at the end of the carriage while her compartment aired. There was barely enough room to lift her elbows, and she puzzled at how she had managed to fit in there earlier with the child. Light and darkness fell on her face from all the wrong angles in the mirror. The naked bulb made her reflection appear gaunt and segmented. Pitiable, and she understood what the crocodile woman had seen.

Another passenger banged on the door and asked her to hurry up.

Find another one, she said, her voice firm.

The passenger continued to grumble and thump, but Katerina refused to budge. She was not ready to face the compartment yet, and soon enough the passenger gave up waiting. Alone again, Katerina was forced to face herself. Around her, everything trembled. It was over. She had failed.

The pain of separation felt the same as it ever did; even after three decades it still bit hard.

Enough, she told herself, and determined not to feel sorry for herself.

She threw her gloves to the floor with disgust and held the gold casing of her powder foundation in her bare hands, no longer caring that the sponge was reddening as she used it to refresh her face. When done, she rinsed the sponge and placed it over the powder inside the compact and clapped the gold case shut. She denied herself a moment longer wallowing over the loss of the child. Lina was now Nina again — their time together cut so very short. The bloodshot streaks in her eyes she put down to a migraine that was setting in. The hole inside her chest would mend as it had before, and with that she replaced her gloves and wiped everything down with the meticulousness of a murderer. The bloodied paper towels she threw into the toilet, and watched them swirl then disappear.

MY NAME IS MOON

ALMA-ATA, KAZAKHSTAN, USSR — 1977

There aren't many words of the old country that survived the homogenisation of Stalin's collective farms. Only the old people harbour much knowledge of the language, but they refuse to speak it. The fragments Antonina hears are the ones her mother hurls in moments of frustration. Angry, alien words spliced inside Russian sentences that somehow never make sense. *Gwisin* is one of these words, carried forward from the Hamgyŏng dialect. Like some little disaster, it causes grown-ups to purse their lips whenever Antonina asks what it means. Shhhh is all they say. We don't talk of such things.

Antonina isn't afraid of the *gwisin* word though, and nor is her best friend Viktor. To her mother, Viktor Andropov is that potato-nosed Russian boy, but Antonina likes the shape of his nose. She likes that his hair is fair and wispy like fluffy clouds too, not Asian-black and flat like her own. And she loves the way he comes for her when he's in the mood to run away. At eight years of age, Viktor is just one year older than Antonina. They've been neighbours ever since the abduction, when her mother packed up and moved to the small village in the Medeu Valley where the Tian Shan Mountains rise abruptly behind their homes and the vast placid steppes spread like the hem of a skirt below. The mountains are a jittery presence. Sometimes they shudder, and sometimes they growl, shaking the dust from the wooden rafters of their homes. Sometimes they send gifts of rolling stones and spongy soil into the valley, and into the river further upstream, but never into the back of the houses of their village, or her mother's workshop.

Tell Antonina why the stones don't hit us when the mountains shake, Viktor says.

His mother has two wooden pegs in her mouth so they must wait. Antonina peers through the gappy limbs of the hedge that separates the two properties, towards the workshop in the backyard, hoping her mother is within range to hear the story. The door is open, which disappoints Antonina. Her mother is always too fixated on the pottery to listen to anything when the door is open.

She throws a weed across the raised mound of the vegetable patch. It seems that all mothers must give children jobs before they're allowed to play. At least with the weeding they are outside, even though it's early April and the ground is still stiff from winter. The chill of it makes Antonina's fingers clumsy, so she digs out a handful of soil as well, and doesn't bother to shake any of it off the roots.

Well, the rocks do come down sometimes, or they used to, Mrs Andropov says and looks up at the mountain. There was a shake that took the whole village with it, and the next one further down. Gummed up the river so much that it set a new path and ran all over the place. Rattled the city so hard that it crumbled to the ground — all except the Ascension Cathedral. Divine intervention that was. Has your mother taken you to see the old church, Nina?

Antonina's mother doesn't believe in church, and Mrs Andropov knows it. No, Antonina says, concentrating harder on the weeding until her row is done.

I beat you, she says to Viktor.

No you didn't. I had more weeds on my side, so we're equal.

No. I beat you.

No you didn't. Mama, tell Antonina—

Have you done a good job, Nina? his mother interjects.

Antonina thinks she has, and she nods with confidence.

Go around the other side, then, and help Viktor.

But Antonina doesn't want to help Viktor. I won, she says so only he can hear.

Viktor scowls and plucks faster. Your weeds were baby weeds, he says. Mine are much bigger.

Antonina tries to turn the rusted knob of the outside tap. It resists her until she's almost ready to give up, then it jerks forward, gushing water on the top of her rubber boots. She stands back, leaning her hands into the spray of it, with no shock from the cold because her fingers are already numb. Viktor throws his weeds onto her side of the garden. She sees him doing it, but doesn't dare complain with his mother there. She dries her hands on her pants the way her mother tells her not to; then sits on the grass where Igor the goat tugs on his chain to reach her. Viktor is much stronger than she is. He loosens the tap with just one twist. They've argued about that before — the way he tightens it too hard.

The way she doesn't. Taps are like that, she thinks — they show the consideration of the girl for the boy, but not the boy for the girl.

Viktor drops down beside her and puffs on a wooden peg as though it's a cigarette. The air is bright with the disinfectant smell of Mrs Andropov's clean laundry. She is a silhouette on the flapping white sheet in front of them. Weak spring light plays around her, rippling her shadow, distorting her shape as it comes in and out of focus. Igor moves in and snatches the peg from Viktor's fingers, and they're both laughing when the clothesline wrenches around, and Mrs Andropov looms between the sheets.

What are you laughing at? Get that peg off the goat Viktor, hurry up.

Viktor reaches back, but Igor is too quick.

Hurry up, before he dies of choking.

Viktor's mother always talks of dying. No matter what they do, they will always die. If they don't eat enough dinner. If they don't put on their shoes. If they let the goat chew on a wooden peg. It's all the same to Mrs Andropov.

Anyway, nowadays the dam stops all the mudslides, Mrs Andropov says once the goat is no longer at risk of dying. She stoops over the clothes basket with her backside high and her head low like an old woman who can't bend her knees. It embarrasses Viktor — Antonina can feel it, and she nudges him just to be sure. Stops the river bursting its banks, says Mrs Andropov. Catches the falling rocks as well. But you never know. One day it could all collapse and take us with it, drowning like little rats, all the way down to the city.

Viktor's dedushka steps out of the back door and lowers himself with a groan onto the highest of three concrete steps.

Don't scare the children like that, he says. We're not going to be flooded again. He claps his hands and motions for the peg.

Viktor takes it over, and the old man lights the end of it with his lighter, puffing like it's a prized cigar, until Mrs Andropov sweeps past and snatches it from his mouth. Viktor looks at Antonina, which, for some reason, makes her giggle.

Careful. Nearly pulled my teeth out, Dedushka Andropov says.

He wears only the top of his false teeth — his chin sunken where the bottom ones should be. He pokes them halfway out of his mouth for the children to laugh at, and they do, not because it's funny, but because they're ugly, all orange around the edges from the tar of his cigarettes.

And you tell *me* not to frighten the children, Mrs Andropov says, but Dedushka Andropov ignores her.

You don't have to worry, he says, his teeth stowed safely away inside his mouth. The snow people protect us.

Antonina prickles with delight. She could listen to these kinds of stories a hundred times over and never tire of them. She catches her bottom lip to bite back another giggle. Dedushka Andropov waits for Viktor's mother to go inside, then slides a jar of jam out of his blazer. He twists the lid and scoops a teaspoon of the red syrup straight into his mouth.

The snow people, he says, words sticky with jam. They protect us from the anger of the mountains.

And that's why we leave the rice, isn't it, Dedushka? Viktor says.

His dedushka doesn't answer. They've lost him already. Something is happening around his feet that has drawn his attention away.

What happens if you don't leave the rice? Viktor shakes the thigh of old man's pants.

Antonina crouches to watch the jam drip from the teaspoon onto the heads of passing ants.

What happens? Viktor shakes his dedushka again, but with less conviction.

Mmhh? his dedushka lifts his head as if resurfacing from somewhere deep. The captain of the submarine, Viktor's mother, calls him, and Antonina likes to think that it was once true. Antonina likes the stories he tells about the snow people, and about the war when they conquered the Germans. He went to Germany once, and keeps a box of trinkets from that time — badges from blazers, medals, name-tags and knives. A miniature Nazi flag rolled up into the size of a sausage. Just small things. Remnants of another life, he calls them.

Dedushka? Viktor says. The snow people. What happens if you don't leave the rice?

Snow people? Viktor's dedushka lifts himself from the step and stomps on as many ants as he can. That, and that, and that . . . you see?

Told you, Viktor says, but Antonina isn't listening, she's watching a poor ant curled on its back, legs kicking for its life.

Fairy tales, Antonina's mother calls the story later that night after dinner.

But they're not fairy tales — Antonina smacks her palms against her forehead — everyone's seen them.

Really? Have you?

Yes, Antonina says, though she's sure she must be the only one in the whole world who hasn't.

What do they look like then?

They're half-human, half-animal. They command the leopards and eat the fruit of wild apples, and berries, and apricots. The rice we leave behind the apple trees keeps them happy. But you have to be quiet to see them because they run away and hide whenever they hear a human voice.

It sounds to me like you're reading from a book. Are you sure you've seen one, or are you just reciting a tale?

And if you don't leave a bowl of rice, Antonina continues with a raised voice, they won't protect you from the angry mountains, and the rocks will come down and squash us like ants. She slaps her hands on the table and makes three good sharp sounds. Like that, and that, and that.

Her mother straightens the knife and fork on her plate, then lines the salt and pepper and her bowl into a tidy row of soldiers. You don't need to be afraid of the mountain, she says. What you need to fear is the ghost who comes in the night to snatch children from their bed.

Antonina can feel herself scowling. She looks down at her plate to hide her uncontrollable face. It isn't right for mother to talk about the woman at the window like that. She wasn't a ghost. Antonina has the small red medal to prove it. It's still as real as it was the night she carried it home on the train, and it's hidden inside the doll Antonina made from her mother's clay. Her rattle. And her mother never bothers with what's inside that makes the noise.

The dinner dishes are piled one on top of another and pushed to the side of the table before her mother walks out of the house without shutting the back door. Antonina knows what's coming — the thing her mother always does when new sightings of snow people come up. Sure enough, she returns with a mound of softened clay and thumps it down on the brown polka-dotted oilcloth that covers the table.

Antonina kneels on her chair, and her mother leans over her from the back to press their hands into the clay as one. They bump together like rowboats moored to the same buoy. The force of her mother's body around her is comforting. It reminds Antonina of how she would sit on her mother's knee at the potter's wheel when she was smaller, her mother's hands working around the obstacle of her child, clay turning on the wheel, wet and messy, bowls forming right in front of them like magic. She can taste the chicken on her mother's breath brushing her face with every huff and press into the clay. Then it's done, and her mother takes Antonina by the wrists and peels her hands free, rolling forward from the heel of her palm to the tips of her fingers. Their arms criss-cross on Antonina's chest, careful not to touch her clothes with muddied hands.

Did you feel the suck against the palms of your hands? her mother asks.

Antonina nods.

That's how much the mountain cares. It wants to keep you close. It will always protect you.

Her mother leans over Antonina's shoulder and runs her fingers around the imprint of their hands. Finger by finger, she traces their shape.

See how the mountain loves you, she says.

Antonina isn't sure about her mother's mud, but she thinks her mother is probably right about the snow people. Sightings always occur in the spring or autumn, when the bears come down to eat apples, either before or after winter hibernation. Short-sighted bears that eat fruit and run away when you yell at them — just like in the myth of the snow people.

Still, it's annoying that her mother doesn't play the way other parents do. That she insists on chasing away any story that has anything to do with her mountain. Her mountain — she calls it that too. She wasn't always like that. She used to read storybooks before bed, but they disappeared when they moved out of the city, all except a worn old version of the crow king. This one book her mother brings out whenever Antonina asks for a story, but now her mother only pretends to read the words. Instead of the real version, she recites one of her own, just as the strange woman had on the train.

In her mother's story, the crow king eats children's fingers for dinner, and for that he sends out his crows to steal children from bedroom windows. Crows that come in the form of old women with black hair, their faces covered in moon dust to hide the feathers, mouths painted in blood to resemble lips.

By late April the snow has peeled back to the shoulders of the mountains, where it stays all summer long. Patches of tulips beckon the children to come and play, and, as expected, Viktor comes for Antonina to run away.

Her mother is in her workshop. That steamy, sweaty place where she often wears only her underwear beneath a man-sized black apron while the homemade kiln cooks the pots she makes for the market. Antonina can hear her mother's song when Viktor comes through the back door. She sings when she's happy, and she's always happy smeared in the cinnamon-red sludge of her workshop. Her songs aren't the kind you can sing along to. They're wordless tunes with low, throaty chords that don't make sense. Songs of appreciation, she calls them — her love songs to the mountain. And there's something enchanting about them that Antonina adores, but when Viktor distorts his face in mockery, Antonina does it too.

Viktor keeps watch out of the kitchen window while Antonina packs a picnic. Two boiled eggs, two chrysanthemum-shaped honey-cakes, two filled pastries that were probably meant for dinner, and one jar of water. Viktor takes the bag and fits one of the straps over his shoulder.

Wait around the side, Antonina says, not wanting him to see her mother's ugly bloomers.

When Antonina enters the workshop, her mother isn't in her bloomers, she is fully dressed.

We're going for a walk, Antonina says.

Good timing. I need to get some clay. You two can come and help me.

But Mama, Antonina complains, you already have some. She points to the corner where the clay is stored under a sizeable damp canvas that smells like sweaty armpits and dog's breath all mixed together. There must be twenty blocks of it, all cut to the size of shoeboxes. These blocks have already been dragged home on the rickety wooden sledge that Antonina is not allowed to play with.

Well, I need more, her mother says. A big order has come in from a restaurant in town. They want all their dishes to be pottery. Isn't that wonderful?

Antonina sours her expression. Something has spooked her mother into needing company again, and Antonina doesn't want to know what it is. She's sure her mother just makes these things up to keep her home. There's the night sky, which she thinks will suck her clear away into orbit and burn her up like Laika, the dog in the space capsule. Writing names in red is forbidden. And there's the ghost who steals babies in the night — all of them warnings made up to keep Antonina close.

Her mother lets out a groan. Come here then, she says, and draws Antonina closer by the clip on her sleeve. What are you wearing? she says, and tugs at the belt of Antonina's favourite corduroy pants. Where are your gloves?

It's too warm for gloves. Have to go, Viktor's waiting, she says in a rush, before her mother has time to think of another reason to hinder their fun.

What about tomorrow then? We could go mushroom hunting. Her mother's voice trails thin as Antonina rounds the doorframe.

It's not long before they're amongst the old apple trees. Antonina loves the wild orchard, the gnarled trunks and arthritic limbs. No fruit are in season — not the tiny sweet pears, not the apricots or berries, not the nuts or the rhubarb. Only mushrooms are in when the season is turning, but the trees are pretty with the last blossoms clinging to the upper branches, the prongs of raw green that will stretch to become leaves. Antonina climbs the first limb she comes to and shakes it. Flurries of petals dance and scatter all around like the snow in a snow-globe inside her make-believe world where everything is perfect. She shakes and shakes again until the petals run out.

Race you, Viktor says, and he's well ahead by the time she gets down from the tree.

Antonina catches him on the second ledge. Way down below, her mother tows the old sledge on the dirt track that leads to the open wound where she finds her clay. She looks so small in the distance, her back set on a tilt, shoulders rounded. Behind her, the sledge ambles along, jerking over loose stones. She tugs the rope, and it races forwards to nip the back of her rubber boots.

Gwisin, Antonina calls out, knowing her mother can't hear. Rocks roll down, voices rise up.

Gwisin, Viktor says out loud too, and they run and hide behind a boulder in case the mountain growls at them.

It never does, though. No tigers come to eat them, no birds peck the eyes from their heads, and no ghosts steal their teeth. It feels good to give the word wings, though it never flies away. Although her mother would never speak of it, the children of the village did. They teased Antonina about her story of the woman who came in the night. Said she was a liar, and their mothers told them so. Petya Alekseev is the worst: he thinks it's funny to slam his body into her 'accidentally' whenever Viktor isn't around. Antonina waited for the woman to return so she could take her to school and show them all, but the woman never came back.

Did you bring it? Viktor whispers, though there is no need to.

Antonina digs deep inside the bag for the clay doll with the medal hidden inside its belly — the doll Antonina made in the image of the strange woman, painted with black-rimmed eyes and a tiny red mouth, a blue scarf and red leather gloves.

It was only Antonina's babushka who dared speak about the train journey. Her finger pressed the paper of the fold-out map from Alma-Ata to Semipalatinsk to show her how far she had been taken away. How easy it would have been for her to have been lost for good, never to return. Semipalatinsk.

Her babushka thumped the place with her fat old finger as if the site itself was inherently bad. Memories of the train ride come to her in pieces, but the last time the strange woman came is clear. She appeared as if from a fairy tale, out-of-the-blue, or out-of-the-white of a page from a bedtime storybook. Poised like a portrait, framed by the window and cast in the dim yellow light of Antonina's bedside lamp. She was beautiful, in a crumbling kind of way. Her eyeliner thick and winged at the edges. Her cheeks pinched pink from the cold, and her shiny black hair swept back from her face and covered in a blue shawl lined with pink and yellow roses. Such prettiness. So unlike Antonina's mother, whose only decorations are the designs she paints on the pottery bowls, though Antonina wouldn't really call them pretty. There's a brooch her mother owns — a traditional Korean Maedeup knot that her babushka made from white silk rope. It folds in and out of itself and forms a rectangle the size of a hand, with four jade beads, one in each corner. For luck, her babushka said. That's as pretty as her mother ever gets, and because of that Antonina was drawn to the attractiveness of the strange woman. Perhaps that's why she wasn't afraid, and it felt safe enough to climb out the window without a single complaint, though her legs were bare in the frozen air, and her mother was only one room away.

Her mother is still only one room away, but now Antonina's window is nailed shut, and so is the conversation between them about the woman who took her on the train. A ghost, her mother called her, after the militiaman had gone. After she slapped Antonina so hard that the side of her face was warm and tingled with disbelief.

A *gwisin*, she said, and you ought to be afraid of them.

Viktor's dedushka has a set of bottom teeth that he wears whenever special visitors come to the house. He wore them the first time Antonina and her mother came to tea. When he tried to speak the words got tangled up like he was drunk. When he ate, they slipped around his mouth and clunked against the top layer, too big for his sunken jaw, and when he laughed, they looked like they might jump right out of his mouth and onto the floor.

Viktor opens the drawstring bag that holds his marbles and the teeth rumble to the surface.

They're like a real skeleton, he says.

Antonina clasps her mouth and stares. You should take them back, she says, but she knows he won't because he never does what she asks.

He's better off without them, he says.

He takes a piece of newspaper from his back pocket and unfolds a story cut from the *Pravda* the day before. Three men have their arms around the back of each other's shoulders, posing for the camera with more emotion than anyone usually shows in public. A thousand golden items are spread out beside the opened *kurgan* where a Scythian prince has slept for hundreds of years inside a mound of dirt. Three men found him in Issyk — just one village over. Nobody knows how he got there, or when. And nobody can read the writing on the silver bowl because no one knows the old language anymore. The lost tribe, the newspaper calls them. Nomads that once lived on the steppes of Kazakhstan, and that's what gave Viktor the idea of burying their own treasure.

Antonina doesn't want to touch the teeth, so she makes Viktor drop them straight into the middle of the newspaper.

Her doll knocks against their ugliness when she wraps them together. It doesn't feel right to leave her doll there like that. She wants it back, and decides to retrieve it when Viktor's mother takes him for a day trip to the city. For now, she will play along. They find a small nook. Their own miniature cave. It's perfect — big enough for the burial and nothing more. A gap that's easily hidden with a pile of loose rocks pushed up against the opening.

Afterwards, they relax on the verge of the rock that spreads like an open palm, where the wind whistles like it's blowing over the top of empty soda bottles. Antonina lets her feet swing free and nibbles the edge of her chrysanthemum cake — around and around until a circle of jellied honey remains. They listen to make sure no one is calling them home, but all is quiet except for the tiny avalanches of loose stones that topple over the edge.

Viktor opens his mouth to show the disk of honey on his tongue, and, without having to say so, they are in competition to see whose will last the longest. Side-by-side, they sit in silence trying not to chew the disk, but it's impossible, and it's gone before Antonina realises she's lost the game. In the lowlands before them, the city of Alma-Ata sprawls out, covered in the day's lazy smog. Above it, the crisp blue sky spreads long and wide and cool and calm; feathered with clouds that seem so close Antonina is sure she could reach out and touch them if she tried. This is her safe place. Here she is away from the taunts of Petya and her other classmates who call her liar. She releases a happy, satisfied little sigh and places her head on Viktor's shoulder. He slips his arm around her back and doesn't mind when she twirls a curl at the base of his neck.

By the end of May, the blossoms have all gone, and the apple forest is flush with leaves and buds of new fruit. The long summer break is so close that school is in wind-down and the children are helping to clean and sort, or playing pointless games to pass the time. There is just one school in their village, located in the community hall, which also acts as a library. For events like the end-of-year show, the partitions are folded flat against the walls, the floor cleaned and lined with uncomfortable wooden pews, with an assortment of orphan chairs placed at the back.

Twelve dancers have been selected from across the female students for the end-of-year celebration assembly. Twelve girls of varying ages dressed in tights with red tulle skirts and ruffled ribbons in their hair. Two of the older girls have used black eyeliner, which flicks out at the edges almost as dramatically as the strange woman's did. Antonina can't stop looking down at the ballerina shoes that tie to a neat bow around her ankles. She has fairy feet. Pretty and magical. Her mother is honoured by Antonina's selection too — she doesn't say so, but Antonina can tell by the time she has taken to prepare the costume, and the money she spent on the ballerina shoes without complaining about their impracticality.

Antonina and Larisa are the two first-year students in the dance. Hand-in-hand they lead the dancers out to line up at the back of the stage — smallest to the centre, older to the sides. Her mother told her to expect butterflies in her stomach that tickle, but when they come, they churn like squirming caterpillars that make her want to throw up. She searches for her mother in the crowd. The hall seems bigger from the stage, and Antonina feels a little desperate when she can't see her. At the last moment, she finds her mother down the back on one of the orphan chairs. She gives Antonina an instructive nod and Antonina pushes out her chest and lifts her chin. She is ready now. She can do this.

It has been three years since the night of the abduction, and Antonina hasn't sung any of the songs the woman taught her. Neither has she thought about the twirl of the dance, but when she looks out over the tops of heads in the hall, she recalls the strange woman who came for her in the night. She was not a ghost. She was real. The adventure was real, and to prove it she decides to show them the dance — especially that Petya Alekseev.

Kanaiji oneora. Antonina hears it in the breath of the accompanying flute, in the flit of her teacher's fingers on the keys of the piano, and in the scuff of her ballet shoes on the wooden planks of the stage. She hears it in the thrum of the pulse in her throat and in the swish of her tutu. She lets go of Larisa's hand, and instead of the dance they've rehearsed for weeks, Antonina moves towards the front of the stage by herself.

Come back Nina, Larisa calls. Her voice hushed and anxious. You're not supposed to be doing that.

Mrs Von Bremzen continues to play the piano, her back to the stage, unaware of Antonina's single-handed rebellion.

Nina, come back! The calls keep coming from behind. You're going to get us in trouble. But it's too late. She is the best dancer, the chosen one, the blessed one. She wears the red tutu and ruffles in her hair. Tonight is her time, and she lifts her arms to second position the way the woman on the train taught her. A rash of giggles sweep through the children sitting on the floor in front of the stage.

My name is Moon, she says, and twirls like a ballerina, but not like a ballerina at all. My name is Moon, she says even louder when the music peters out. She has wings, she is sure of it. She will leave the stage very soon and fly up into the rafters. She twirls and twirls. My name is Moon, she says over and over, and the room seems to be falling away. All except a single chair that screeches against the wooden floor with the ache of urgency she can feel in the back of her teeth. It's the sound of trouble, and she stops twirling in time to see her mother clamber up the front of the stage in her best dress without bothering to take the stairs.

Antonina tries to run from the stage, but her mother corners her and throws a coat over the top of her head. One of the girls behind her bursts into tears, then another joins in. Antonina can't see anything. She has a coat over her head like a puppy ready to be thrown into a river. She tries to punch her way free, and her mother squeezes tighter so Antonina's arms can't swing anymore. The air is heating up inside the coat, the wool messing with Antonina's red ribbons, tugging at her hair. Her mother doesn't seem to care about any of this — she holds Antonina sideways like a plank of wood, her shoes slapping against the floorboards as she marches off stage. Antonina kicks at the air as hard as she can, and on the way down the stairs, she hits her shin against something hard — a doorframe, or a step, or the edge of a wall — something that doesn't like her. The cold night air pinches her legs, and her shin screams with an indignant pain.

I hate you, Antonina yells, and the ropes of her mother's arms tighten. I can't breathe, she says in a softer voice, but there is no pity coming her way. She is pushed into the back seat of a car, where she tries to pull the coat from her head to see who's there, but her mother is beside her and clasps her tight again. There is the jangle of keys and the sound of someone getting into the front seat. The rain rattles on the roof, and the cold engine starts up with a shiver.

Turn around, Mr Andropov growls, and Antonina burns more from embarrassment than heat or anger. It could only be Viktor he is talking to like that.

Antonina is captive inside her bedroom for two weeks without even the air of the mountain or the songs of the birds to keep her company. Her babushka has travelled up from the city to bring them food and take the pottery to market for her mother, and Antonina presses her ear to the door to listen to them speak.

Mr Andropov drove off the road on the way back to school the night of the show. Antonina already knew this. Viktor had come to the window two days afterwards with his arm in a cast. Everyone is talking about the dance, he said, as if that could be the cause of a dog on the road that made the car clip the kerb. His father's head broke the windscreen, but Viktor couldn't remember it. He couldn't remember anything past the scream of tyres, then the lift as the wheels left the road — the slight pause before the fall he motioned with his hand, and Antonina couldn't help thinking of a cartoon character with its legs wheeling in mid-air before plummeting off the cliff. Not that Viktor's father plunged off a cliff, and not that any of it was funny in the slightest. Her mind works in strange ways like this.

Who taught her that dance? her babushka asks her mother.

You think it's that woman? her mother says. The one who took her from the window?

Must be. Useless militia we have. Why didn't they catch her?

There is a moment of silence.

It's shaman, isn't it? her mother says. That dance?

It's the dance of the ancestors — if you believe in that kind of thing. It's not harmful, just strange, that's all. Moon, you said? Nina called herself Moon?

Another pause. Then her babushka is mumbling.

Who is she? her mother says, her voice heightened. Where does she live?

She left the area a long time ago. It could be. She was a dancer. I don't know about the shaman business, but you never know. We didn't have much to do with her after—

She stops short.

It probably isn't anything, but I'll tell the family to watch if she returns. The elders will talk to her if she does. They'll figure it out. This is so annoying. Every time we bow to our ancestors, they think its shamanism. Now, this. In front of the whole school. Makes the Koryo-saram community look stupid.

This was to be the summer of their greatest adventures. Viktor and Antonina planned to spend as much of the upcoming holidays on the mountain as they could, but it wasn't to be. When Antonina is released from her bedroom, she runs to Viktor's house to find it locked. No one locks their doors in their village. She rattles the door to be sure it's not just stuck, then kicks the skirting board beneath the lowest glass pane. Through the windows, she can see all their belongings. There is the couch with the bubbly orange fabric that Antonina likes to drag her fingernails across. A cupboard door is open a fraction in the kitchen with dishes stacked as neatly as ever.

Viktor's toy soldiers are lined up in tidy rows on the floor. Nothing is gone, except the Andropovs.

A few weeks later a truck arrives to take the Andropovs' furniture. Then nothing. They may as well have rocketed off into space, dropped off the face of the earth, burnt up in the atmosphere like space dogs. No one knows where the Andropovs have gone, or at least they aren't telling. The villagers mutter about Mr Andropov's head not healing, but Antonina's mother will have none of it spoken about around her without a vile reproach.

A curse that set in the night of the school show, Antonina picks up in shards of whispered words. The night of the wrong dance that her mother now calls the forbidden dance. Antonina hadn't meant any harm by it. It was just a dance. A stupid dance, she yells at the children when they refuse to let her play. Her mother is right. The world of imagination is too strong inside her mind. Fairy tales that blur the line between what's real and what's not. Snow people and crow kings. Rice farmers and Scythian warriors.

Now everything's wrong. Sitting on the lip of the rock that spreads out like the palm of a hand is wrong too. The air up there feels different without Viktor beside her. The sun hangs at an angle that annoys her. The city doesn't look hazy, it seems dirty, and she doesn't want to be there anymore.

Gwisin, she yells so hard that it hurts, hoping it will cause an avalanche that will bury her like the Scythian warrior, where no one will find her for a hundred years. But the mountain doesn't growl. And when she returns home, she takes the crow king storybook and throws it into the furnace of her mother's kiln.

NO PLACE FOR UGLY
ST PETERSBURG, RUSSIA — 1994

Last Wednesday, Oleg Kulik stripped down in broad daylight to a collar and chain to be led around like a dog on Malaya Yakimanka Street, near Marat Guelman's gallery. Actionism they call it, and the mix of protest and art has taken off in the larger cities. There was an article about it in the newspaper — a large shot of Kulik on all fours, with the caption beneath stating: Mayor promises to ban naked hooligans from the streets. A video has made its way to St Petersburg. A current of shocked whispers ripple through Antonina's class about the dog-man. No one mentions the screening at Pushkinskaya-10 later that afternoon, although they wouldn't really. They don't speak of the nonconformists within the Academy of Art unless the discussion is comparative, or detrimental.

Antonina knows she may not be the only one who has heard about the video's existence, but she's probably the only one daring enough to cross town and view it. *The crisis of contemporary culture via the violence of a dog.* The discussion sounds provocative — too good to miss. Antonina sits amongst the bubbling chatter of the Academy lunchroom and fidgets with her sandwich with the pretence of feeling ill. A headache, she tells Galina Vasilievna, the art history professor, and it isn't exactly a lie — the high-pitched babble of female students competing for attention during the breaks has been annoying her more and more recently.

The professor is an easy touch. Yes, she says. I thought you looked pale.

There is so much empathy bound up in the touch of the professor's hand that Antonina has to turn away to hide a singe of embarrassment.

Go home. Rest, the professor tells her. But make sure you catch up on your work tomorrow.

Nataliya sends a shrewd, hard stare Antonina's way. She knows. Perhaps Antonina will see her at the viewing too, though it's hard to imagine Nataliya at Pushkinskaya-10 with her father's informers everywhere. Such behaviour would concern the Academy as well, if they knew one of their prized students was interested in the antics of the nonconformists. There is a lot they wouldn't like about Antonina's artistic desires.

With her coat zipped, her bag on her back, and her paper-wrapped sandwiches ready to be eaten the minute she's out the door, Antonina makes her way down the cascading staircase like a tsarina late for a ball. She imagines long petticoats brushing against the mosaic flooring as she crosses the foyer, the clopping hooves of horses pulling up outside the heavy wooden doors ready to sweep her away. But no guard opens the front door for her as a gentleman would — he's too busy thumbing a magazine down in the cloakroom.

Antonina emerges into the busy streets like the pauper that she is, wholly and delightfully ignored. Lucky to be free of the bourgeois restraints Nataliya has to adhere to. Under the radar, as Tatyana says — the best way to live.

They're such unlikely friends. Antonina first noticed Tatyana in Ostrovsky Square, when she overheard a discussion about works by underground artists. She was immediately fascinated and followed the group to an apartment exhibition. The room was no larger than twenty square metres, walls cluttered with paintings of all different sizes. Some framed, some not. Nudes, mostly, in the neoclassical style draped with fabric over one shoulder or another, sometimes covering the genitalia, sometimes not.

The models displayed the typical distant expression of the romantic gaze perfected by the masters Raphael, or Leonardo; retakes, or remakes, of familiar compositions that included a great deal of self-portraiture. There were others in the paintings as well, faces Antonina recognised in the audience as she moved around the room — spectators, both on and off the canvas — an added dimension to the spell of displacement, and transcendence — the familiar within the unfamiliar.

On a few smaller canvases, the stance of the artist as the sole model was painted deliberately askew, suspended mid-air, arse facing the viewer, or some likewise awkward and challenging position. All still within the framework of the classical style. New-Academism, Tatyana called it. To Antonina, the work felt bold. Brave. Infused with romanticised hope and purposeful destruction. At the Academy, she is expected to adhere to a strict protocol of traditional form in content. Anything controversial or contemporary is not welcome. The nonconformists, by comparison, have energy, and more importantly, they have voice — something Antonina longs to bring to her work.

Antonina quickens her pace to cross the bridge. Soon she's marching past the Bronze Horseman, the Academy across the Neva on Vasilyevsky Island behind her. She has no idea of the time, but it must be at least half past twelve. The walk to Pushkinskaya Street will take half an hour. The ding of a trolley-bus bell sounds behind her, and Antonina does what she hates doing; she wastes her precious *kopeks* on the price of a ride down Nevsky Prospekt.

The trolley-bus is already packed, and Antonina has to push her way on. She stands at the end holding the rail, hoping the bus-girl won't see her, but they have eagle eyes, and Antonina scrambles for the correct change inside her bag when the bus-girl aims for her. There's no heating on board, but the air is thick with sweat and wet wool, the windows fogged with recycled breath.

Two stops down and the bus-girl comes for Antonina's *kopeks* again, as if she can't remember the face of a Koryo-saram among the Russians, although, the fact Antonina is Koryo-saram could be reason enough the bus-girl is trying to make her pay twice. Such racial contempt shocked Antonina at first, but after almost four years in St Petersburg, she is numbing to the disappointment it causes her. Kazakhstan was a more accepting mix. Russian, German, Koryo-saram, Uzbek, Ukrainian, and ethnic Kazakhs. They never seemed to mind each other, not that she could tell. Antonina is sent into a fluster searching for the paper ticket. She finds it scrunched in the bottom of her pocket, glad she didn't throw it on the floor and she waves it in front of the bus-girl like a victory flag.

Garbage has built up all across town. The air is spiked with fermenting sweet and sour smells from the overflowing bins inside courtyards, and plastic bags breaking open and left scattered in clusters on the kerbs. The collectors can't have been paid again. Small people on government wages seem to be the last to get their money in the current chaotic economic climate.

Even the Academy has struggled to stay open over the past few years, or so administration says whenever the art supplies run out. The Academy has been propped up by the philanthropy of alumni, and Antonina can't help wondering what these generous artists will do with their money now the government is taking back the financial reins of the institution. More money for student funding, she hopes, and sometimes she even prays. The value of the government monthly stipend used to be enough for modest living, but now it only feeds her for one of the four weeks. She's subletting her student accommodation to feed her for another two, which is illegal, but she isn't the only student to stoop this low. The rest of the week, her survival is dependent on Konstantin for miscellaneous odd jobs, the sale of icon paintings in the markets, and the sharing of a single-sized room divided in two in an old converted factory.

The other avenue of raising funds available to Antonina centres on her end-of-year marks. The higher the score, the more money the student is allocated. Receive a mark of just acceptable, and you get nothing. The competition for placement is intense, and it would make sense to stay away from the nonconformists. Every time Antonina crosses the bridge to visit Pushkinskaya-10, she risks enough distraction that could cost her the high mark she needs. Just one year

Antonina has known Tatyana, but life on Vasilyevsky Island now feels too bland without her in it.

Antonina steps down from the trolley-bus to a footpath full of commuters piling out of the metro doors like ants scrambling from a rained-out nest. She catches an opening and merges with the stream heading towards Pushkinskaya Street. Tatyana is up ahead waiting. She is a tall, dark figure in her oversized duffle coat and unisex hairstyle that's short on the sides and long in the fringe. Newly hatched from the subtropical temperature of the centre's radiated rooms by the look of her hunched shoulders. A plume of smoke escapes her lips, and she turns in Antonina's direction, cigarette held in her mouth Viktor Tsoi style. She nods when she sees Antonina and is all cool and calm, no urgency about her, though the video must be starting any minute, and mid-winter is no time to be standing on street corners.

Antonina takes her by the arm, and they make their way down Pushkinskaya Street, Tatyana on the inside, like a gentleman protecting a lady from falling icicles that drop from the guttering from time to time. Neglected baroque-style apartments line the street with thick stone in varying clay-coloured hues, darkened by dampness and decades of exhaust fumes. Five floors high, with rectangular slabs that protrude from the wall in chiselled horizontal lines that create a rippling effect. The regimented windows and doors are deep-shadowed sockets. The detail of scrolled plasterwork above darkened doorways and antique-style street lamps project a gothic eeriness in the bleakness of winter.

In the middle of the street stands the lonesome statue of Pushkin, arms crossed with snow pooling up his chest, across his shoulders, and on the top of his head. The stupid waste of his talent perplexes Antonina. Death by duel — what was he thinking? Such lofty ideals have made him a demigod, but how many nights did his wife lament the chill of her empty bed?

Antonina tucks her scarf under her chin, uncovering her mouth. Did Pushkin's wife ever remarry? she asks, her words breathy clouds pushing through the air in front of her.

Not sure, Tatyana says. I wouldn't have if I were her.

I guess it depends if she was able to support herself, financially I mean, Antonina says.

Still the same today, isn't it? Women marrying for financial security.

Do you know someone who's done that? Antonina asks.

Everyone knows someone who's done that. It's easier to share the burden between two, don't you think?

You don't have to marry to do that, says Antonina.

No. You can just be friends, Tatyana says. That's why you should move in with me. Get away from that creep.

Konstantin's not a creep; he's just . . . shady. Anyway, I don't see you turning away when he's got something you need.

Antonina's feet slide on the frozen path, but she doesn't go far, Tatyana has her arm, and they draw closer together, linked by their difference in height — Antonina's elbow tucked under Tatyana's and held there firmly against her hip. Just like an old, well-accustomed couple. No one would know they weren't lovers by the shape of them.

They will never agree on Konstantin. And truthfully, if Tatyana didn't live with so many crazies, Antonina might consider sharing a room. Two artists splitting the cost of living is a good concept. But the environment of the nonconformists makes her nervous. Anyway, she has her mind set on getting her own room back at the student hostel. All she needs for that is a perfect mark. Students do get them, though not her, not yet anyway.

When they enter the archway of Pushkinskaya-10, Antonina waves at the mirrored glass window on one side for no good reason, except that there's someone in there, hidden-away, watching. Two motorcycle mirrors are screwed into the wall, aimed towards the street, so she knows whoever it is can see them coming.

Don't do that, Tatyana tells her. We don't know who they are. I think they're going to try taking over the squat.

Can they do that? Antonina asks.

Good luck to them, Tatyana says. The original residents have been through decades of persecution by the government trying to get them out. Winters without power in freezing temperatures, fires deliberately lit in studios, arrests and exiles, even the odd 'accidental' death. And still, we are here. None of us are going to give up our home to a bunch of thugs.

Inside the courtyard, two men in pyjamas burn a pile of boxes that are going up in high flapping flames that reach almost a storey high. Tatyana pulls Antonina along as if that kind of behaviour were commonplace, nothing to stop and stare at.

See? Antonina says as they pass the fire. Look at them.

See what?

You live with crazies, she whispers.

I know. Isn't it great?

Precisely what a nonconformist would say. They stop outside the door to the centre while Tatyana fishes for the key in the back of her jeans, under the heft of her jacket.

The Academy of the Three Noblest Arts — that's what they called Antonina's academy when it opened, which she mentions to Tatyana.

Really, Tatyana says. And that makes you feel noble?

Antonina doesn't say so, but it does, more than she would like Tatyana to know.

Tatyana fits an oversized archaic-looking key into the lock. With each rotation the bolts of the door clunk as they edge out of the thick concrete wall.

Well, she says, this one used to be called The Academy of All Kinds of Art.

All kinds of art? Antonina says.

They're all noble, aren't they?

Antonina looks down at her shoes. I guess the ambition always is, she says.

The antique-looking keys to these thick wooden doors were one of the first things Antonina noticed when she moved from Alma-Ata to St Petersburg. Almaty. She has to remind herself that her hometown has been renamed. Just as Leningrad has now become St Petersburg again. So many things have changed since the fall of Communism.

Almaty, she says to herself to try to make the new name stick.

They arrive late to the viewing of the video and slink into the seats at the back. Artwork is piled up against the walls — large paintings with their backs to the room. Naked French linens in some places, cheaper bleached canvases in others. The scribble-styled handwriting of painters is made to look unintentionally significant as if the titles had been laid down in a flash of inspiration, which isn't true, as Antonina knows for herself.

Students that fill the rows of chairs in front appear to be in period dress. They wear bodices and bohemian velvet, silk pocket squares, lapels, and cravats. Tatyana removes her coat, and even she has dressed for the event, in a white button-up shirt with a mandarin collar and voluminous billowing sleeves. Over the top of this is a silky-blue waistcoat that she usually reserves for dance raves.

There is a quiet discussion going on up front — two male teachers lean over a projector, pushing buttons, ejecting the video, putting it back in again, pushing more buttons, and checking plugs. The room is as over-heated as Antonina expected. She shuffles out of her coat and scarf, then her sweater and hat. One of the teachers turns around on her seat to size up Antonina. The teacher's cheeks are red as autumn apples with thin purple veins visible, even from three rows back.

Am I allowed to be here? Antonina whispers, feeling self-conscious and rather conspicuous all of a sudden.

In response Tatyana waves at the teacher.

Don't worry, she says. She's fine.

What's wrong with her face?

Antonina's seen chilblained cheeks before, but they never look like that.

Rosacea. Tatyana tilts her head as if to prevent her lips being read. A lot of oldies at the hospital have it. Nothing you can do.

One of the teachers manning the projector stands upright and bites the end of his thumb, pauses, then re-engages with the machine, nudging the other teacher to make him move away. The students grow restless, and a gentle murmur of small talk spreads from row to row.

Ah, that seems to be it, the thumb-biting teacher says. The over-exposed image of a gathering appears on the front wall with people paused like statues. Get the curtains, someone, please.

The room turns semi-dark, with the daylight still evident but filtered.

I think the oldies with red cheeks are beautiful, Tatyana says as if Antonina had said otherwise. Makes them glow.

The video starts up, and the room quietens. A near-naked man is leading the naked Oleg Kulik, who is on all fours. Sit, the near-naked man says, and roll over. He rubs the dog-man's chest and scratches his ear. There is nothing in the square for the dog-man to cock his leg against, but he urinates with his leg up anyway. Then he sees something he doesn't like and becomes the angry dog, the dangerous dog. He runs towards the crowd and bites a man in a suit on the thigh. Laughter skitters through the room.

The video flicks to another scene outside a metro station, where the dog-man digs his nose into a woman's crotch, making her squeal with a mix of fright and delight. Then he notices a flood of commuters coming through the metro doors into the square. He chokes on his lead trying to reach them, his front lip raised to a scowl, teeth bared, growling with menace. The few daring commuters trickle past, but the rest cower behind the glass doors. The dog-man situates himself on the top step so no one can get in or out. He scratches his ear with his hind leg the casual way that real dogs do, ball-sack jiggling.

Tatyana's face flicks silvery-blue in the light of the screen. She squints with concentration as though she were trying to make out the smallest letters on an eyesight test. Antonina has lost interest. The dog-man feels more sensationalist than intriguing to her, and the back of the paintings lined against the nearest wall beckon her. She tries to read the titles in the darkness. The room goes quiet again, until two militiamen appear on the screen and the students come alive. They yell for the militia to leave Oleg alone. Tatyana sends abuse hurtling towards the screen as well, so Antonina joins in, happy just to be doing something. The two militiamen smirk at the camera — part of the game Antonina suspects. Bribed to perform. Neither of them in a hurry to take the dog-man away.

The video transitions to a series of snapshots that roll in from the side for a moment of glory, full-sized and unavoidable. Slides of the dog-man letting a real dog mount him as if they're about to copulate. Another with a sheep, its back legs tucked into his half-mast trousers, the dog-man's penis hard and intentional. Antonina fixes her stare into her lap. Barbaric sex is one thing, but animals she considers innocents. She knows he's saying they are all just animals, but it's distasteful. Art for shitty art's sake.

When the curtains open, the students stand to applaud the entrance of Timur Novikov. Novikov the dandy, dressed like Eugene Onegin, or how Antonina imagines Onegin would look in a black top hat, long black coat, and walking cane.

They're doing Novikov's 'Secret Cult', Tatyana says.

It feels conspiratorial that Tatyana didn't tell her there was to be a second show. The curtains close again and Antonina considers leaving, but she takes too long to decide and the play begins.

All the way through, Antonina remains only half attentive. The criticism of the lost golden age is engaging enough, its ideology of beauty seems eloquent, as does the depiction of the battle between the beautiful and the ugly, but there's no dislodging the taint of the bestiality scenes she just witnessed.

Afterwards, they make their way to a cavernous cafeteria with mismatched chairs and pockmarked concrete walls painted dirty mauve and army green. Glasses of sweet cherry wine are passed around, which Antonina turns down, not sure if she's expected to pay for it. Tatyana lights a cigarette. Antonina doesn't smoke, but a shared cigarette with Tatyana now feels natural, and she motions with two scissor fingers for a puff.

The cafeteria is alive with voices that merge into the same high-pitched sense of overstimulation as the lunchroom of the Academy.

What did you think? Tatyana asks.

I don't get the sexual innuendo at the end, Antonina says. I understand the critique of the overly refined cultural language. I get that. I agree with that. We get too much of that at the Academy, but it isn't respectful to treat animals like that. Looked more like sexual fetishism to me.

Tatyana shifts in her seat, turning her body to angle away from Antonina.

The conversation's different, Tatyana says. Her lip twitching. She does that when she's annoyed. There's no room for ugly in your beautiful world, she says. All you do at that Academy is re-create tradition.

You're wrong about that, Antonina says. You haven't seen my recent works. Have you given any thought to my idea of a combined show?

Tatyana runs her fingers through the length of her fringe and sweeps it back to one side.

Actualism is dead, she says. You need to bring your work into the now. Then we can show together.

You haven't seen my recent work, Antonina says again. I keep making these crazy figurines. They're the little people. The Koryo-saram. We've been here a hundred years now.

That's not long, says Tatyana.

Long enough to lose ourselves.

That's rubbish, Tatyana says. You're not lost. You're Russian.

Not true. I'm not Russian. I'm not Kazakh. I'm not even a real Korean — what do I know of that place? We don't even speak the same language.

That gives you something much more interesting to work with, Tatyana says. You're like a lost tribe. Or a new tribe made of many parts. A blend of lived experiences. It's not always just about blood, and it's not always about separation. Think about it, she says.

The rosacea-faced teacher wheels a trolley in and the smell of warm, savoury food blooms and fills the room, the same way it does in hospitals stretching down corridors with the ability to make a stomach rumble with anticipation whether you feel hungry or not. A cluster of students forms a queue, but King Timur is served first. Antonina reaches into her backpack for the brick of black bread and jar of pickles she was saving for later.

Compliments of our favourite black-marketeer, she says, and drops the goods on the trolley.

Konstantin didn't give you that, Tatyana says once they've nestled on the window ledge with their soup.

He did, Antonina says. Only he doesn't know he did.

Antonina takes a spoonful of soup. Borscht with tiny

pork dumplings and sour cream — worth watching the play for. The sourness of black bread infused with the chicken beetroot broth is a harmony of delight. As good as her mama's. Fresh and full.

After the soup, Tatyana joins a conversation and moves away. She motions Antonina over, but Antonina's had enough. There are times when the art talk is just too demanding in an environment where buying bread seems like enough trouble for any given day.

The concrete stairs that run through the centre dip in the middle from centuries of tread. On the first landing, the original mosaic floor is missing most of its teeth. On the second, the walls resemble a spray-painted tropical garden. On the third, a wall is coated with photographs of cockroaches, each with the head of one of the centre's artists. *All artists are cockroaches*, the banner says. *Where you find one, a million follow* — a squatter's proverb.

Tatyana's image will be there somewhere, saddled on the back of a cockroach, but Antonina doesn't stop to check. To be honest, she is a bit agitated by the visit. Disappointed, and baffled too, that her friend didn't seem to find the screening at least a little bit disturbing. There is safety in the conformity of her Academy that feels like protection at times. Communism was a bit like that, too.

She leaves through the rear of the building and the archway that feeds through the middle of the centre, out into a smaller courtyard where the free library is unloaded from boxes every Wednesday. Up another half-level of steps, and she's inside the entrance to the middle building. Up the last few steps and Antonina escapes the labyrinth to emerge into the ever-busy Ligovsky Prospekt.

There, Antonina joins the late afternoon race for home, wrapped against the cold and the noise of horn-blowing, placard-wearing street advertisers trying to off-load brochures and discount vouchers. Amidst the chaos of the street, Antonina keeps her eyes down, careful not to kick the heel of the person in front, content with anonymity like the gangster behind mirrored glass. She's aware of how lucky she is to have the freedom to float between the parallel worlds of art in the city. There is only one world she can't inhabit, and when she reaches the corner of Nevsky and Vladimirsky prospects, she pulls out from the flow of walkers in front of the Moskva restaurant, where she is reminded of the freedom that money can bring.

The window of Moskva looks like the setting of a fairy tale with its plump red velvet upholstery and the warm glow of chandeliers. A woman sitting in the window wears white drop-pearl earrings the size of marbles that contrast against her gypsy-coloured hair. She is caught in the intricate weave of a daydream, impassive and graceful. It reminds Antonina of the snow tunnels she dug as a child: the solid cocoon all pearly lustre around her, the words of her mother filtered in the soft, gauzy light. The woman rests the lip of the cup against her mouth and when she takes a sip of her tea, their eyes meet. Antonina pretends to look past the woman then away, and conscious of feeling like a beggar, she moves on.

The bells of Petrikirhe ring out as Antonina reaches the Green Bridge on the Moika River. She leans on the steely bannister and muffles her mouth while she listens to the dance of the chimes that announce the time. Five o'clock. The afternoon lessons at the Academy will be ending. Beneath the bridge, the city lights are little more than blanched spectres reflected on the frozen canal. She leans over further and sees the shape of herself among the ghosts — impressionistic in style. She wonders about painting through the filter of this kind of otherworldliness and decides to play with it next time she's in Tatyana's studio. She walks on. She has missed the practice sketching class at the Academy this afternoon and decides to stop in to see what work she will have to catch up on. She's passing by on her way home anyway.

Inside the live sketch classroom, Makar is still in session. She hadn't expected Makar; he must have stepped in for the professor. Through the glass panel in the door, she recognises the line of his back, one of the long-sleeved black t-shirts he likes to wear, the way the pocket of his jeans indent and the dimple in his butt when it flexes. So gorgeously familiar, and so off-limits these days. She tilts around expecting to see a few lingering students, a naked model, but there's only one other person in the room with him. Between the obstruction of canvases on easels, she spots Nataliya. Her hair pulled back, accentuating the strong angle of her jaw. She is all put together today, her fingers idling a red beaded necklace that matches her earrings. The boldness of their colour contrasts with her striped t-shirt and a green camouflage over-shirt. So casual. So confident. So blonde-haired Russian charming and spoiled for choice, and there she is biting the end of her pencil, making a play for Makar. Everything he says seems to warrant a reaction — a smile, a raised eyebrow, a nod. So obvious.

Antonina looks down at the pallid floral print of her own dress. Old-fashioned. Romantic. Her hair long and black drapes around the small moon of her Asian-shaped face.

Renaissance-style, she likes to think. Her legs are not as long as these lofty Russian muses, but they are just as slender. The thing she inherited from her mother that she likes the most is her legs. She presses a few fingers to her lips and peers back through the glass door. Makar likes the fullness of her mouth, or he used to when they were allowed to see each other. Back when he was still a student. Now he's a teacher, and the story of their relationship has sunk away into the boggy marsh that harbours the bones of slaves beneath their city. Sometimes she imagines she can hear the bones of the dead moving around beneath the granite foundation blocks, tapping against the old oak piles that hold up the city, but that's probably just the symptom of a lonely bed.

Nataliya alters millimetres of line with her charcoal pencil. Beauty is like gravity, and Antonina can feel the energy in the space between them, the current of desire that feeds all the best parts of life. Makar steps closer to point out an area to strengthen in the sketch, indicates invisible new curves with that soft-handed sweep of his, as though he were tucking a strand of loose hair behind the charcoal girl's ear. Makar has entered the dreamscape. Usually, he is so scattered with projects that he fails to focus enough on the class. They all complain about it, though never to anyone who matters. But when he enters this dreamscape his eyes change — they click over. When that happens, they all know to let him go, dive deep and find the treasure. And he does — every time. He finds the gold. He sees with a clarity they are all envious of, moving beyond the frustration of their current technical limitations. Antonina desires to touch him as she used to, even just to place a hand on his and absorb some of his knowledge like an osmotic transfusion.

The door creaks and opens a fraction, which causes Antonina to step back. She hadn't meant to lean so hard. The distraction is enough to bring Makar back from the depths. He claps his hands — a sure sign he's rounding up their conversation, trying to get away.

There is no way Antonina can hide if Makar turns around and sees her. She can't hide her desire for him either, she never could. It hasn't wilted away as he no doubt hoped it would. Before he can make it through the maze of canvases to leave the studio, Antonina moves down the corridor and tucks herself into the shadows of the passage that leads to his office. Her senses are on hyper-alert. She can smell the turpentine and oil of the paints, the coils of freshly planed wood, the earthiness of drying clay, even the wax polish of the floor. She can see charcoal and dust motes floating like fairies in the air, and she feels the weight of her own breath pushing through her lungs with the desire to claim him as her own again — or claim his favour at the very least. She needs him. And she needs the high grades as well.

Makar and Nataliya speak outside the studio in the low hush usually reserved for promises and secrets. Antonina strains to hear, but the conversation is indecipherable, then it perks up, and they say goodbye. Nataliya's voice carries an edge of disappointment, or perhaps that's just Antonina's imagination. It's jealousy, of course, that slants her perception. She knows this. She also understands the lingering effect the dog-man screening is having on her. Primal. Lustful. Shameful. She will retake her old lover. Just once more. No one will know. She is embarrassed that the video is affecting her body this way, but it's not very often that she feels this greedy, this selfish.

The clap of Nataliya's footsteps fade and the soft pad of Makar's trainers move towards Antonina. He rounds the corner and sees her. Stops. Goes to take a step towards her and stops again. She should be ashamed, but she's not. She heads in the opposite direction, not to get away, but to cause him to follow. He knows what she wants, she can feel it. She unzips her jacket and pulls her arms free. Her body is electrified. Desire is burning her up like a spacecraft re-entering earth's atmosphere, hurtling through space. If he doesn't follow, she will surely die sad and hopeless like the little dog Laika. Would he do that to her?

He follows as she hoped he would, catching up with the longer length of his stride. She turns into the small, out-of-order toilet the caretaker uses for storage. Inside she has time to kick off her boots before he enters, but that's all. He stands by the door with the vulnerability of fear all over him. Before he can back out, she takes his mouth in hers, smothering his pitiful plea.

We're not allowed, he manages to say. We can't, he whispers when Antonina reaches behind him and locks the door.

Too late, she says and unbuckles his belt.

GHOST TRAIN

VLADIVOSTOK, RUSSIA, USSR — 1937

The Primorsky Krai on the far eastern edge of Russia was their home, and Nikolai was proud their first-born child would be a Soviet. A boy, he hoped, and often cupped his hands as he spoke to her belly as if the father and child already shared secrets. Both Katerina and Nikolai's families crossed over the border in 1910, when Japan annexed Korea as a colony of its own and the famines took hold. Katerina was the first generation of her family to be born outside Korea, and as a display of willing naturalisation, she was given a Russian first name.

During the Stalin period however, suspicions spread. Articles in *Pravda* regularly accused the Koryo-saram of disloyalty and spying for the Japanese, though there was never any evidence given. Because of the close proximity of Vladivostok's port to the threat of Japan, and the Koryo-saram's Asian ethnicity, Stalin became paranoid and decided they could no longer be trusted.

Some were offered money to leave, but very few took up the offer. Nikolai believed it was honour that kept them in the Far Eastern Krai of Russia. He said they were displaying loyalty to the new government that had accepted them as one of their own. In truth, the only options offered were Manchuria, Japan or Korea, and they knew they would be marginalised as Soviet spies in any of those countries after living so long inside Russia.

The first of Katerina's losses were her father and her brother. The NKVD came for them in the night — two very tall, middle-aged men in the khaki uniform with red stripes on their collars took them away. Her father was a delegate rising in the ranks of the Communist Party who had met Stalin several times. The prized photograph of him sitting two seats behind Stalin at the 17th Central Committee of the Communist Party meeting hung above the mantle of the fireplace in the front room that was used for special visitors. Below this, his medal sat proud on its cushion of red inside an open case. Nearly all of the delegates in the photo were later executed, their gold teeth missing when the bodies were returned for burial.

Nikolai was from a family of rice farmers, but since their marriage he gave up farming and became her father's assistant, hoping one day to wear the white clothing of the leaders for himself. Katerina had hoped the marriage would take her away from her father's house and the constant flow of independence fighters and politicians who visited, but instead the excitement drew her husband in.

The night the NKVD came for her mother, Katerina and Nikolai climbed out the window and hid in the dog kennel. The next day they packed their belongings and moved out to his family farm in Khabarovsk. But that didn't stop the NKVD finding them, and taking her Nikolai away as well. She clung to his arms and begged the officers for mercy. They were not the same men who came for her parents, but they had that same numb look on their faces, eyes distant, refusing to engage with the pleas of a pregnant young wife. She held on until one of the officers wrenched her arms free of Nikolai and threw her to the floor. Nikolai's mother had stood on the stairs with his father, and they moved only when Katerina fell. They ran to her, not to Nikolai, which embarrassed her. Katerina shook off his mother's hands and tried to stand on her own, ready to grab hold of Nikolai again.

Stop it, Nikolai yelled, not at the officer, but at Katerina. Think of the child. She fell back against the wall, drew her hands to her mouth and tucked in her legs beneath her body, helpless as a beaten dog. Her hands moved up to cover her face, then across to her ears, unsure which sense they needed to block the most. His mother retook her arm, and this time Katerina accepted the help.

With Nikolai gone, Katerina wasn't sure she'd made the right decision in staying. That first night, she lay awake reprimanding herself for not going with him. The second night, she pushed herself hard against the wall with her face right up against it, as if Nikolai were to come in later and slide in beside her as he usually would. However, her subconscious could not be so easily tricked, and she tossed and turned in her husband's childhood bed all night long, the last image of his solemn face staring back from the car, bearing down on her. The cries of his mother from the room next door were a constant accusation of the guilt she already carried — the daughter of an intelligentsia, the daughter their son should never have married, the ambition of her father a contagion that spread like a fatal disease to anyone he spent time with.

I'll come for you, Nikolai had called out as he waited for the car door to open. The light from the house doorway filled with the shadows of three people, shocked into silence, while the dogs barked and barked and pulled at their chains in the yard, all full of anger and sharp teeth. I promise, her Nikolai said. No matter where, I'll find you, and we'll be together again.

She believed it to be true, but at the heart of his words, Katerina could feel their co-joined fear that it wasn't.

The next day, Katerina smoothed her hair and tied it up into a French twist and dressed in her most respectful clothes, then caught the train back to the city. All the way, the words ran around inside her, filling the void with a prepared argument that she hoped would convince the authorities to release her Nikolai. In her mind, it was a robust conversation. They had naturalised — their own nationality had been neutralised. They were loyal Soviets. Her father fought with the Red Army for the Bolsheviks and was awarded the medal of the Order of the Red Banner for extreme bravery. It should count for something. Katerina was a quiet person by nature, used to having strong men to stand her ground, cut over her sentences, finish her stories, but she was sure she could push through this time on her own. The strength of love for her Nikolai was the confidence that would surely steady the tremble at the base of her ribs.

When the train arrived at the station, the number of freight carriages that cluttered the tracks went unnoticed by Katerina. There was no way she could know that the carriages usually intended for transporting animals, or stocks brought in through the port, were to be used for the deportation of her entire community. Her focus was whittled too thin to consider anything other than her husband's plight. She came armed with her father's medal and the photograph of him sitting behind Stalin, and she marched straight into the NKVD headquarters to find the highest-ranking superior she could that didn't bare the ferocious look so many of them threw at her.

Please, she said with her head bowed, the medal and photograph held out to him. My father is a good man who has served this country well.

It was all she could manage in the end, the words of her lengthy speech turned to chaos in her head and she burst out crying. The two items she held out seemed to be enough to grab his attention though, and he took her into a side room to talk. She told him her father's name and he scribbled down his details in a rush until she mentioned he was already with them, arrested and taken in. That's when he lost interest and laid the pen flat.

My husband is a good man too, she said dabbing tears with her handkerchief.

The officer looked at her, his eyes deep-set and icy blue, calculating behind the stillness of his face, the straightness of his silent lips, tense behind the mask of calm. Later she realised she should have said he was a rice farmer, but she didn't. She should have never gone back to the city, but she did.

There are others who haven't been arrested, she blurted out like an idiot. Teachers, lawyers, accountants — all of them are loyal in their service to the administration, and they are free to walk the streets while my husband is locked up like a criminal. Nikolai is just a clerk. An assistant with too much ambition. He is not an enemy of the state. He is no threat to anyone. You must see this?

Your husband is with us as well? he asked.

Yes, she said. Also my mother, father and brother.

But not you?

She hitched her breath, unprepared that she might have put herself in danger, the baby too. Think of the child, her husband had said, but she hadn't. Again, the shame crossed her face, made her turn away from the stare of the officer.

You think we have been unfair? the officer said.

Yes, she said, rounding the mound of her pregnant stomach with her hand to accentuate her vulnerability.

Like who? he asked and sat back in his chair. Who are these lawyers, accountants and teachers you mentioned?

She began to name a few, and he handed her the pen and paper. This is when she should have realised the deception. Somehow the young captain had lulled her into a place of trust with the soft roll of his voice. How could she know it was a trap? They had never been enemies before. Just months ago, they were fellow countrymen. Most recently this became a different story — a story of missing men and women, of misunderstandings and allegations, mistrust and fear, and there was no escaping that. So, perhaps she did know what she was doing. Perhaps a red beacon blared at the front of her brain, where she refused to look, the kick in her gut was not the baby's feet pounding, but the knowledge that she was trading four names for one, four others for her own, the value of her husband as subjective as that. She was already too far down the track to pull out. Or was she? Either way, she carried on, and when she handed the names over, she not only looked like a dim-witted young woman, she felt like one too. But if it played to her Nikolai's benefit, she didn't care.

Are these what you would call the pillars of your community? he said.

The ones who have not been taken in, she replied. And my brother-in-law, Stanislav, he is a teacher, the husband of my Nikolai's sister. He is a good man too.

Well, all right, the officer said, lifting the piece of paper to read the names for himself, each one neatly hyphenated with their occupation running after the last name. I'll look into it.

He shook her hand good and hard. She pointed to her father in the photograph so he would know his face, then left for her parent's house to wait for word of her Nikolai's release.

Her father's house was sad and empty when Katerina returned. It lacked the smell of dinner cooking that overtook the pipe smoke of her father in the early evening. It was missing the sound of happy feet, tired feet, feet up and down the stairs, the clink of cutlery on the table being set for dinner. She lit the fire with wood chopped by her husband not long ago, placing each stick of kindling into the tepee shape he showed her. Each stick of wood was like a piece of her Nikolai now, each one carried the history of his touch, just as her body did, and it felt wrong to light the paper and send part of him away. He will be back soon, she assured herself, and caught the match on the flint to set the wood alight. There will be more wood. More time. More of Nikolai to infuse the items of their daily lives with memories.

When word came the next day, it was not what Katerina expected. The neighbour crossed the road to let her know that Stanislav had been taken in the night before. Katerina was struck rigid with dread. Have any been released? she asked.

The only way they return is ready for burial, the neighbour said. The woman opened her mouth slightly, ready to continue a line of thought, but stopped herself, drew her lips together tight. I'm sorry, she said, and patted Katerina's arm. Do you want to come over? It's not good to be here alone. Or I can send Liza over if you prefer, to keep you company.

I'll be best on my own for a while, Katerina said, and the neighbour seemed to understand.

Katerina closed the door and stood there for the longest time studying the grain of the wood as if it held some ancient truth in the lines that marked its age. What had she done? She tried not to formulate the word that was circling like a predator, and turned away from the door. The little man with the blue shorts and braces was out of the weather-house that hung to the left of the door. It would be a cold day, grey, possibly some rain. The little blue man always announced the worst kind of weather. Her legs shifted and she knew she was moving, but the knowledge was only loosely connected to her mind. She stopped within the doorframe of the front room where the fire's greedy licks were already eating the wood her Nikolai had cut, turning it to charcoal, to death, and she understood all of a sudden, the full, devastating result of her actions. The trickery. The deception she was not wholly unaware of when she handed over the names, and it wasn't shame that overtook her at that moment, it was fear.

What would happen to her if the remaining elders found her list? she thought. With the names written in her own proud scrawl. How would she ever be able to look Nikolai's sister in the eye again if she knew? And what would Nikolai think of a wife who was — the word circled and landed — a betrayer?

No one knew the train was headed for Kazakhstan. Gather your belongings, your personal documents and all the food you can find in your home and follow us immediately. You are all being deported. This was all they were told before being chased from their homes.

Katerina packed for her husband as well as herself, expecting to see him wherever it was they were being taken to. One bag of food, the other a mix of clothing for herself and Nikolai, her mother's jewellery, and her father's photo. The medal, she tucked into the pocket of her coat, and over this, she wore her husband's thick tweed coat.

It was autumn. The time of harvest, but the farmers were forbidden to work the fields. Teachers were forbidden to teach. Office workers were forbidden to write and organise appointments. Stores were forbidden to open. And the entire community of Koryo-saram sat on the streets throughout the Primorsky Krai, forbidden to return to their houses. Without exception. All they were allowed to do was to wait, for what, none of them knew. That first night spent on the street, Katerina's neighbourhood huddled together and lit fires from fence pales while the armed guards kept their distance beside a fire of their own, two of them taking turns to watch over the group.

By lunchtime the next day, Sasha, another neighbour, snuck into his house after deciding it was better than having to listen to the nag of his wife about the fur coat she had left behind while she shivered through the small hours when the wood ran out. It was as he headed back to them, down the side of the house under cover of an apricot tree, that he was spotted.

Katerina remembers the way the neighbourhood of street squatters stood with a communal sensation of disbelief. Sasha was marched around the back of the house, hands clasped behind his head, elbows out, the fur coat left in a puddle under the apricot tree where he dropped it. The sun was not hot, but warm enough to create wavelets that rose from the side of the house and made Sasha and the soldier appear as though they were crossing into another dimension, into a dream, into a nightmare. Just a few seconds and they were out of sight, the street silent as if the neighbours had collectively forgotten to exhale. The clap of a gun bounced around the surrounding hard surfaces of empty houses and sheds, closely followed by the scream of Sasha's wife as she collapsed into the arms of her neighbours. A band of sparrows darted upwards with panic, then circled and sunk back into the foliage of the trees, the fur coat still as a dead animal in the shade of the apricot tree.

Late afternoon the trucks came, and the neighbours were herded together on board so tightly that no one could sit. They jostled and swayed like the laden heads of wheat left behind in the fields, moving as one in the breeze, with travel bags and sacks of rice tucked between their legs.

At the railway station, they climbed out of the trucks to be shunted forward onto an already crowded platform.

The chain of train carriages that lined the closest track was the longest Katerina had ever seen, with at least fifty carriages in tow — several up front: a kitchen carriage, one that looked like it held sanitary facilities, then a couple of open platform carriages, but none of these was intended for the Koryo-saram.

They passed all of the carriages, the crowd pressing in the elbowing turmoil of the platform where passengers had recently spent happier times. All the while the cries of babies rose above the commotion.

Katerina couldn't see the officer she spoke to a week earlier at the NKVD headquarters, and even if she could, there was no way to break herself free from the group around her that shuffled forward. She gave her name to the soldier with the clipboard, and he found her on his list, ticked her name off and waved her past, but she refused to move.

My father, she said, holding the Order of the Red Banner medal for the soldier to see, as if it contained the passport to her freedom. He's a good man. My family shouldn't be here. What of my mother — surely, you'll not hold onto women? She said their names, spelling the family name so it wouldn't sound like moon. M.U.N. The soldier checked and shook his head. She held the medal out again. There must be a mistake, she said. Please, check again.

Another soldier pressed his gun into Katerina's shoulder and made her skip forward. You can buy those for coins, he said, which wasn't true. The Soviet star, Katerina knew, you probably could, but not the Order of the Red Banner.

My husband? Nikolai? she pleaded from the end of the line, and she called his name. The soldier with the clipboard checked, then shook his head.

Katerina put her bags in the corner of the cattle-car, thinking it would be best to be able to sleep with her face to the wall, curled on the hay behind the blocking board, where the shadows could wrap around her as she quietly sobbed, away from the children at the other end. But there was no getting away from each other in the restricted space, and they all cried as they left their homeland. Some stood by the mesh windows that ran along one side, the smoke of the engine billowing in on the crosswind. Some sat in the shadows, as Katerina was, recoiling from the reality of what was happening, as yet not filled with the full level of remorse she would face when the train rolled into Khabarovsk for more passengers.

Had she known her husband's sister, Bora, and his parents would be added to her corner when the train stopped to load up in Khabarovsk, she would have insisted on being placed in a carriage with her uncles and aunts. Not her husband's family. Not her Nikolai's sister Bora, who took Katerina in her arms like a sister when they came on-board, and who, thanks to Katerina's list, was now as husbandless as Katerina was herself.

LIQUID ROUBLE

ST PETERSBURG, RUSSIA — 1994

Antonina lugs Konstantin's trolley bag behind her, the same way her mother pulls the rickety sleigh across the mountain for her clay. Every time Antonina has to take the trolley bag out, she feels the ache of old woman's bones, as though some part of herself is prematurely ageing — her back bending just that little bit further, her chest sinking inward, and her hip bones chafing ever so slightly in their sockets. It's unfair to be burdened with the humdrum of daily life when she's an artist. To have to battle for bargains when she could be in her studio creating new works. But today is Konstantin's party, and she must join a queue to get her supplies.

The new supermarket with its giant orange logo flashes up on advertisements all around the city, promising *better selection*, and *the freedom to choose your own items from the shelves*. Faster processing, they say, but so far nothing seems quicker. Feels like half the city has crowded in for the supermarket's opening-day deals. The woman behind

Antonina in the queue taps the trolley bag with the tip of her boot in a passive-aggressive manner. There's half a step between Antonina and the man in front, but she ignores the prompting to move closer.

The queue waiting to go into the supermarket snakes around a series of metal barriers at the entrance to form a rectangle of shoppers, all neatly contained like marbles in a maze. The usual Soviet-style queue doesn't have barriers. It would stretch all the way around the corner, possibly even the block, restricting discussions and political debates to hot spots, but the metal-barrier version makes it easier for contact between the front and the back, and everything in between. There's an argument going on, shawled women in coats cinched at the waist versus young men in jeans and gym shoes.

The government hasn't changed quickly enough, one man says, his words projecting like a good spit. It's still run by the same men who were there in the years of Communism. The same ones who stole from us before, still steal from us now.

They need to go, another says. Let us get on with it.

You wait and see, one of the women yells. The Soviets will rise up again. They'll squash this Boris Yeltsin. He's no good, you know.

The woman behind Antonina taps the back of the trolley, and again Antonina ignores it. The arguments rage on all around, viewpoints flung about like beer bottles in a bar brawl. If Pushkin were here, there would be a challenge. A duel to the death. His wife did marry again. Antonina looked it up. Silly woman. Antonina bites on the *pyshka* she bought from a street cart with a few *kopeks* she'd found in the pocket of Konstantin's washing — another of the chores she does to earn her board. She would rather be responsible for washing

Makar's pants. If he were to ask, she knows she would be a silly woman too — if he held his hand out for her to take, she would leave all her friends behind to join him.

Move up, will you, the woman behind says.

Antonina takes half a step forward. She remains silent, eating her *pyshka* and staring straight ahead at the orange logo above the door in the distance. She keeps her opinions to herself and shuffles forward only when she needs to. The new world feels like a brittle place. The new regime is as tentative as thin glass. Antonina would like to explore her politics on the street like everyone else, but the last time she joined in she got called a dirty Korean dog-eater. It's just one of the insults used to punctuate the new pecking order. Russians are the new gods. The Koryo-saram are interlopers with no claim to the land. Like squatters who no more belong than they did the first day they crossed the border over one hundred years ago. Unless you're Viktor Tsoi. Everyone loves him.

Used to be, they were all one as Soviets. Not anymore. Being pregnant to a Russian should change that, but Makar doesn't know about the baby yet. No one does except Konstantin and Tatyana. The nugget, Antonina calls it. Reminds her of buried treasure. She likes the idea of a golden baby lying hidden inside a small mound that no one notices. The gold that might just sway her Makar into committing to their relationship again. She is not like Pushkin's wife. She does not want any other, and if he refuses her, she is sure she will spend the rest of her life on her own. Like her mother.

Konstantin nudges his way through the crowd to get to Antonina.

Hey, you can't push in like that, the woman with the kicky-boot says. There is a flash of steel in the woman's eyes when Antonina turns to confront her complaint. She is younger than Antonina expected. Mid-twenties, like herself, but already she carries the worn-out look of the disillusioned in her long grey overcoat and washed-out scarf.

I'm not staying, Konstantin says, his hands held up in mild surrender. Just giving the girl her money . . . Here, he counts the roubles into Antonina's palm. That should be enough. Show me the list.

Antonina taps her pockets and feels the crunch of paper. She hands the list to Konstantin, and he looks at it, calculating the cost in his head.

Plenty, he says and hands it back.

There's never plenty, Antonina says.

Enough then.

There is never enough, she says.

You're lucky to have that.

Luck is a chance thing. She flips the words off her tongue like the scorn of an old woman.

Really, he says turning to face her. Some of us work hard for our luck. Others just get pregnant.

Antonina blushes and turns back to the queue, more angry than embarrassed. She takes one step forward, and he does too. Her banter was meant to be a quip, but underlying resentment seeped through and stole the playful tone of her voice. Her pregnancy was not intended either, though it was also not avoided. She was taking birth control pills when she was with Makar, but when the relationship ended, she saw no reason to continue.

There is too much emotion in her face, but she would rather the tears run as if the cold wind has caused them, than wipe them and acknowledge her weakness. Konstantin steals glances at her, his face always so unreadable, but he doesn't leave.

She catches herself almost prepared to apologise, surprised that his opinion should mean so much to her.

You're disappointed in me? she says.

He huffs. None of my business, is it?

There was a time I would have been congratulated for falling pregnant to an educated man, she says. When my mother was pregnant, the local party leader came in person to award her an apartment in the city and a brand-new pram.

Back then, men were in short supply, and Antonina's mother chose to sleep with a university professor from Tashkent — behaviour that was encouraged by the Soviets to promote good genes and population growth. The professor was Koryo-saram, and Antonina wonders if the leaders would have celebrated a mixed-race child the same way.

Communism is dead, Konstantin says. No free prams for anyone anymore.

Did you hear the arguing when you came in? she says lifting her voice and forcing a smile.

Konstantin shrugs and draws heavily on the last of a cigarette before stomping it out in that rogue manner he has. He is what Antonina would call a handsome Russian, and there aren't many of those. Something happened to the gene pool during the great patriotic war, her mother used to say. It killed off all the good ones. Konstantin's hair is fine and short and swept to one side, the colour of a muddy puddle. The tenseness around his eyes makes him look as if he were continuously deep in concentration. It's his birthday, but she has no idea how old he is. He could be late twenties, mid-thirties, even early forties with a stretch. She assumes he's made a habit of looking older than he really is. Good for business. The sheepskin-lined stonewashed-denim jacket he wears makes him look much more substantial in stature than he is, too. It's all deception.

Seems there are others who would like the return to party-state as well, she says.

I only heard the ones who want the equality of the open market, he says. Listen, they're still going. Capitalism. Like the Americans. See?

Do Americans trick the elderly out of their apartments, and sell them for profit?

Konstantin looks at her as if she's asked the most stupid question, and she is glad the water in her eyes has drained away. It's just business, he says. It's the way of the progressives. The old ways are obsolete. You should move on, let it go.

The queue moves forward and the woman kicks Antonina's trolley from behind.

Whoa, leave the trolley bag alone, Konstantin says to her. That's mine you know.

It was an accident, the woman says.

Antonina stays where she is, hoping the woman kicks her trolley again, waiting for Konstantin to let her have it. He is her Rottweiler, always on the lookout for trouble, and she feels safe in his company.

Okay, I'm going to leave you to it, Konstantin says, which disappoints Antonina. I've got other stuff to do.

More important than keeping a pregnant friend company in a line?

Fraid so. He turns to leave, but Antonina catches the trim of his jacket and gives it a tug.

Well, at least I have a heart, she tells him.

What are you talking about now?

Anyone who wants to return to the old ways has a heart.

Ha ha ha, Konstantin says in fake-laugh style. Never going to happen.

Anyway, Antonina says. How many candles do we need for the cake?

You know what your problem is? he says, punching two fingers in the air in front of her. You're too used to being pampered at that university of yours. It's not the real world. Look around you. He raises his arms half-mast. This . . . is the real world.

Look at the line, the woman behind says. If you can't keep up, I'll overtake you.

Plus, anyone who wants to go back to the old regime has no brains, he adds.

Konstantin shoots the same two fingers at the complaining woman before he shoves his way out. Antonina moves forward, still leaving half a space between herself and the man in front. Just one candle then, she decides. One big white ugly one from the emergency box. That will teach him for being so annoying.

The woman behind her taps the trolley bag again, and Antonina turns around. You kick my trolley again, she says, and I'll ram it where it hurts. She jerks the trolley bag forward a couple of times in lieu of her Rottweiler, a dog-bag ready to charge at her command.

You should go back where you belong, the woman says.

I belong right here. Antonina points to the ground as if that were the very spot she was born.

The woman scoffs. Just watch the line, she says. I'll mind my business if you mind yours.

This seems like a decent proposal to Antonina, and she turns back and moves up a step, keeping her focus on the orange logo ahead as if hope could make the line move faster.

Sobakoyed, the woman mutters under her breath — dog-eater. Antonina thrusts the trolley bag back hoping the lower bar catches the bone of the woman's legs, and she smiles to herself when she feels the hit that has the woman swearing the way they say Russian women never do.

An hour passes before Antonina reaches the supermarket doors. Inside she is delighted with the warm and well-lit interior — much nicer than the dirty, windy markets. The smell of fresh paint lingers, and the usual foodstuffs, found in any common kiosk, sit alongside new products brought in from America. Items like packages of chicken legs called 'bush-legs', and beans in a tomato sauce. But Antonina must stick to her shopping list. She pushes her way towards the baker's counter, arm raised, voice pitched for attention, determined to get a loaf before the woman with the kicky boots, but she is taller than Antonina, a Russian whose long arms win the competition. Democracy, Antonina thinks, does not deliver the bread any more than Gorbachev could.

Such a waste of her time, but it's one of the ways she remains valuable to Konstantin. Tonight, they will celebrate with his friends at their *kommunalka*. She has enough money for the sugar, butter, eggs, the bread, flour, oil, and the *nastoyka*. Miska candies she hadn't planned on, but she can't resist slipping a small packet into her string-bag. A birthday gift for Konstantin in the morning — if the sweets last that long. She unfolds her wad of rouble notes and counts out what she needs. It means spending more than she's supposed to, but she is in a good haggling mood and can make the money stretch further when she reaches the market.

Someone yells abuse outside the shop front, and it carries through the entrance doors. Antonina tiptoes to see over the heads of the checkout queues. Everyone is looking towards the window, and some join in the tirade.

Can you see what's happening? Antonina asks the man beside her.

The government just kicked us again, he says curling his lip. As if we hadn't given enough. My father fought to save this city from the Germans. Should be worth something.

Antonina doesn't know what to say about that.

A currency-exchange man can be seen outside the window as he rises above the crowd on a stepladder. The cursing increases to a roar when he replaces the old wooden numbers on the converter board with new ones. No one leaves the queues though, and when the man climbs back down his stepladder and moves on to spoil someone else's day, the uproar diminishes to a melancholic murmur.

Antonina stands on her toes to see the new numbers, but they don't really matter. In the end, it just means less, and she pulls the candy from her bag, placing the packet on the floor for the store boy to collect. She recounts the notes in her hand. Liquid rouble — they all have a name for that phenomenon.

Half an hour later, and she still has the market to reach for the mushrooms, and, if she's lucky, some marinated fish, and maybe some caviar. She runs through her recipes on the ride down the escalator to the metro platform, careful to keep the trolley to the right so the runners won't trip. She would run too if it weren't for the trolley bag, but today she is Konstantin's babushka, and she will return to Vasilievsky Island to cook and bake and clean for his birthday. Then, on a weekend of her choosing, he will belong to her. She will let him sleep off the Saturday night hangover until noon, and bring him black tea and bread with no Miska, but that's all she will give him.

Vladimir's room is the largest of the tobacco factory. They're all squatters, equal in rights to the bathrooms, the kitchen, and the designated size of their rooms. All except Vladimir, who was the first to pick the locks and claim the abandoned factory for communal living. For this, he gets the room at the end with the windows that let the sunshine in. Nobody else gets the sunshine.

Parties are always held in Vladimir's room because of its size, and because Vladimir loves any excuse for a good time. His latest project stands in the corner — a mannequin, sequinned with thousands of silver drawing pins. Next to it, Vladimir poses with a swirl of barbed-wire, using it as an umbrella, a mask, then a crucifix hung on the wall, commanding all who pass to bow and pray to the god of art.

Konstantin's not going near it. He's in the corner with Sofiya, the ageing beauty queen, who was once the mistress of a mini-garch. She has half a room full of gowns and shoes to prove it, purchased between pedicures and chocolate mochaccinos at expensive cafés before he ditched her.

Konstantin's grinning like he's in for a romp, but Sofiya is thinking only of herself, twiddling a string of pearls and looking at her glass absently, then up into the air, as if some fond memory lurks there that she must recount. Ivan, the cook, takes his family over to meet them. At first, his wife looks impressed with Sofiya, but when they realise she's doing her monologue of how important she used to be, Ivan moves his family on. Their two children come to the table, a pretty girl, blonde with pigtails tied with pink velvet scrunchies, and a shy boy — both with stunning honey-coloured eyes that match the colour of their hair. Antonina wishes she had the Miska to give them. All she can offer is cake and lemonade. They settle on the gingerbread and scuttle away.

Antonina can't imagine how Ivan lives without them. Perhaps he had an affair, and the wife kicked him out. His hand touches the middle of his wife's back every now and then as though they still belong together. One of the Marias — the fat one — has sweets for the children. They come back to dump the gingerbread on the table, then rush off for the sweets. Who could blame them?

Hey, Tatyana says, catching one of them as she comes in the door. Get me a sweet, too? But they run off and don't even pretend to try.

Vladimir places the barbed-wire around the head of his mannequin and Antonina thinks he might actually have something.

Look, now it's working, she cups her hand and aims her words towards Tatyana.

What shall we name it? Vladimir notices them looking and pinches his chin.

Untouchables, Tatyana calls across to him.

Vladimir raises his arms in his usual dramatic way. Eureka! he says.

I wouldn't do that. Antonina nudges Tatyana. He's likely to hunt you down for more.

Hunt me down?

If he remembers your comment, he'll come for you later, and you'll be stuck in his floodlights, forced to defend yourself until he drops in a vodka coma.

Sounds like fun. I hope he does.

Trust me, you don't.

I can handle it.

Antonina moves the plate of blini on the table, so it's closer to the mushroom sauce. The cherry jam and sour cream are there as well, but the mushrooms and the marinated fish are the stars since she failed to find any caviar. The other Maria turns the music down to let Semyon play a song on his guitar. He's a good singer for a decommissioned soldier. Or, at least, that's what Semyon calls himself. Konstantin says he has the tattoos of a convict. He must have hidden them well to get his security guard position at the fancy apartment block. Semyon probably isn't even his real name, according to Konstantin.

Everyone claps when Semyon's song is done. They ask for more, but he's had enough and turns the stereo back up. Vladimir poses with the barbed-wire again. He places it over his head, and slips, cutting a finger as he tries to stop the fall. He looks across to Antonina with puppy-dog eyes, but Antonina has no intention of playing nursemaid.

Tatyana, she says, go help him, will you?

Why me?

You work at the hospital, don't you?

Being an orderly hardly makes me a nurse.

Geriatrics, isn't it? Well, he's old enough. You said you could handle it.

That's not what I meant, and you know it.

Tatyana guides Vladimir towards the kitchen with his

bloody finger leading the way. As soon as they're gone Konstantin ramps the music up, and the volume of conversations rises in competition. The room is filling up fast. The new album recently released by The Fantom is pulsating, and the *nastoyka* is starting to work its magic.

Come dance, Sofiya says, but Antonina doesn't like to stand too close to her. Looking up all the time hurts her neck. She declines and points towards a new bunch of men who have just arrived. Sofiya looks them up and down, then waves them away.

The new men follow Tatyana to the kitchen. By the time Antonina joins them, the room's full of blue smoke and laughter. One of them offers her a chair at the table, and she takes it. Be nice to get a bit drunk. Be nice to have Makar by her side, looking after her, offering her a chair. He used to of course, but . . . Makar, Makar, Makar. Stop it. She feels sick of herself thinking about him all the time.

The kitchen is divided into several food preparation surfaces, most made from old cupboards brought in from elsewhere and covered in floral oilcloth. Above these are makeshift shelves that look as if they could fall any minute from the weight of hanging pots and stacked plates. There are two ovens and three bench-top mini cookers, but there is only one sink, and it's down the end of the narrow room beside the table with its three mismatched wooden chairs.

Tatyana's smoking a brown cigarette that smells like a cigar.

What's that? Antonina asks.

A cigarillo.

Give me a puff?

You're not allowed. Tatyana holds the cigarillo away.

Oh my god! I'm going to whack you if you don't give it to me, Antonina says still holding out her hand.

Tatyana shakes her head. Nope. It'll make you sick.

Just before midnight, Antonina leaves the kitchen gathering to light the church candle on the honey cake. Konstantin manages to blow it out without too much spittle landing in the cream. The cake slices beautifully, with the multiple layers staying intact. She tries not to feel offended when only a few take a slice. It's often that way, and Antonina isn't sure why they leave the cake till last. At her next party, she will have it first. Not that she has any parties of her own. Good for breakfast though, if she gets up early. Honey cake and strong tea. Yum.

Konstantin decides its story time. Take a seat, he commands and motions for everyone to sit on whatever they can find, half of them opting for the floor and crossing their legs.

There was this time I spent in Nevskaya Dubrovka digging for war trinkets when I was a child, he says. The shadows would cross the trees right in front of me. Dead soldiers from the siege, they were. Sometimes they would guide me with blinking lights to a spot where the skeleton of a hand poked through the mud, sometimes a boot, sometimes a helmet, or a gun. I was sure they were having a laugh at my expense, could almost feel them laughing and I was scared, but I wouldn't show them. One night a ghost followed me home. He whispered his name in my ear as I slept. Rafik, he said. I woke in the night screaming, convinced he had me by the shoulder, shaking me so hard that it hurt. Dream or not, my father had to knock my shoulder back into the joint. Like Jacob in the Bible, he said. Wrestling with an angel.

Only Rafik was no angel. It gave me such a fright that I wouldn't go back into the woods. A few weeks later another boy was killed by an undetonated hand-grenade going off, buried not far from where I had been digging. It was the ghost of Rafik that saved me, he says. Maybe the other boy was too stubborn to look for the signs. Or didn't hear Rafik's name whispered in his ear at night. Still hurts, he says, rounding his shoulder at the joint.

Now, who else has a story? A true story?

One of the new men is a writer. Peter, the poet. He looks Antonina's way as he makes his way to the front. She should be interested, but she's hooked on Makar like Velcro, so there's no point. He recites a poem from memory called 'Black Raven'. It's about the disappearances in the night of the diplomats from the House of Government in Moscow. *The house of shadows*, he calls it. Antonina likes that name. He looks at her again when he's done, and she turns away. Good name for a show, she suggests to Tatyana.

Who else has a story for me? Konstantin says.

Antonina thinks about it. No one else is coming forward yet. She could.

Come on, Konstantin says. It's my birthday. Tell me a tale.

I have one, Antonina steps forward. She tells of the time she was abducted as a child. How a strange old woman her mother called a *gwisin* took her from her bedroom window, onto a train, where she was taught the dance that calls up the ancestors' ghosts.

Did it work? Sofiya asks.

There were strange shadowy shapes inside the train when we crossed the bridge. They could have been the ancestors, I suppose. They told me the story of the crow king and the rice farmer's wife, but they muddled the story up, said the wife lied so much that her fingers burnt to charcoal. But that's not the real story.

Ghosts that tell stories? Sofiya says. Is that the best you have?

Konstantin hushes her. Show us the dance, he says. Maybe we'll get some visitors tonight.

Antonina isn't sure about doing the dance. She remembers the last time she did and the trouble it got her into. The room cheers her on, and space is made in the middle of the gathering, the rugs pulled back ready for her performance.

I'll tell you the story of the crow king, she says. She lines herself up in the middle of the circle. Once upon a time in the land of crows, she says, accentuating the gesticulations of her hands and arms as the story grows. Her legs move like a dancer and she plays with the expressions on her face, points her fingers and weaves the story with the same controlled voice and graceful rolling rhythm the old woman had used. The audience laugh and sigh on cue like puppets, her hands tugging at the strings of their emotions. The dance comes as naturally as a gift. The process of retelling a joy she hadn't expected.

The applause at the end warms her so much that she takes a bow.

Show us the other dance, Sofiya says. The dance of the ancestors.

No, Antonina says. Time for someone else.

She heads for a spot on the floor to sit, but Konstantin starts a rhythmic chant. Dance, dance, dance, he says, clapping in time with foot stomps until it is impossible to say no. She shouldn't have mentioned that dance. The forbidden dance, though, she never did believe it was the reason Viktor's father had the accident. Her mother over-reacted, and that's why the villagers called it a curse. It's just a dance, after all. A simple dance. It'll be fine, she tells herself as she moves to the middle of the circle again. Her hands lift to second position like a ballerina, but not like a ballerina at all, and she begins to twirl. Is she really doing this? The worms are in her stomach, just as they were the night of the school dance. She pushes the thought of her mother aside and focuses.

Kanaiji oneora. Antonina hears the words in the rhythmic clap of her audience, in the scuff of her boots on the bare concrete floor, in the pulse in her throat and the swish of her skirt. She lets go, her eyes rolling back in her head. My name is Moon she chants, louder and louder, this time without a mother to stop her halfway through. The dance pulls her mind away, reeling her in like a fishhook through the heart, and when she resists, the taut line tugs at the flesh of her right atrium. She has wings, she is sure of it. She will leave the ground very soon and fly up into the rafters. She twirls and twirls. My name is Moon, and the room seems to be falling away, shrinking to a small curl of light no bigger than her brown irises. Surrounding her is darkness, and she has no idea if she still twirls below in that circle of light, or if her body has stopped and fallen on the floor. So distanced from her body now. Flying, she is flying. *Kanaiji oneora,* she hears, but this time it is not the voice of the old woman at the window, it is the voice of a man, in a place that feels as if it could swallow her whole.

Antonina stops and unhooks her heart. She does not want to enter the dance any further than that, or to know who is speaking to her. And she does not want to believe that the dance was anything more than a stupid dance. A stupid dance that she should not have dared to do again. The darkness retreats and her eyes roll back to the room. She feels warm and drowsy, as though she's been woken from the blissful state of sleep and can't quite place the enormous gravity of concern in Tatyana's expression as she comes into focus.

You all right? Tatyana says taking hold of Antonina's arm.

What happened? Antonina asks, expecting something horrible by the way Tatyana is behaving.

That's enough, Tatyana says. You shouldn't be doing that.

Did we have some visitors? Antonina says.

I think we scared Tatyana, Konstantin says, and laughs.

We didn't have any visitors, did we? Antonina says. It wasn't meant to be serious.

Nope, Konstantin says. No visitors, but we saw plenty of your knickers.

She hadn't thought of that.

Not to be outdone, Vladimir starts up a new ghostly tale, and the attention is drawn away.

It looked pretty serious to me, Tatyana says, leading Antonina towards the corridor. Like you were about to pass out. I've seen that look — just before my mother has a fit she gets it. The eyes roll back, and she's off.

Oh, I thought you were mad about showing everyone my knickers, Antonina says.

Why would I be angry about seeing your knickers? I like your knickers.

You weirdo. Anyway, I'm fine now, Antonina says, and releases her arm.

A few people that Antonina doesn't recognise are playing poker in the kitchen. Tatyana pulls out an unoccupied chair, but Antonina pushes past and sets herself at the sink, pressing her legs against the cupboards so she won't look tiddly, though that's exactly how she feels — the room undulating either side of her. The metal bench-top is solid though — cold to her touch, and the plug fits in the drain without trouble.

You sure you're all right? Tatyana says. You're not going to be sick, are you?

I'm fine, Antonina says. It was just a dance. I got a little giddy, that's all.

The sink fills ready for clean-up. Antonina's had enough of the party. Even the sugar of the cake isn't enough to keep her from feeling weary. Fear of clean-up is enough to scare anyone away — even card players in the middle of a game. Soon they've packed up and gone. But not Tatyana. She sits at the table with a tea towel ready for wet dishes to be passed over. Antonina swirls the dish liquid in the sink. She feels a bit more than giddy if she's honest. A bit agitated as well. It's probably just the memory of her mother's coat being thrown over her head the last time she did the dance. The feeling of being the puppy in the sack. The sense of shame. Calm down, she tells herself.

She starts with the flat plates and sinks an entire pile into the water leaving a hole in the suds that soon closes in like clouds. One by one Antonina scrubs the face and back, and hands them over, dripping on their journey across the corner of the room. By the time she is on to the second pile, the turbulence has lost its energy, and the waves in the air have gone too. Her legs are sturdy enough without the cupboard's support.

So, how are the geriatrics? Antonina says.

They're fine.

Tatyana dries two more dishes in silence. Antonina wipes her hands on Tatyana's towel and finds the hidden whisky, and a glass, which she slides across the table to Tatyana then goes back to the sink and starts piling the dishes on the bench while Tatyana takes time to enjoy a drink.

I was taking an old guy down to X-ray the other day, Tatyana says, and he asked if I was taking him to the crematorium. I thought he was joking and laughed. It wasn't a joke though. He was serious, and he couldn't understand why I thought it was funny. He actually thought he was already dead.

That's so sad.

I know. You never know what they're going to come out with. Maybe you could come in one day. They like visitors. They would think you're their daughter, or son, or mother. Sometimes they even believe they are talking to angels.

Antonina loves the way Tatyana chatters about work when she's drinking. Usually, she is so quiet about it that Antonina forgets that she works.

Do you ever really connect with them? she asks.

Sometimes. There's one old darling who keeps saying she knows my papa. I must have mentioned him, and she's remembered his name. They go in and out of reality, hard to tell if they're fully there at times.

What does she say about your papa?

Not so much my papa, but she thinks I have a lost brother in Semipalatinsk.

Ivan's wife leans in the doorway to say goodbye. The children have been sleeping on the bony refugee sofa in the hall. The girl in Ivan's arms has her head on his shoulder, the boy leans into his father's legs, none of them wanting to let go. Only the wife smiles.

Say goodbye, Ivan's wife says.

Ivan turns so the girl can see without having to lift herself. She yawns. Thank you for the cake, the boy says.

Antonina waves at the girl as they leave. Tatyana starts up where she left off. She says they were friends before I was born.

Who does?

The woman in the geriatric ward.

Antonina's dish pile is getting too high, so she hands Tatyana a bowl to dry. But your papa isn't old enough to have friends her age, is he? she says, unsure how old Tatyana's parents are, having never met them.

No. Tatyana's face brightens with the revelation. So, they can't have known each other, can they?

You were bothered about it before, though?

Before Tatyana has time to continue, Konstantin is suddenly there, standing in the doorframe, arms crossed like he means business. Tatyana slides the bottle of whisky from the table to the floor without catching Konstantin's attention.

So, he says, did you know there was a tank in Palace Square today? His words elongate and mesh at the edges. He sways to the left and lands a shoulder against the wall as if that's what he intended.

The fat Maria pushes him out of the way, and he rushes forward with the loss of balance. Maria holds out the stand Antonina borrowed for the birthday cake. While Antonina cleans it, Maria searches cupboards muttering about not being able to find anything, and dishes being put away in the wrong place.

But that's enough of that, she stands upright and clasps her hips as if to reprimand herself for being so dull.

What are you missing, love? Tatyana says as though Maria's one of her geriatrics. And she probably will be soon enough.

A green plate. It was my mother's. Shaped like a teardrop.

Of the two Marias, Antonina is fondest of this one. The other has tiny feet and clippy heels that echo in the corridor day and night, and all around the kitchen her belongings are labelled with pink ink on brown packing tape to make sure no one else uses them, though everyone does.

Cleaned bowls and plates are piled up on the table, waiting for owners to claim them. Amongst the pile, Tatyana finds the green dish.

Oh, there it is, Maria says. She hugs it to her chest like a hot-water bottle, and Antonina can almost see the monsters packing up and moving out of her head — for the time being at least. Maria collects her cake stand and departs with the treasure that's too precious to leave in a communal kitchen.

You know what? Konstantin moves closer. Antonina tries not to inhale his drinky-breath. If you want to stay in St Petersburg and do your arty stuff, I could arrange for someone to take the child for you. Permanent like.

The 'p' of the word permanent has some spit attached and it sprays the side of her face. She wipes her cheek clear and pushes him away.

I'm not giving away a baby, what are you thinking?

No, he says, and he rounds the side of her face again. She holds her breath. Not give it away, he says. Sell it.

You're serious? she says, her hands suspended above the dishwater.

Yep, he says and nods slowly and intentionally like a child.

Don't worry about him, Tatyana says. He's drunk. Go back to the party. We're busy working here.

Antonina washes another dish, but the water is oily and brown, so she leaves it to come back to. She takes Tatyana's tea towel to wipe her hands, but it's too wet. So she finds another.

Konstantin hasn't gone back to the party. He's still in the doorway when Antonina takes a seat. What she would do for a smoke right about now, or a shot of that whisky Tatyana hid from Konstantin.

I don't think Makar would be too happy with selling his nugget, she says.

Tatyana asks if Makar even knows.

Seriously, Antonina says. Are you ganging up with him? She points towards Konstantin.

Tatyana sits back, crosses her legs and kicks her foot out and in, out and in, the way she never does.

I'll go see him if you like, Konstantin says.

No, you won't. Antonina glowers at Konstantin. Don't you dare. Like you said, this is none of your business, and I'm not — she stops herself and reduces the volume of her voice — I'm not selling.

The beauty queen moves into the kitchen to empty her samovar. Antonina's not sure how much of Konstantin's suggestion she heard. There is no way of telling beneath the lobotomised smile.

There's no room here, Antonina says. The sink is full. You'll have to empty it in the bathroom.

Sofiya looks across at the sink. I need to rinse it, though, she says.

Tatyana reaches for the samovar. Leave it here. We'll clean it and bring it to your room.

Their curtness must come as a surprise because Sofiya retracts so Tatyana can't take hold of the samovar.

Go use the bathroom then, Antonina says.

But it doesn't fit under the tap in the bathroom, Sofiya complains.

Oh, for God's sake, Tatyana says. Here, and she hands Sofiya a pot.

Sofiya just stands there blinking, so Antonina takes her by the arm and leads her towards the door. We're not finished in here, she says. She pulls Konstantin inside the room and shuts the door, leaving Sofiya out in the hall.

So rude, Sofiya says, loud enough to be heard, then she trots away, her heels clipping like Maria's.

That's just typical, Antonina says to Konstantin, her voice a mix of fierce and calm, and she's comfortable with that. Now you're into human trafficking? One of your gangster connections, I suppose?

That's my girl, Tatyana says.

Antonina sends her a reprimanding look. She must understand she's being patronising. She's not stupid. Tatyana's leg kicks too fast to be comfortable, and her foot takes over instead, jittering side to side.

I'm not part of the mafia. I know other people. Nice people. He moves away, trying to appear casual, though he shifts his shoulders like he's bothered.

Nice people, who want to buy nuggets to use as what? Tatyana says.

Nice people, who want nuggets for their own, he says. He picks at his thumbnail without looking down.

Like an adoption? Antonina asks.

Exactly like adopting. Legit adopting, Konstantin says. Only they'll pay for it.

Antonina crosses to the sink. Her friends are quiet behind

her, but she can feel them staring at her back.

It could be a way clear, she says. Tatyana's foot stops twitching and Antonina doesn't dare look up from the leg. But there's still Makar, Antonina says when she should be thinking instead. And, well, you never know —

Makar? Tatyana's voice suddenly booms. You don't need Makar.

I agree. Konstantin puts his hand up like he's in class. Where's pretty boy been the last two years? I'm the one who's been looking after you, not Makar. He pats his chest as he speaks, then coughs.

That's not true, Antonina says, the fierceness back in her tone. I look after myself. I don't owe you anything.

Good girl, Tatyana says.

And I don't owe you anything either, she says to Tatyana.

I didn't say you did, Tatyana says. I said you don't need—

Who have you been talking to about this? Antonina says.

No one, Konstantin says. He backs up to the fridge, bumping it so the bottles inside rattle, then he slides down onto the floor. You're meant to be being nice to me, he says. It's my birthday.

They both ignore him.

Anyway, he babbles on like he's having a discussion with himself, I just heard it gets done. Lots of people want our babies. All these Westerners with weak semen. They can't have any of their own, so they come into the orphanages and our government sells them ours.

So, you thought you'd expand your business into baby-selling, is that it? Tatyana says.

He looks up, engaged with the room again. Just trying to help. That's all. You haven't seen a doctor, have you?

No, Antonina says. Not yet. Her hand instinctually lands on her belly and rubs it.

See, it's not even registered. Easy. Just think about it then, why don't you? He stretches one leg out in front, then unhooks the other as if with considerable effort from beneath his butt.

Why haven't you seen a doctor yet? Tatyana says.

Antonina rolls her eyes. Don't you start.

So, you don't even know how far along you are? says Tatyana.

Around three, three and a half months, I think.

You think!

Antonina pulls the plug and watches the funnel of swirling water until it's gone, then wipes down the clear side of the counter. Konstantin is right. She needs to talk to Makar. But it's too soon. She doesn't want the possibility of hearing the word 'abort' come from his lips. He wouldn't do that, would he?

You're not really considering Kostya's offer, are you? Tatyana says.

Just give it some time, Konstantin says.

It's not for sale, Tatyana says. It's going to her mother, isn't it, Nina? That's what we decided.

Tatyana's 'we'. Now they're getting too loud.

She's expecting it, right? Tatyana says.

They both know her mother doesn't know about the baby yet.

Konstantin drags himself up with a groan and scuffs towards the door. It's an option, that's all I'm saying. He points two fingers at her. You wouldn't need to scratch that stupid teacher's back for funding if you sold the nugget to a good home. You'd have enough to keep yourself going at that university for a couple of years, maybe more.

I don't scratch anyone's back for funding, Antonina shoots back. But I'll think about it.

Konstantin ploughs his arm through the air like a shooting star and makes a whistling noise that would be funny at any other time. Antonina has no idea what he means by it. But that's that, and she's glad he's satisfied enough to head off for bed. Tatyana is another matter. She says nothing, but Antonina can feel the kettle inside her friend coming to a boil. Slow and sure. They listen to Konstantin's stumbling down the hall. Antonina lifts herself to sit on the bench-top. The chill of stainless steel penetrates through her skirt. The party has quietened down, but there's still chatter in Vladimir's room. Another couple of guests pass by the kitchen door on their way to bed. Antonina would dearly like to go to bed too, but Tatyana is pacing, and she dares not leave the room.

Tell me you're not going to consider it, Tatyana says when the coast is clear.

Antonina hadn't meant she would think about the adoption, she thought it might be a good idea to send Konstantin to talk with Makar. But now that Tatyana mentions it, maybe adoption is not such a bad idea.

But what if they're good people? she says. They'd have to be good people.

You can't trust him, Nina. Don't. You've got a shot at a good mark, haven't you? And you're going to talk with Makar about it?

I wasn't thinking of blackmailing him.

Tatyana shakes her head and whistles silently.

Antonina doesn't want to hear what's coming. Doesn't

want to see Tatyana's face when she says it either. She is afraid she might see the hardness of judgement in her friend's expression. Or worse, the soft quiver of pity.

Seriously, Nina, Tatyana says. You don't still think he's interested?

Antonina hangs her head. What if, she says and stops. Tucks her hands beneath her thighs on the bench that has warmed to her. Well, if he isn't interested, then I will blackmail him. She lifts her head. What if I got the extra funding from the Academy, she says, and a reasonable payout for adopting the nugget? Kostya's right. It could carry me right through. No more odd jobs. My own room back at the hostel. Would that be so bad?

To what end? says Tatyana. So you can complete a degree at that bloody Academy? How could you live with yourself knowing strangers are out there raising your baby? That's just bullshit.

I know, Antonina says, still thinking. But it's an option. Let's call it plan B, or maybe C. If everything else fails.

Tatyana folds her arms across her chest and stares at Antonina, her eyes wide with disbelief. Disappointed. Pained. It's the first time Antonia has ever seen that face on her friend. If you do that, Tatyana finally says, then you're no different from the rest.

What do you mean? Antonina tries to sound calm, but she can feel herself tightening. She shouldn't have asked.

Greedy, Tatyana says, hard as a bashing ball. A sell-out. That's what I mean.

Emotion rises like mercury up the back of Antonina's throat. She tries not to cry when Ivan returns from delivering his family home and pokes his head in to see what's up. He looks as nervous as a robin come to steal a crumb. No one's seen Antonina and Tatyana argue before, because they never have.

Are you trying to tell me that you would throw your art career away for an unplanned nugget? Antonina says. How would you even know what you are capable of unless you're in the same position?

Hey Tanya, Ivan says, Vladimir is looking for you. A swift glance in Antonina's direction is enough to spot the fear. Typical males. They can fight bears, but they can't handle the tears of a woman.

Tatyana is supposed to stay the night, but Antonina doesn't try to stop her when she leaves for home. It doesn't matter. It's not her baby. That 'we', she keeps talking about. Antonina has no intention of becoming a 'we' with anyone but Makar. She leans forward and wipes her wet face on the edge of her skirt, feeling so alone, and hating herself for her need for company, for love and acceptance. This isn't the way adults are supposed to behave. Her mother wouldn't.

She has no idea what's right or wrong anymore. Everything is upside down. The heel of her boot taps against the cupboard door below the sink and a cockroach scuttles across the squares on tea-stained linoleum, into the dark recess under the fridge. Where there's one, there's many. An infestation. They still say that about the Koryo-saram. Feels like someone keeps kicking at her trolley bag, and she's getting tired of the fight.

THE NUGGET

For months now, Antonina has been rising early to get to her clay before the day starts at the Academy. There is just one month left to complete an end-of-year show strong enough to get the high mark required for next year's funding. Either that or she needs to grab the attention of the art patrons she hopes will attend. Makar will be one of the hands they shake. One of the trusted voices to give opinions on the up-and-coming artists, and it's time to convince him that she has what it takes. The nugget, she hasn't brought up yet. She is four and a half months now, and lucky it has taken some time for her belly to round. Not too much that it's noticeable beneath loose clothing, but enough, and she can't believe she didn't take up the option of abortion while she could. It's too late for that now, and still, she can't find the courage to bring up the nugget with Makar.

Rising early should have become automatic by now, but it still takes the alarm clock to wake her. Konstantin pounds on the freestanding wardrobe that divides the space between them and it shakes like a little earthquake even when he stops. She ignores his complaint and fumbles for her clothes. There is a light, but their conjoined spaces were once one room, now they're each the size of single beds with one bulb that serves both halves. The torch isn't where she left it, on the floor beside the door. She reaches through a gap to Konstantin's side, trying not to inhale the smell of his sweat and stale breath. Various objects line the small bedside table, and she touches them with the gentleness of a mosquito on skin until she comes across the shape of the torch. Just when she has hold of it, Konstantin grabs her wrist and laughs.

Wake the whole place up, why don't you? she says tugging her hand free.

His bed creaks with the sound of a body turning over. The luxury of going back to sleep would be tempting if her clay didn't wait for her on the stainless-steel bench of her studio, and the eagerness to be there with it overrides the warmth of her blankets.

Down in the bathroom, the light sways on a long-drop chord in the constant draught. The whole place was once a bustling tobacco factory. Now it's a sleeping factory, with a loading dock that Konstantin uses for storage. Whatever he can find to fill the old military truck comes through the place. Whatever he can peddle on the black market to earn enough money to live on.

Three splashes of icy water from the tap shock Antonina into full wakefulness. Above the sink is a length of opaque mirror with dark pools where the paint on the back is peeling. It gives the room an old movie look, with the film burning away in places. In the reflection her doppelgänger brushes her long black hair, her features softened in the haze. A romantic version of herself, spoiled when she pulls her hair back and covers it with an army-green beanie. The movie-star version of herself gone in a flicker, and it's all right with Antonina — she would rather verge on the unnoticeable than the conspicuous.

Back in her room, she places a single cigarette in her mouth, checks her gloves are in her pocket, her bootlaces are tied, and her bedroom key is inside her bag with her lunch. In two well-practised movements, she switches on the light and whips the blankets off Konstantin, dumping them on the floor. He could pull them back while they're still warm, but he doesn't. She hears him searching for his boots as she takes flight through the door, his cussing behind her in the corridor, the clatter of a tin bucket and the clumsy clop of his unlaced boots as he follows.

Antonina bolts through the back door and stops when she reaches the cut-wire fence. Konstantin comes no further than the open door, and Antonina throws him the cigarette with the torchlight guiding its safe landing, the way she always does. He catches the cigarette, puts it in his mouth and holds out his hands for the torch. He's almost cute with his hair more mousy than blond, sticking up like static, his sleep-angry crumpled expression. She throws him the torch and the beam of light cartwheels between them. She then turns into the darkness to wait until her eyes can sift out the details of the alley before she moves. Behind her is the *fsst* of Konstantin lighting a match, the whip of his jacket zipper, and she knows he'll stand in the doorway until the cigarette is finished. He doesn't need her smokes. He doesn't have to listen out for her the way he does. But it's an unspoken rule of their cohabitation that he will.

There don't appear to be any foreign noises in the distance, just the gentle hum of a sleeping city, so she ventures out, moving fast. By the time she's out of Konstantin's earshot, the worst of it is behind her, where the factories sidle up, and the alleys are narrow. Beyond this are the housing developments of the old city, with internal courtyards that offer more security in the darkness than the streets with their roving gangs.

Antonina makes her way through the square at the back of the Academy. There is no point heading around the front as the doors will be locked for several hours yet. There is a broken path through the square, but no lighting other than the luminosity of thin spring snow that clings to the edges, and the gauzy purple of early dawn — night starting to peel away so Antonina can make out the edges of the world around her, in a two-dimensional way at least.

At the far end of the building is a small window above the toilet that Antonina unlatched the day before. It's a game she plays with the caretakers without them even knowing — one of them locks the windows at closing time, and she unlocks the toilet window before leaving.

The window pivots open with a quick tuck and tilt of the blade from the box cutter she stores in her bag. With a secure grip of the sill, she climbs the ridges of the stonework to squeeze herself through the narrow frame. It's a trick that's getting harder by the week thanks to the nugget. She sucks in her breath and elongates her torso, scraping her back along the ridge of the window so the baby won't be harmed.

The toilet is more like a closet than a bathroom, small

and cluttered and used for storage. Half-empty paint cans stock-piled for future use, boxes of toilet tissue that Antonina helps herself to when there's enough that it won't be noticed. Brooms and mops lean against the wall and occasionally change position. She is never sure exactly what time the security guard comes in. Sometimes there is one. Sometimes there's not. There is no pattern to their presence. When she is satisfied no one's there, she heads out into the corridor with hardly enough light to scare the darkness away. She makes her way by feel, fingers trailing along the solidness of the wall, trying very hard to ignore the thoughts of moving shadows the way they did on the train. Which is ridiculous, she always tells herself. You were a child with an imagination as big as the moon. Though it's hard to ignore the sense of being watched that makes her flesh prickle.

Inside the studio, she feels safe enough to turn on the lights. The fluorescent bulbs blink then settle into a hard light with their usual hum. Above two rows of curtained studio spaces, a life-size plaster-cast copy of St Isaac's Jesus Christ with angels protrudes from the end wall. They look set to be lifted out of the world into heaven, raptured and saved from the presence of pagans.

Good morning, she says, palms pressed together in appreciation of their company.

Dawn is never the best time for moulding clay. As soon as Antonina touches the lump on her bench, it returns the chill of her morning hands. Resentful, perhaps, at being left alone in the west wing of the Academy, unformed. Or perhaps the clay prefers to be left alone altogether, snug under the wrap of its damp sacking. Whichever it is, the resistance is always obvious in the beginning.

The clay has a smooth clammy sheen to it. Her mother would approve. Critical as she is of the impracticality of Antonina's sculptures, she has nonetheless taught her daughter how to care for the parcels of clay she sends all the way to St Petersburg for Antonina's work. Each week a new package arrives. *A gift from the mountain*, her mother labels them. And she's right; they are — the clay is good, rich, and dark with minerals.

The metal of the studio radiators ticks with the promise of heat. One of the caretakers has arrived too early. She must begin her work before the distractions set in. Class. Cleaner. Makar. Even the thought of Makar is sometimes still a distraction, though he has avoided being alone with her for months now. She opens up the volume of her tape recorder and lets Chopin fly out over the partitions that reach halfway up the towering walls. Up and out the music expands, and fills the entire room all the way up to the ridiculously beautiful vaulted ceiling.

With a cutting wire, she splits the mound of clay into three equal parts. Russia, Kazakhstan, Korea. Perhaps she *can* embody them all. Claim herself and her baby as part of the new tribe, just as Tatyana suggested.

Be careful of that word *blend*, Makar warned her in front of the entire class when she brought up the idea. Diversity is our strength — his new mantra.

But Antonina isn't sure the diversity of being Koryo-saram without a motherland is the kind of individuality that gets celebrated. What if the work is about what I am, rather than what I'm not? What if that's where the voice is strongest?

Makar said she was talking in abstracts, and that's not what they were here to do. Other schools teach to provoke and shock, he said. You can move into that kind of work after you graduate. Four years complete, another two to go. The Academy of Art's training is a lengthy process — too long to wait before she can express these ideas. This abstract part of herself she has managed to separate from the formal training of the Academy, and she creates a responsive work in the hidden hours when only the caretakers are there to see.

She lets herself centre, allowing the energy to rise through her core before she pushes down on the clay. She lifts and pushes again. And again. The earthly chill of the clay transfers to her hands, numbing her fingers in a duel between her mother's mud and her own hands. At first it appears the mountain will win, but eventually, it thaws to her persistence. With one last rise, she plunges splayed fingers deep into the softened clay, feeling that old familiar suck when she pulls away.

See how the mountain loves you? she says, just like her mother used to. She stands back to take in the handprints that mark her existence. Caveman-like. The shape of one living human being left behind.

Within the hour a caretaker moves in with the lazy sashay of his wide-head broom working its way around the studio. The tap of it against the parquet flooring outside her closed curtain is irritating. Must be to expel dust from the bristles, either that or he's drawing attention to the fact that they both know she's in her studio outside regular hours.

Her Chopin cassette picks the worst time to come to an end, the recorder clicking off to the suddenness of shocking silence with the caretaker still on the other side of the curtain. Antonina flips the cassette over. The broom taps on the parquet flooring again. What will he do? Report her? Makar will make it go away anyway. He's good like that. Perhaps the caretaker wants a bribe, but she has no sugar for the donkey. He has the wrong student if that's what he's after. She lets the music fill her mind again and comes back to the clay.

Good morning, Antonina. The caretaker pulls the curtain aside; he's Asian, his head slightly bowed in a pensive stance that's not typical of Russian servitude.

The clay doll in Antonina's hands turns into a series of finger dents and nail bites — its personality flitting away.

Nothing needs doing in here, she says.

The caretaker pushes the curtain open more, and she can see the entire length of him.

Chopin's number one. B flat minor. *Larghetto*, if I'm not mistaken? The caretaker's voice bounds over the top of the piano chords.

His irksome smile is radiating intrusive energy. Antonina can feel it, and she flicks him another glance, nods, then curls her shoulders deeper, to concentrate on the small figurine in her hands. With a pointed tool, she carves one tiny perfect face into the clay, her own face so close that her breath rebounds off its surface.

The caretaker is gone from the corner of her eye, then he's back holding a package the size of a tea tin towards her. He's never done this before. Never come to the sculpting studios before the others arrive. Never personally delivered parcels from her home. The clay doll slips in her hands and loses its shape.

Sorry, she whispers to the figurine, then squashes the tiny perfect face with the pressure of just one thumbprint. The clay thumps onto the bench, where it remains stoically standing, though it tilts enough that it should fall.

You're new, are you? Antonina says, wondering if this is the usual caretaker she passes during the day. What happened to the last one?

It reminds me of my wife, he says. The music. A long time ago now. He looks down at his feet. She hopes that's the end of it, but his attention sweeps back towards her. May I have a look at your work?

Antonina shifts to see what he is looking at, and that seems enough of a cue for him to move in. On the trestle table at the back of her studio, there's a week's worth of work lined up in varying stages of drying and painting. She is not accustomed to being addressed so directly by the caretaker. Usually, they manoeuvre around each other. Notes from across town dropped on desktops. Packages left inside studios without a mention. Even in the corridors, they avoid eye contact. There's natural synchronicity that lacks the need to acknowledge one another, and today he's decided to break it.

Chopin still blares, and she resists the obligation to turn it down. The handwriting on the small package is her mother's. There's nothing unexpected about that, so she places it beside the cassette recorder, then squashes the lopsided figurine into a ball of clay that squelches through her fingers.

The caretaker is at the back going over her work, and she watches him. Attentive — both of them. There is something about him, something familiar that she can't quite pick. While his Koryo-saram identity is evident, the poise of his diction is unusual — the considered emphasis of vowels here and there, that gives an air of diplomacy that's unfitting to a caretaker. Maybe this position was a demotion during the Soviet period, a punishment — he's old enough for that. Might have been a politician who barely escaped the coal mines in Siberia in a former life, and now he's too afraid to do anything else.

Do I know you? she asks.

My name is Nikolai. He stands as if waiting for something, a tip most probably, or a reduction in noise so he can speak.

I have nothing for you, she says, opening the palms of her hands to display the empty value of her clay.

The caretaker turns back to the trestle and leans in to consider each face of the figurines on the bench. No one else has seen them before. She covers them before class with an old tablecloth.

Your work, he says, tilting his head towards her, suggesting her pieces are too important to leave unattended. What do they represent? His interest appears to be genuine, so she turns the music down to a background vibration.

I don't know yet, she says.

They look lost. Sad and lost.

Antonina feels suddenly concerned. There must be fifty of them there, though there are more in large cardboard boxes in a storage room as well. Hundreds of them, varying in size from the width of her palm to three quarters the length of her hand, each with its own unique features, its own personality. She's not sure why she keeps making them.

They're the little people, she says, and no, they are not sad. She checks some of the faces to be sure, and no, they are not saying sad. They're waiting, she says, and with that, she knows what they are not — they are not a part of her future; she will leave them behind after the apartment show with Tatyana.

Yes, they wait, he says, and they're also sad.

Antonina draws a breath as though to defend something,

but there's no way of answering. The caretaker sees what he wants to see, and there's no reason to be anxious about that.

What do you think of that one? She nudges her chin in the direction of her largest piece, a life-size torso of a man pushing himself up from a plinth.

He is one of her masterpieces for the Academy examination at the end of the year. Well defined. The piece that will rake in the marks. Emotive. Evocative. Perfection of balance and skill.

A huge grin spreads across the caretaker's face, showing his teeth. Of course he has teeth, but to see them like that, so white, and so surprisingly open to the air, makes him look like an idiot.

This one is the ghost train, he says.

Antonina looks for evidence that he's teasing, but he doesn't give the impression of a jokester. I don't see it, she says.

You know the story of the ghost train? The caretaker pauses when she doesn't respond. He places his hand on his chin as if contemplating whether it would be wise to proceed. He is close enough that Antonina can smell the same brown soap her mother used to hand-wash their clothes with when the washer broke down.

I remember my mother saying something about deportation on the trains. Is it the same story?

How much do you know about our people, our history? he asks.

We're Koryo-saram . . . and Korea doesn't want us back. We were Soviet, like everyone else, and we aren't like anyone else anymore. I suppose there's more to it than that. To be honest, I'm having trouble figuring it out.

It surprises her that she is having this discussion with a caretaker, but why not? He's there, and he seems interested.

He sighs, folds his arms, the little people still holding his attention. He has a smooth round face; his age would be indiscernible if it weren't for the buckle of folded skin beneath each of his eyes.

My parents crossed the border into Russia to avoid the famines, he says. You know about that?

Antonina shakes her head, even though she has heard of that part.

Vladivostok became their new home, he says. That's where I was born. He stalls after saying this.

What about your wife? Antonina says, hoping to kick-start him again.

He stares into the space above the figurines now, his expression downcast, and she can see it — the lostness, the sadness. It doesn't belong to the little people, it belongs to him. It's tempting to reach out and touch his arm, but no bond between them would warrant such an exchange of empathy. She tries not to look. Gives him space to say what he wants to say, and opens herself to the muse within herself — that flitting shadow that likes to stay in the periphery without acknowledgement. A bear that runs when you yell at it. A muse that scatters if you look for it. A caretaker that can't be rushed. They all feel like the same thing.

Your music, he says. It hooks me. Chopin's melancholic nocturnes belonged to my wife long before you ever played them.

The music plays on behind them. The caretaker closes his eyes and sways to the memories that come to dance.

I still see her in the play of the piano, he says. Her smile.

Her laugh. Her mischievous fun. But that was before. As the music winds into a cluster of urgent notes, he says he also remembers the after. The ghost trains that took them away. You wouldn't know. Your generation doesn't understand. But look. He motions towards her piece on the plinth. It's in your work. It's coming up through you instinctually.

Is it? Antonina says. I don't see it . . . tell me more.

He picks up one of her little people and holds it close. Trust me, he says. It is. And trust is more important than belief.

—

Nikolai stops himself going on. It's not really his place to tell her the history of the Koryo-saram. That's a gift her babushka should already have given her.

The little person he picked up is an empty cone of dried clay that is just smaller than the palm of his hand. A woman with no neck, no body, no arms. Her face is tiny and perfect. All the work has gone into her features, and the cobalt blue shawl, which is meticulously edged with diamonds in yellow and green, each one framed with a hairline strip of gold. Her lips are precise little red curves at rest, and her eyes are as serene as any good Virgin Mary icon.

He slips the little woman into the top pocket of his overalls while the Sharm girl is busy trying to find the connection between her sculpture and his words. She concentrates so much that her face has stiffened with concern, her lips tight, her brows pressing in above the nose. His passion is confusing her. He will have to be more careful next time. Perhaps it wasn't a good idea even introducing himself, but he couldn't help it — so long he has waited, and for some reason there was excitement there, to see her in the flesh once again, all grown up.

How many years has it been? He tries to think, but the years no longer feel like years to him — they come and go unnoticed. Age defies comprehension. And now the girl is no longer a child, her age is a perplexity as well. One he really shouldn't care so much about. He hopes she appreciates the indulgence of time strolling by in the way it should, as he wishes he had when he was young himself. Back then he thought ambition was everything. He wasn't as attentive as he should have been. Back then he wanted time to pass quickly so he could get to where he was going, and here he is doing it again.

He should get on. Leave the girl to her work. To his delight, the little clay woman taps against a rivet as he walks away, a tiny repetitious thud like the beat of a heart. A small secret that brings him such unexpected pleasure.

Can you tell me the story of the ghost train some time? Antonina calls after him.

He presses his hand to his chest and feels the comfort of having a little woman there to touch.

I don't know much about the train. I was taken away before that happened. A lot of us were. I can tell you about Vladivostok, but maybe you should ask your babushka first. I'm sure there are stories she would like to share with you.

She's never spoken about it before.

Write to her, he says. Ask her. If she doesn't want to talk about it, then, of course, I will help you.

She nods.

Yes, it was probably a mistake to introduce himself so soon

— still, he is here now. And he can help where he can. He has taken something of hers. Now she must take something in return. It's only fair. He leaves the keys on the trolley and heads out for a walk around the building with his little woman. Tap, tap, tap.

———

The caretaker has left Antonina in a baffled state, while he moves around the room all calm, the broom held like a staff. Black rubbish sacks splay outward from his grip on the wooden handle. His other hand rests on his chest as if he were taking an oath. Allegiance perhaps. Or some other act of earnestness. She studies the clay man on her plinth. There would be a striking resemblance if the caretaker were younger.

Ghost train, she whispers and draws in close to see if the caretaker's words have poured any new substance into the source of the matter. Matter. We are matter amongst matter. But none of this is helping. If anything, his words are leading her even further away from the theories she should be studying for the oral exam. And this bust is destined to be broken down into reusable clay dust, just as soon as she gets her mark. It gives her an idea for the show with Tatyana though — an extra dimension that might be interesting.

She is still at the plinth when the caretaker passes her cubicle and heads out the door. He is just movement in the corner of her eye again, where he belongs. But there is something else. His trolley. Her eyes flick from the swing doors that swoop in and out, to the trolley, to the glint of the keys these people usually wear on belts, so they clink on their hips as they walk. The door stills, and there is no footfall in the hall. Her eyes move from the door to the keys. From the door to the keys.

The largest keys must belong to the outside doors. She aims for these first to find they are marked, the words *Front. Back. West. East*, soldered, one for each key. Her heart does a little jump, and she could almost giggle with the rush it gives her. What luck! She can't believe it. The hinged metal ring unhooks, and she takes the key marked *West* and gets back with her work as though nothing were amiss.

Before long, she hears the echo of the caretaker's boots in the empty hall. The doors swoop open, and he comes to claim his trolley.

I'll be locking the toilet window from now on, he says. It's not good for you to be climbing through windows. You must take care of the *aga*.

Aga. Antonina doesn't know that word and instinctively looks down. She is small, and the nugget has been hidden for the most part, but her plastic apron pulls tighter than it used to around her middle. She doesn't feel ready for what her body is doing, and has tried as much as she can to ignore it so far, but there is no doubt the secret is leaching out of her. That doesn't explain how he knows about the toilet window, though.

You know, you really shouldn't sneak in on people while they're working, she says. The caretaker is already leaving. She lifts herself up on her tiptoes as if to help her voice pole-vault the top of the partition. You usually whistle, she says. When you whistle, I can hear you coming.

There's the sound of puffed air — an attempt at a dry whistle that finishes with a slight groan. I think that's the other caretaker. Perhaps I'll just stick to my stories. Let me know what your grandmother says. The swing doors flap in and out, and it's only when he's gone that she remembers the phone in the head of department's office. She could have used it to call her babushka, if she had thought to look for that key as well.

Ghost train. It's a good name. Perhaps she'll suggest it to Tatyana for the show. The play button on the cassette player snaps off, causing a small avalanche of echoes that bounce around the stone walls, the statues, the vast panes of glass windows, and the baby flutters inside her for the first time.

ST ISAAC'S IS SINKING

The days are getting lighter as they head into summer. Antonina doesn't need Konstantin to stand by the door any-more, but he's out there anyway.

Not for the teacher, he says, before letting a large green pear drop into her hand.

Thank you, Papa, she says and shoots off towards the Academy, leaving him swearing in the doorway that he ain't nobody's papa.

It's too early for fruit crops in Russia, and she has no idea where the pear could have come from, or how much it potentially cost him. This makes her appreciate it all the more, and it's gone before she reaches the apartment buildings — chewed to a thin core, the sweetness still sticking to her lips and her fingers when she reaches the clay on her workbench.

Today, Antonina will complete the last of the figurines. She can't wait to see how they will look filling the floor of the apartment exhibition, but she will miss the mindlessness of the repetitious work. She is at her happiest with her hands in the clay, and the little people have allowed her a state of pleasant emptiness where thoughts can come and go freely like dreams that don't linger. Her mother must experience this every day. Pot after pot. Dream after dream. No wonder she is so reluctant to change. Art is not always as much fun as people assume. It has its pressures and pains. The little people, however, have been nothing but joy for Antonina, and she will be sorry to let them go. Unlike her mother, she must move on.

The central piece for the apartment show is what she will make next, and for that she needs a bundle of glass sand. What do they call it? She strains her brain to think, then releases it to work on the figurine in her hand. Frit. The name comes to her when it's ready. That's it. She'll make her own from glass bottles. Only, they aren't easy to come by since refunds on returns became available. She could ask Konstantin. Or there's the dumpster in the courtyard of Pushkinskaya-10 that the nightclub in the basement feeds. The only problem is the padlocks. She'll need bolt-cutters. Konstantin to the rescue after all. And Tatyana. She will need Tatyana as well.

During clean up, Antonina discovers another package left in the corner of her bench. It's wrapped in brown paper and tied with four knots in the Maedeup design that is always a shame to slice open. Inside are three vials of powdered pigment, each with a hand-written label — the turquoise is called *Big Almaty Lake*, the fuchsia *Tulips in Spring*, and the white *Mountain Peaks of Home*. Antonina places the pigments aside and opens the hand-painted piece of folded card in the bottom of the box. Three money orders flap onto her bench like escapee butterflies.

Dearest Nina.
There should be enough here that you can fly home this time. I've had a good season. So much to catch up on. Coming soon to see your show. I am looking forward to being there with you. Miss you, as always. Be good. Mama. P.S. Your babushka has asked me to send on her letter for you. She received your questions about the Koryo-saram's travels to Ushtobe. I'm not sure that part of our history is worth turning over again. We move on. Never mind, what's done is done.

To receive money of any sort would typically send Antonina out in a spending frenzy before the value dropped, to pay a debt, buy a treat. But the last time she went to the post office with one of her mother's money orders they refused to cash it. The new Kazakh currency is something modern Russia can't seem to manage. She will have to sell the money order to Konstantin for a tenth of the value. Or send it back.

Dear Mother

Antonina writes in the blank space of the same card. There's a lot of space, and a stamped envelope, so her reply will be swift.

The end-of-year show is coming together well. Please don't bother yourself coming to this one, it really isn't very interesting and not worth your time travelling here for it, especially since you hate to fly. I'll bring photos when I come home in the break.

The baby. Should she tell her about the baby? The thought of it makes her mouth dry. She takes her cup to the sink and pours a drink. The water is soothing and cool. She pours another. No, she won't mention it. She hasn't decided whether to put it up for adoption, or not. And if she doesn't, then surprise would be the best tactic, anyway. Delay as long as possible. The last thing Antonina needs is a mother crossing the continent to round her up and take her home before she's ready.

Thank you for the money order. I'm not able to cash them anymore inside this new Russia, but don't worry, I will cash them when I come back. I will be working through the holidays and will have enough to come home in August before the Academy starts again.

By August the child will be six weeks from birth. By then Makar would have covered for her at the Academy so she can return late with a good excuse. A car accident perhaps. Something that will take time to heal. It would cost him in *vziatka*, but she is not going to feel sorry for him — he will have to make it happen. It surprises her how easy it is to slip into the mode of bribery. The art of persuasion. Good business skills, Konstantin always says. Twist the arm enough so it hurts but doesn't break. As for her mother, she will leave it open-ended. News of a baby would not make her happy. It took considerable effort to get her mother to support her leaving for the academy in the first place. To peel away her mother's over-protective arms. No, she couldn't face the shame her mother would demand she feel. Not yet.

I know you will be disappointed I'm not coming home sooner, but I have a surprise for you when I do. You'll like it, I promise. I am doing well, enough to make you proud, I hope. Love Nina x

Her babushka's letter is thick inside a sealed envelope. A slip of glue along one edge could be evidence that her mother steamed it open before sending. A ruckus of noise distracts her. The clapping of urgent shoes where they shouldn't be, at least not for another hour yet. Nataliya's voice — Antonina would know it anywhere. She places the letter inside her bag for later and closes the curtain to her studio. As if spying, she listens for clues of who the others are. They aren't students. They're older, their voices sunken the way the octaves do as people age. She peeps through the curtain.

Nataliya carries on in her usual unflappable way. She motions towards her sculpture, and there's a shuffle of helpers — a tall man, her father most likely, with strong, blond hairy arms, a gold watch with a broad strap, and the weight of the world gouged into creases in his forehead.

The mother has the Bahama tan Antonina has only heard of. She is slim, attractive, and all those other aspects of the moneyed Russian wife that defy the typical Soviet stereotype. She wears knee-high suede boots, jeans, and a cream silk blouse. Around her neck is a simple silver chain, but on her finger is a ring with a tsarina-sized sapphire that's hard to ignore.

There is also the cliché character of a tall, lanky man-boy, who's trying not to be there — a brother perhaps, his face a complaint, shoulders pinched, saying nothing.

Antonina has already seen the piece they're moving

from the studio. The Dvina, Nataliya called it. The class workshopped it a few weeks ago in dry clay form. Nataliya said it was the primitive state of the finished work, and Antonina assumed it was to be remodelled in porcelain, but it isn't. This work has been carved from wood.

The mother flaps around with blankets while the two men groan at the weight of The Dvina. Steady the trolley, will you, the father says, and the two women take hold.

On the blanket, the mother says, and the father's hard look is as effective as a swear word.

Antonina likes the way the father's jaw clenches, the ridge of muscles on the boy-man's forearms, taut with the pressure, but still lean and almost hairless, just like the arms on her ghost train. She should have clenched the jaw more, and she admires the strength of the father's features again.

Shit, the boy-man says — a word usually reserved for street bums, and to Antonina's surprise no one rebuffs him.

Nataliya holds out her hands when The Dvina tilts on its side, as if she could save it from a fall.

Get the trolley. The father's voice is a whip now. Hold the bloody trolley.

Nataliya retakes the handle, and The Dvina comes down to lie lengthwise on it.

Well done, the mother says, clapping her hands.

Mr Yermilov, one moment please? One of the security guards holds a swing door slightly ajar, and when he knows the father is coming he closes it and moves deeper into the corridor.

Antonina had just enough time to make out the shape of the guard. He is the middle-aged one with the worried frown who likes to read magazines instead of doing his rounds. It's time for the returned favour for letting Nataliya's family in. Antonina can imagine the scenario unfolding in the security guard's tale. Contacts. They all need them.

The mother takes the opportunity to look inside other cubicles, which makes the boy-man complain that she's disrespecting privacy.

Ah, says the mother, discarding his concern with the flip of her hand. Who's going to know?

Antonina stands back from the curtain and waits for the mother to peek inside her studio. The mother lets out a small shriek and jumps when she does, and Antonina can't help laughing at her.

So, who let you in so early? Nataliya says with wild accusation in her words. Was it Mr Volkov? Or should I say, Makar? You seem to get all the teacher's favours these days.

Antonina's hackles rise at the mention of Makar's name. Not everyone pays for favours, she says, and the mother turns their way with a sharp glare.

That's not what I've heard, says Nataliya. She runs her fingers along The Dvina's arm.

Antonina hopes they drop the thing. Hopes it snaps in two. It's didactic and dull anyway.

It's called St Isaac's is Sinking, Nataliya says.

That's a bit weak, Antonina says. I thought you were working on a porcelain piece.

I was, then I was offered one of the oaks used as piles under the city. It's over three hundred years old. Touch it. It's beautiful, the wood, I mean.

Antonina moves in to stroke the wood. It can't be one of the original piles, she says. Wouldn't it fall apart after that long in the bog?

It's authentic, the mother says, and Nataliya gives her a shut-up look.

Not from St Isaac's? It can't be. Antonina knows the stories of St Isaac's Cathedral sinking, whether there's any truth to it, but there is no way you could remove one of the piles from under the weight of that much marble and gold.

It wasn't even in the bog, the boy-man says with a scornful tone.

But it was one of the oaks that was meant to be, says Nataliya.

So, it's just a random old pole then, says Antonina. Could have come from anywhere.

Nataliya is about to defend herself when the father comes back, the swing door flapping violently behind him. We don't have time for this, he says in a manner that means that *he* doesn't have time for this. Come get the other door, will you? Don't just stand there yapping.

Nataliya's mother holds the swing doors open, and the father guides the head of the trolley through, with the man-boy stationed at the end. The piece really is remarkable, though Antonina would never say so out loud. If she'd known what was in Nataliya's studio, she would have spent some time in there with it.

You should keep the name as The Dvina, she says.

You have no idea what you're talking about, Nataliya says, sending the words flying over her shoulder. And they're off, the grind of unoiled wheels in the corridor bearing the weight of The Dvina, swing doors settling with the beat of butterfly wings, Nataliya and her entourage gone. Just the singe of jealousy lingering.

Makar will soon be in her studio. He's doing the rounds, working his way closer one student at a time with checks, commendations and recommendations, all the while toting that massive mug of coffee, no doubt. It has become his constant companion throughout winter. Ugly. She can't imagine him picking up a navy-blue giant mug with green dots all over it, carrying it to a counter and paying good money for such a thing. It must have been a gift.

That new distance in his voice gives her the creeps. The all-important transplant of a voice that rumbles up from the chest. Sounds grey, with a non-emotional, non-judgmental, pneumonial grind that is supposed to sound authoritative. He made a much better mentor than he does a teacher. One day he will settle back into himself again.

He wears a docile smile when he enters her studio, and she wonders if Nataliya whispered in Makar's ear about Antonina's break-in to the Academy earlier in the morning. Bribery is illegal now, so Antonina feels safe with a weapon of her own to throw back if she needs to. Nataliya's not stupid. She would know this.

Makar lets the air settle before they acknowledge each other's presence, and Antonina hangs her head forward as if in concentration, but really it is to allow the length of her hair to hang — a veil she uses to hide the blush when the whip of longing jumps behind her ribs with the fizz and bloom of fireworks. She doesn't rise to greet him, but remains crouched, leaning against the side of the box she's preparing for the other show, a different show, one that he knows nothing about.

She hears the toe-heel clink of his cup being placed on the bench above her, and catches a glimpse of him sliding her essay from the faux-leather folder he holds under one arm. No words needed. He has edited her work as she expected, probably more than she expected, and she nods in silent appreciation.

What are you working on? he asks.

She tucks her hair behind her ear so she can see him properly now that the heat is dying from her face, grateful the ugly mug isn't between them. It's just storage, she says.

You're not going to break the pieces down after the show?

Yes, she says. I just thought of playing with a mould first.

Do you have time for that? You've got a lot to get finished. This isn't what you're supposed to be doing.

She shrugs.

You've been distracted lately, he whispers. I think you should get back to the curriculum. Forget the extras. They aren't going to help your final mark.

You could help my final mark, she says, immediately sorry she let that slip. She glances through the curtained opening. There's no one visible, but the sound of the class busy with their projects is all around.

Don't get your hopes up too high, he says. Antonina follows his eyes to the essay, and he mouths *needs work*.

He crouches beside her, places the folder on the ground, and continues in a whisper. The springs of his brown hair are longer than they have been in some time. Used to be she could twirl a finger in them, and she longs to reach out and run her hand along the side of his head.

Things have changed, he says. He looks at her and sighs into the next sentence: There's no longer the strict ethnic quota there was. Positions aren't held open for the children of farmers. You must keep up.

I'm not the daughter of a farmer, she says. I'm the daughter of the great artist, Professor Valerii Shin. And he vouched for my work himself on the application.

You're not the only spawn of the great Valerii Shin who's been vouched for through the years, he says. And Antonina knows he's right; only her mother could make copulation with a member of the intelligentsia sound so important.

Truth is, many want-to-be mothers travelled to Tashkent to visit Mr Shin for the donation of his sperm. It was no secret he was a man willing to do his duty with more than just one pretty young Koryo-saram with skin the colour of cinnamon clay, dark eyes bold with ambition, lips coloured ruby-red especially for the occasion of a quick romp in a book-laden back room. Tweed and dust-mites. At least, that's how Antonina imagines it. And that is where his fathering duty ended. He returned to his wife and children, she supposes. Like any good farmer after sowing the fields with seed. Anyway, she's not sure what Makar's point is in bringing all that up, unless . . .

They won't send me back, will they?

Of course not. But you can't expect leniency.

I never have, she says. She points to the essay. We used to do this before. Why is it now considered anything else but friendship?

He gives her a pitiful look — head tilted, forehead forward. No more, he says.

I need to talk with you, she says. We need to talk.

He picks up the folder, places his hands on his thighs and stands. Antonina wants to reach out and take hold of one of his legs like a child, so he can't leave.

The silence is heavy between them.

What about the scholarships? she stands up beside him. I've heard the patrons are looking for other ways to support the university.

I don't know anything about any scholarships, he says. Anyway, what is this? A shakedown?

She frowns at him. They both know he gets to mark some of their assignments, though she's not sure he gets to choose which ones. How hard would it be for him to give a little nudge? That's all she's asking, not leniency. She's not a beggar.

He picks up his cup and holds it just above his navel like a shield, his slim body erect in its defiance of their shared past. She pauses to watch his lips close over the rim, his sip without flinching, though the coffee must be stone cold by now.

These are good, he says, moving over to the sculptures of the horse, the life-size human leg and arm. Come back and finish these. Forget about that, Makar says and waves with a flick of his hand at the box. You need to build on the detail here and here. The line is out down here, can you see?

I'm pregnant; she wants to say so everyone can hear. Everything inside her wants to blurt the secret out in his face. He doesn't look under the tablecloth. He doesn't really look at the horse, the leg, or the arm. He's just making excuses, so it sounds like he's being the tutor. He doesn't stop at the ghost train, and he doesn't stop to look at her properly either. If he did, he would see the change for himself.

Later in the day, Antonina heads towards the main entrance like an ordinary student, no longer having to out-wait the security guard to unlatch her toilet window. She descends the beautiful stone stairs that curve around the walls. A couple of students are embroiled in a passionate kiss on the landing. The sun from the atrium windows backlights their moment of passion and hazes the details of their faces, giving them the appearance of darkened statues.

The Academy of love. She remembers being warned about that in the first year. Students meet. Students fall. A couple she knows has even married. And here she is, pregnant to a teacher who isn't interested in anything but his career. Perhaps it was the dance she did the night of Konstantin's party that turned him away. First Viktor, and now Makar. Perhaps every man she loves is destined to be lost to her. But that's just paranoia. It's just a dance.

She steps down into the foyer and crosses the circle of mosaicked flooring filled in with concrete scars where the tiles are missing. A few students have set up half-sized easels around the central circle of the foyer, with a couple on the stairs. All of them are seated on small stools, drawing either the pillars with their surrounding wall decorations or one of the many statues. None of them sketches the concrete scars, which, to Antonina, carry more of a story than remakes of classic architecture.

To the right is the ceremonial hall where their end-of-year exhibition will be displayed, and inside, positioned perfectly on a short, white plinth beside the nearest window with its ruffled white curtain, is Nataliya's Dvina. It really is a stunning piece of work. Antonina stops to admire it in the distance.

She leaves through the heavy wooden front door, aware

that although Nataliya doesn't need it, she will no doubt be the recipient of one of the rumoured scholarships for the new year. Probably one paid for by her father. St Isaac's is Sinking, she says to herself — maybe it is a good name, after all.

GHOST TRAIN

SEMIPALATINSK, KAZAKHSTAN, USSR — 1937

Although it is the nature of the Koryo-saram to band together in support, to help each other as brothers and sisters, to provide hope and aid, it was Katerina who pulled away into self-imposed isolation.

The train travelled for weeks along the Trans-Siberian railway, stopping frequently to allow them to relieve themselves on the side of the tracks, to gather water, and to light small fires to boil rice — though there was hardly time to cook anything properly.

A bucket was set up in a corner of the carriage for anyone who couldn't hold on until the next stop, which became more common as dysentery took hold. At each stop they switched corners for the bucket, but it didn't make much difference — the smell of stomach acid and shit permeated the dampness on the walls. Her clothing, her hair, every breath that Katerina took was entwined with the particles of someone else's defecation, someone else's heat, someone else's germs, and it wasn't long before she was spilling from both ends as well.

Katerina watched through the wire-mesh window as they passed towns with warm glowing lights and smoke rising from chimneys. When they finally crossed over into Kazakhstan, she saw the wide-open steppes for the first time, and every now and then she could see the yurts of the Kazakhs and their animals huddled in the security of small clusters. So many aeroplanes crossed the sky — a constant rumble that flew in formations like flocks of bald ibises. The cold she remembered the most, the mesh keeping nothing of early winter from blowing through the carriage. They were like wild animals in a cage, staring out into the blank-faced snow-clouded sky; staring through bars where the icicles grew, anchored to the cold metal.

The adults cut back their food intake to feed more to the children. All the food was combined at the start of the journey, and they worked out rations. Bora offered half of her own to Katerina at every meal, but Katerina couldn't accept it. For the baby, Bora insisted, but she had no idea what Katerina had done. Bora's husband's name may well have been on a list already, he may have been destined to be taken away like her Nikolai, but there was no way Katerina could accept the kindness of a sister she had betrayed so terribly, so thoughtlessly, so selfishly.

Supplies ran out within two weeks. At every stop, they begged the soldiers for food, but the soldiers were not willing to share. The mother of the children at the other end of the carriage had not been taking anything for herself. They only learnt this when she fell ill, then died, and the children became the responsibility of the remaining adults. Water they had plenty of since winter had set in and the snow was deep enough to collect and melt, but food proved more difficult to gather. Katerina sold her mother's jewellery for supplies at the stations, and this kept them going until the jewels ran out. She even considered selling her wedding band, but could not let it go. Nikolai had given it to her following the Russian tradition, back when they believed that Russian traditions were as much theirs as Koryo-saram. Her father's medal she also refused to sell, and kept it hidden, tucked deep inside her brassiere where it wouldn't be dislodged in the violence of vomiting.

Her arms and legs thinned, while her stomach swelled disproportionately by comparison. At every station, the stops took longer since the dead had to be unloaded and stacked beside the platforms. No one knew what became of them, where they were to be buried, or if they were to be buried at all. So much energy was wasted on tears, but there was no avoiding it. Even if the dead ones were unknown to Katerina, the tears came. As they left the stations, the survivors sang. An entire convoy of carriages on the snaking train sang, sending the dear ones love through the power of heartache. They never spoke of the curse in Katerina's carriage, but there was the belief that the lost souls left behind were doomed to roam the earth forever in search of loved ones.

Arirang, Arirang, their voices harmonised in song alongside the rhythmic clank and rattle of the buffers and coupler chains. *Dear ones who left us here, shall not walk ten ri before their feet will hurt*. It became their beautiful, heartfelt lament, and they all understood the burden they would carry for the rest of their lives — lost loves, as well as lost pride.

After a while, Katerina accepted extra food from Nikolai's

parents, though even that turned bitter when her father-in-law died. Soldiers back in Vladivostok had beaten him, and he had never fully recovered. His death made Katerina want to die too. To join her husband, whom she assumed had been shot. But there was the talk of men being sent to the mines in Siberia, and he had promised to follow her. Hope enough that kept Katerina holding on.

There was nothing any of them could have done to save Katerina's baby. The pain started in her back like water coming to the boil. She tried to quieten the contractions by smoothing her hands around her stomach, the same movements that had soothed her over the past few months. It was too soon, her hands told her body, but her body didn't listen. Katerina lay as still as possible, enveloped in the darkness of night, holding on to the scream inside.

Her father-in-law's body was laid out across the side of the carriage. His head faced the door, ready to be taken away from the horror of the cattle-car, and she was glad he didn't have to watch her give birth before her time. There was more space now in the flattened hay. The whole carriage slept, as much as they could with the constant shove and shake around them, as much as they remembered what sleep was like when it was deep and satisfying. Now it was only half-sleep, just as the days were spent half-awake — the energy for both commanded too much to be entered into fully.

By the time the morning sun lightened the blues in the sky, the pain had Katerina in its clench. The contractions were coming more quickly and stronger — the last one like a punch to the back that unlocked the scream from within and startled Bora beside her. Katerina's waters broke with a gush. She wanted it all to stop, but her body was acting of its own accord. Bora sang to calm the two of them, her voice shaking and breaking in places until she merely hummed while Katerina's mother-in-law was locked away in mourning for her husband, disconnected from what was happening.

Soon Katerina's pain was so constant and so punishing she felt she was drowning — submerging and emerging with barely enough time to swallow a mouthful of air before being driven down by another belting wave of pain. She called for Nikolai, and her fingers tingled as though his ghost were present, but it wasn't. Katerina's blood rushed through her veins, and her temperature rose. Her fingers hurt to bursting and when she held them up in the dimness of dawn, they looked black at the tips as if frostbitten.

Katerina rolled forward and clasped Bora's shoulders when the contractions strengthened — no longer like a wave, but a blinding light that poured in and out of her. Passengers in other carriages joined in the song to comfort her. Katerina placed her chin on Bora's shoulder, so the vibrations of the song were closer than the rattle of the train. There was no doctor. No nurse. Just Bora inside their boarded section. She would have welcomed death if it came for her, just to be free. She let go of Bora's shoulders and lay back as if she were letting go of the only thing keeping her afloat.

Hold on, Bora said, gripping Katerina's hand. Please, hold on.

But Katerina couldn't. Every secret Katerina had ever held on to was pushing its way through her. The guilt of Bora's husband cracked open in the innermost part of her heart like a vial of poison, throwing every good thing out of its way. Katerina turned away from Bora, furious with herself, and knew she would never allow herself to be comforted again. Never accept a shoulder to sleep on, or the sympathetic hand of her family on her arm. She didn't deserve it. And it was with this thought ravaging her brain, and the caw of the words no, no, no, coming from her mouth, that her child was born.

It was a boy. Her baby. Such a great honour he would have been for her Nikolai.

Hello, Katerina whispered when he opened his milky eyes to his first minute of his last day. A heavy silence filled the carriage, the shadows of faces Katerina couldn't bring herself to acknowledge, shrunk back behind the blocking boards, giving her the respect of privacy. Bora handed her a cotton dress to wrap the child in, but Katerina refused it. Instead, she took the two silk shawls Nikolai had once given her and wrapped the baby in those — white for honesty, orange for the safe journey ahead. She stroked the small curve of her baby's back before she covered his body like a loaf of warm bread.

His tiny hand clutched her finger as he inhaled air with lust. Cold air that had travelled across the emptiness of a Kazakhstan steppe. Cold air that mixed with the stink of bodies that had remained unbathed for weeks. Cold air that mixed with shit and vomit, and she didn't blame him for the disbelief that exploded in an enormous wail. A wail shrill enough, she hoped, to call his father to them, to lead Nikolai to their side. The baby struggled on, trying to take the air into his unformed lungs, into his body that refused to let life enter, his cry diminishing to a gurgle within minutes.

You're going to be fine, she told him. Mama is here, and mama loves you more than anything.

She held him firmly until his eyes closed for the last time and his body rested, his heart beating on, like a wound clock slowly running down. His hair was black as a wet rock, like her own, but the long fingers, they belonged to her Nikolai, and to his father before him. She kissed each tiny finger as she unfurled them from her own, then tucked his bluing face inside the softness of her best silk shawls, and curled over the top of him to cry.

Semipalatinsk. White paint on green board. The sign seemed proud of itself, but it was a name Katerina would never forgive. Men who had enough strength left, lifted her father-in-law from the open carriage and lugged him to the side of the platform, along with other bodies — children, old people, and other babies too. Bora offered to hold the baby as Katerina placed a trembling foot on the concrete of the platform, but Katerina didn't want anyone else to touch her baby. A soldier took a cursory look inside the shawls then waved her on, stepping back, disgust spread across his face like white paint on green board. Katerina's head felt light. She thought for a moment that she would collapse as she walked. Colours splashed before each step like ghosts of a migraine and continued as she rested the baby of silks inside the arms of his dead dedushka. She had no idea where they would be taken, or if they would be given a proper burial. But at least her child wasn't alone.

Can you see the blood? Katerina held her hands open to Bora, and she could see the concern forming in Bora's eyes.

Bora took hold of Katerina's hands and placed them together in front of her. There is no blood on your hands, she whispered. But she couldn't have been more wrong.

Katerina climbed back into the carriage without taking any food or water. In her corner, she curled into the hay under the heft of the tweed coat that no longer smelt of her Nikolai. The shadows welcomed her powerlessness, the betrayal of her body, and she let the tears run unattended until she exhausted herself and fell into a sleep so deep that she didn't hear the carriage doors slam and shut out the light of the day. Nor did she feel the hand of Bora sweeping back her hair from her face as she sang quietly, praying to her father, her husband, her brother — asking them to take care of the lost child.

CANDELABRA LIGHT
ST PETERSBURG, RUSSIA — 1994

Neither of them has money for the metro, so Antonina and Konstantin walk from the back of Vasilievsky Island to Palace Bridge, the wheels of the old woman trolley bag rumbling behind them with the bolt-cutters inside. The sunlight hurts Konstantin's eyes — Antonina can tell by the protective way he hunches his shoulders. She stops deliberately in the middle of the bridge, so the tiny shards of reflection dancing across the water have the chance to penetrate his hung-over brain. Tatyana would have found that amusing if she were there. He doesn't stop, though, and he's almost off the bridge before she catches up.

Do we really have to do this? he asks. It's Sunday.

You'd prefer to go to church?

Pfft, he says, and mumbles about a waste of his time. He would be shaking his head if it didn't hurt so much.

Millions of basalt bricks have soaked up the warmth of spring sun in Palace Square, and the crowds have come out to enjoy it. Pavel from her class is in the centre of a small gathering, crouched crab-like, drawing on a flat area of asphalt. He could be any one of the street-chalkers, but she knows his sneakers — Converse Cons, originals in white, red, and blue — the colours of the Russian flag, but also the colours of America, from where his uncle has returned bearing gifts. Only recently have the defectors dared to return home to show off their new life in America. New wives. New apartments they don't have to share. Apartments with their own kitchens, their own bathrooms, and even a separate lounge.

The colours of Pavel's chalks take Antonina by surprise. They're not the usual rainbow-colours she has seen before. His are more subdued. More honest. Similar to the pigments her mother makes. He is finishing a three-dimensional kitchen that looks as real as a bunker built beneath the road, with the asphalt peeled back at the corners like a chocolate wrapper. There's a steaming kettle on the stove with no one to tend it, creating the expectation that any moment a chalk figure might cross the room to switch it off.

It's too glary here, Konstantin complains. Can we get going?

Antonina ignores him.

Come on, Konstantin says. I need a drink.

Just a minute, she says, but a minute is too long for Konstantin, and he heads off.

Where do you get your colours? Antonina asks Pavel.

He raises a chalky hand, but his eyes don't lift all the way to her face; they rest on the curve of her belly. She self-consciously covers herself with the bottom of her cardigan, and he averts his eyes. Antonina reminds herself not to wear this dress again without a jacket.

Do you make them yourself? she asks.

No, they're from Germany, he says.

The colours feel sincere, she says. I like it.

Like it is something they're taught not to say when they critique each other's work.

Thanks, Pavel says, and she's relieved he doesn't challenge her on the *like* comment.

Konstantin is back wearing a newsboy cap and dark sunglasses.

They did that during the war, Konstantin butts in. He lights a cigarette and finishes the sentence with smoke curling around his words. His two pointy fingers are out again, this time with a cigarette lodged between them. The bombers thought they were hitting buildings, but they were just painted images in squares.

Pavel isn't interested. He gets back to his work.

Antonina turns to leave before Konstantin says anything else, but it's Konstantin who doesn't move this time. He draws heavily on his cigarette. She follows his stare to a few guys across the other side of the square. None of them older than her, all dressed in the same blue Adidas tracksuits.

I thought we had some shit to make, Konstantin says, his voice prickling. We shouldn't have even stopped here. Come on.

You mean the frit? she says.

What?

We have frit to make, she says.

Yeah, that's what I said.

So, who were the guys in matchy-pants? Antonina says once they hit Nevsky Prospekt.

I don't know, he says with too much emphasis to be convincing.

And where did you get that stupid hat?

You don't like it?

His eyebrows arc above the sunglasses, his humour returning.

You look like an old man, she says. Thought you had no money.

Someone owed me a favour.

So, how old are you anyway? she asks.

Why? Are you interested?

No! she says, mortified by the idea, and quickens her pace to move away.

The last time Antonina was at Pushkinskaya-10, the hedgerows inside the filigree fences were freckled in spring buds. Now they're covered in leaves so new the green has a fluorescence to it. The scaffolding is new too. Two rows of metal pipes and wooden planks cover the front of one of the apartment blocks further down the street, like braces on old teeth. Apart from the nonconformist centre, all human life seems to be vacating the area, and it's the same right across town. Old squats turning into fancy apartments. The rise of the bourgeoisie, she says, but Konstantin doesn't want to engage in her mild sense of self-pity. He marches on and turns into the archway that leads to the centre.

Inside the courtyard, there's already an industry of residents involved in the making of her frit. Antonina hadn't expected Tatyana to round up so many helpers, but there she is, conducting the process like a professional foreman.

The courtyard is a suntrap. Four walls of apartments enclose them. Most windows are open as if the building itself has decided to take deep, healthy breaths of fresh air. Antonina removes her cardigan and looks up at the sky between buildings. Black power-lines reach across the rooftop like liquorice straps. Sweeps of clouds blanch the blue sky. They could be anywhere. Tuscany. Venice. Or any other place that looks dreamy and warm in travel agents' windows. Behind the line-up of frit-makers, the backdoor to the nightclub is shut. No windows on that level. No signage. No lights. No one would know it's a bar from this side, apart from the noise that starts up late at night.

Tatyana fishes for bottles in the skip, and Konstantin leans against the wall, already doing nothing, next to Sasha who is thumping a metal pole into the hole of a concrete block, looking like a maniac in a gas mask, with clear plastic wrapped around his trousers, for protection.

Antonina inspects the mayonnaise jars of coloured frit. White, brown, green, and even a small amount of blue. It's exactly like the coloured sand she read about.

Not bad for an hour's work, Tatyana says.

Is this your way of apologising for avoiding me? Antonina says. I haven't seen you since Kostya's party.

Tatyana scratches her head. Glances at Konstantin, then down at her feet. This is about as coy as Antonina has ever seen her.

I don't know, Tatyana says. I meant what I said. Just promise you'll think about it. That you'll be open to finding another way to carry on. Even thinking about selling a nugget must bring bad juju.

I don't know if I can manage another year of this constant

hustling, Antonina says. And it's true. Maybe it's the pregnancy, but everything feels harder.

Tatyana points to the workers. Look, she says. They like you. You'd be welcome here if you had to leave that Academy.

There must be a dozen of them. Even the babushka that runs the free library is there; the one who never speaks to Antonina, and tells her dog to come away whenever Antonina tries to pat it.

I'm not leaving the Academy, Antonina says.

Why not? They don't have anything we don't.

Actually, yes, they do. Antonina doesn't say it, but for one they have reputation. Tatyana just doesn't get that. The Academy is authorised. There, that's another word. Funding they both have, and Tatyana seems to be an expert at winning scholarships and awards from random patrons. Must be easier here than on Antonia's island to do that.

When does the bar open? she asks.

We've got four hours. Best to be gone by three. Tatyana takes control of the trolley bag, removes the now-redundant bolt-cutters, and fills the bag with the frit-filled jars. They won't be happy to find us stealing their bottles.

How'd you get into the bin?

Barmaid's a friend of mine. It seems she forgot to lock it last night, Tatyana says with a grin so deliciously wicked that Antonina can forgive her anything.

We're running out of bottles over here, Sasha calls.

Konstantin leans into the skip and clunks about, then resurfaces with a couple of green bottles.

Not like that, Sasha says. Get Tanya to take the labels off.

Antonina goes to help the library babushka, who is

feeding pieces of glass into a food processor. Chunks of brown bottle spin and clunk inside the transparent bowl, making the machine jump, even under the weight of the old woman's heavy arms and breasts that anchor it down.

You know you won't be able to use this again? Antonina says, and the old woman looks up, the loose skin under her chin quivering.

No matter, she says, her voice a warble. Konstantin can get me a new one, and she shoos Antonina away as if the frit-making had nothing to do with her.

Sasha hands Konstantin a pole for thrashing glass in another concrete block, and he pounds it so pathetically that it's frustrating to watch. A couple sitting on a window ledge two floors above decide to cheer him on. Tatyana has her video camera on the dangly feet, then with one big swoop, it's on Konstantin.

Konstantin, Antonina says, so it echoes around the court-yard. The food processor. You'll get her a new one, won't you?

Where am I supposed to find one of those? he says. I can't even find enough bread to eat!

Tatyana moves right in, but not close enough that he can swat the camera away, though it seems he would like to.

Only if I can go back to bottle washing, he says, always the negotiator. This pounding hurts my head.

Antonina takes over from Konstantin, but Tatyana takes the pole and hands her the camera.

Documentation, she says. The process is just as important, plus you never know, you might have to give a talk one day.

Konstantin takes his place on an empty beer crate next to the girl in charge of the bottle-washing process. Antonina zooms the camera in on the bottle washing, Konstantin hiding under the brow of his cap and his dark sunglasses, his denim jacket rolled up to the elbows, his hands in suds scrubbing bottles. She turns the camera off and rests on her haunches in front of Konstantin's bucket.

You remember when you offered to talk to a certain someone about the nugget? she says.

His fingers stop scratching at the glue of the wet label, then start up again. Yes, he says, elongating the word, ready to hit Antonina with a smug look to let her know that he was right and knew all along that she would come to ask him.

Would you mind? She catches the outline of his eyes through the dark glasses and holds the glance until she knows he understands.

You sure?

I'd really appreciate it. She gives him an embarrassed smile, even though she isn't really embarrassed at all, and certainly doesn't feel like smiling. Konstantin, the negotiator. If anyone could get Makar to play fair, it would be her Rottweiler Konstantin.

For two hours they pound away, then, as if cued, all the helpers drop tools and disappear indoors. Even the swinging legs from the window ledge have gone, the window closed, curtains drawn. The sky above is still blue, but the temperature is dropping. The walls of the courtyard no longer look Tuscan warm or Venetian clean, but more sepia-toned and slightly chilled. Antonina puts on her cardigan, and Tatyana takes hold of the front of it in the way Antonina's mother used to when she was about to button her up. This is too small, Tatyana says. She takes off her own jacket, one that looks deliberately over-sized, and gives it to Antonina. She rolls the sleeves in a fashionable way and tucks the collar up. That's better, Tatyana says. And look, she waves at the front of it. You can do it up too, just like magic.

Konstantin takes hold of the broom and drives it like a maniac.

Look at you, Tatyana says. A hooligan with a broom. You missed your calling.

He drops the broom and throws the concrete blocks into the skip. Then the metal poles, the burnt-out food processor, even the buckets go in.

If the bar staff aren't angry about the missing bottles, Antonina says, they're going to be seriously miffed about that.

Her comment doesn't stop Konstantin. He obviously wants to get home.

Antonina's thrilled with the frit. Twenty mayonnaise jars full of it. Too many to fit in the trolley, so Tatyana stacks it up and ties down the overflow with a length of netting and twine. Around this, they wrap thick silver duct tape. It's an ugly mess, but the jars are secure. Antonina can't wait to get started on the new piece now. Sunday afternoon. The Academy should be quiet enough to get it started without anyone around to share the kiln with.

Hang around for a bit, Tatyana says. Stay for dinner.

Thanks, Antonina says. But I have art history class in the morning. And an oral exam in a week, so I better not.

Sounds really interesting. Tatyana's voice is deliberately toneless.

Well, it's compulsory, so . . .

I can walk you over in the morning. Konstantin can take the trolley home.

I'm not taking that thing anywhere, he says pointing at the overladen trolley.

It does look ridiculous, the same way the trucks did back in Alma-Ata, heading in from China. So overladen that on the odd occasion one of them would topple sideways. Then the men of the village would run to fetch tractors, while the women slipped around the back to help themselves to spilt goods. A lot like Konstantin, now she thinks of it.

I want to talk to you, Tatyana says. Konstantin, you're going to have to take it anyway. She can't. It's too heavy.

Shit, he says. Give it here then. And hurry up, I haven't got all day.

Now he looks ridiculous too. Antonina swallows the desire to laugh and cause him to abandon it altogether.

Take it to the Academy. I'll meet you there, she says.

Konstantin wasn't going to wait for her anyway. He jerks the trolley bag into motion, the bolt-cutters over a shoulder, and leaves with the sound of his cursing echoing in the archway.

So, what's up? Antonina says.

Come up. We can talk in my room.

I really need to go. I probably won't get another chance at an empty kiln unless I go in today. Can't you just tell me now?

Tatyana runs a slow hand through her hair. Her eyes are glazed and peaceful, but Antonina knows there's turmoil behind them. The bolts of the bar clunk, then the door swings open and the owner steps out, squinting in the daylight as though he's been asleep inside a coffin. Wouldn't surprise her. He's always pale, and so skinny.

What the hell! he calls out. You two know anything about all this rubbish in my bin?

Antonina tries to look as innocent as possible when he lifts the buckets, the poles, and the concrete blocks out of the skip and drops them on the ground. The food processor he lingers on, but it's beyond restoration, and it gets thrown onto the concrete where the plastic bowl breaks away from the motor and tumbles with a clatter.

Tatyana behaves as if he isn't even there. I need to know what you think, she tells Antonina. It turns out the old woman in the geriatric ward has photos of my father. So, she did know him. And she's adamant they had a son while they lived in Semipalatinsk. Do you think I should call my parents and ask them about it? Or just try and find him for myself?

There's a blank space that's punctuated only by the sound of the skip-bin lid slamming shut and the bar owner swearing.

I'm calling the militia, he says, but he won't. A bribe to the militia would cost him more than the bottles are worth. Then he's gone, the bar door slammed shut behind him.

Semipalatinsk is that nuclear place isn't it? Antonina says.

They don't do the tests there anymore.

Antonina imagines Semipalatinsk as a ghost town, where only mutants live. Perhaps Tatyana's brother is a mutant. A freak. Antonina likes to visit the Kunstkamera museum with its deformed babies. Bones of a two-headed toddler. Humans and animals. All sorts of freakish and hideous specimens. They even have Rasputin's penis on display at the moment. These things she is fascinated by, but Antonina is not sure how she would feel about having a living brother mutated in a similar way. Tatyana's very own nuclear disaster walking around, waiting for her to find him. It seems too awful to be true.

I think you should call your parents, Antonina says. Just

because the woman knew your father doesn't mean her story is your story. Could belong to someone else. You said they get confused, these old people.

Tatyana picks up the broom with a groan. I'll see you Thursday then, she says.

Antonina knows she should stay. Be there when Tatyana calls her parents. But there's the frit, the sculpture to make, and the possibility of an empty kiln. And Konstantin is heading towards the locked Academy doors.

Thanks for today, Antonina says. I owe you.

I love you, she almost said, surprising herself. So often their relationship feels the way things did with Viktor when she was a child, and she doesn't understand what that was either.

There are many different kinds of hunger, and on the way back down Nevsky Prospekt, Antonina embraces the hunger of a memory. She should have crossed the road as she typically does at Corinthia Canal, but her thoughts had wandered off aimlessly, with scant consideration of the hollowness that overwhelms her whenever she passes the door of the Corinthia restaurant.

The food was the best she has ever had, as was the lovemaking afterwards. Makar was in his final year of study. She was still new to the city. Wine glasses were set out on the tables, twinkling in candelabra light, and the white fabric napkins with damask roses seemed brand-new. They ate salmon *kulebiaka* with the crispiest buttery pastry she's ever tasted. There were fried potatoes, and beans in a salty cream sauce as well. It was decadent. Makar even tipped the waitress. Like an American, he said on the way home.

They could hardly afford a meal like that, and they survived the rest of the month on out-of-date sardines, coffee, and the infusion of that beautiful meal in their memories. Now it's just the memory that makes Antonina's tummy rumble — like a sensory postcard from the past she's trying hard to forget.

Konstantin doesn't wait as Antonina hoped he would. She can't believe he was so impatient that he took the trolley bag with her jars of frit all the way home. She checks the front door of the Academy just in case he's inside, but it's locked. No extra time for students needing to finish work, even when there's only one week left before completion date unless they have a key to the side door, but Konstantin doesn't, so there's no point going in. No frit for the frit man, so the frit man will have to wait until morning.

By the time she reaches the factory, Antonina is relieved not to be working. It's a mellow evening, and Vladimir has his room open. Semyon strums his guitar in the corner, humming as if to himself, but his tunes pour through the room lulling the small gathering into a quiet, reflective mood. The sun is going down. The colours stretch, casting orange and red blooms that follow a neat line across walls and up towards the soaring ceiling where the colours get tangled with the metal rafters and cobwebs. Antonina sits on an oversized cushion against the back wall. Over to the right is Konstantin with his head rested into a nook, fallen asleep while sitting, his hat and dark glasses gone, his face much gentler than she has ever noticed, the vulnerability of him almost an innocence, and a desire wells up that she hasn't known before — a nurturing desire. Could it be that she wants to look after him? Care for him? It can't be. Her hormones are playing tricks. He is not a man who needs care or nurture — she stops herself, realising this isn't true. Why else does he keep her around? The bravado is a cover, just like the puffy sheepskin jacket. Beneath both, she suspects there is a much smaller personality, a much more ordinary man than he would like to think she can see.

Semyon sits to her left, and as soon as she pulls her stare away from Konstantin, she knows that Semyon has been watching her. She squints at him in a 'don't you dare tell' glare, and he lifts his chin with a half-smile that hints at her secret. The sun is going down, mellow and orange and the soft strum of Semyon's guitar strokes and soothes and releases the stress from Antonina's shoulders. She leans back, rests her head against the wall, and lets the responsibility of two shows coming up in the same week shrink to unimportance.

DEVIL AS HE MAY BE

At four o'clock the next morning, there is no darkness when Antonina sets out for the Academy — only varying shades of first light, the milkiness of the in-between already melting away. Soon the nights will be completely white, and the summer festivities will take over, while most of the residents draw blackout curtains to maintain regular sleeping hours. No need for blackout curtains in the factory though, with the only window in Antonina's room on Konstantin's side, and even that opens into the storage area where he keeps watch on the big fat truck that stinks the place up with diesel whenever he heads out. He's not a native city man, his roots lie somewhere in the countryside. She's asked him several times where he's from, but he always replies with the same answer, and much like his age, he is reluctant to give any sense of history to his presence. I'm from here today, he says. And Antonina can respect that — home as a choice, a place of present existence. She feels the same way.

It's a mistake to cut across the park; the spring snows are long gone, and the mud is unavoidable in places. Thick black tips of new grass crunch beneath Antonina's boots. It's a sacrilege, she is sure of it — the snap of new life, like the crunch of baby bird bones.

The first time she used the stolen key to the side door, the seal cracked open with decades of dried dust acting like glue, and she had to force it to unstick from the frame. Now, there's no surprise, and it opens with a bored yawn. She makes her way to the bathroom, where four tubs line the wall, four clean, pine-fresh molars — a stark contrast to the rusty versions back in the factory. Antonina unlaces her boots and wipes away the residual mud with wet toilet paper, then removes her socks and carries her bundle away from the mess of the sink. She turns at the door. She should clean the mess. No, it will be her calling card to the caretaker, and this morning she needs him for the lifting.

The wind whistles around the corner of the building, coming and going with that high pitch that signals impending doom in movies. All the way to the kiln, Antonina pads the marble floor in small, quiet steps, the cold climbing up her heels towards her knees, grit catching between her toes and sticking to the soft naked undersides of her feet. She keeps watch for shadows that shift or lights that flicker in case some terror rises from the foundations to harm her, but all she notices when she turns on the light is a breeze that plays with a sweep of dust in the doorway to the kiln.

The kiln is empty, and Antonina is relieved she doesn't have to touch anyone else's work and risk leaving traces of her surreptitious movements. She removes two shelves and sets the temperature — too hot, and the frit of her glass man will melt and slide to a glob, too cold and it won't melt, midway — perfect. At least, that is what she read, and she hopes the information's correct.

On her way to the studio, the lights come on overhead and hover in amber half-power before they whiten. The corridors are narrow and lined with up-lights that give the appearance of daylight to the repeating geometric patterns on the vaulted ceilings. Her caretaker has arrived early, and for the first time in months Antonina is reassured to know she is not alone in the building that looms around her like a crypt.

Good morning, she says, greeting Jesus Christ in his perpetually frozen state of awe, hands and eyes lifted towards heaven, the pagan at his feet.

Nothing has moved inside her studio since she left on Friday, with no extra work completed over the weekend as she had hoped. Ghost Train, Antonina says softly and runs her hand over the clay man. Work for Academy examinations is not to be given abstract names — their titles are merely the representation of anatomical studies. That doesn't stop the students naming them though.

Ghost Train has shrunken by about a tenth in size during the slow natural drying process, and the colour of the clay has lightened. His eyes are fixed straight ahead on some distant desire. His upper torso pushes against the restraints of the plinth like a spirit arising from train tracks, as if the earth itself has hold of him, gripping his lower half in a battle between worlds. She rests her hands on his shoulders, then on the knotted muscles of his biceps. Touches the curve of his neck, and the top of his head. He is perfect. Life-sized and intricately formed. She strokes his cheek. It will be hard to break him down into reusable clay when the marking's done, as they do with all their sculptures. Dry, dead clay is all anyone thinks of them here, and Antonina usually does too, but this one is different. This one has clipped a piece of her on the way out. She sweeps a length of hair around the left side of her neck and draws intimately close to the clay man's face. Is Ghost Train your real name? she whispers, but the clay man doesn't respond. What about The Bones of St Peter? Do you like that name better?

A title like The Bones of St Peter would counter the glossed-over version of Nataliya's Dvina and the foundation pole story. Only, the clay man isn't Russian. He's Koryo-saram, and Koryo-saram had nothing to do with the construction of St Petersburg. From what she's heard they did a little work on the building of the Trans-Siberian Railway, and just like that, she has another reason to call it Ghost Train.

She leans around further and takes in the length of the sculpture's torso. The line of it leads her eye to the corner of her studio, where she is surprised to see the old woman trolley bag, laden with its jars of frit. How on earth did Konstantin get that in here? He really is a strange man, but she is delighted. Antonina had a complete blank about it herself — not registering it wasn't at the factory, not remembering she needed to bring it in this morning for the glass man. Semyon's music must have spun a spell on her last night. She releases a little snort at the silliness of the thought. Pregnancy fog brain is more likely.

The mould waits for her under a tarpaulin beneath her bench — a negative that was a huge task to make. It took two of them to lower Ghost Train into the moistened clay. Twice they failed, and she nearly gave up when Pavel left her to get on with his own work. The caretaker had the patience she required in the end. He jostled the clay man free on his own, and the negative finally remained neatly in place. The mould lacks detail, but the outer edges are clear — the top and back of the head, the neck, the back and shoulders, the outer sides of his arms. A blanket effect — but she is happy with that.

It doesn't take long to wash the sides of her mould with adhesive and slap white frit all across the wet surface in a haphazard fashion, careful to leave good-sized gaps, so the frit doesn't form a solid piece of glass when it melts. Half an hour to rest, and the adhesive should be set. Long enough for her socks to dry on the radiator, soon enough that she won't be caught wearing Anya's felt boots.

One of the swing doors open and Antonina anticipates the caretaker.

I thought I could hear you whistling today, she says.

Her curtain is closed so she can't see the door. Chopin is playing at medium volume, and she turns the music down, hoping it is the right caretaker she's talking to.

I think you're hearing things, he says. I don't whistle.

Must be the wind, then, she says and opens the curtain.

Right on time, the wind whips around the building with its apocalyptic song and the caretaker smiles as if to himself.

He doesn't seem so interested in her work today. He dips in and out of cubicles with his broom, checking bins without comment. She moves past him to fetch the half-brush and shovel. Still, he says nothing. She sweeps up the loose frit that scattered during application and tips the residue into an empty jar for use another day. Then she tests the inside of her mould with the tips of her fingers. It's probably too soon to move, but the frit seems firmly stuck.

Would you mind helping me to get this into the kiln? she says.

He groans and parks the broom beside the door and scuffs out of the room looking much older than he did a few weeks ago. He might be ill, so Antonina decides to help him and sweeps from the back of the wing all the way to the doors until he returns with the large trolley.

You left a fine mess for me in the bathroom this morning, he says. I won't be helping you if you act so dishonourably again.

Dishonourably? she says with bewildered mockery.

Honour is one of the strengths of the Koryo-saram. Remember that, he says. Remember who you are.

I know who I am, she lies, and she tries to slide the mould clear of its crate on her own.

He groans again, and pushes her aside. Watch the *aga*, he says with impatience.

He loads the mould onto the trolley and together they take it out into the corridor, the caretaker leading from the front, Antonina holding back one of the swing doors. Déjà vu. Only, the caretaker isn't her family as Nataliya's was when they did the same thing with The Dvina. The mould tilts while rounding the corner and they both stop to hold it still. The caretaker takes his time to align the trolley with the walls, then they head towards the kiln with as much care as a patient being delivered to surgery.

When did our people settle in Vladivostok? she whispers, conscious there may be a guard lingering in the strange hours of the morning too.

I thought you said you already knew who you were, he says.

I asked my babushka, she says. I got a letter, but she didn't talk about why we left Korea in the first place, and she didn't mention any famines.

Your mother hasn't spoken to you about this?

No, I didn't think about asking her. Funny though, whenever Mama wants to swear, she says Vladivostok instead. Always sounds like a cuss to me now. Vladivostok. Can you hear it?

My parents left in 1910, he says. When the Japanese invaded Korea. They were animals. Brutal. Our families crossed the Russian border to escape the famines. We set up new lives. Good lives. It was a respectable place, the caretaker says, then he pauses. I don't think your mama should use Vladivostok as a swear word.

Probably not, Antonina says, sorry he couldn't see the humour in it. What about the ghost train, though? Babulya wrote about the deportations and the people who died on the journey. She said Koryo-saram tried to re-establish their pride by becoming the most successful crop growers in their new home in Kazakhstan, but they could never prove their loyalty to Stalin, he continued to treat them like outcasts. And they could never get back to the way they were in Vladivostok. Our honour was stolen, she said. And we've never been able to reclaim it. Is that what the ghost train means? Lost honour?

The echo of heavy boots vibrates through the corridor as if the shoes precede the man. The jangle of keys unmistakably announces the advance of the security guard. Antonina leaves the trolley and tucks herself in behind some chairs. The caretaker stays by the trolley. Perhaps he will take the blame for the noise, for the disturbance out of hours. The guard's footsteps pass on by without coming in their direction, down another corridor, up a flight of stairs, and then he's gone, swallowed by another floor, and it's safe again to move.

Antonina doesn't speak again until the mould is in the kiln. The firing will take forty minutes, she says. There's a new urgency in her desire to know the story. More information to attach to her apartment show with Tatyana. A show that has much too much of her attention at present, but she can't help it. You promised me the story, she says like a child at bedtime. I need to know who I am, for the work. It's important. I can help with your rounds while we talk if you like.

The caretaker smiles and blinks in that endearing way her mother does whenever she catches Antonina doing something she considers as 'right' or 'good'.

Come with me then, he says, but instead of getting Antonina to help with the cleaning, the caretaker signals up with his thumb in the air, and she assumes he means they are going to the top floor.

Carrying a full mug of tea is a bad idea. It spills over the rim as Antonina tries to keep up with the confident steps of the caretaker. They're in the dark recesses somewhere between the third floor and the rooftop. There's another small flight of stairs in a squatty attic, and the whole place feels eerie. The smell is oppressively old; dust and damp, mice and mildew. Step after step she follows obediently. He climbs a ladder before her, and belts open a trap door that releases a billow of dust into her hair. Antonina stops to ask herself if she really does trust this caretaker with the sky now behind him, whether the story was worth her putting her life at risk up on the roof of the Academy. She grips the mug and stares up at this man she hardly knows. This man who could throw her over the edge if he wished, and for the first time she understands her mother's fear of the open sky.

He holds out his hand to help her up. *Kanaiji oneora* he says, and something within those two words overrides her concerns. It's the same phrase her babushka uses. The same one the strange woman in the window used too, and she likes the sense of protection it gives her. A sense of safety. Since meeting the caretaker in her studio, Antonina has felt some indefinable connection she can't name. Similar to the strange woman in the window, and the same response rises up inside her as it did when the woman took her from the bedroom — the desire to discover more, the desire for adventure. No harm came to her then, and no harm will come to her now. Anyway, she has always thought of herself as brave. Bold enough to leave her mother's mountain and make it on her own. The roof of the academy could be no different than sitting on the lip of the mountain, so she will trust this strange man, devil as he may be.

Out on the roof, the wind whips her hair all over her face, and a slight vertiginous spin threatens to destabilise her steps. She leans against a chimney and tucks her hair into her collar. Down through a long stretch of a skylight is a magnificent two-storeyed hall. There's a double-sided marble staircase sweeping up to a landing with columned archways that line a mezzanine floor that wraps around the entire room — all of which is decorated with plaster fretwork and hanging ironwork lanterns. Around the circumference of the lower level are alcoves that showcase sculptures from the Tsarist period. Antonina can almost see the swirling dresses of young women being led around the room by gentlemen of past centuries. So very Anna Karenina. Doomed love affairs. Just like her own, but she is not about to put her head under a train wheel because of it.

It's a crazy place for a chat, but she follows the caretaker's lead, and they sit, side by side like two pigeons between brick chimneys. The golden statue of Minerva is to their left, perched on a dome with its cherubs, and its owl. It feels surreal to be so close to it. Across the Neva, the golden dome of St Isaac's emanates its own sunshine. The smallness of life totters by, like some part of a Potemkin village. A couple lingers way down below where the embankment in front of the Academy opens to broad granite steps that invite passers-by down to the river. They seem particularly interested in one of the matching sphinxes that recline on tall plinths facing each other on either side of the steps. Ruins of another civilisation brought in from Egypt by one of the Tsars. Half-human, half-animal — like the snow people of Kazakhstan. It's the perfect place for the telling of a story. She sips her tea, the grit of dust left on her tongue after a swallow.

The ghost train, the caretaker says, and he tells her the myth of the curse. He tells her the myth of the screaming bridge as well, where the dead gather, and when she asks him if he believes the stories, he says yes, he thinks they are real. She is a child being told fables, similar to the fables of the snow people on the mountain back in Alma-Ata. And she tells him the snow people story. But it doesn't feel as important as the ghost train or the screaming bridge. The crow king, he already knows, and soon the only stories remaining are the ones that would hollow out Antonina completely. She decides to hold on to the one about the dance, and the strange woman at the window.

So, what did your babushka say in her letter? the caretaker asks.

She says the Kazakhs opened their arms to us, and we are lucky to have an indigenous people so willing to share their home. You never went to Kazakhstan, though, did you?

No, he says. I was taken away before that. A lot of us were.

Babulya says some of the Koryo-saram went back to Vladivostok as if to their motherland. But what about Korea? Why didn't any of them go back to Korea?

I don't know. I guess when you've been born to a country, that land becomes your home. You speak the new language. You grow a new life. I can understand why some went back to Vladivostok when they could.

I asked my babulya where she wanted to be buried, Antonina says. I thought she would say Almaty or Vladivostok, but she didn't, she said Ushtobe, next to her husband. She had a husband before that one, but he was taken away in Vladivostok before the transports. Maybe you knew him? I don't know what his name was. Actually, I don't even know what my babushka's first name is. Always been just Babulya to me. Is that odd? Anyway, Antonina continues, without waiting for an answer. I thought she would want to be buried with that husband. Not the second one. I thought first love was meant to be the strongest.

You see, the caretaker says. Your babushka has had more life spent with the second husband than the first one. He became her new home. And yes, I did know your family. A long time ago. I knew your babushka's first husband. He was shot in a line-up and thrown into a mass grave. I don't think she would like to be buried anywhere near that, so she's made a good choice.

He was shot in a line-up? Antonina finds it impossible to stop her voice vaulting skywards.

You haven't heard of such a thing?

No, Antonina says with a little more control. No one has spoken about that to me. Or the mass graves. I mean, of course I heard about the purges, but I've never really thought about our history in those terms. I grew up thinking we were transported, and that was it. Started again. But it was really more warlike, wasn't it?

How have you managed to stay so protected from your own history? he says, a chuckle curling around the edges of each word. Did your mother cover your eyes and ears this whole time?

I amuse you, I see, she says. I'm sure I'm not the only one who hasn't bothered to find out more.

He lifts his eyebrows and smudges a small tear in the corner of his left eye. You do amuse me, he says and nods.

Antonina shouldn't be surprised by the shootings. Or the mass graves. Stalin was a crazy man. The caretaker's right, though. Her mother had secluded her up there on the mountain.

You knew my family?

This shouldn't have surprised her either. It explains the connection. The trust she feels. It's as if he were an uncle. But this doesn't actually explain who he is. He must have been so young back then, or else he is much older than he seems now. A few strands of hair catch in her mouth when she turns to puzzle at him, and she doesn't have to say anything for him to laugh at her again.

Yes, I knew your family, he says. I knew your great-aunt also. Katerina. What became of her? Did she marry again like your babushka? Did she make a new home?

I don't know any Aunt Katerina. She checks the clock of the Peter and Paul Cathedral, but there's no telling the time from that distance. It's probably best to check on the glass man in the kiln, she says. Thanks for bringing me up here. It's an impressive spot, and a bit scary too. But mostly impressive.

Ask your babushka, he says.

She is caught gulping cold tea when he says this, and she forces herself to swallow quickly, then tips the rest out of her cup onto the roof, so it shoots off downhill on the metal. Ask her about what?

About Katerina, your great-aunt. I'd be interested to know where she went. It's important. Like these stories are for your work. You understand?

She nods, then heads off, leaving the caretaker up on the roof, sitting and staring into the distance — a lonely figure in a dull grey uniform, the tips of the city glinting in morning light in contrast to his sombreness.

The glass man is done, and Antonina turns the kiln heaters off. He's too hot to move, so she heads to the room where she hides her work to make room for him while he cools. There are so many rooms in the Academy that remain unused. She cannot lock the door to this one, but in the labyrinth of halls and rooms, her stockpile has not yet been discovered. Just for a month, she told herself when she first took possession, but there was no knowing how many little people she would keep making, and the glass man was a complete afterthought — work that came through the process of work. Towards the back of an over-sized shelving unit, she finds her eight boxes, but not as she had left them. They had been taped shut and stacked neatly, but now one of them sits on the floor, its lid ripped open. Several smaller, cardboard boxes have been unpacked from inside the open box and placed beside it. Two of them have been emptied, the figurines from within smashed to pieces and scattered across the floor with violence. A wooden baton lies abandoned, its work of vandalism cut short.

For a long, numb moment Antonina stares at the mess. When she brings herself to move, she steps cautiously through the field of dismembered bodies until she comes to the perfect little face of a perfect severed head. Her eyes are crisp baroque blue. Each cheek is a dip of coral pink from the smallest flathead brush. Her lips are pursed to speak in the crimson pigment of her mother's *Tulips in Spring*. Antonina cradles the broken woman gently and draws her close.

Who did this to you? she asks, but the figurine's little stone mouth is still.

Antonina imagines Nataliya bashing her figurines, then Yeva, Sasha, Sofiya, and even Pavel. She can almost see her entire class looking on while her little people are brutalised. It's a ridiculous idea. Sensationalist. But someone must have found out about her illicit production and decided to punish her for breaking the rules. Did it warrant such vindictiveness, though? The twist of Nataliya's jealous words come to mind — the biting comment she made about Makar the day they caught each other arriving early. Anger begins to harden inside Antonina, quickly turning into the cold hard metal of revenge. All she can think of is The Dvina — pushing it over and beating its face in with a hammer. But then what? She'd be reported. The caretaker and the guard as possible witnesses. That kind of dishonour she couldn't deal with.

Her mother. Makar. Nataliya. They would all know her shame if she did that.

Antonina scans the scattered pieces on the floor, not knowing what to do next. There must be at least fifty severed heads amongst the rubble. Makar would know what to do, and she strides up to his door, not sure why she's expecting an answer so early in the morning. He is never there when she needs him, not lately anyway. She tries the door, but it's locked. Why can't he be here, just once? she thinks and kicks it, then shakes the handle like it's the door's entire fault.

Quiet girl, the caretaker calls from down the corridor with a mix of surprise and frustration on his face. What are you doing?

Antonina has slumped down on the floor, her back against Makar's locked door, her body shaking with anger, trying to figure out what to do about the figurines. She can't report them, and she can't leave them. They should have been taken to Tatyana's studio already, only she hadn't realised she would have to protect them from a thug. Antonina picks herself up off the floor and leads the caretaker to the storage room so he can see the mess for himself.

This is who I am, she says when they are inside. See what they think of the Koryo-saram here. See how they still treat us. I get this kind of prejudice fired at me every day. My Babulya is right, we have lost our honour.

He shakes his head and draws in some clay dust with the edge of his shoe. How many are damaged? he asks.

Does it matter? she says and starts to cry so unexpectedly that she doesn't understand the tears are true tears until she wipes her face on her sleeve and realises there is no grit in her eye to cause it.

Shhhh, the caretaker says, but she doesn't care who hears her. You're upsetting yourself, he says. It's not good for the *aga*. Look, they're not all broken. He bends down and cradles the decapitated head of a figurine. Such a shame, he says, and hands the head over to Antonina. Perhaps they can be used for something else?

I can't let Nataliya get away with this, she says. It's just going to keep on happening. If not to me, then another Koryo-saram. You were right, she says. It is coming through me, I have inherited the trauma of the deported Koryo-saram like a curse, and it's seeping out of me through my work.

The caretaker looks like he's listening, but with a surprising restlessness, as though he's not interested in her words but is searching for something behind them she doesn't understand. Are you sure it's prejudice? he says, which just makes her feel stupid. Like an angry, stupid child that she has every right to be at this time. It is only fair she be allowed to be angry. And are you sure it was the Nataliya girl? he says.

Antonina looks around as if the answer lay in the crumbs of her dolls. No, she says.

Can you report it? Tell that teacher of yours?

She can't answer that question. Not because it's not a reasonable thing to ask — it's just more of what he would call 'dishonour'. Her fingers lace together, and she places her hands on her forehead with a squeeze at the temples, unable to think clearly.

Then we'll move them, he says. We'll put them in your teacher's office, for safekeeping.

You have a key? she opens her eyes.

Not for that door, but I have an idea. I'll be back in a minute.

I'm sorry, Antonina says before placing the little clay head carefully inside an empty cardboard box, then another perfect little face, and another, and another. In the other cardboard box, she places every piece of broken body that isn't smashed to dust. When she closes the lid, she wipes her tears in the crook of her elbow, snorts back the drips in her nose, and orders herself not to weep anymore — which half works. All that's left on the floor is the baton the butcher used to kill her dolls. She picks it up with a hard grip and squeezes as if it were a neck. She will take it. Throw it into the Neva. And she will hide the little people where it can't hurt them ever again.

This is her voice, she realises. Her weakness and her strength. The point of her diversity. The caretaker, the crow king, the ghost train. The stories of her ancestors need to be told, and the Academy is not the place to do it. She must stand up. Reclaim the honour of the Koryo-saram for herself. She must disrupt the sense of displacement and turn the mirror on the perpetrators. This is her story for the apartment show, and it is good. Right now, it feels far more important to her than her work at the Academy, and she knows she must be careful not to let the passion overtake her completely. Stay in control, she tells herself. You can do both.

The caretaker returns with a trolley and a length of wire. Once they have some of the boxes at Makar's door, he bends the wire backwards and forwards at right angles until the heat in the bend makes it snap.

Is this that honour you were talking about? she says as he threads the end of the wire inside the lock, pulling it out to straighten it, re-bend it, and pushing it back inside, twisting and not answering until the bolt clicks over.

You're right, he says. Sometimes, we do need to defend our honour. I don't think we Koryo-saram have been very good at that in the past. But look, here we are. He opens the door and wheels the trolley in with her boxes of figurines.

Over there, Antonina aims a finger, deciding its best to line the boxes up against the window so Makar can still access the bookshelf. Books are more important than sunlight — she knows this of him.

I don't think he's my teacher anymore, you know, she says, slipping the caretaker a quick glance to make sure he understands her meaning. He straightens up, studies the chair behind Makar's desk as if to eyeball the man himself. Then nods and guides her out of the room.

When all the boxes have been moved to Makar's office, the caretaker asks if there is any other work that shouldn't be here.

Just the glass man, she says. My last piece. The rest is all Academy work.

He heads off to collect the last piece to store in Makar's office, and she takes the dustpan to the storage room where she sweeps up the clay dust and places it inside a rubbish sack for use at another time. The torn box she leaves in the middle of the floor where she found it, and across its side, she writes *I can see you* in red paint, so it drips like blood. Ominous. She likes it.

Back in her studio Antonina turns on Chopin and tries to focus, but her thoughts are scattered now, broken into pieces she can't pull back together. It's six-thirty. Another hour before the doors open to the Academy, but she can't face the onslaught with all the emotion still boiling inside her.

All the bad energy will infiltrate her work, and it won't come together with her anger festering like this. It's a strange phenomenon, but she knows this from experience. Whatever she is feeling presses itself into the shape of her clay. Better to head back to the factory than to let the students see her red eyes. Best to tuck herself away in the darkness of her blankets and cry out all the self-pity. The indignation she can channel through the second show. But self-pity is useless. One day, she will allow it. Just one day.

THE CHIMERA

Antonina wakes with a start, even before the alarm. The toilet window. She hadn't thought of checking that. It may not have been Nataliya who broke the figurines after all. She brushes her hair and teeth with urgency, her brain filling in new spaces of possibility. An outsider. If it was, it was probably just a random act of vandalism. She isn't sure if that makes it any better, but at least it wouldn't be personal.

Antonina throws Konstantin's blankets back in the usual way, but this time she doesn't run. Hurry up, she says. I need to get some work out of the Academy before it opens. Tit for tat, and she won't leave him alone until he agrees.

Konstantin moans that he already did the tat yesterday with the glass shit. He sits up and scratches his scalp with such violence it leaves his hair sticking out. Antonina holds out the denim jacket, and he snatches it from her.

His hands are on her when he guides Antonina up and into the cab of the truck. She is left with just a few seconds to hide the rush of blood to her cheeks before Konstantin jumps in himself.

Park at the side of the building, she instructs him as they draw closer to the Academy, and she makes sure to jump down from the cab onto the pavement before he rounds the front to offer her help. She leads him to the side door.

Where'd you get the key? he asks.

There's no way she's going to tell him, so she says someone owed her a favour, and he throws out an easy laugh.

The first thing on her mind is to check the small toilet window. It's locked, but that doesn't mean it was yesterday. Makar's office is locked as well, and she searches inside her backpack for the piece of wire the caretaker used to unlock it. While she's hunting, Konstantin flips open a set of skeleton keys that open like a Swiss-army knife. She gives up her search and raises her eyebrows, fully aware that he knows she is no better than he is, at least when it comes to illegally entering the premises of the Academy. But that's as far as she will accept their likeness.

Inside Makar's office, the boxes of figurines are still stacked neatly and remain untouched. The glass man inside the mould is on the trolley too, thanks to the caretaker. While Konstantin moves her boxes to the truck, Antonina searches the drawers of Makar's desk. She is in the middle of the bottom drawer when Konstantin comes back and catches her.

Getting good at this I see.

She motions him over to unlock the top drawer. Inside are typed sheets of a paper Makar is putting forward for publication. A pair of sunglasses she has never seen him wear, pens, rubber bands, scissors, and tucked to the back she finds what she assumes she was looking for — a blue box of chocolate plums with a small gold bow on the top right corner. He has a taste for small luxuries, so he probably bought them for himself. There is no evidence that they have been given to him by Nataliya, or any other female. No signed note, or love heart or photograph anywhere, not that there ever was when they were seeing each other.

Find what you're looking for, Konstantin says, then he stops, frozen, listening with his head partway out into the corridor, his body leaning against the doorframe. Antonina tucks the chocolate plums inside her jacket and feels the baby shift.

We should go, Konstantin says when he unfreezes.

There is only the glass man left to load. When it's in the back of the truck, Antonina secures it with rope tied to the ribs of the canopy, while Konstantin thrusts the trolley into the corridor of the Academy so it sails away unattended, then he locks the door. He skips in front of the truck in that funny way he does when in a hurry and trying not to be obvious about it. Probably doesn't even realise he's doing it. The Academy key please, Antonina says holding out her hand when he climbs in the cab, and he fishes it out of the inner pocket of his jacket with reluctance.

Tatyana isn't up when they arrive in Pushkinskaya-10. This early in the morning, Antonina is unsure anyone will be awake to let them in. So they sit in the cab of Konstantin's truck on Pushkinskaya Street, facing the noble statue in the middle, watching as the pigeons come and go messing up the ground looking for breakfast. Antonina is dying for a cup of tea, but she isn't going to pay for one. Anyway, it doesn't take long before Konstantin gets tired of the wait and goes in search of a hot drink. Too early for street vendors, so she wishes him luck in finding a café open this early. As always though, Konstantin is resourceful. He returns with a bag of *sochniki*, one coffee that smells like a dream, and one cup of black tea.

Can I have a sip of your coffee? Antonina says. Can't remember when I last had one.

Nope. Not good for the nugget, Konstantin says, and he places the cardboard cup on the dash without its lid, just out of Antonina's reach, where the hot coffee steam is as tantalising as a belly dancer.

Just a taste wouldn't hurt, she says.

Save it for something to celebrate, he says. And make it vodka.

Antonina rolls her eyes.

What? he says. My mother drank vodka the whole time I was in her belly. Nothing wrong with me.

Oh, no. Absolutely nothing wrong with you. She sees the smile he tries to hide. To be honest, the sweet cottage cheese pastries are enough of a treat. Antonina hasn't had any of those for months either.

One of us needs to go over and wait, she says. Someone should come out soon, and we can catch the door.

Konstantin bites another pastry in two and agrees. There is a half-beat before he catches on. Why me? he complains. You go, this is your delivery.

Not good for the nugget to stand outside in the cold, she tells him, and he grumbles, slamming the driver's door so hard that she's sure there's now a rectangle of rust in the street the width and length of a truck.

Eventually, someone does come out the door, and while Konstantin props it open Antonina runs up and rouses Tatyana from her bed. Konstantin has already stacked the boxes of clay figurines outside the back door when the two of them come down. Antonina is anxious to make sure Konstantin is careful with the glass man, so she watches while he unloads it from the truck and follows him all the way to Tatyana's studio.

You're going to make me drop it with all your fussing, he says.

Tatyana holds the door for Konstantin, and while the rest of the boxes are being brought up Antonina sits on Tatyana's windowsill with her legs pulled up. Apart from Konstantin, the courtyard below is still quiet. Feet cross the floor above. A chair drags — people rising for the day, while for her it feels half over already. Konstantin insists on leaving the moment the boxes are all safely stored. You coming? he says.

There is no avoiding the Academy today. She has to set up the show for marking, only she needs Tatyana's strength beside her, so she doesn't appear wounded by the figurine massacre.

I need a shower, Tatyana says. And some breakfast.

I'm only waiting five minutes, Konstantin says, and he makes his way to the truck.

Antonina fishes out the chocolate plums. Compliments of the baby's papa, she says.

Let me guess, he doesn't know he's giving them to me, does he?

Antonina half-laughs then stops. Thank you, she says in all seriousness.

Tatyana hands her back the plums. We'll eat them later,

she says. Together. I'll meet you at the Academy. I won't be far behind you. You should go, catch your ride.

They are almost at the Schmidt Bridge when Antonina tells Konstantin to pull over and let her out. She was right — she doesn't dare walk through the doors of the Academy alone. Konstantin slaps the truck into gear when she's out, and pulls into morning traffic, squeezing into a space that's too small, trusting that the cars will make room for his tank, and they do. Antonina stamps her boots on the granite steps of the English Embankment to knock the chill from her toes, and positions herself against the side of the bridge out of the wind, where she can see Tatyana when she comes. This has always been Antonina's favourite aspect of the Academy. Across the Neva, it sits solid and proud. Only three storeys high, yet it dominates the riverbank in both size and grandeur. The soft apricot hues of the building blush in the early morning sunlight, confident of its style, and projecting a tone of imperial elegance over the entry to its island.

An hour passes, and Antonina just about gives up fighting the wind, when she sees Tatyana's figure in the distance. There is no mistaking the stride — even when she's anxious her walk seems relaxed. Antonina waits for Tatyana to arrive before she stands up.

Hey, they say, greeting each other, and it's so good to see Tatyana that Antonina could almost hug her, but she won't do that in public.

What's going on? Tatyana says as they walk across the bridge, the wind trying to steal her words away.

Someone found my items for our show and started smashing them.

Who would do that?

I don't know, but I have suspicions, Antonina says.

Why would someone do that to you?

Antonina doesn't want to go into it again. She stops at the middle of the bridge and pulls the baton out of her bag. They used this, she says and throws it into the Neva. Tatyana leans over to see, but the baton is quickly lost under the bridge and floats away like a giant turd.

And you tell me off when I flick my cigarette butts over there, Tatyana says.

I thought art academies would be free of the prejudices on the streets, says Antonina. But they're not. All the typical characters are there: jealousy, corruption, ambition, racism. Pick one. It could be any of them that caused someone to sabotage my work.

I think your world is a bit more judgemental of that sort of thing than mine, to be honest, Tatyana says.

I always assumed artists were exempt from that; above that. And the schools I thought of as sanctuaries.

Some are more than others I think, says Tatyana.

You don't get it at your academy?

Jealousy is unavoidable anywhere, but, as you know, we're all a bit unique at Pushkinskaya, so we're probably more accepting of differences. I get plenty of prejudice on the street, though.

But you're Russian, Antonina says. How is that possible?

Tatyana laughs and opens her arms to display her body. Look at me, she says. Of course, people are going to be threatened by the way I am.

Antonina only sees the beautiful Tatyana she knows and loves, and has to struggle to acknowledge the large blocky awkwardness and plain features that strangers might veer away from.

Together they enter the Academy like typical students — through the front doors during open hours.

Morning, Jesus, Tatyana says with a small salute that mocks the statue on the wall above Antonina's studio. Then she pulls the curtain aside. Dissatisfied with the lack of clear space, she then throws the curtain up and over the rail, so it looks more like a decorative canopy than a curtain. Welcome to the sanctuary, Tatyana says with annoying glee.

Antonina is slightly uncomfortable that her studio is open to full view, where students are already on the go, moving objects out to the exhibition hall. But it's the right approach. She has nothing to hide. Not anymore. They eat a few of the chocolate plums and joke about farting all afternoon, which Antonina has been doing a lot of lately anyway, plums or no plums.

Antonina has been allocated a partitioned corner of the great hall for her display. It's a small corner, with a narrow entrance and a broader end, but she doesn't mind that. There is a window that could act as a distraction. Other students with exhibits along the front side of the hall have lowered the frilly white curtains behind their works. Antonina will have to put her curtain down before she leaves too, but for now, she likes the view of the Neva through the window. The constancy of its surface ruffled by the wind makes her think of new beginnings.

Tatyana absconds with the large trolley, even though it's not their turn. Antonina is waiting for her to return with the Ghost Train when Makar's footsteps sound in the hall.

She knows the sound of his footfall — she spent her first two years in St Petersburg listening for them, then another two trying not to. She alters the placement of a few smaller anatomical pieces, a leg, a bust, then the model of the horse they call Chunya, who comes to the Academy for visits and stands for hours while students draw her. Antonina's movements are smooth and methodical as if she were unstirred, but her senses are wired for Makar, they always are, and they stretch away from her body desiring his attention, his approval, far too intensely.

Makar stops at one of the exhibits where a student lingers, making adjustments to their presentation. There is a small exchange of conversation, and some encouragement given. His voice is not what it used to be. She knows the sound of his real voice. The vulnerability of the quick temper caged beneath the academic veneer, the desire, the moan of ecstasy, the whispered intimacies.

He moves on from the first student to another, then comes to the end of the hall, to Antonina, as she knew he would. Only, when he arrives he merely asks to speak with her for a moment, then moves out without commenting on her exhibit.

Tatyana arrives as he leaves. You want to give me a lift? she asks him, but he passes by without acknowledgement. Rude, she says, her eyes following him.

I'll be back in a minute, Antonina tells her. I think the caretaker is about, ask him to help you, or Pavel is up the front. He's nice.

Makar waits for Antonina in the corridor, and when she catches up, he takes her by the elbow to lead her towards his office like a naughty child being brought to the school director. She tugs her elbow free, resenting this treatment.

She remembers the dread, the shame of her mother being notified of unacceptable behaviour in school, and she doesn't need to feel that kind of guilt again.

Antonina presses her back against the bookshelf trying to take up as little room as possible inside Makar's office. He paces the narrow space between the desk and Antonina, passing so close that she can taste the deliciousness of coffee and peppermint chews on his breath.

I'm sorry, she says. I had no choice. Someone vandalised my work. I had nowhere else to store them. I left you a note. She points to his desk. He must have seen it. I know the boxes were an inconvenience, she says. But they're gone now, and to be honest I hadn't expected you to be so mad about it. As she speaks, she tries to catch his glance, but he has entrenched himself inside his indignation, his eyes glazed and dark as she has never seen before. This isn't about the boxes.

The bookshelf smells of dust mites and the air in the room is thick and stale, heavy with that sweet scent of the cologne he started wearing once he got the new position. It's hard to take him seriously when his hair juts up on the side where he has failed to wet it down properly. Antonina reaches up to pat it down the way she used to, and he shakes his head and bats her hand away like a pestering fly.

Has Konstantin been in to speak with you? she says, but he's not listening, not even when he looks up at her, grey eyes meeting chestnut eyes, and there is nothing that she can read in between.

I try really hard to help you, you know that, right? Makar leans in close, an arm either side of her on the bookshelf. She doesn't pull away when he rests his face into the crook of her neck. He inhales through his nose, taking in the smell of her too.

You have been good to me Makar, she whispers.

Smoky voices pass through the corridor followed by the confident trot of what sounds like other professors. Makar stiffens, listening in case one of them comes towards his door. He springs away leaving her cold, the bookshelf gently shaking.

What is it? she asks.

He presses his hand to her belly. I take it that this is an *aga*?

The word lacks the endearment the caretaker infuses it with, and Antonina is overwhelmed by the coldness, the hardness of the word from Makar's mouth. Taken aback that the caretaker thought he had the right to let Makar know about it too. She's not sure how she should answer Makar's question. He can see she is startled and moves away, flops into the swivel chair behind his desk and stares hard at a clear space on the blotter in front of him, saying nothing for the longest moment. He looks up at her stomach with genuine concern and says quietly that he hadn't even noticed. How could he have not noticed? Then his countenance changes. The Makar she knows switches back to the teacher, and she loses him again. He is distant when he speaks now.

Perhaps it's time you returned home, he says. Have the baby in Almaty. Take some time off and make pottery bowls with your mother, then come back to the Academy when your head is clear, when it's old enough to be left with your mother.

You've given this some thought, Antonina says, but there is nothing wrong with my head. And the baby isn't an *it*. She feels like a hypocrite, considering her own dehumanising term for the nugget.

He doesn't respond.

Has Konstantin been in to speak with you? she asks again.

Makar scowls. Why would he do that? he says. The scowl unfolds to wide-eyed disbelief when he realises he is about to be blackmailed.

Antonina can't believe she has to do her own negotiating. That damn caretaker.

I would come to visit you in Almaty if you wanted me to, Makar says sounding a little desperate.

That's not exactly what I had in mind.

She takes a deep breath, holds on to a rung of the bookshelf behind to steady her nerve.

I am going to work here in the city during the first half of summer break, she says. Earn some money. She almost tells him how but decides that it's none of his business.

I'll head home in August. No one will know about you being the papa. What I need is a cover for the first two months of next semester. A good mark would help me financially if you have access to that. Maybe a word in the ear of one of those philanthropists for a scholarship as well. I need some money to see me through the next year.

How am I supposed to cover you for two months?

Think up an illness that will keep me away. It's all I ask of you, Makar. The rest is my responsibility.

You can't prove it's mine, he says as though a light bulb just whacked him on the head. And I've told you before, I don't know of any scholarships.

She gives him the 'don't be stupid' look. He's seen that one before. He can read it. People know about their past relationship. She doesn't have to remind him of that.

Have you been seeing someone else? she fires at him.

How did you get into my office? he fires back. Has that

caretaker lent you a key? You know it's breaking and entering. A chargeable offence.

Where's the evidence I was ever here? she waves her hand at the empty window space.

He just shakes his head. Looks as if she's lost the spot of most favoured student. Nataliya will be pleased.

Tucked away inside the staff toilet, there isn't a single noise except for the sound of Antonina blowing her nose into a bow of toilet paper. Then the gentle click of Makar's door echoes out in the corridor, as does the tread of his feet as he makes his way towards the foyer without her. He's thinking hard already, most likely, of an illness, an excuse to cover her while she dispenses of the nugget. Dispenses — his word. He doesn't seem to care how she does it. She is now just a problem to be solved. In return, she agreed to give him the estrangement he requires. Just like her own papa, and his hands-off approach to fathering his tribe of children.

The teachers' soap smells of lilac. Antonina lifts her foamy fingers to her face. From now on, the smell of lilac will remind her of finally relinquishing her connection to Makar. Lilac. It's the colour she will use in her work to represent duplicity. Duplicity — that's a nice way of putting it.

They may not be together ever again, but because of the baby they will forever be merged. Antonina told Makar that. Connected, she said. Like a chimera — part him, part her, part baby, part Russian, part Koryo-saram. Some things can never be separated once they've been joined. He corrected her. The chimera is made up of separate species, not races, he said. We are not part of each other's futures, and we will never be merged again. He strangled the word *merged*, squeezed his lips so tight that it almost stayed in his mouth. He is not the Makar she used to know. He has become a species all his own, and she is now part of him. A chimera, she insists. She is the snake's head in his tail, and if he isn't careful, she will bite.

She rinses her hands and wipes them dry on the roller towel before placing the bar of soap in the pocket of her skirt. She doesn't care about the wet patch. She wants that smell near her for a while. The failure is not her own, but Makar's. She will get what she needs by way of the nugget. Already she has some of Makar's money freely given so she can get away, enough to last the summer break without having to hang around to work, and a little more on top of that as well. He had been pre-prepared at least for that part of the deal, and gullible enough to think that's all she would expect.

Tatyana is waiting in the studio, and Antonina puts on a flippant expression, opens her pocket with the soap inside it and tells Tatyana to smell it.

Old woman smell, says Tatyana.

Antonina sniffs it for herself. Yes, it is, isn't it? she says with mild elation. Old man smell too.

Antonina fetches the backpack and is ready to leave after one last check of her exhibit. She changes her mind though when she sees Makar in the centre of the hall, his attention caught in close discussion with Nataliya's father.

Is everything finished? she asks Tatyana, thinking she might be able to avoid re-entering the hall.

Come have a look, Tatyana says, and before Antonina can say no, Tatyana is already marching past Makar and

Nataliya's father, making them scatter like birds in a park when a dog charges through just for fun.

Antonina walks through the hall knowing full well she is being measured up by Nataliya's father while Makar has turned his attention elsewhere. Favours for favours and Antonina can't help wondering what Makar's up to. Probably just the promotion of Nataliya's work, as Antonina has already suspected. She is too tired to think about Makar anymore, and anyway she has an oral history examination to study for. So, she leaves them to it, and exits out the front door feeling grateful for the loyalty of her Tatyana, and yes, even Konstantin. True friends come in strange guises.

I AM NOT KAZAKHSTAN

The central city streets are littered with neon-coloured flyers the size of greeting cards. They flap like flags on doors, bus shelters and windows, being no respecter of receptacle — any stationary object will do. And it's not just the young ladies eager to make the acquaintance of paying customers who advertise this way. Both men and women can be seen in the early hours of most mornings gluing fresh notes high up, where the old ladies who are paid to peel and shred have to stretch to reach them. Theirs is a futile occupation. The old women half-heartedly throw their scrapers around, knowing full well the persistent three-metre tide of coloured notes arrives fresh every morning, offering sexual services, apartments, home improvements, cash loans, help with drug dependency, or whatever else the city needs. When the glue dries, the flyers are difficult to completely remove. The names and numbers of mysterious women may disappear, but the residual scrapings turn pastel as they weather and are then covered over by newer lurid notes.

To Antonina, the flyers add texture and grit to the streets. They create a pattern and a rhythm that would otherwise be lost to the blankness of dull concrete walls. They trace the needs and wants of the city, and to her eye they create one great, beautiful abstract painting that depicts the precarious balance between order and chaos.

Antonina creeps into her bedroom without the aid of the light bulb so she won't have to listen to Konstantin's complaints. It must be midnight, but the lighter nights are deceptive and time runs away before you know it's getting late. The room in the factory is its usual dense blackness no matter the brightness outside. Konstantin's there, on the other side of the wardrobe — the rasp of his sleep-breath working its way to a gentle snore at the tail of each exhale. The light isn't necessary — she knows which side the bed is on, how not to trip over the old woman trolley bag and her box of clothing, and where the edge of the mattress is.

The bed jerks like an unbalanced dingy on rough water when she sits to remove her boots. Then someone screams, and Antonina is thumped in the ribs of her back by the kick of a mule. She tumbles to the floor gasping to fill her winded lungs, and as she gropes for air she scrambles to get away before the mule finds her again, tucks herself into the corner and forms a ball to protect the nugget. Some kind of weapon is waving around the room, searching for the solidness of her body. Her mind goes to the baton she threw into the Neva, but this is bigger, and its determined blows are not designed to smash little clay dolls, they are aimed for the breaking of bones. She bites back a shriek when the sharp, evil breaths of it slice the air around the tiny room, whacking the wardrobe, the bed, the metal handle of the trolley bag that lets out a ring of complaint. The attacker grunts with the effort of each swing — a strained, high-throated pitch that could only be female. When the weapon claps the wall above Antonina's head, her heart does a leap. She should tackle the woman, grab her ankles, but there is the nugget to look out for. She should call out to Konstantin, but the weapon would find her quickly if she does. The noise must have woken him, surely, but she won't wait for his intervention. When the weapon hits the wall furthest away, she decides to escape through the door, but just as she finds her legs, the light is on.

Blinking yellow light half-blinds her with its sudden brightness, but she knows the shape of Konstantin's back, the charcoal grey of the t-shirt he wears to bed, and the shock of his pale, naked legs with their soft blond down.

Polina, he says. Cut it out. You're waking up the whole bloody island with that racket.

Antonina leans around Konstantin to see a woman standing defensively on the other side of him, blinking hard against the light as well, her hands gripping and re-gripping a metal pole as if preparing herself for the pitch of a ball in the game of *lapta*.

Put that down, he says. It's just Nina. I told you about Nina.

Polina lowers the pole. She is young, maybe eighteen or nineteen. Her hair is tied up but tousled in a bountiful blonde movie-star way. But she is no movie star. Her bottom lip is split and swollen, her eye and arms bruised from a beating.

Antonina pushes past Konstantin and slaps the woman hard. Look at me, she says, pointing down to her stomach. Look what you could have hurt.

Polina collapses onto the bed, the defensiveness slides into convulsing, catastrophic sobs that rouse a few other tenants in the factory who yell at them to shut up. Antonina stands in front of Konstantin, expecting an answer, fury oozing from her. She could slap him too, and he knows he deserves it. She sinks her hands into her hips babushka-style. You told her about me, she says, but you didn't tell me about her.

It wasn't planned, Konstantin says. He scratches the front of his scalp, the way he does when he's nervous, then waves his hand towards Polina. She needs someone to take care of her. You can see she's had a rough time of it.

Take her into your room then, Antonina says.

Konstantin replies that he can't do that, that she is, you know, a street girl.

Antonina can't believe he's brought one of them into her room. It's one thing to admire their advertisements as artwork, but quite another to have one of the mysterious ladies in her bed.

Since when did you become so particular about the company you keep? she says.

If that's what you think, then it's not a good reflection on you, is it?

Antonina huffs and folds her arms. What are you doing bringing her here then?

Antonina checks Polina, but Polina isn't listening. She's barricaded herself inside her grief — too busy crying to hear the insults.

Take her into your own bed, Antonina insists.

I can't do that. Konstantin straightens his back as if offended. I don't use their services. She's not here for that.

Antonina is taken aback by the sensitive language Konstantin is applying to a prostitute, his usual armour, a hard-boiled vocabulary he has allowed to slip, and yes, she can see him, the country boy with his animals, caring for the new babies, crying when they are taken away to slaughter.

He lowers his voice. A gang raided the hotel she works at, he says. The security guard was beaten unconscious with knuckle-dusters, the girls robbed of their takings. Polina was their primary focus, I think. She's had a relationship with an American, a non-paying relationship that goes beyond the professional. Someone to blackmail, and they tried to kidnap her.

Konstantin doesn't say how, but he apparently stole her away, and Antonina is surprised to feel a burst of pity for the girl.

Polina lies down facing away, and covers herself with Antonina's blankets.

Did they see you take her? Antonina asks, wondering if it's even safe to be there, in her room. Will they find us here?

No, he says. I made sure they didn't see anything. I snuck her out the window while they were taking their time with some of the girls.

What were you doing there if you don't — you know? She mouths the words 'use them'.

I was doing a delivery, he says. Honest to God, that's all I was doing.

Antonina is not convinced. It's not any of her business, though. She considers crossing town to stay with Tatyana, but it's late, and she's tired.

All right, she concedes, but just for tonight.

She pushes Konstantin out of her room and climbs into the end of her bed without a pillow, trying not to touch the legs of Polina, but top-and-tailing is impossible in a single bed. She closes her eyes and tries to stop the adrenalin wheeling. Several minutes pass before the tremors cease from Polina's sobs, and Antonina assumes the street girl has fallen asleep. She thinks about the rainbow of leaflets pasted to walls throughout the city and the names with phone numbers spray-painted onto sidewalks. The women risk imprisonment with the sentence of a murderer if they're caught soliciting. What a precarious life.

I'm sorry, Polina says. I would never hurt a baby.

Her legs come to rest against Antonina's back, and neither moves away.

It's all right, Antonina says. You gave me a fright. We'll sort something out in the morning, she says loud enough for Konstantin to hear.

Antonina doesn't usually believe in prayer, but she sends a plea up to the sky to notify whoever is up there in office that two women are in need of rescuing down here. Two women trying to survive, and she could do without any more obstacles to deal with, thank you. Her life feels like it has suddenly switched into a constant state of chaos, and she wonders about the repercussions of the dance again. It's just a dance, though. And life is an annoyingly persistent pressure-cooker for everyone at the moment. They are not so different — her and Polina. Doing what they must to survive.

After a night of half-sleep and trying not to fall out of bed, the pain in Antonina's neck and lower back gnaws all the way to Pushkinskaya-10. The wheels of the old woman trolley bag grumble and catch on the lip of every concrete ridge and kerb on the way. The trolley is heavier than usual. Inside are books and clothes, as well as an antique tsarist tin from the city of Odessa complete with painted red roses that are still whole and beautiful even though the tin itself is badly dented. The shape of it is more the size of an ammunition container from the Great Patriotic War, with a leather handle on top, and room enough inside for a hundred chocolate bullets.

The tin is too old for food items now. Too rusty for clothes too. Antonina keeps her trinkets inside instead. There is the doll with the rattle she made in her childhood. The Maedeup knot her mother has probably noticed she has taken. The various pigments her mother has sent. The sable paintbrush she stole from Makar early in their relationship, which he is not getting back. And the key to the side door of the Academy. In her backpack are all the remaining clothes that could fit, along with her toiletries. There is no knowing what a street girl will steal. Even what Antonina has left in her room doesn't feel safe, and it would be just like Konstantin to offer some of her belongings to Polina as if they were his to give.

When she arrives at Pushkinskaya-10, Antonina is relieved to find another troop of unconventionals already clearing Tatyana's studio. They've formed a production line, very similar to the day of the frit-making. The centre's very own chain of ants, carrying more than their own weight. These artists aren't cockroaches — they got that wrong. They're ants. Lovely, wonderful, helpful ants.

The second room of Tatyana's studio has been opened up at some point, the doorway widened inclusively — the two rooms becoming one, yet partitioned and defined by the frame of the opened wall. Such extravagance of space for only one resident thinks Antonina. Stinks though. Can't be healthy to live in the fumes of paints and thinners for too long. Lucky the room doesn't spontaneously combust with the heat of the radiators.

The area is soon empty. Even the bed is gone. The two rooms with the opening in between are ample space for an apartment show. All they need now are the beverages, and Konstantin is yet to show up with the supplies he promised.

Glass is stronger than clay, Antonina reassures Tatyana when they are trying to pull the glass frit man free from the mould. This isn't exactly the truth, but it stops Tatyana fussing about the edges. If he breaks, he will take on a new conversation, Antonina says. I'll use him anyway, so don't worry.

The sculpture doesn't break, though. Antonina worms her fingers down the sides, and the glass peels away all at once. They place the glass man on the plinth in the centre of the farthest room and Antonina draws the blinds. The pendulum light above casts a tremor of stars across the length of his spine, and when she pushes the light slightly, the glass man's filigree shadow flutters in circles around the plinth like dandelion seeds blown in the wind. Tatyana follows the shapes cast around the floor with her video camera rolling. She circles the glass man, raising the focus until the camera is pointed up at the swaying light, then lowers it to Antonina's fingers that are running over the rough surface of his arm. This is how she will show her glass man. He is so much more impressive than she expected. She laughs into the camera.

He's prickly, she says, elated at the success of his form. She is beaming, and she knows it. Smiling into the eye of Tatyana's camera like an idiot.

Tatyana adores the idea of making the audience step on some of the little people as they enter the room.

Most of her own work is hung and ready for the show by the time the last box of Antonina's little clay people is opened. The dolls are placed around the entire area of her space, circling the plinth with just one narrow, clear strip left, to the side between the door and the small table that is waiting for Tatyana to set up the video camera.

Tatyana stands in the entrance to the second room while Antonina is on her knees, her back bent as she stands doll after doll on the floor, their tiny faces like sunflowers turned towards the light-bleached room where her own work hangs. There must be hundreds of them. What a process they must have been to make.

Do you think they'll break easily enough? Tatyana asks.

Pass me that hammer, and we'll find out, says Antonina.

Tatyana has the hammer nearby from hanging her artworks, but she's reluctant to hand it over. I believe you, she says, thinking Antonina is going to sabotage one of her pieces. Which is ridiculous — there's plenty to spare, and they are all about to be stood on and broken anyway.

Get me the hammer, Antonina says.

Antonina is up off the floor when Tatyana comes through to hand it to her.

Hold him still for me, Antonina says. She stands in front of the glass sculpture; hammer casually tapping the side of her thigh, the glint of mischief in the small stretch of her smile.

I'm not going near that again, Tatyana says. See what it

did to my sweater last time? She points to all the loose threads pulled away when she helped to lift the glass man out of its box. The sculpture was light enough but positively vicious.

Antonina doesn't turn to look. She raises the hammer with both hands.

Step away from the glass man, Tatyana says, but she knows Antonina is determined. Just wait a minute, Tatyana says. You'll break the whole thing if it slides to the floor.

Tatyana wraps her arms around the back of the glass man and waits for something terrible to happen. Tiny shards of glass hook onto her clothes. She can feel the suck of them like dry coral.

Not like that, Antonina says. Turn your back and rest it against him, so he doesn't slip.

Tatyana pulls herself free of the glass prickles, carefully unfastening the longest snags that refuse to let go. Her sweater is ruined, and she groans at the state of it.

Come on, Antonina says. Down the back. Lean into him.

Tatyana positions herself obediently. She doesn't see the hammer swing, but the shock of the blow travels through each notch of her spine, and she freezes, expecting to feel the piece shattering.

Are you done? Tatyana asks.

Yes. Come have a look. It's perfect.

Tatyana unhooks the back of her sweater from the glass man again. Her hands shake, the vibrations of the hammer-hit still rippling through her. Antonina has her hands lifted away from her sides as if she were expecting to be raptured any minute, taken up into some skyward place. She stares, mesmerised by her work, the light from the single bulb above reflects off the glass onto her face, and she stands before it radiant. The glass man, on the other hand, has the head of a hammer sunk in its skull, which makes Tatyana burst out laughing.

What are you doing? she says. Are you going to leave it like that? To which Antonina just nods.

Look, Antonina says looking at her feet, thoroughly enamoured with another new aspect of her work. The glass, she says, and points to her feet. It looks like rice.

And it does. The glass has shattered into hundreds of white shards. It has fallen onto the heads of the little clay people nearby and in the spaces between them.

It's perfect, Antonina says, and she sweeps the shards from the tops of her feet before she tiptoes away from the glass man with the hammer in his head. Antonina is right. Glass is stronger than clay — Tatyana gets it now. The exhibit wouldn't be so vibrant if the piece on the plinth were clay. The juxtaposition is brilliant. They stand together at the opening to the second room and admire the power of the work before them.

What a shame we didn't have a sickle as well, says Antonina. But I guess that would be too obvious.

You have no idea how strange you are, do you? Tatyana says. You say I live with a bunch of crazies, but I think you actually top them all.

You don't like it?

I love it.

If Tatyana could, she would wrap Antonina up and keep her all to herself. It's maddening to have to share such a spontaneous, sensitive mind like hers. She doesn't belong at that Academy on the island — this, Tatyana is sure of.

Antonina's thighs and back will hurt tomorrow from the slow crab-crawl across the floor to put the figurines in place. It should be safe now to put the video camera on the side-table and set the timer so that no one can see it. The element of surprise when they break the figurines has to be natural. Anything acted will spoil the documentation.

Tatyana sets the timer and covers the camera with a small wooden nail box, the lens facing through the cut-out handle grip, which isn't ideal because it's only half as wide as Antonina would like it to be. It will add to the drama, Tatyana assures her. The hidden eye, peeping through a keyhole, without hiding the keyhole. Deliberate stealth, and that's precisely what it is.

Antonina fills the floor area with the last of the figurines when Tatyana has gone off to class, then pulls up some blankets and catnaps in the sun beneath one of Tatyana's self-portrait compilations. Day sleeping is a strange phenomenon. In her dozing state, the urgent sounds of footsteps in the corridor are distant enough to be irrelevant. Chatter in the courtyard. A trumpet hoots somewhere nearby, but not close enough to offend. All of this she is aware of, but none of it matters in the sanctuary of rest and warmth. If these same sounds came in the night, she might be annoyed. But during the day they dance around in the place of light without disturbing her peace. All except the clinking of bottles and Konstantin demanding her attention when he enters the room.

Hey! he says like he's expecting a welcoming parade. Wake up, sleepyhead. Look what I brought you. He lands the box of drinks on the trestle table, and the bottles' clatter is annoyingly loud.

Antonina lifts herself up on one elbow, her body heavy and reluctant to move. She is not sure how long he stays. He mutters about aspects of the show, but she's not sure which parts he is referring to, because she has already settled back into the blankets and half drifted away.

When Antonina wakes later, the noise of the world around her is at full volume once again, and Konstantin is no longer there. The memory of excitement in his voice comes to her, and a little sadness flutters around like disappointment; disappointment that she didn't engage with his interest in the work. Her backpack sits in the corner beside the old woman trolley bag, and she considers the study for art history she had planned, but it's getting late, and there is still the artist's statement to write for the apartment show, and it's this that she decides to give her attention to.

The old typewriter Tatyana told her to find in the office area down the corridor looks as if it has serviced two great wars already. Some of the Times Roman letters don't press properly. Others stick, slowing the typing of her artist's statement, especially when she has to dive into the middle and pull the keys back. The s and f letters press hardest, giving a distortion of colour throughout the page. It's not until the page is pinned to the wall and she stands back to admire the work as a whole that she decides she actually likes the uneven press of her words. The ghost letters lend an air of mystery.

I am not Kazakhstan
Artist abstract: by Antonina Sharm

The phenomenon of displacement in contemporary society,
made manifest through the visual art of a minority citizen

The abstract tells the tale of the rice farmer and the crow king — or at least one of her stories — as she has decided she has many. The one she recites for the show relates the trauma caused by Stalin stealing her people away from their homes, their paddocks, their offices, and exiling them with the command to grow rice in a barren, foreign land.

During the opening, Antonina explains that the crow king story is a personal adaptation of an old Korean fable, mixed with the mythical beliefs of the Koryo-saram. She speaks of the deaths and the hardships of the deportations that her babushka told her about, but she also tells them of the ghost train and the curse of the unburied souls that either roam the track or linger at the screaming bridge just south of Semipalatinsk. As she continues, a wave of acceptance tingles up her body with a shiver as if an ancestor has touched her knee with appreciation. This gives her confidence, and her voice rises, more powerful, more determined, and before she knows it she is speaking with the rhythm of a drumbeat, the words bounding from her lips in nice neat columns, pauses, emphasis and eye contact where they should be.

I am not Kazakhstan, she says. I am not Russia. I am not Korea. I am not the displacement of my people. I am not the lost. I am a part of the new tribe. I am Koryo-saram and my place is here.

She has done well. The audience's applause leaves her with the sense that she has re-established respect — if not for her people, then at least for herself.

The anxiety the show causes the visitors is evident — most of their faces crumple and grimace as they crush the clay bodies beneath their shoes. Initially, they adhere to a trampled line that leads from the door and around the plinth of the glass man like a track cut through dry grass, the strip of broken dolls returning to dust the colour of burnt sienna; their delicately painted faces now invisible.

Vladimir has come to the show unaccompanied — no Sofiya, no Maria. Not even Semyon has bothered to cross town to see her work. Never mind, Vladimir is enough of a showstopper on his own, stomping around, smashing as many figurines as he can, like a child on bubble-wrap. Tatyana's self-portrait, Oscar Wilde-style, is the centre of attention in the first room. All night Tatyana joins the conversations in front of it, capturing the words of her audience, the unpacking of potential layers she hadn't thought of, then turning to her work with new awe, new resolution that the work is good. It's inspiring to watch. Konstantin would have enjoyed the show, and Antonina is disappointed he had to head off for the night before it got started. It would have been fun to watch him dissect one of Tatyana's paintings. The clay dolls would have stymied him for sure.

Tatyana catches Antonina watching her and moves to lean against the wall next to her.

A good night, Tatyana says, all energy and elation.

They love your Oscar pose, says Antonina.

No, I think the night was yours, says Tatyana.

Pfft. Antonina scoffs and straightens herself to peer around the room once again. Just in case Konstantin managed to complete his nightly loop and come back early.

You haven't seen Kostya, have you?

Konstantin, Konstantin, Konstantin, says Tatyana. Anyone would think you two had a thing going on.

Antonina laughs and gives Tatyana a slap on the arm for being so ridiculous. Deep down though she is a little stunned to realise that it is Konstantin she's thinking of and not Makar — the black-marketeer's nod of approval she seeks, not the assistant professor of the prestigious art school on the island.

Konstantin said to feed the dog tonight, says Tatyana. I didn't know you had a dog.

Antonina didn't either, but then she clicks. Polina. He wants her to feed Polina while he's away for the night. She will have to hit him up about calling a woman a dog. Prostitute or not, she shouldn't be given that kind of label. Antonina has had it thrown her own way often enough to know.

When it comes to breaking down the last of the clay figurines after the show Antonina decides she doesn't have the heart. Only one hundred of them survive intact, and she feels they have earned the right to be kept. The glass shards that at first appear as rice she quite likes too, so she scrapes them up into a small box. Rice and little people. A gift to take back to her mother perhaps?

Ksenia helps Tatyana hustle the mattress in through the door, trying to keep the sheets and blankets attached so they don't have to make the bed from scratch, but the blankets loop away from their grip. The mattress flops onto the floor where residual clay dust scatters, and Tatyana collapses on the bed even though the room is filling up again. It's the after-glow of a show that will soon develop into a full-blown party.

Stay with me, Tatyana says, waving her hand over the mattress like a one-armed snow fairy.

Stop it, Antonina says. You're giving people the wrong impression.

Two of Tatyana's friends bring in the chest of drawers, then jump on the bed as if that's all the furniture moving they can be bothered with.

At least someone still loves me, Tatyana says and wraps her arms around one of her friends in that clingy way she does when she's had a few drinks.

Don't be so smug, Antonina says. Anyway, I can't stay. I have to go feed the dog while Kostya's away gallivanting. Looks like you won't miss me, though.

That's the problem, Tatyana says. I always miss you.

The old woman trolley bag is hidden beneath the trestle table, and Antonina is not sure if she has the energy to traipse across town with it again.

Can I leave my stuff here? she asks.

Does that mean you're moving in? Tatyana responds, and her two friends laugh out loud like the tipsy idiots they are.

Antonina gives up. She heads to the table and pulls out her belongings. She has only just put on her jacket when Tatyana comes up beside her.

Leave it, she says. I was only joking. I think all these hormones are making you too serious.

You'll look after my stuff? Antonina says, ignoring the hormone insult. She juts her chin towards the bed. You won't let the monkeys touch it?

God's honour, Tatyana says, which is good enough for Antonina. Not that Tatyana believes in God, but there is always the fear of thunderbolts if you lie about such things.

Antonina widens the string of the trolley bag and opens the lid of her Odessa box without drawing it out. The only thing utterly precious she won't leave behind is the doll with the medal inside, so she takes it out and places it in the inside pocket of her jacket where she can feel its rattle close to her heart. She contemplates the backpack, and only because of her toiletries, she takes it.

On the way out of the building, there is no one around in the corridors. She stops in the middle of the stairs and listens. Nothing. She leans over the rail and looks up the stairwell. No noise apart from the gathering instalment of party-types inside Tatyana's room. So, she heads back up to the communal kitchen. The place is warm and soft with the light of the evening filtering through a row of net curtains. The benches are much cleaner than the ones in the factory, and here there is enough cupboard room for every dish, pot, and spoon to be put away in its own place.

The fridge door has a squeal that seems worse the slower it opens. Two drawers are full of vegetables, so Antonina helps herself to two carrots, some cabbage, and a good meaty bone. In a metal bowl are a dozen cooked potatoes still in their skins and whole. She grabs two. It's enough to make a good soup for the prostitute and herself. Bread would be good, but potatoes will have to do. She puts the food in her backpack and checks the corridor is still empty before leaving.

By the time she reaches the factory, Antonina is ravenous. She heads straight for the kitchen, unloads the food and immediately sets a pot of salted water to boil with the bone already in it. To this, she adds the chopped vegetables. There are some onions in the fat Maria's basket. She knows there will be trouble if she takes one, but she does anyway. She chops it quickly and scrapes the pearly white squares into the soup, then hides the dry skins inside her bag to be discarded when she next goes out on the street.

After a while, the fat Maria comes into the kitchen and starts fumbling on the other stove. Antonina guards her boiling pot, ready to lie about the onion if it's mentioned. Sofiya comes in too, her hair in rollers. She lays a blanket over the table and covers it with a sheet to iron her dress. With her are two others. A man and a woman who are both much younger than Sofiya. Shabbier too. Sofiya likes taking the young ones under her wing, teaching them how to take care of themselves. She has even tried instructing Antonina on the art of eyeliner, to no avail, and Antonina boggles at the challenge of ironing Sofiya is pointing out to the pair. It's another of those instruments that Antonina will never use unless she has to. For a wedding perhaps, but nothing less.

Antonina ignores the two guests and their comments on the wonderful smell of her soup. They aren't getting any, and with that Antonina decides not to wait any longer. She puts two bowls in her bag with two spoons and a cup, then grabs the pot, the hot handles tucked inside a tea towel, and takes it down to her room. She is about to put the pot down on the concrete floor to manoeuvre her way into the bedroom when the door opens. She carries the pot through, not expecting to see Polina on the bed. Antonina turns to see who is closing the door behind her. It's the security guard from the Academy, the one Nataliya's father bribed. The middle-aged, large, worry-faced security guard, inside her bedroom, where he doesn't belong.

What are you doing here? she says sharply.

Is that any way to greet a visitor who brings gifts? Sit, he says.

She thinks about the hot soup in the pot. The guard sees her eyes going from him to the pot.

I'll take that. The guard reaches in and seizes it. Don't want you having an accident.

Polina is curled into the corner of Antonina's bed, her back pressed against a wall with the blanket pulled up to her mouth, sucking an edge of it like a scared child. Antonina sits on the end of the bed nearest the door, between the bully and the prostitute, wondering if she's interrupted some kind of business that shouldn't be going on in her bedroom.

I can come back, she offers.

The guard laughs and tells her to relax. He's not there for that.

No one seems to want Polina for that.

The pot is just beside his feet, where she can still reach it if she needs to. He pulls up next to her in an old cane chair she has never seen before. The chair creaks at the weight of him lowering himself into it.

Look, he says, I thought we could spend some time getting to know each other better since we both seem to be keeping odd hours at the Academy. He shows her a breadboard he prepared before she arrived, with a cob loaf of fresh bread, sliced meat and cheese. He pours a small glass of whisky, and she passes it on to Polina. He pours another, and Antonina shakes her head.

You wouldn't refuse me the courtesy of just one drink, would you?

She takes the glass, and he pours another for himself.

To life, he says and downs his drink in one. Antonina takes a sip from her glass. Don't insult me, he says, and holds the glass up, so she has no choice but to swallow its contents.

When he glances past her to check on Polina, Antonina sees the door behind him. She thinks about the door, thinks about the soup, the nugget, Polina. He is back, his face a moon in front of her, his enormous body taking in all the air of the room, so there is hardly any left for anyone else. He draws a hunting knife from a holster in his belt. Stay calm, she tells herself. This isn't what Makar would have arranged. He's not going to hurt us. The guard holds the knife like he's about to stab a pig in the throat. Instead, he sticks the loaf of bread so hard that the knife hits the board and stays there when the guard lets it go: blade half sunk, handle jutting straight up in the air, a loaf of bread stabbed in the guts.

See, he says. I am no brute. Won't you eat something?

Antonina thinks about the knife. It's so close. But so is the guard. Adrenalin rushes through her. She turns to check on Polina, but she has zoned out, into the safe place Antonina imagines they all go during the servicing of men, her eyes disconnected from the real-life happenings of the room. The guard takes the knife and saws a piece of bread, adds some meat and cheese, and hands it to Antonina. They may as well be alone because he doesn't offer anything to Polina.

I've been asked to come to tell you to leave Mr Volkov alone.

Has Makar sent you to intimidate me?

No, Mr Volkov has not. But someone else has. Eat.

Antonina takes a small bite of her sandwich. It is good, but she chews only half-heartedly and tries not to swallow in case it gets stuck in her throat if either of them makes a move. The guard takes a big bite of his, half the sandwich gone in one go.

This girl, he waves the knife in the direction of Polina, his voice doughy through the food in his mouth. I've seen her before. Someone's looking for her, I think, yes?

Antonina shrugs. Chews. Holds the sandwich in her hand and tries not to look at the knife.

It's good. The guard refers to the sandwich, not Polina. He nods and stuffs the second half in his mouth, chews a few times and swallows, his eyebrows raised as if to make room to let it slide down his throat. Antonina nibbles hers like a mouse.

I think, he says tapping the tip of the knife on his knee before stabbing it in the bread again, I think you should tell your friend Konstantin that it would be better not to disturb Mr Volkov again at the university.

Antonina swallows. Konstantin? she says.

Oh, he says. You didn't know? Yes, he's been skulking around the Academy too.

She forgot to tell Konstantin that she'd already spoken to Makar. Her fault. There have been so many distractions lately.

How did you know where I live? she says suddenly unnerved by more than just his presence. No one knows where she lives. Do they? Not at the university, and certainly not Makar.

He smiles — an attempt at endearment that makes him

look more of a creep. I'll go now, he says. Let's think nothing more of it. Just leave things be, yes?

He packs the food into their original wrappers and places them inside a paper bag. The loaf of bread Antonina reaches across to snatch for herself, maybe stupidly, and he pulls the knife from its head before she gets the chance. She should have just grabbed the knife. Instinctually she went for the food.

So, we are agreed? he says holding the knife mid-air.

Tell him our original deal still stands.

The guard pulls back, confused.

No more Konstantin, she says, but our original deal still stands. Just tell him that.

He tucks the knife back into the holster and lifts his chin towards Polina. See that your Konstantin gets the girl out of the city, he says. It won't be long before they find her here, and you don't want to be tangled up with that.

Antonina's breath comes all at once the minute the guard leaves the room. It's as if she'd run a block when she rushes to lock the door. She rests her hand on her chest to calm herself as the guard's footsteps fade. She is infuriated by his visit to her home, but there is a swell of gratefulness too, that she now knows the danger the prostitute poses. Polina must be aware of the guard's leaving too, because the blanket drops and she asks if he has gone. Antonina kicks the closest leg of the cane chair, then picks it up and throws it into the loading bay so it clatters and lands right in the middle, where Konstantin will have to get out of his truck and move it. No space for chairs in her tiny room. No space for prostitutes either. She sits on the bed hard enough that

Polina bounces at the other end. Konstantin may not have been seen rescuing the prostitute on the night, but now her whereabouts are known, and he's out of town.

Don't worry about it, she says. Kostya is a good man. He will take care of you when he returns. But tonight, without him to guard us, we need to move.

She collects the pot of soup from the floor, placing the loaf of bread on the lid.

Follow me, Antonina says, and they walk down the corridor like another two chicklings for Sofiya to take under her wing and watch over for the night.

PEOPLE OF THE TIGER

VLADIVOSTOK, RUSSIA — 1994

Katerina prefers the safety of the back seat. The Japanese imports that flood through the port are too light — everything bounces when they hit a pothole, and there are many potholes in the city of Vladivostok. For years, she hasn't driven a car for herself, and today Katerina is a guest in the local *mudang*'s car. Jeemin was keen for Katerina to come along for the fishermen's blessing that the shaman community will perform on a boat in the harbour of Vladivostok. The last time Katerina dabbled in shamanism it did not go well; the ghosts of the screaming bridge in Semipalatinsk still haunt her. But here she is, two decades later, full of hope once again that she will hear from her Nikolai now she is so close to their old home.

Jeemin's instruments are wrapped in bed sheets and tucked within boxes that fit snugly inside the boot, but still the tiger bells chime whenever the car jolts. Toyota Corolla. Even the name sounds aluminium. Not like her Zhiguli, slowly rusting in the shed back home. Seventy-seven. Katerina forgets her age at times. On the inside, she remains the same, and her mind still believes she's only twenty. She is a slow-rusting vehicle, the engine of her brain solid and dependable — it's just her body that's not keeping up.

Katerina ignores the glances in the rear-view mirror. Jeemin is too enthusiastic for her own good. Trying to anticipate everyone else's moves leaves Jeemin without the conviction of her own ideas, her own instincts. That will make for a very dull companion, for the week they will spend together in the city.

Watch the road, Jeemin, she tells her. I'm not ready to leave the planet yet.

There's a sudden smoothness as the car leaves the unsealed road for proper asphalt and it comes as such a relief, even amongst the congestion of Fadeeva Street. Cars, buses and trucks all travel the same arterial route into Vladivostok as they always have, but since the city opened to the public the traffic has become heavier, more aggressive, the drivers less forgiving. The highway is wide enough for order, but the lanes remain unmarked, and it takes assertiveness to negotiate the chaos.

Jeemin jerks the steering wheel to the right, and a bus comes so close to Katerina's door that she leans away instinctively as if that would help the car keep balance. The tiger bells chime in the boot, and beside Katerina the ceremonial costumes that hang on a wire rack shuffle and lurch.

Sorry, Jeemin says. Another ditch in the road.

Katerina would tell the woman to slow down, but in her experience it makes no difference. She readjusts the seatbelt across her chest, and the silks settle on their hangers beside her with a shush that sounds like relief.

After a while, they pass the security checkpoint that was once part of a military ring that protected the naval base from outsiders. Now its empty shell weeps a stain the colour of henna from rusted, vandalised windows. A year ago they would have stopped to hand over passports. Now it's just a marker. Twenty minutes to downtown.

Jeemin has dressed beautifully for the celebration. Katerina still can't persuade the woman to wear makeup, but her hair is oiled and tied back, shiny and neat, the sheaths of her under-costumes pressed and pristine white. She smells of the scent that will always remind Katerina of Communist Party workers and strict teachers. Red Moscow —a woody, floral, hefty mix. So many other perfumes come through the port now, but for some reason there is this nostalgia for the old Kremlin bottle.

Has your boy's knee recovered? Katerina asks.

Mostly, thank you, Jeemin says. The doctor thinks he should give up sport though, in case it happens again.

That must be very upsetting for him.

We're all upset by it, says Jeemin.

Perhaps he could do something else? Use his mind instead?

A computer would be a good idea, Jeemin says. I told Borya last year to get him one.

Katerina doesn't know much about computers. A chess game probably wouldn't do, so she decides not to suggest that. She closes her eyes to rein in the energy. She tires so quickly these days and isn't sure how she will last through a whole day's celebration. And then there is the hospital visit for tests. Can she be bothered? The illness is the end coming for her, and quickly. She doesn't need to be told by a doctor what form it takes.

Oh look, Jeemin says. There's a blow-up mouse in the street over there. Can you see it?

Katerina had nodded off as they approached the city, her head hanging forward, and she snaps it upwards at the sudden perkiness from the front seat. Out in the street is the giant blow-up face of Mickey Mouse that caused the spike of elation, its mouth the widest, stupidest grin she's ever seen, the eyes too large to be trusted, and she holds her hand to her forehead to shield herself from the enormity of its brazen gaze.

Sportivnaya Gavan. Katerina recognises the bay.

The blow-up is not for us, I hope, Katerina mumbles.

No, Jeemin says and laughs a little.

They're taking the scenic route, but they're not far from the wharf on the other side of the ridge. Golden Horn Bay — she remembers that place too.

The mouse looks like it's for a new restaurant opening, Jeemin says. Lots of Chinese coming in and opening up shops these days.

I think these ones must be Americans, Katerina says.

Lots of Americans coming in too. The foreigners are over-running us. I liked it best when the region was closed.

Katerina disagrees. Closed minds restrict the freedom of the spirit. People should be free to follow their hearts. It sounds like a Confucian chant when she says it, but it's her own truth.

When they pull into the entrance of the wharf, a security guard steps in front of the car with his hand held up.

Don't worry, Jeemin says. Dmitry's here to help us get through. She gets out to speak with the Dmitry fellow, who's playing with his moustache in a way that suggests he is worried. A second guard picks up the telephone inside the booth. Could be trouble. Katerina rolls down her window.

What's happening? she asks.

The mayor gave us permission himself, Dmitry says. They can't stop the barge going out. Won't be long, he's calling the mayor's office now.

Katerina wonders if she will get her money back if they cancel. It wasn't cheap securing a place on the outing, and she wouldn't have bothered if it weren't the last-ditch effort to reconnect to her Nikolai before she passes into spirit herself. Not much the rest of them can do to her — the cursed souls that roam can pluck her backbone all they like, there's not much they can take from her now.

The guard outside the checkpoint booth motions for Jeemin's documentation, and she pats herself down as if there were some secret pocket in her ceremonial costume, which there isn't. Katerina reaches through the front seats for Jeemin's internal passport inside the middle console, then waves it out the window with her own.

The guard in the booth is taking his time, fluffing with imaginary numbers no doubt. The pressure builds as other cars line up behind theirs, and Katerina can hear the impatience in the pats of the acceleration pedals, the small revs in neutral that keep the engines from falling asleep.

We're here to perform the blessing for the fishing community. Jeemin directs her words to the guard outside the booth. We were given permission months ago. Why are you holding us up?

It's too dangerous, the guard says. We can't let you take all these people out on a barge. Container ships come in and out of the port all the time. You'll get us in trouble. Big trouble. He emphasises the 'big'.

Go back to the car. I'll take care of it. Dmitry directs Jeemin towards the car, and she doesn't argue. They know the ritual required for the placation of guards, and Katerina winds up her window, pretending not to notice the hunch of Dmitry's shoulders as he pays the illegal *vziatka* that will iron out all their concerns.

Twenty years ago they wouldn't have meddled in the business of a *mudang* like that, Jeemin says. She takes in the details of their faces and closes her eyes to send their images on to the other side. Katerina has seen her do that before, and it sends an involuntary shiver through her shoulders.

The barge is not the ugly slug Katerina expected it to be. Today it has been transformed into a floating theatre that reminds her of the travelling Korean theatre during Soviet times — the fold-out stages with colourful scene-drops that shut out thoughts of dreary, repetitive work in the fields. Although this show isn't free. These patrons have paid millions of roubles to receive their warnings, blessings or messages. Be they good or bad, everyone wants to read the future. The stage has been set up with folding screens that run along the back, forming a wall covered with images of deities. To invite the helpful spirits, Jeemin says. Her face beams as she explains the rest of the set-up, though Katerina knows it all already; she saw her first *mudang* ceremony before Jeemin was even born. Outside this, Jeemin says, is the sacred bamboo with red and white fabric that keeps the malevolent spirits from entering.

They move to the front of the stage where the pine branches define the sacred space of the altar, and flags made of coloured paper depict the five directions: north, south, east, west and centre. To the back are tables loaded with food offerings, and giant incense sticks that are already into their slow burn; tips of ash like unflicked cigars. To the sides are two tents for the *mudangs* to change costumes, and helpers are already unloading Jeemin's belongings from the car, passing the stage with hats and beads and belts, along with at least twenty changes of robes. Then there are the swords and knives. Katerina wasn't expecting swords and knives.

Is there to be a sacrifice? she asks. If there is, she wants no part of it. Bloodletting is something she knows shamans do — chickens, goats, sheep, or whatever — but she certainly doesn't want to see any of it.

Jeemin assures her the swords aren't for bloodletting. They're used to call up the war hero Chungoon, she says. Don't worry. Most of my patrons are usually the wives of businessmen. They like the proceedings to be civil. She nods towards the guests coming on board. Look at all the fishermen who have turned out, she says. I can feel the energy of their belief already. It's so strong, and we haven't even started.

Can you feel mine? says Katerina.

Not yet, but I'm sure it will come through. And again, she says not to worry.

Katerina hadn't considered she was worrying. Her hands are fussing she notices, wringing the red leather of her gloves like wet cloths, and she is somewhat anxious. But not worried.

Dmitry is keen to cast the barge out to sea quickly, in case more authorities demand favours. Within an hour of the ropes being released, the barge floats in the middle of the harbour and the ceremony begins. Jeemin is the local *mudang*, so she performs her dances when she chooses.

Between her performances, the other *mudangs* take the stage, but while Jeemin rests, she remains connected, sitting to the side of the altar encouraging the audience to clap and dance, to laugh and banter. The visiting spirits like to play, and Jeemin tells the audience bawdy jokes that supposedly come through from the dead, and when the time is right the dead whisper secrets in her ears. Katerina has a privileged position in the front row of the fold-out seats, and the secrets fly out. Not one of them for her though. If she had the medal that belonged to her father, there would be a connection, her aerial for the souls of her family, but that's now long gone.

After a while, Jeemin takes her place on the stage again. She waves coloured flags up and down as she spins, and they resemble the currents of the sea, the tentacles of jellyfish, or the sway of seaweed. The chant is a simple counting repetition that goes up to twenty, then starts again. When her twirl comes to a stop, Jeemin offers the ribbons to a weather-beaten fisherman with skin as thick as tanned hide. He is to choose one, and, dependent on the colour he picks, the forecast of the year will be determined. He picks green. The year ahead will be good for the fisherman. The chant and twirl are performed again, and again, with no story to entertain Katerina's imagination. She is supposed to sit there with simple hope to carry her through the monotony. They wouldn't get away with that in the travelling Korean theatre, she says to herself.

Katerina can't stand it any longer. The noise of the drums and cymbals feels deliberately calamitous. They're penetrating her head and making her ears ring. The pressure has been building for at least an hour, with the pain of a headache squeezing the front of her brain. There are no messages here for her. She shouldn't have been so foolish as to think there would be, and she heads to the back of the barge for a reprieve.

Way up above, the frosty trail of an aeroplane stretches across the pale blue, the craft already long gone. The half-moon that kept a watchful eye on the procession all morning has faded away and left them to it. A whisper of breeze is rising, lifting the robes of dancers when they twirl, adding drama to the supernatural, and from the distance, the dancers seem serene. Across the harbour, the strip of Golden Horn Bay curves towards the peninsula of the city. It's not as pretty as when Katerina was young. Large frigates that were once the Navy's pride now rust side-by-side like dying insects whose antennae no longer twitch, the life leaving their dull husks ashen grey against the cityscape behind them.

Katerina is in a daydream when Jeemin comes up and offers her a banana and a slice of cake in a napkin. She takes the banana to reassure Jeemin. To be honest, food gives her very little pleasure anymore, but Jeemin is right, she should eat.

We're heading deeper into the estuary so the barge will be still for the performance of the *Chakdo t'anda*. It's the dance with the knives when I call up the great warrior Chungoon. You should come back to your seat. He might just have something for you.

Soon, Katerina says. I'll be there in a moment.

Jeemin squints up at the sunlight, then down at the churn of white-water that follows the moving barge. Give me your wedding ring, she says waving her hand with a small, demanding gesture.

Katerina doesn't budge. It won't work, she says, half-sigh,

half-voice. I tried that once before. Don't worry about it. I should have known better.

Give me your ring, Jeemin insists. There's someone here. I can feel an energy.

Before Katerina knows it, her heart is beating like the irregular drum in the ceremony, pelting in her chest so hard she could die from it. She peels off her red glove and tries to remove the ring, only it's wedged. The finger swollen with age has created a natural trench for the gold ring. There is no removing it. Katerina gives Jeemin a pained look and almost bursts into tears at the sudden build-up of expectation that has collapsed into disappointment.

Give me your hand, Jeemin says, and she wraps the entire ring finger in the palm of her hand.

Katerina's fingers tingle. Something they've been doing a lot lately.

There is a spirit kneeling before us, Jeemin says. He has his hands in his lap, and he smells like charcoal and rain. Wet burnt wood. Are these things familiar to you?

Katerina doesn't know that smell, though it doesn't sound altogether unpleasant. No, she says. Who is he?

Looks like he is the block to your husband, but he won't say why. The name Bora is coming to me. Does a person named Bora mean anything to you?

Golden Horn Bay is slipping away into the distance, and Katerina could almost lean over the rail and throw up at the thought of Bora's first husband. She lets the banana fall into the churning white-water. Is he with Nikolai? she asks. They were together, weren't they?

He's gone, Jeemin says and lets go of Katerina's hand. That's all I can see. He wouldn't speak.

Who told you about Bora then?

I don't know. But I can see a baby floating above us. A new soul waiting to come through. Someone you care about is pregnant. Does that mean anything?

Katerina grips the railing and allows the sun-baked heat of the metal to soak into the nakedness of her ungloved hand. Her fingertips stick, and she knows without looking that her fingers have begun to bleed. The throbbing of the barge's engine whines down and settles into a comfortable idle. Small waves lap softly, coming to their end against the metal of the hull. When the barge stops, it begins to sway beneath her feet.

A child that isn't born, she murmurs. Someone I care about.

There aren't many people that Katerina could say she cared about. The Sharm girl is one. She shivers at the possibility of the unborn child belonging to the Sharm girl. The guilt of taking the child from her mother back in 1974 still rakes her.

I have to get back, Jeemin says. It is time for the dance of the knives.

Why is it so hard to find my husband? Katerina asks.

Jeemin offers her arm for Katerina to take, and they head towards the front of the barge. Whoever the man was, he seems to have reason to be angry with you, Jeemin says. You will need to find a way to make amends. Perhaps he will come again during the ceremony of the knives. If he does, shall I send on a message?

Katerina doesn't know what to say. Every night her brother-in-law enters her mind, filling in the silence with an imaginary argument — Katerina explaining the trickery of the NKVD. The apology she would give. The depths she would bow to. Conversations carried on even in her dreams. Words and sentences that expand with every round until she wakes and realises it has all been in vain. Her fingers still bleed. Her husband still doesn't come. The apology has not been received, or perhaps just not accepted. Perhaps now he will hear her.

Yes, she says. If he comes again, please tell him I am sorry. I am so very sorry.

Mickey Mouse is gone from Sportivnaya Gavana by the time Katerina arrives the next day. In its wake is a long queue for a new ride in the amusement park. Even though the wind is driving in from the Pacific and stirring sand in their faces, the line stands rigid against the elements, each person patiently waiting for a turn. The weather is too wild for Katerina. The wind has always unsettled her, messing with her hair the way it does. She tightens the shawl around her head and shoulders, clasping it firmly in a fist, and makes her way across the width of the peninsula.

An army of Japanese businessmen marches out of the Vladivostok Hotel as she passes. Probably another bomb-threat evacuation, because there's no fire alarm going off. A bit of excitement during a boring convention by the look of them — all black and white, ties and shiny shoes. Several flagpoles line the front garden of the hotel with the proud flapping flags of hotel occupants: Japanese, Chinese, American, Canadian, Russian, Korean, as well as a couple of others she doesn't recognise, and of course there is the tiger of Vladivostok in the centre, where it belongs.

Jeemin was right. The city does seem to be overrun with foreigners. Katerina saunters through the streets and picks up the fringes of conversations in languages she doesn't recognise. Just a few blocks from Dmitry's apartment an Asian couple approach her. The man says something in Korean. Katerina listens for words she can understand. But Korea changed its language somewhere along the way, and the languages of the old and the new Korea do not fit together very well.

Cherry? Katerina answers his inquiry. No cherries yet. Too early, she says.

The man shakes his head and repeats his phrase. All she can hear is cherry.

I don't understand, she says.

The woman says something about being Korean. The tone ends on a high, so it must be a question.

Yes, Katerina replies. I am Koryo-saram.

The woman's handbag is strapped across her body defensively, and she pulls it to the front and rests her hand on top for extra security. She speaks louder and more slowly. Speak, Korean, she says and repeats the word 'cherry'. That's all Katerina understands. The woman turns to the man and says something in ruffled tones.

Speak Russian, Katerina demands. You're in Russia, so speak Russian!

The woman's hair is cropped too short. Her eyebrows are untamed, and the baggy blue sweater makes her look like a middle-aged frump. In the reflection of the woman's owlish sunglasses, Katerina feels proud of her enduring elegance. It's you who is a disgrace, she thinks. Not me.

The man seems frustrated, but his voice is kinder than his wife's. Katerina listens. Where are you from? he asks. Why can't you speak?

It feels like an insult.

I am Russian-Korean, she says in the old dialect. *Koryo-saram*.

But she may as well be speaking in Martian. They shake their heads. The woman unclips the clasp on the zipper of her handbag, which takes some fiddling. If the hawkers didn't know she was a tourist before, they'd know it now. She pulls out a book and secures the zip again. The pair exchange some quiet chatter while searching for a page, then they turn the book to Katerina and point. Casino, it says in Russian. He says 'cherry' again and taps his finger on the page.

Hearing it again, Katerina can decipher the word casino. *Kajino*. Cherry Casino.

No, she shakes her head. Don't know, and she moves on, knowing the iceberg of a building is just one street away.

Katerina aims for the old Communist Party headquarters as she crosses the peninsula. It sticks out like a colossal white tooth, and she is relieved to be heading downhill towards Central Square, towards Golden Horn Bay, towards the spot where Nikolai stole his first kiss. The wind can't reach her on this side, and soon she grows warm in her coat. She removes her shawl and straightens her hair, then checks herself in a mirror, as if Nikolai still waits. Her feet already complain, but she refuses to stop until she reaches their spot on the embankment. She lowers herself onto a seat. Behind her, a park spans what used to be dry docks, along with storage for enormous machinery and building products. The once-sheltered alcoves are now open to public view, and it's a popular place. People sit all around, murmuring and eating picnics. A papa is trying to teach his toddler how to kick a ball.

Kick, kick, he says. Like this, and he lifts his arms in triumph when the child's boot meets the ball.

The smell of sewage is a little sharp with no wind to push it out to sea. Across the way, a dozen stowed vessels remain motionless. Small patches of oily slicks stretch from their hulls in colours that resemble the northern lights.

The way her memories of Nikolai come to her is beautiful. The press of his hands on her hips. The warm, soft shaft of his neck against her cheek. His voice a wing beating in her ear, here, in this very spot where Nikolai asked her to be his wife.

He promised he would come for her, and his failure has bled through the tips of her fingers for half a century. After yesterday's final disappointment, all that is left of her hope is an ashy heap with a few deep red embers that need stirring to find. She resigns herself to saying goodbye. This is the real reason she has come. Not for the shaman ceremony. Not for the hospital visit. The illness has drawn her here to say farewell. What they had is lost. Her rice farmer cannot find her, and she cannot find him.

The colours in the oil floating on the water change to blue, then purple, then grey. Katerina's neck is suddenly cold, and it's only this that causes her to look around and realise that time has played a trick and disappeared. All the picnickers are gone. Globe lights pop on in the dimming light all along the embankment. She should have left long ago, and she gets up to follow the globes, each one a goal to aim for, each one a fraction of the journey back to Dmitry's apartment on feet that complain more and more. She carries a heart that hangs low with the threat of falling away altogether.

THE UNCONVENTIONALS

ST PETERSBURG — 1994

Konstantin was never interested enough to find out what lay behind the façade of a higher education facility before Antonina came along. Never had the chance to discover a talent he could advance into a career either. Perhaps if he were a poor Koryo-saram from Kazakhstan he would have been given the opportunity to develop academically. But orphans aren't meant to linger long in school. And outside of it, the only driver is the month-to-month needs of staying afloat. This he has done on his own since he was fifteen without help from anyone. To get ahead is a dream. The kinds of opportunities that would allow him that require connections he either doesn't have or doesn't want. Ambition he has. Ideas, he is never short of, and at the moment there is one that keeps circling that could change his situation for the better, or for the worse if he doesn't tread carefully. What he isn't sure of is whether it's worth the risk.

The Academy is an unnerving place. The foyer alone

is bigger than a dozen rooms in the factory combined. Size has always mattered with these types of buildings, designed to remind the workers just how small they are. Tsarist or Communist, Konstantin is never in doubt of his insignificance when he steps inside one. He stops in the centre of a circled entrance with doors and stairs that lead in all directions. The domed ceiling belongs in a palace, but the many white statues positioned around the area give the place the sombre mood of some human disaster — like the Pompeian village where people turned to stone while going about their daily business.

No one notices the vulnerability of the statues' nakedness. Their empty stares are just the backdrop to a crowd dressed like colourless blackbirds, all pecking at crumbs of conversation within tightly guarded circles, just like the days of school, and the thought of it makes him uncomfortable. No one notices Konstantin either, standing with his posy of drooping tulips wrapped in soggy newsprint that drips like a slow leak. He embarrasses himself. Surely, he would embarrass her too. He could turn back and walk out. Antonina would never need to know he was even there. He checks to see if she's within sight, but he can't see any Koreans.

She asked you to come, idiot, he tells himself. She wanted you to see her show, and you've already missed one, so suck it up. It's all the drive he needs to push his way through the crowd clotting up the entrance and go find his Nina.

The tulips were a mistake. He bought them from a street vendor on the way to the Academy. It seemed like a good idea at the time — almost fate-like that they were there. Tulips are from Kazakhstan, he was planning to say, but no one else has flowers, and just when he's about to lay them down to the left of the main doors, he sees Antonina, as lovely as she always is. Small and perfect and exotic. Her hair is down. He is not used to seeing it so full around her shoulders. Hadn't noticed how long it had grown over winter. It's smooth, and dark as night sprinkled with stars that shine in the light of the chandelier. Her skin is pale and perfect — a little makeup around her eyes. Her mouth. He likes that the most, like perfectly set waves — two at the top, one beneath. At rest, it's almost as wide as it is deep. For the longest time, he has imagined what it might be like to touch those lips.

She faces his direction with a tender sadness in a dreamlike gaze. It's not him she sees, but the wooden carving that draws the attention of a group who close in around it with focused interest. Beauty is a seductress, but the statue is dead. True beauty is only in the living, and as far as Konstantin is concerned it stands right in front of him. He waits to see if Antonina will feel his presence.

The moment their eyes connect, the backs of his shoulders let go of tension he hadn't been aware was there. Antonina crosses the floor with a mousey squeal of delight that surprises him. Her head tilts forward and she holds out her arms in an unnecessary show of emotion. She wears a stonewashed denim jacket over the softly pleated fabric of a white linen dress that catches the small mound of her belly when she moves. She is radiant like he has never seen, and he leans down to kiss her on the cheek, careful not to linger too long in her warmth, but sneaky enough to inhale the smell, and store the details with fondness.

Here, he says, and hands her the flowers. They're from your mother.

A moment of shock registers. Antonina's eyes enlarge, a sharp intake of breath.

My mother? says Antonina. Is she here? She scans the room in a slightly contagious panic that makes Konstantin look around as well.

No, he says. Well, actually, I don't know. The flowers are from me. I just thought you might like it if they were from your mother. I don't know why I said that.

What an idiot, he thinks. Tulips are from Kazakhstan. What happened to just saying that?

Oh, Antonina says, you should have said. Thank you. She lifts the tulips to her nose, cradling two of their hanging heads, sniffing one, then the other.

Do they smell like the ones from your mountain?

Nothing smells as good as the mountain, she says. Anyway, look at you all dressed nice.

It's true; he did make an effort. He wears a button-up blue shirt, tan canvas pants, and black polished shoes. He tried very hard not to look as though he had tried too hard to impres by untucking the shirt. He shouldn't have bothered. The room is a mix of suits and dresses, and jeans and t-shirts, with him stuck somewhere in the middle in a kind of limbo-land where he is neither one nor the other. He scratches the front of his scalp and thinks about leaving again, but Antonina won't let him escape so easily, she takes him by the sleeve and jostles a path through the crowd towards the back of the hall. When they reach the far left corner, two of the tulips have lost their clothes. Crumbs in the woods, or pebbles for the path back to safety. One of the lost petals has been pressed into the floor by his foot, its colour leaching like a skid of blood.

My exhibit, Antonina announces with wide, introductory

arms. Before you look at this one, though, watch this. It's the show we put on at the nonconformist centre. I wish you were there to see it, she says.

I did see it.

Antonina opens the side flap of a portable video camera and holds the screen out where they both can get a clear view.

You only saw the set-up. This is the show. Watch it.

The floor is a carpet of clay dolls, just as he remembered. From a distance, the individuality of their faces is stripped away. The colours are there, but the eyes, the noses, and the mouths are indistinct.

Amazing how their personalities are stripped away in the over-crowding, he says. They look all the same. Like rolling hills of faces that have become one larger entity.

Antonina lowers the camera. You see that? she says, looking bewildered enough to cause Konstantin to run back over his words, wondering if he's said something stupid.

I didn't expect you to see that, she says.

He shrugs and rubs his lip to hide the pleasure of surprising her. She lifts the camera again, and he listens to her speech, sees the passion of her fist. Fighting words. Tatyana is having an effect on her. It's good, he thinks.

Hey, he says pointing to the screen. What are they doing? A member of the audience steps onto the heads of a few clay dolls, crushing them as they walk towards the glass thing in the middle. Hey, Konstantin says again, this time with indignance, as if they could hear him. A few more people join in, treading carefully at first, then stomping their feet hard. He recognises Vladimir who stomps around the room, obsessively destroying dolls. They fall like dominoes, but still, his boots show no mercy.

He must appear concerned because Antonina pats his arm and tells him it's all right. They're meant to be broken, she says. Tread on the small people. It's part of the message.

What a shame, he says. They had such pretty faces.

I have some left. If you really do like them, you can have one.

I do, he says. I like this one too. Konstantin walks to the large clay sculpture in her Academy exhibit. I saw this one the other day in your studio.

To his eye, this one looks like real art. A piece that showcases Antonina's talent. Apart from the rusty clay colour, it could be an ancient Roman statue, highly realistic — a life-size man pushing his way out of the stand as though stuck in drying cement.

I know how this guy feels, Konstantin says.

Well, you can't have that one, Antonina says. I need his clay for next year.

You break him down? That must hurt.

Tatyana appears before Antonina can reply, and the hall quietens as a glass is clinked with a spoon, and everyone moves out of the booths into the middle to see who's speaking. A middle-aged man with a greying beard and silver-blue suit introduces himself as the head of department. Konstantin spots Antonina's baby-papa and weighs the measure of him from the distance while the slow drip of a speech goes on and on.

Antonina stands on her tiptoes to whisper in his ear. Stop looking at him, she says. It's done. You don't need to visit him anymore. I've sorted everything with him myself. All right?

She flattens her feet and waits for his acceptance. At first, he is reluctant, but then he nods. He doesn't accept her decision though, and when Antonina's focus is back on the speaker, Konstantin's glance slides to the skinny excuse of a man who doesn't look like he could grow a beard if he tried. The teacher can feel his glare, Konstantin can tell, by the way he rubs that side of his neck and lifts his collar like a shield.

When the bullshit speech is over, Antonina leads Konstantin and Tatyana out, through a labyrinth of stairs and unlit passages into a musty attic where nothing but cobwebs are stored, then up a final flight of steps where they climb out onto the roof. He doesn't need to ask if they are supposed to be up there to know they're not.

Woohoo! Why haven't we been up here before? Tatyana says. This is amazing. She points out the domes of St Isaac's across the way, then Peter and Paul Cathedral to their left. The three of them stand in a line taking in the view, the wind pressing the fabric of their clothes to the fronts of their bodies.

Look at us, Antonina says. We're like those heroic bronze statues of Soviet workers.

Konstantin stands firm, arms crossed on his chest on one side of her; Tatyana's long black jacket flutters around her legs on the other, and Antonina's white dress presses around the mound of her stomach.

We're the new frontier, Tatyana says. The new tribe of unconventionals.

Unconventionals all right, Konstantin agrees.

Antonina sits and pats the space beside her. Konstantin expects cold tin, but it's surprisingly warm. Now the three of them sit in a row, beside a gold statue with cupids and an owl that Konstantin has only ever seen from a distance.

You think it's real gold? he asks, and Tatyana goes over to check.

Meanwhile, Antonina is opening a half-sized bottle of vodka.

It's brass, Tatyana says when she comes back. Hey, what are you doing? she says to Antonina.

Celebrating the end of the year, Antonina says and hands Tatyana a glass.

You're not supposed to drink alcohol.

It's just one, Konstantin says. Won't harm her.

How do you know? Tatyana says. You've been pregnant before, have you?

And you have? Konstantin fires back.

Tatyana stares hard. Steely and penetrating. Konstantin locks on, projecting murderous intent in her direction, but she doesn't break away. It's Konstantin who pulls out of the glare-wrestle first, his eyes drifting back to Antonina, who seems unaware of the intensity that passed through the air right in front of her.

To life, she says holding out her glass in a salute, then swigs it in one gulp before anyone has time to stop her.

Not wanting to offend, both Tatyana and Konstantin down their drinks in one as well, and while the cringe of horrid homebrew clearly has Tatyana in its clutch, she waves for the bottle to be handed over.

No more for you, she says, like she's holding her breath. That's really bad.

A strange flavour, Konstantin says. Where'd you get this shit? It's harsh, even for my taste.

Horseradish and lemon, Antonina tells him. Came in from Finland.

Konstantin doubts that very much. As a rule, Finnish vodka is much smoother than Russian. Well, it's bullshit, he tells her. Don't buy it again. Tastes like methylated spirits. They used to make gin from it. God knows what they put in bootleg vodka. If you need anything like this, you should get it from me.

Tatyana takes Antonina's glass and tucks it beneath her own.

It is horrible, isn't it? Antonina says, and Tatyana nods with enthusiasm.

———

There is a small grass fire in Antonina's chest where the vodka spreads its wings. It's strong as well as horrible — just one toast is making her light-headed. There is a tapping on the left side of her stomach, but she won't acknowledge it, in case it's the nugget reacting to the vodka. She hopes it's all right; knowing she shouldn't have had that drink.

Do I look any different to you? she asks.

No, Konstantin says, flapping his hand around his face at a mosquito.

Antonina's convinced that the pregnancy glow is still missing. She suspects it only occurs when one is happy to be in that condition. The only maternal bloom she has noticed is the size of her belly. A balloon that's uncomfortable in anything other than the type of industrial cotton underwear her mother wears. Ugly, romper-style, but surprisingly warm. She can see why her mother wears them, and it hasn't taken much to get used to, hidden away under layers of clothing, where no one sees her anymore.

Anaemic clouds ride east over the city, and the sun is a blinking orb behind them, weak as torchlight in fog, never truly breaking free. The city is a sepia-coloured postcard of flushed pastel and faded pigments. Reds that are more like washed-out terracotta. Blues that appear more teal, more green. Pretty, but she could do with some sunshine and mountain air.

Can I stay at your place a few days, Tanya? she asks. Kostya rented out my bed to a prostitute.

What? Tatyana says. Why has Kostya rented out your bed to a prostitute?

I have not rented out your bed, Konstantin leans behind Tatyana's back, his expression that of a parent silent-scolding a child for telling tales.

Antonina ignores him and fixes a blank stare into the middle space in front of her, focusing on nothing.

Lone child syndrome, he says. Most children grew up knowing what it's like to share a bed.

Share your bed with her then, says Tatyana, and she reminds him that Antonina is pregnant, after all.

We're leaving soon, anyway, he says. I'm taking Polina to Novosibirsk, so you can have your bed back in a couple of days.

What's in Novosibirsk? Tatyana asks.

An American. He works at one of the universities. He loves her. Apparently. Konstantin does a poor job of hiding his scorn, and Antonina wonders if it's because of the love, or the American.

What's in it for you? Antonina asks, and it's enough to make him stand up in a huff.

There must be some money in there somewhere, Antonina

thinks. Why else would Konstantin go all the way to Novosibirsk? American dollars. Everyone wants American dollars.

Is there a reward for her return? Tatyana says, apparently thinking the same thing.

Back off, Konstantin says. You don't know what you're talking about.

But they do, and there's an awkward lapse of discussion between them to prove it. Time enough for a dog to burn up on re-entry.

Did Polina tell you about the visitor we had two nights ago? says Antonina.

What visit? he says, flapping away another mosquito.

The Academy security guard. She didn't tell you he came?

A guard from here? he says with a look of genuine surprise. Did he see her?

A scourge of mosquitoes sets him off swearing and leaping about. Antonina sits nearer to Tatyana. The bugs usually prefer her blood. Something to do with the heat, she suspects. They all slap at the air, their arms, their necks, anything that's bare, until the ambush of bugs has flown off. Konstantin has swallowed some of them. He spits and curses. Spits again.

Sit down, Tatyana tells him and pulls his shirt-tail. Here, she says and passes him the horseradish vodka.

He waves it away. Throw it out, he says. It's rubbish. He looks across at Antonina for the answer to his unanswered question. She nods.

So, when are you heading for Novosibirsk? Tatyana asks him.

I think, he says like an idea is warming, I think we'll be going in the morning. First thing.

Feel like company? I can help with the driving. What do

you think, Nina? Are you done here for the year? Let's take off, go find that brother of mine. Be easy to jump on a train to Semipalatinsk after the drive.

Yes I'm finished. Had my oral exam this morning, Antonina says.

So, then? says Tatyana. Shall we go?

I suppose I could use some of the money Makar gave me, says Antonina.

Good girl, Tatyana says and soft-punches Antonina's arm. You got something out of that sucker.

It's not much. What about your job at the hospital?

I haven't been paid for two months. Maybe some time off will remind them to pay the staff.

Might lose you your job too, says Antonina.

Tatyana's excitement eases. She scratches at a mark on her jeans slowly. Yes, maybe, she says. I guess I'll find out.

Do you know for sure you have a brother in Semipalatinsk? Konstantin says.

Yes. There's a record of his birth, but no death. The only way I'll find out is to go there.

Konstantin kicks his plastic cup, so it scuttles across the roof as he stands, his fists thrust deep into his trouser pockets so his shirt bunches up in the front. There's a woman interested in your baby, he says. She wants to meet you. I thought you could come to Novosibirsk and meet her.

Double-dealings, Tatyana says. Then turns to Antonina. I didn't think you were going ahead with that.

I'm not sure I said I was.

Yes, you did. Konstantin says. You said, go ahead with arrangements.

Antonina has to stop and think. Her mind swirls and races

like the Neva. No, she says. I meant with Makar.

So, you don't want to sell the baby? Tatyana says.

Oh, God. Here we go again, Antonina thinks. Her hesitation is enough to set them off again.

Yes, or no? Konstantin demands. Don't be pressured by Tanya. It's your decision.

I suppose I'd be interested in meeting her. And, it would be good to get out of St Petersburg for a bit.

I'm definitely coming too, then, Tatyana says. I'd like to meet this woman as well.

Antonina says nothing. If there is to be a meeting, it won't include Tatyana. If there is to be a meeting.

Oh, shit, Tatyana launches herself straight up from sitting like an exclamation mark. She takes her time to read the clock, and she must have better eyes than Antonina because she's suddenly cursing. Got to go.

Antonina stands to catch her before she heads for the trap door. So, I can stay tonight?

Yes, yes, she says. You know you don't have to ask. Are you coming now?

Antonina's not in the mood to run across town on the end of Tatyana's arm, so she agrees to meet her later. Truth is, her stomach is a bit upset, she might have to take it slowly. She leans against one of the many redundant chimneys to steady herself. Down below is the great hall she noticed last time. Three layers of decadence, and right in the middle is the caretaker, staring up at her. He looks younger than before. He has no broom, no overalls, no trolley. He is dressed in a suit, with a trilby hat. For the end-of-year exhibition, she presumes. She waves and waits for him to move away. But he doesn't, he just stands there, arms crossed, staring up at her like a reprimand, but she is not sorry she brought her friends up onto the roof.

A rush of people leaves through the front doors of the Academy as if the exhibit hall had been emptied in one great flush. Konstantin and Antonina sit side-by-side on the rooftop watching as Tatyana breaks away from the crowd below and runs across the bridge. Antonina can't help being reminded of sitting next to Viktor on the mountain when she was a child. Konstantin has no curls at the back of his head to twirl, but there is the temptation to lean her head on his shoulder.

You're worried about the guard visiting the other night? she says. Is that because of Makar, or because of Polina?

I'm not worried, he says. I'm just tired. It's good you're staying with Tatyana tonight, though. Get a good night's sleep before the trip.

Their eyes follow Tatyana until she becomes the size of a black ant and disappears in the park. Swallowed, as her mother used to be, by the foliage of trees. Viktor. Antonina thinks of him again. He never did come back. He has remained lost to her ever since the night of the dance. She looks at the side of Konstantin's face and wonders whether the same could happen to him.

The nugget, he says. You know there's no pressure? I'm just trying to help.

No pressure, Antonina says. It's a process. I'm trying to figure out what's best. I think I'll know what to do when I meet your lady.

Is it just the money you need? Or is it, he rubs his forehead, then stops mid-motion as if he'd fallen asleep holding his head.

What? The papa? Antonina lets out a breathy laugh. That's well and truly over. No, I don't care about him anymore. I grew up without a father, so I know the nugget would be just fine without one too. The money would be convenient, but I have to admit I'm becoming a bit attached. She rests her hand on her belly. Feel this she says, and places Konstantin's hand where the nugget kicks.

Haha, his voice skips inside a little laugh. That's incredible, he says, and leaves his hand there until the nugget stills. I grew up without a father as well, you know. And look at us. We're doing all right.

Antonina doesn't move. This is the first time he has ever opened up about anything personal, and she waits patiently for more delicious divulgence. Allows the space for him to talk, interested for the very first time in who this man really is.

PARALLELOSPHERE

No one answers her banging on the door of the nonconformist centre, which isn't unusual. Tatyana's Academy recently opened a museum on the first floor, but Antonina can't fathom the randomness of its hours. Sometimes it's open for exhibitions or musical events, sometimes it's not. Today the door is shut with no sounds of life inside, and most probably many of the students have already left the city for family time in country dachas.

It's early evening. Lights are on inside parts of the building. The sun isn't due to set for hours yet, but the day is grey enough that extra illumination is required to brighten most rooms across the city. Tatyana's studio is three floors up. Her curtains are open, and there are no lights on, but Antonina yells Tatyana's name anyway.

No response.

She hadn't meant to take so long. Turns out, Konstantin can talk, and he isn't a country boy after all. Grew up in

Moscow. Mother died of chickenpox. Father a few years later when the canning factory caught fire. She's never met anyone from an orphanage. Never heard of anyone dying of chickenpox either. Family is important, he said more than once, and she assured him she does indeed appreciate her mother. Hearing about his loss makes her feel like a sad excuse of a daughter, but she gets the impression he includes the nugget as well, which is odd for someone who has been arranging a sale.

A new sculpture climbs the corner of the courtyard — a mountain of polystyrene cut into large cubes. Antonina's been dizzy off and on since leaving Konstantin on the island, and the toxic smell of the polystyrene sets her in motion again, this time with a spin like a curveball. It causes her to salivate too heavily and her spit curdles in her mouth. The creator of the polystyrene mountain wouldn't be impressed if she defiled it, so she backs away to support herself on the solidness of the wall, and slides down to a crouch. Up above, various grey clouds pass casually over the building, the tip of bird wings flap in the gutter sprinkling rainwater over the top of the polystyrene like a holy blessing. The nausea is just settling when the key turns in the lock with its distinctive sound — the bolts deep inside the wall clunk once, then twice, a third time and the door opens.

Hold the door, she calls.

The babushka with the black dog steps out. She is dressed without a coat, just a thick cable-knit cardigan and sheepskin boots. Her curved upper back gives her a forlorn widow appearance, forever looking down and slightly to the front as if that were as much of life as she could manage.

Good evening, Lida, Antonina says, pleased to have

remembered the old woman's name. She reaches to catch the weight of the door and trails the tips of her fingers along the back of the dog as it passes. The black fur shines despite the dog's age, and it doesn't seem to mind her touch.

Lida doesn't even lift her chin. There is no verbal acknowledgement, just a mutter to the hobbling dog with the swollen arthritic paws, calling it away, down the poster-plastered archway that leads to the front of the building. The clack of dog claws on concrete stops inside the arch of the tunnel.

———

Tatyana sits across from Sergei at a kitchen table that doubles as a desk placed in the middle of his room. The frame of her body is a comfortable fit in the worn leather padding of the chair, her arms the perfect length for the wooden armrests. She likes the way it swivels when she moves, the way it makes her sit straight up, important as a judge in a private chamber, or a librarian with the power to command the volume of noise.

She lets her legs stretch out, ankles crossed, careful not to knock the artworks stacked beneath the desk. The whole room is crammed with layers of canvases, yet Sergei always knows where a particular piece of work is when he needs to show her some style, some story, some protest he took part in years ago. He either has a meticulous memory, or he's a damn good liar, able to apply random theories at a whim.

Parallelosphere, he says, rocking back in his chair. Do you know what it is?

Tatyana knows what parallelism is. She experiences it every

time she crosses the bridge and enters Antonina's world. She also knows that isn't what Sergei means, and she is the student, welcomed into the room of a founding member of the centre, being given the privilege of a private audience, so she better come up with a suitable answer.

It could be related to the Stalin period. What we show, and what lies beneath are two different worlds, she says, trying very hard to impress.

We aren't in the Stalin period anymore, are we?

No, she says. Then you must be talking about something larger than the individual. The —

We are all individuals, he cuts in, and she feels her confidence waning.

She sits up even more impossibly straight, tucks her feet onto one of the wooden claws beneath the chair, more pensive, then she tries another approach.

Is it a protest movement?

We are not political dissidents. This centre functions within the declaration of human rights.

He's enjoying the deliberate evasion and raises his eyebrows in expectation of another answer. Feels like a trap. Like he's ready to pounce, yet his hands are relaxed, folded one over the other on top of the paunch of his belly. He grins slightly, giving away nothing, with the glint of amusement in his devious eyes. A gentle tap on the door disturbs her thoughts, and she hopes Sergei won't answer it. Lida enters the room without an invitation, but his focus remains on Tatyana and her struggle.

It's cultural opposition, Tatyana fires at him, and he affirms the remark with a nod, then lifts his chin to the direction of the open door.

Your friend is having a baby. Lida leans over the lintel and waves a hand for Tatyana to come.

A baby? Tatyana stands, prepared to defend Antonina's innocence if need be. What baby? . . .Who?

Your friend. The one from Vasilievsky Island, says Lida. You know who I'm talking about. She's in the toilet being sick. You need to come help her.

The glint in Sergei's eye ignites to a definite sparkle. He knows. They all know. Poor Nina. Secrets don't stay secrets around the nonconformists for long. Sergei lifts his hand towards the door. Tatyana is being dismissed — the private audience she has waited for all month is over.

Perhaps we should offer her a key? he says, his words buoyant with mischief.

The dog groan-yawns and hops from foot to foot. He wants to go home, to his mat beside the radiator.

Sorry, Tatyana says. I thought she must have decided not to come. I'll clean the mess up.

I was just joking, Sergei says. You know she's welcome here if she needs a place to stay. Anyone is.

Lida nods and grunts with agreement, then she's off, marching as much as she is able, the dog tottering behind, wide-legged and stiff.

Antonina is lying down in the corridor humming when Tatyana finds her, the soles of her boots beating a soft tune on the door. One of her clay dolls is the recipient of a song, as though a child in need of soothing.

Do I need a password to get by? says Tatyana.

Antonina gives a short laugh and tentatively makes her way into a sitting position, tucking her legs beneath her.

Lida said you've been sick.

So, the old woman does speak, after all, Antonina says, her voice slightly distant. Her face flushes, and she tries to hide it away with the end of her scarf.

Where's the mess? Tatyana says. Do we need to do a clean up?

The old woman's going senile.

Don't say that. Tatyana looks around as if Lida were lurking nearby. She's actually a really lovely lady. She was worried about you.

Was she really? Antonina says. Worried about me?

Tatyana nods.

So, there's no sick to clean up? says Tatyana.

No sick.

When the door is unlocked, the smell of paint rushes to escape. She helps Antonina to her feet, then heads in to open a window. One of the downsides of painting where you sleep is the constant hangover of fumes and the headaches it can cause. Babies need fresh air. She remembers her mama saying this by way of explanation when Tatyana found a photo of herself as a toddler inside a cage hung outside the window of her babushka's apartment. Sunshine for babies. The belief that air rising from the streets below was not polluted now seems so ignorant. But they were gullible times. Surprising she didn't die of pneumonia.

Tatyana feels slightly shy about the Oscar Wilde pose of the self-portrait on the easel when Antonina stands in front of it, drawing up to the canvas, so close that Tatyana almost expects the painted image to lean forward and kiss her.

Why do you use this style? says Antonina.

Tatyana moves away to light a cigarette beside the open

window. Why not? she says, fanning out the match. It's taking back the ownership of the gaze. Neo-classicism offers the kind of innocence that allows the body to be observed in the purity of beauty.

But this feels more like self-aggrandisement, than the purity of beauty, Antonina says.

You mean because I've painted myself as a man?

You always dress like that. Like that guy . . . What's his name?

Oscar Wilde?

No. The Dandy. Timur. That guy. Anyway, where's all the old work gone? I really liked your abstracts.

Antonina peeks behind the easel where a large piece of canvas is covered in a sheet of oilcloth. What's that? she asks.

Here, hold this.

Tatyana gives Antonina her cigarette to hold while she takes down the Oscar piece and lays it carefully against the wall. No one's seen this one, she says, hoisting the covered canvas onto the easel. Just, don't laugh, she says, holding one corner of the oilcloth slightly open. Promise?

You know by asking me not to laugh, that you make it impossible for me not to, don't you?

Tatyana catches Antonina taking a puff of the cigarette. She drops the oilcloth to snatch it back and flick it out the window.

Antonina sinks to the floor with her hands on her belly. That could catch alight, you know, she says. Set the polystyrene into a slow smoulder that will burn us all to death in our sleep.

Now you sound like my mother, Tatyana says. Stop it.

Antonina blinks, then nods. I think I'm going to be sick, she says. It's that horseradish vodka. It's poison.

Vodka and cigarettes. It's no wonder, says Tatyana. I'll make you a cup of tea. See if I can find some crackers. You okay if I leave you alone?

Now you sound like *my* mother, Antonina says. Stop it.

———

Antonina cups her mouth and tries to hold onto what little is left inside her stomach. Footsteps scatter in the corridor, and Antonina hopes one of them is Tatyana returning with that cup of tea. A sugar cube would be nice as well. Right now, a sugar cube could solve a thousand woes. A couple of chairs scrape in the studio above, and laughter ripples through the floor from early arrivals in the club below. Her mouth waters and she swallows, the heat stampeding up her neck, her cheeks, her forehead, her skull. Get to the tub, her brain screams, and she hopes like crazy it's empty of Tatyana's paintbrushes.

Only a patch of thick foamy bile with the odd bit of noodle is dredged up from the depths. Behind her, come the clink of mugs and the click of a lamp switch.

You all right?

Antonina is too drained to speak. She lets the lamplight filter through her and sooth the tremulous aftershocks of vomiting. Her consciousness is surfacing when a bolt of light dazzles and blanches the colours of the room to a misty montage of coloured orbs.

Nice, Tatyana says, and her camera flashes again. Stay there, just like that.

Antonina gathers her strength. No more, she says as weighty and severe as she can.

Tatyana steals one more shot. That's it, she says. No more, I promise.

She places the camera down and raises her hands as though she's just lowered a gun in front of armed guards.

Some friend you are, says Antonina, making her way through to the bed, arms out-stretched slightly, as if blind and weary.

A rip of electric guitar riffs up through the floor, the band in the nightclub plugging in. Check, check, check, on the microphone. A wail of sirens washes over the outer building that usually buffers the noise of the street. The band stop-starts and stop-starts, a song that sounds like blues, but it isn't, and when Antonina wakes up later in the night, the radiator is ringing to the vibrations of techno dance music. Tatyana is in the other room, painting, wearing men's Y-front underwear and a singlet. It reminds her of the ugly bloomers she is wearing herself, and she hoists herself up on her elbows and laughs. It's too funny. Tatyana catches the laughing in the corner of her eye and turns around, a wounded expression on her face. By way of explanation, all Antonina can do is pull up her dress, and show Tatyana her ugly underwear. She points to Tatyana and watches the revelation bloom.

Tatyana puts her paintbrush down, and Antonina knows what's coming. She lies back in wait for the click of the camera. She pushes the elastic of her underwear down and cups the base of her swollen belly as if acknowledging her condition for the first time, not as an ache, not as indigestion or some other dreaded thing, but as the child she carries in her womb. It scares her — the shape of it, the gentle tapping, the brand-new being growing inside her. The responsibility of it, should she decide to follow through with keeping the nugget.

The flash of the camera lights up the red curtain of Antonina's closed lids. There's another, then another — then it's gone. The floor is alive with music that ripples through Antonina's body, and when she gets up she finds herself dancing to the repetitive thump of it. Tatyana returns to her easel where she retains that tightly measured stroke as she paints. Her body sways like seaweed in a gentle tide, her head tilting this way, then that, her shoulders adjusting ever so slightly, embodying every stroke and curve of the brush. A dance to the music inside her head. Clever how she can tune the world out like that.

The painting is a remake of Venus in the clamshell — only it's not Venus, its Antonina with her baby belly, much bigger than it really is. Konstantin is moving in from the side to cover her with a cloak, and on the other side are two angels, holding each other, arms and legs entwined, both with Tatyana's face — one female, one male.

It's beautiful, Antonina calls out over the music.

Really? Tatyana pulls back to take in her work from a distance.

What's the one in the courtyard called? Antonina says.

What one?

The polystyrene sculpture.

Polystyrene? That's not a sculpture. It's going through to a class next week for carving practice.

Oh, Antonina says, amused by her mistake.

Tatyana comes to sit on the bed. She catches a piece of dried paint on the wooden end of her brush with the nail of a thumb. So, this woman who's interested in your baby, she says. Are you really considering meeting her?

Sure. Why not? She might be nice. Like Konstantin said.

I don't know, just feels wrong.

Antonina flops back on the bed. For you, or for me? she says.

Pretty weird. Giving away a perfectly healthy baby.

You're thinking of your brother, aren't you?

I guess so. I just don't know how you could give up a baby like that.

Me, or your parents?

Both.

And there it is. Antonina knew this discussion was looming. Tatyana leans over the top of Antonina with a sad expression, mouth in a soft frown. Her skin is the colour of virgin canvas — naturally pale, beautifully bare. Antonina feels privileged to be close enough to see the tenderness behind the veneer. They are the same in that regard — Tatyana and Konstantin. Maybe they all are. Hiding away their real selves from the world.

Why don't you forget about that, and just come to Semipalatinsk with me instead? Tatyana says. I can pay your way; you don't have to worry about that.

It's just a simple meeting, Antonina says. Can't hurt anything. Kostya's set it up already. I owe him.

Owe him what? What do you owe him?

Antonina holds her tongue, wishing the discussion over.

Tatyana's bottom lip pushes her top lip, so her mouth curves upwards from the middle — a fault-line on the move. She's trying to think of another way to approach the argument, and Antonina decides to stop it before it starts. She sharpens her voice.

I'll come to Semipalatinsk with you. But first I'm meeting the woman, and that's that. No more discussion.

Tatyana fans the paintbrush against the edge of her palm causing tiny specks of flesh coloured oil to splatter across the floor. The fault-line has turned into a straight line.

Did you speak to your parents about your brother? Antonina asks.

I did. Made my mother cry. She said that we lived in Semipalatinsk when I was born. I already knew that, though. Dad has radiation poisoning because of it. I've never told you that before, have I?

What do you mean, poisoning? Antonina says. You're not just saying that so I won't meet the woman, are you?

Tatyana stands up. What would I do that for? she says. She switches off the main light and throws a red shawl over the lamp in the corner. Takes her place in her favourite chair by the open window. I'm not sure what you think of me to even suggest I'd manipulate you like that, she says.

There is a rest in the music. The band taking a break, and the sudden quietness comes as a relief.

You'll ruin your paintbrush if you don't wash it, Antonina says.

There is an audible huff from the chair. The details of her friend's body are lost in the deep red hue of the room. There's the crinkle of the cellophane wrapping being removed from a fresh pack of cigarettes; the slip of the silver tongue being pulled out and screwed into a ball and thrown on the floor.

Antonina lugs herself up the bed on her elbows towards the pillows. Tell me about him, she says. Your brother. Tell me what you know.

That's just it, Tatyana says. A flick of a match and the head of Tatyana's smoke glows deep amber. I don't know anything, she says blowing the smoke afterwards, then takes another puff. I think my parents abandoned him. Put him in a home and left him there. That's what they did back then with the bad ones.

Because of the radiation?

It causes birth deformities. And cancer. Mum says Papa hasn't got it, but he's always sick.

Did your dad work there?

In the armed forces. They detonated bombs all around Kurchatov. They thought they were safe in the distance, behind shields, inside bunkers. So, when my brother was born, there must have been something seriously wrong with him. I've got it too, but it doesn't show, well, not much.

But you're not deformed? Antonina says.

The clubbers downstairs are clapping, louder and louder it grows until the DJ comes back 'for just one last bash', he says into the microphone.

And your parents told you this? Antonina gets in before the music belts out again.

Hell, no! Tatyana says sounding a little put out, but that might just have been the necessary increase in volume over the music. They still deny any brother exists. Mama begged me not to go to Semipalatinsk. She got really distraught, so I said I wouldn't go.

But you are going?

What would you do?

Antonina thinks about it. Yes, she says. I'd go too.

Antonina is tired of yelling above the music again. She assumes Tatyana is too, because they say nothing for a while, the two of them inhabiting their own space until the music goes quiet for the last time. All the activities of the night are grinding down to the last shuffle — bodies beneath the floor finding their coats and scarves and making their way home. It must be three o'clock. She will wait a couple of hours. The bridges won't be down until five a.m. anyway, so she might as well get comfortable, and try not to fall asleep.

The net curtains swell and deflate, ghostly and luminous in the night air. Against this, Tatyana is a black charcoal etching — a body in a chair, smoke twining about her face, then she stubs the butt out inside a teacup on the sill and shuts the windows. Antonina moves over in the bed and turns to the wall. She tucks her knees up and places her hands between her legs. The press of her clitoris brings a spring of unexpected pleasure that shoots through her. She tries it again, but the joyful spasm fails to ignite. Much like the muse, she ponders — comes when you're not expecting anything. Hard not to go searching for more, demanding more, though you know you've already had the best of it.

She hears the whisper of Tatyana's clothes as she undresses, then feels the bounce of her settling into the bed. Tatyana wraps her arms around Antonina from behind and tucks her legs in too. They are an ill fit like this, but still, somehow it works. Matryoshka dolls. Tatyana, Antonina, the baby — big, small, smallest.

It's not still poisonous, is it? says Antonina. Semipalatinsk, I mean.

Yes, but we won't be anywhere near that part. I wouldn't put the nugget at risk like that, or you.

Torrents of bottles tumble into the skip-bin down in the courtyard — a clinking avalanche that's evidence of the evening's sales.

Do you need money for travel? Tatyana asks.

No. Makar gave me some. I'll be fine for a little while.

Good, says Tatyana. Then she softens her voice as if someone else were in the room listening: We don't need them you know. The men. Makar. Konstantin. I'm glad Makar isn't getting let off, but we could do it by ourselves without any of them. Tatyana's voice lowers until it's just the breath of a whisper stroking the back of Antonina's neck. We could keep the baby. You and me, she says. I can look after you. I promise I could.

Antonina pats Tatyana's hand, then lets their hands rest, one inside the other on her belly.

So, Antonina whispers. Are you sterile from the radiation?

I have no womb, she says. No nugget for me. Our kind aren't meant to reproduce, anyway.

No wonder she wants to keep the baby. Antonina waits until she hears the pattern of Tatyana's sleep-addled breathing, then makes her way to the chair by the window. Don't fall asleep she tells herself, and when she catches herself falling, she jerks her head up. This happens a few times more before she succumbs.

Antonina sits in the chair with her head resting on the rim of the windowsill and enters the inner world, where she is the foetus and her mother's heart pounds like a tribal drum, picking up pace, becoming ominous and loud. Antonina wants to look away, but she is frozen, expecting some distressing tragedy, when a thin slit opens in the lining of her mother's belly like the pupil of a cat's eye — phosphorous white against the encompassing red of the womb. She must wake up, that's all she knows when the beat of her mother's heart comes to a stop, and the slit widens. What happens next, she doesn't want to know, and wills herself to wake

— rolls her eyes from side to side and forces them open. When the red of the dream-womb folds away, she wraps her arms around her stomach and squeezes gently, anxious to feel some movement from within. The nugget is still, in a secure way. Safe and sound. Nothing to be concerned about. No slit opening. No blood. No drums. She has not harmed the child. Not aborted it, as so many girls do. With that peace of mind, the knot of anxiety loosens.

Antonina thinks of her mother, and all of a sudden she misses that mud-ridden woman and her mountain. Will the baby bring disappointment or delight? she wonders. At least the father is intelligentsia, Antonina will tell her. Good genes and that counts for something. She lifts her head off the windowsill and feels the neat indented line where her temple rested against the wood, rubs her eyes and blinks. Tatyana is splayed across the bed, taking up all the room. Outside the day has already started. The sun gilds the very tips of the building across the courtyard. Time to get going. She gathers her backpack, puts on her boots and buttons up her jacket, then quietly sneaks out of the room.

Antonina doesn't have to wait long for the mechanical hum of Schmidt Bridge's lowering to start up. The guttural churn of the bridge's belts and cogs grow louder than the idling of queuing cars. To her side is the hiss of a cigarette tossed into a puddle, followed by the urgency of a car door slamming, then two more. The arms of the bridge begin their smooth descent, and the cars inch forward, positioning themselves for take-off. A cluster of young men overtakes Antonina on her way towards the mouth of the bridge, and out of habit she tightens her grip on the straps of her backpack.

It is good to see the sun after a week of consistent white nothing clouds that have stretched from one end of the city to the other. The air is stiff with petrol fumes that stifle the prettiness of the morning, but the sunlight skips like stones across the rushing river, and in the corner of her eye she sees the dance, feels the dance, as though some part of her has gone out to join in the play. It's not until her feet touch down on the asphalt of the island that she feels herself gathering back together again, ready for the pack-down of her show. Young-man voices carry down the street even though they are now half a block away. Amongst their banter comes the slapping of shoes against concrete.

Nina, a ruffled huff of a voice calls out, and Antonina knows it's Tatyana even before she lands next to her, feet flopping to a stop. Tatyana bends over, hands on her knees to catch her breath.

You are funny, Antonina says. I wasn't sneaking out on you; just thought you'd like the sleep before the drive. I think Konstantin wants to head off early.

Tatyana stands, her hands tucked into her mid-back. You think, she says between deep, raspy breaths, you think I'm going to let you have all the fun breaking down the show? Ah, ah. She shakes her head.

One hammer each, and the breakdown starts when Antonina thrusts her weapon into the skull of the ghost train. There was no nice way of saying goodbye, and the sever is immediate. She doesn't stop to let the pain of it blossom, she keeps going, thrashing and thrashing until all that's left is powdered clay. It's done, but there is an itch that smashing anatomical body parts won't satisfy, so she leaves Tatyana to finish and heads for Makar's office. He had seen her making the dolls. He knew only too well that she had claimed the unused toilet as her own. Had he been the one to smash the dolls in storage, hammering the small people now he was a big person, hammering what they once had into powdered clay? He must have laughed that she thought his room a safe harbour for the remaining small people. She collects the box with the dripping letters on the side — *I can see you* — picks the lock of his door and places the box on his chair. Inside the box, she sets the ugly, over-sized mug, blue with green dots, and smashes it to pieces. It feels too good, but she could do a lot, lot worse, and she has to leave before the urge takes over.

SIBERIAN WEASEL

NOVOSIBIRSK, RUSSIA

Tatyana and Konstantin take turns at the wheel in the non-stop trek towards Novosibirsk, while Antonina and Polina share yet another bed — this time a double mattress laid out in the metal tray of Konstantin's old VAZ truck. Sleep should be impossible what with the canvas cover that trembles like a tent in a sandstorm, metal ribs that stretch and retract with a clatter, and the jarring suspension. Yet, sleep has an undertow of its own, drawing Antonina down into the soft seabed of unconsciousness before they even leave the city.

She wakes to snapshots of Polina in the early stages of the journey: brushing her freshly cleaned hair so it glints in the sunlight that pours through a vent in the canvas; kneeling with a transistor radio to her ear; forming dance moves with her upper body; crinkling snack-food wrappers; singing — song after song. Like a caged bird that knows it's about to be freed, Polina won't shut up. When they stop for their first road-trip meal, Antonina is ready to jump into the passenger side of the cab and sleep against the jerking window.

Lunch of noodles, spicy lamb, peppers, tomatoes, onion and bread is so surprisingly good that by the time they are ready to set off again, Antonina returns to the back of the truck having forgotten her grievance — until the next stop, when Polina races into the toilet ahead of her, taking all the squares of newsprint on the nail for herself. Easy for Konstantin. He stops wherever he likes and unzips his pants. Tatyana doesn't mind squatting in the grass, but that's not a desirable option for Antonina because her pee squirts forwards instead of back, and her underwear ends up wet. Pregnancy changes the shape of things like that.

Two and a half days it takes to reach Novosibirsk. One moment Konstantin is snoring in the back with Antonina, Polina yapping in the front with Tatyana, then it's Tatyana's turn in the back, and for the last stretch it's Polina who sleeps, curled up like one of the skinny stray cats they see that look like miniature Siberian tigers. Cute, but feral. Not something Antonina would ever try to domesticate.

When they finally arrive at the hostel at the end of their journey, Antonina's brain is foggy from too much sleep, and she stands beside the truck feeling slightly dazed. Konstantin, by comparison, has come alive. He is like a blowfly zipping past in the glazed, manic state of someone who's had too much coffee. The box of dolls has travelled with them, and Konstantin disappears with that first, returning empty-handed for Polina.

Hurry up, he yells.

Polina is the last to climb out of the truck, and Konstantin takes her hand as she jumps from the open tailgate, landing on the asphalt beside him with a grunt. Her cheeks are still pink and warm, her carefully brushed hair now all mussed by sleep. She dips her head away from people passing by as best she can. The swelling has died down around her eye, and the bruises are more yellow than blue, although the split on her lip has tightened and pulled to an ugly, hardened scab that will be difficult to hide beneath lipstick.

You could have told us we were close, she says as though Antonina, too, is in on the complaint. I need to tidy up.

Do it inside, he says.

Tatyana sucks back quick drags on her cigarette, letting Konstantin unload their bags on his own. When she finally squashes the butt with her heel, Konstantin and Polina have already registered and made their way upstairs.

Three nights up front, the receptionist demands.

Day in advance, insists Antonina.

You run the risk of losing the room if I get another booking, the receptionist says. We don't have many small rooms. If you lose it, you'll be in the bunks. Her green suit is too large for her figure, and the fabric buckles beneath a thick black belt like a turtle in a shell sitting there without sunshine behind the desk.

We'll take that chance, Antonina says. She counts out half the cost of the room, and Tatyana does the same without argument. No point in paying more if things change overnight, and with Konstantin that's always a possibility.

They have their own twin-share room, but it's not one of the better ones. It faces the back of another building. Konstantin must have ordered cheap as well, because their room is right next door. His excitement is clearly audible through the thin wall. Polina's mood is picking up by the sound of it too, responding to his instructions with a series of quick steps down the corridor towards the bathroom. Antonina sits on the bed in a state of expectation; both she and Tatyana sit upright, listening and waiting for Konstantin and Polina to head out.

They must be meeting the American soon, Tatyana says in low volume.

Then she'll be off, out of our lives for good, says Antonina.

And out of your bed, Tatyana stutters with a weak little laugh.

The prostitute with the glass slipper, Antonina says. Is it crazy that I'll miss her?

No. She is cute.

Antonina sweeps her hair into a ponytail, and some of it escapes and hangs against the dampness of her neck. The room is too warm. She feels hot and thirsty, and more than a little hungry. It's still light out, they could go find some food, but the need for sleep has priority for Tatyana, and she already lies flat on her bed, arms raised above her head in abandon. Antonina leaves her to rest, makes her way to the communal bathroom where the steam is quickly fogging up the room from Polina's shower. Inside another cubicle, Antonina hangs her towel and undresses. She fills her hair with shampoo and watches the lather slide down the skin of her breasts. They're heavier now, her stomach round enough that the suds split and curl around the sides like curtains. By the time she's done, there is only the ghost of Polina lingering in the bathroom — the smell of hairspray and a mirror wiped in the shape of a fan, and she does miss her, Antonina realises. The energy. The annoying joviality. Affection wasted, Konstantin would tell her.

Back in the room, Tatyana snores to a snort and stops,

swallows, then turns towards the wall and tucks in her arms and legs. Antonina throws a blanket over her, then sits on the bed going up and down with a couple of foamy bounces. She listens to the shuffling of Polina through the wall, voices muffled like a television in the next room, a small drama playing out at half-volume. She's not ready to sleep, so Antonina makes her way downstairs in search of a real television.

Dinner is being served in the main room, and Antonina decides that pork chops, potatoes and cabbage are well worth spending some of Makar's money on. She receives two plates, even though the receptionist insisted that meals be pre-ordered. Lucky there's enough left over, the cook says. Eating for two?

Yes. Thank you. Antonina lifts one of the plates in a small wave of gratitude.

She sits at a small table on her own, tearing at the flesh inside the elbow of pig bone when Konstantin and Polina cross the foyer for the front door. Polina is an exotic bird in her shiny yellow dress and bright pink scarf. Konstantin looks like Konstantin in his washed denim sheepskin jacket, even though it's far too warm for it.

His eyes dart around the lounge, and when he finds her he is like an arrow aimed with such determination in his stride that she wonders if he's angry at her, but it's probably just nerves about the American. The parakeet waits for him in the foyer tapping her thigh impatiently with a clutch bag.

Here, he says, handing Antonina a square of paper then poking the air above it with an impatient finger. It reads: *Semipalatinsk railway station, noon, Tuesday — look for the doll*, in his spidery scrawl.

What is this?

The woman who wants to meet you. Didn't take her name, and didn't give her yours. So, you're both anonymous.

Semipalatinsk? I though we were meeting here?

I changed it. I thought it would be easier, for you I mean, not her. Not so rushed.

How will I know her?

I sent her one of your dolls. Just look for that. You can meet, or you can forget about it. Up to you.

You sent her one of my dolls?

He shrugs. You have loads of them, don't you?

Where are they by the way? The moment the words leave her mouth she feels callous, and Konstantin stands up straight, a slight distance between them. He points to a room beside the reception desk. It's locked, he says. No one will steal your precious cargo.

I didn't mean— She cuts herself off. Re-considers her words, embarrassed. Thanks, she says, and waves the note with a roll of her wrist.

Antonina takes the extra plate of food up to the room. Tatyana is still out to it, so she leaves it on the table between the beds. This time there are no Polina distractions to keep Antonina awake, and she sinks away to a healing place, only to be woken hours later by the violent shaking of her shoulders that is not Konstantin's truck, but Tatyana.

Shhh, Tatyana says, her face a pale shade of grey in the black and white room. Listen, she says.

The voices through the wall are no longer that of Polina and Konstantin, but someone else and Konstantin. There's a different kind of excitement going on. A shuffling, thumping, groaning type of commotion, coupled with the menacing voice of an intruder.

Where's the rest of it? a man says in a low, confident tone that wavers just at the point of another thud that sounds like meat hitting meat.

That's all there is, says Konstantin. His voice is tremulous, strangled.

A solid object hits the wall beside Tatyana's bed. Antonina is on the other side of the room, but she feels the vibration of the particleboard as it cracks. Konstantin is so close that he could be right beside her. A sharp panic enters the pit of Antonina's stomach, and suddenly she needs to pee. The wall cracks again with the threat of breaking right through. If it does, they will be caught. Tatyana scuffles onto the floor to hide under the bed and orders Antonina to follow. There is another whack, and Antonina wets herself a little. She thinks about making a run for the door, only there might be another intruder out in the corridor. Best to pretend they can't hear anything. Pretend there's no one home inside the tiny room.

Antonina shifts as quietly as she can across the dust-laden floor beneath her bed into the arms of Tatyana.

One hundred thousand American dollars we were to be paid for the girl's delivery, the voice says. One hundred thousand dollars you took on our behalf.

I didn't take her to the American for a bribe, Konstantin says. She said they were in love. No money was mentioned.

Is it hot yet? the intruder says. Antonina realises there must be two of them in the room.

She squeezes Tatyana harder when they hear the resistance of Konstantin kicking, the sound of his body being dragged across the room.

Hold him still, the intruder says.

There is a ghastly pause before Konstantin pleads for them to stop. A strange hiss and another cry belts out so loud that Antonina's heart clenches. Tatyana's body is the steady quiver of a frightened dog beside her. Five thousand American dollars is all I got, he says. Antonina knew there was money in bringing Polina to Novosibirsk, and, like an idiot, Konstantin has put them all in danger because of it.

Between gasping breaths, he explains once again that there was no bribe. It was a reward for bringing the girl. The intruders are quiet, listening, contemplating while the violence pauses. It's all there, Konstantin says. Take it. His voice is breaking now. Antonina unfurls a little from Tatyana's grip. I thought the American was helping her, he insists. The American was grateful, Konstantin says, then bursts into a cry. She's never heard him cry before, and she wants to rescue him from the pain. Take it, he says in an out-loud bawl. Take it all. I never meant to cross anyone.

Antonina embraces Tatyana tightly again, trying to muffle her ears inside the fabric of their sleeves. They know he is pleading for his life now. It would be so easy to kill him. They have already alerted most of the hostel to their presence, and like well-trained ex-Soviets no one will do a thing to stop it. Murders have become commonplace in the past few years. The battle between gangs is constant in the re-establishing of street-level control since the market opened up. Please, no, Antonina prays. Please don't. The entire building seems to be holding its breath with her, waiting for the final moment of butchery to be over.

As expected, there is one last crash, then the weight of a sack of potatoes hitting the floor before the heavy-booted footfall of intruders heads out. Konstantin kept his mouth shut about their involvement, but they can't offer him the same loyalty until they know that no one is coming back to press a gun against his temple. He could lie dying, bleeding to death in the next room, but Tatyana and Antonina stay huddled beneath the bed for a long while before they dare come out.

Antonina leans cautiously around the doorframe before venturing out into the corridor, but Tatyana rushes past her and barges straight into Konstantin's room. The light blares boldly from the single bulb inside a broken plastic cover. She expects blood smeared across the floor like the petals of a tulip, but there's no blood, only the hotplate of an iron thickened with a smoking black char. Tatyana's first instinct is to switch the iron off — Antonina's is to rush to Konstantin, who is crumpled between the upturned bed and the wall, the back of his favourite denim jacket torn with sheepskin jutting through opened seams. The stench of scorched flesh makes her stomach turn. She presses the fabric of her shirt to her nose and mouth and tries not to retch. The room could self-combust with the heat of the scuffle, but she won't leave without Konstantin.

Stay down, Tatyana tells her, and reaches up from a crouch to open the window — just enough for a crosswind, but not enough to alert anyone outside of their presence. They turn Konstantin over, and baulk at the state of his burnt cheek. Antonina starts to weep.

Shhhh, Tatyana says, and she gives Konstantin a good shake. He comes to and opens his eyes just enough to see them there.

See, Tatyana whispers. He's not dead. She shoots a weak smile in Antonina's direction.

We'll take you to the hospital, says Antonina. Where are the keys to the truck?

No, he says, grabbing Antonina's wrist.

His bedroom has been turned upside down, the mattresses slashed, his bag emptied on the floor, and in the midst of all this, it is surprising to see Konstantin draw several hundred rouble notes from the inner pocket of his jacket.

Go meet the woman, he whispers and squashes the money into Antonina's hand. Find the doll, he says, and his words press into her ear, hot and hurt. But, you don't have to sell the nugget.

Antonina shakes her head. It's the wrong time to be talking about that. Tatyana tries to roll him up onto the mattress, but he pushes her away with a force that knocks her backwards. She pulls herself up to sitting position, legs crossed, staring at Konstantin in wild surprise.

You stupid arsehole, she whispers. What have you got us into?

She doesn't wait for a reply before she gets to her feet.

We can't leave him like this, Antonina says as fiercely as she can in a whisper.

Go, Konstantin says. Think of the nugget.

I can't, she says, but Tatyana is pulling at her arm. We're family, Antonina insists. We can't leave you here like this.

I'll come to you, he says, which causes Antonina's chin to crumple again.

Konstantin is still collapsed on the floor when they head for their room. Once inside, Tatyana places her hand over Antonina's mouth, removing it only when she stops crying. They sit on the floor without speaking or daring to turn the light on, their body weight pressed to the bags against the door in the long wait for dawn. The smell of Konstantin's beating has followed Antonina, permeated her clothes and her freshly cleaned hair, embedding itself into all of her senses, and she is sure she will never be free of its horror again.

Konstantin moves before they do. He gets up, packs his bag and drags it down the corridor. Antonina tries to join him and is pulled back down to the floor. It is light now, and Antonina can see Tatyana's face shaking. No, she mouths. Stay. They sit there, side-by-side in silence for another agonising hour, then rise, late enough that Konstantin will be long gone, early enough that they will miss the morning rush of hostel stayers queuing for bathrooms and porridge.

Outside, there is a dry rectangle against the kerb where Konstantin's truck was parked. Otherwise, there is no sign of him.

This way, Tatyana says with a slight jerk of her head.

On the way to the railway station, she stops for only one thing — a newspaper, which she promptly folds and tucks under her arm.

Antonina remains contemplative while Tatyana hands over Konstantin's roubles for train tickets to Semipalatinsk, then a few more for a pot of tea, and a plate of pork dumplings. The dumplings they devour — two forks emptying the plate quickly. Better than any porridge from a hostel kitchen, and afterwards Tatyana opens the newspaper and turns the first pages with quick, snapping glances.

There, she says, leaning in.

What happened? Antonina says, slow and mild.

Tatyana keeps the paper held up, and they read the article

together. American shot inside local café, it states. Several paragraphs describe the incident with the American and Polina. A street girl, they politely call her. The speculation is that both have been killed for escaping her pimp. It feels as if a fist is embedded in the top of Antonina's stomach. They couldn't have it any more wrong. They were in love. They wanted to start a new life together, away from Russia. The fist in her stomach twists when she thinks of Konstantin. All morning, tiny shock waves have been hitting her with disbelief. Had he been in the restaurant, he would be dead too. But someone saw him anyway. Someone followed and beat the daylights out of him. The article goes on to focus on the government's gang-bribe crackdowns, and tells how the militia are in hot pursuit of a lead on the gunman.

Konstantin was right to leave her and Tatyana at the hostel when he did. The lead in the article could possibly implicate him. And if the militia weren't chasing him, the gang was probably watching still.

Where do you think he's gone? Antonina whispers.

Tatyana snaps the paper shut. Who knows? He has your mother's address, doesn't he?

I guess so. Would he go there? Should she let her mother know? Thoughts come in a rush. Turbulence she can't negotiate, and she leans into the thundering fall of worst-case scenarios.

What if he's dead? she says.

He's too smart for that, Tatyana says. She clears her throat and folds the paper in half, then a quarter. Don't worry. We'll probably see him in Semipalatinsk.

The dolls, blurts Antonina, remembering they've left them behind.

Too late to go back for them now, Tatyana says.

Antonina is busy reprimanding herself for forgetting the dolls, then for thinking about them when they really don't matter. She stares into her cup and swirls the last of the tea and swears in a whisper.

You can make some more when you get home, can't you? says Tatyana. Anyway, there's no way we could have got them here without Konstantin and his truck. No point worrying about it.

Antonina shifts in her seat. Tatyana's right, she can make more of the dolls if she wants to, and she's not exactly sure why it was so important to bring them along in the first place. She should be relieved to be free of the burden of lugging them across the span of another country.

You're not going to make us go back and get them, are you? Tatyana asks.

Antonina drinks the last of the tea, then manages a re-assuring smile. It's fine, she says. It's just clay. I didn't know what I was going to do with them anyway.

Tatyana's shoulders roll back and she releases a puff of breath. Antonina slides the newspaper closer, leans on her elbows and tries to sink into the first line of a small article, but the words are just meaningless tracks, the disappointment of leaving the dolls behind won't dislodge, and it's still simmering half an hour later when they board the train.

The idea of travelling by train to Kazakhstan comes with a sense of déjà vu. Antonina's childhood abduction by the strange woman and the return to Semipalatinsk today are almost twenty years apart, but they run parallel in Antonina's mind. Two sides of a single train track, both headed for the same destination. This time there is no first-class cabin. They are in an open-ended booth with a walkway that passes right through their allotted space. They settle their bags beneath their cots. Tatyana has a last-minute panic and darts back outside to buy food for the journey, believing the onboard cafeteria is overpriced, and she's probably right. Antonina lies down and covers her legs with a blanket and tries to ignore the passengers passing through.

Poor Polina. She was so excited about going to America. Love was a life-changer for her, only not the way any of them expected. Konstantin. She sends a prayer up for his protection. Imagines him slinking his way through the countryside, remaining out of sight, out-running gangsters, and perhaps the militia as well. Tatyana is right — he is smarter than he appears. He will come. He will find her and come to her, like he said he would, and she believes it — she has to. He's been right there in front of her, looking out for her. All this time she's thought of him as callow, untrustworthy, and yet he's the one who has stood by her, no matter what. And the worst part is that beneath the vanity of her academic arrogance, she is no different — only, so far, he appears to have a better heart.

Tatyana returns with paper bags of food, which she drops on her bed. The loudspeaker hisses, then a crackle of a voice announces the impending departure of the train to Kazakhstan. A last surge of travellers makes their way past the open-end of their booth. Antonina stares out her window until the train starts moving. For the first time in as long as she can remember, it feels like she's returning home. Such a shame she couldn't have brought her little people with her. To Antonina, it would have been a significant circular journey to return her little people to the mountain. But that's sentimentality. Don't turn into your mother, she tells herself. It's just clay.

GHOST TRAIN

USHTOBE, KAZAKHSTAN — 1937

Thirty-four thousand Koryo-saram were dumped in the barren landscape of Ushtobe in the early winter of 1937, without warning, without provisions, without shelter. What they did have was the mandate, direct from Stalin himself. Grow rice, it declared. But the arid conditions were so different from the Primorsky Krai region that rice proved difficult to grow, and the establishing of irrigation was slow when most had only their hands with which to dig.

If she could, Katerina would have chosen to return to Korea during this time. She regretted the lost opportunity of not taking Stalin's initial offer to leave voluntarily while still in Vladivostok. If they knew what was coming, the entire community would have likely packed up overnight and returned to Korea. To be outsiders in their motherland of origin would have been preferable to the poverty of Ushtobe. Once in exile, though, it was too late, and they were denied the right to travel. Those deemed most untrustworthy were sent the farthest away, the luckiest were dropped off early in the transports and housed in warehouses and abandoned buildings — this was not the luck of Katerina. *Disasterstans*, they called the lower regions of the USSR — with families split-up and sprinkled throughout the area.

Katerina tried to imagine what could be worse than the initial emptiness that faced them in Ushtobe, but nothing compared. There wasn't a single tree in sight. The land was flat and dry. One naked hill was the only redeeming feature that offered a measure of protection from the worst of the harsh winds that flew along the steppe. Katerina, her mother-in-law and Bora followed the others in their group and dug hollows in the ground to sleep in. Over the next few days they covered the holes with a straw-mud roof, and on the floor they cut a pit for a fire. *Ondols* they called these mud huts. They were like graves, yet this scant protection from the freezing elements offered at least a chance of survival.

The nearest settlement was two hundred kilometres away, and they were forbidden to travel there. The only kindnesses were the occasional nomadic Kazakhs who passed through and fed the worst of the sick Koyro-saram, housing new mothers and children in their yurts until it was time to move on. Bora was good at communicating with the Kazakhs, but Katerina held back, not just from them but from her sister-in-law. The constant reminder of Nikolai taunted Katerina, and her guilt at causing Stanislav's death would not let her rest.

When Stalin rounded the Kazakhs up like cattle and put them to work in their own collective farms, the Koryo-saram of Ushtobe were left completely abandoned. Thousands died within the first few years, whittled away by starvation, hypothermia and dysentery. Katerina's mother-in-law was among them, found one morning with her lips blue, hands clenched into frozen balls against her chest.

After her mother-in-law died, Katerina dug out her own *ondol*, desperate to be away from the eyes of Bora. Three winters the Koryo-saram lived huddled in wind-gnawed isolation on the open steppe before their first full crop of rice took hold. Their only comfort, the handmade mud huts with fires built beneath the floor kept alight with rushes. Fires that were their constant obsession — if the fires went out, so too did their lives.

Children were expected to work in the fields as well. They all knew Stalin expected them to die or to turn on one another in the hardship, like dogs. He expected to break their spirit, only he didn't. He underestimated the heart of the Koryo-saram. They were determined to maintain dignity and prove their worth in the Soviet system, by not only beating the harsh environment that became their new home, but to go on to become the most successful crop growers throughout the entire Soviet Union. Surely, Stalin would see their efforts — the work, day and night of children, mothers, fathers, and the grandparents as well. Not only did they meet the quotas, but they surpassed them, time and again. To this Stalin reacted with a show of fanfare and acknowledgement, then he quickly moved to devastate their community once again.

Katerina was a schoolteacher in the early stages of the *kolkhoz*. Her small village was taking shape, buildings were made from dried grass and mud, water wells and irrigation brought in fresh water, the crops took hold. Although many felt the loss of honour due to the stripping away of all they had built in Vladivostok, they still had their schools and books that enabled education in Russian, as well as the original language of the Koryo-saram. They still had their own stories and myths, the dances, the celebrations, the religious beliefs.

As a teacher, Katerina was expected to work the fields in the afternoons and evenings. The farm work she resented, but not as much as the forced egalitarianism of the shared community. Everyone was seen as the same — one heaving entity of working ants. She endeavoured to undo that message in the classroom, singling out children for special praise and attention. And in teaching the new generation, Katerina began to let go of the past. She would never let go of Nikolai, but there were days when she could focus on the future lined up in front of her, in the faces of her young pupils.

But Stalin was not done with them yet. Overnight, he commanded the Koryo-saram schools to stop. He burnt all the Korean books and banned the teaching of their language. After the soldiers had gone, Katerina sifted through the remains of her upturned classroom in the hope of finding at least one book unharmed. What she would have done with it, she wasn't sure. Bury it like treasure to hide it away? Hold it up to the soldiers and be shot for it? What would Stanislav have made of that? Dying for the cause of preserving their culture. But in truth she didn't have the strength to sacrifice herself like that. She sat among the torn and charred books, overwhelmed by the constant punishment, and having to endure it, year after empty year.

All that remained of the Koryo-saram culture was their travelling theatre. It alone could move between *kolkhozes*, providing stories and dances that retained a small portion of their heritage in the native language. It gave Katerina the way out of Ushtobe, to travel around Kazakhstan as a performer hidden behind the makeup, the costumes, the characters and songs. And behind the veil of the performer, Katerina learnt to glean information about those left behind and those who had been exiled. She listened out for any news of Nikolai, but none ever arose. Sometimes the theatre would return to Ushtobe to perform at Bora's settlement. On one visit she found Bora had a new husband, and on another there was a baby. It was cause for celebration. Of course. Katerina was the only one who couldn't bring herself to look at the child. To Katerina, her sister-in-law's moving on should have been a release from the past, but it only reminded her of what she had lost. Only once, she slipped. Just once she caught the bubbling, laughing face of the child as she was bounced on a babushka's knee, and saw exactly what she expected — her husband's beautiful cinnamon eyes, the eyes her own child would have had.

For most Koryo-saram, Kazakhstan became the new homeland. When Stalin died in 1953, their bonds to the *kolkhozes* were released and they were free to move away. Katerina, however, could not settle anywhere, but continued to roam with the travelling Korean theatre. After years of reciting stories to audiences throughout the communal farms, Katerina knew her husband had not made it into exile. The only place she found his face was on the child born in Ushtobe. She gave up watching for him in the crowds, but she did not give up the expectation of seeing him again. He said he would come for her. Her rice farmer. And she believed he would.

POLYGON BABIES

SEMIPALATINSK, KAZAKHSTAN — 1994

The train stops in a small town just before the Russian Kazakhstan border, and the main lights switch on inside the carriage. Antonina is already sitting upright, but the sudden glaring light has her blinking to refocus. Tatyana turns over on her cot, covering her face with blankets as if she could escape the conductor stomping through to open the exit doors at each end of the carriage. A surprisingly cold draught rushes through their cocoon, which makes Antonina reach for her blankets too. The carriage has been uncomfortably warm since they left Novosibirsk, and it grew even stuffier during the night, making sleep difficult, for Antonina at least. The sunrise was worth being up for, though. A haze of red stretched across the horizon, burning for an hour before surrendering to the solid soft blue of the morning. She was able to enjoy a wonderfully private hour while the passengers slept. Now they all grumble as they rise.

Tatyana sits up, her blanket wrapped around her shoulders

like a shawl. She leans forward to see what is happening out the window. Where are we? she asks.

The conductor's voice is thin and hazy when it comes through the speaker. Difficult to understand, but Antonina knows they are at the border.

Lokot, the conductor says. Prepare your documents for customs checks.

Lokot, says Tatyana. My first-ever Kazakh town. She zips her jacket against the chill seeping in through the door. Any teabags left?

Antonina cannot remember where the box is. It was on the table the night before, but then they were playing cards, and . . . She looks under the table and there it is, half-squashed under one of Tatyana's discarded boots.

Usually, the conductor serves hot tea, but today they are switching the dining carriages around — all the Russian staff will join the northbound train while they are replaced by Kazakhs.

The ribbed tea glasses are ringed brown from previous use, however Semipalatinsk is only hours away, so there's no point in washing them. Tatyana takes the glasses to the samovar and returns with them full of steaming water. Soon the teabags release their amber goodness, and the soiled ring-marks disappear beneath the high-tide mark. Antonina settles at the table by the window and squeezes the teabag with a spoon, trying to make the tea as intense and black as possible. A band of officials walk along the platform, peering inside each window as if checking on prisoners. When they reach Antonina's window, she tries not to pay any attention, but it is hard not to notice the cupped eyes beneath the military-style visor hat and the face held firm, solemn as granite.

Two guards enter the carriage, one from each end, and begin the baggage checks. Antonina and Tatyana are the first at their end of the carriage. They stand, holding their faces still as the guard compares the passport photos to the real thing. Tatyana's backpack is the first to be emptied. A guard splays her belongings across the bench-seat with his stick.

What are you carrying? he asks.

Food and clothes, they each answer.

The old woman trolley bag is not so easy to upturn, and Antonina prickles with embarrassment when the guard asks her to hurry up. The sniffer-dog is outside on the platform. Antonina can't see it, but she hears the clicking of its nails on the concrete, circling its controller on a short lead, alert and ready to pass through the carriages on command. She keeps moving, unpacking shirts, socks, underwear, and, among her clothing, Antonina finds Makar's sable paintbrush, her mother's Maedeup knot brooch, the doll with the medal inside its belly, and the glass cylinders of pigments. She slips a surreptitious glance towards Tatyana to see if she is aware of the tampering of her bag. No acknowledgement of guilt is returned, no concern that Antonina's items have been out-turned from the safety of their tin box. Tatyana is oblivious. Her focus is fixed on piecing her bag back together now the guard is done with her.

What else is inside? the guard says. He taps the side of the trolley bag with his stick, and in the slight panic of the moment, Antonina forgets to lift the Odessa tin straight up, and it jams on an angle against the side of the trolley bag.

What is that? The guard points to a vial of pigment with a lid that has come loose, apricot dust sprinkling across the shoulder of a white cotton shirt.

Pigments, Antonina says. She picks the glass cylinder up and pushes the cork in tight, the colour fanning across her fingertips. See, she says and points to the label. *Summer harvest*. I'm an artist. I use these to colour my pottery.

The guard picks up one of the vials and shakes it close to his face, then another. You make those big Kazakh bowls? he says. We have one of those. My wife keeps potatoes in it.

Antonina thinks about how to answer. He is referring to the type of pottery her mother makes.

I make art, she says. She shows him the doll with the medal inside. This is an old one, but it's kind of what I do.

Well, I don't think you are very good, he says with an amused huff. Should probably stick to the bowls. What's in the tin?

Antonina tries to unjam the Odessa tin. She thumps the top of it with her fist, but it will not budge. The guard looks for more vials in her clothing, finds one, shakes it and checks the bottom of it like he is panning for gold.

Perhaps you could try? she suggests to the guard with a motion towards the tin. He looks down into the bottom of the bag where the tin's lid has opened, and her mother's letters sit neatly tied with black shoelaces. He pulls out the entire bundle and flicks through them like a deck of cards.

It's fine, he says. You're Kazakh. But don't expect it to be so easy when you go back to Russia. Step aside.

Antonina and Tatyana step out of the space of their booth and the guard checks under the cots. Antonina wants to argue that she is not Kazakh. She is from Kazakhstan, but she is not Kazakh. She wants to, but she doesn't. She is more concerned about who has been inside her bag. When the guard moves on, Antonina uses her foot inside the trolley bag to stamp on the Odessa tin, so it comes loose from the side and settles on the bottom. There is an envelope with her name on the top of the pile of letters that wasn't there before. She sidles up to Tatyana.

Did you put something in my bag? she says as if speaking to the stack of letters in her hand.

Tatyana stuffs the last of her tangled clothes into her backpack and thumps the sides to get the zip shut. Depends what you've found, she says. If it's gold bars, then, yes, they'll be mine.

Antonina sinks her thumb into the glued flap of the envelope and is about to tear it open when an Alsatian jumps inside the carriage, followed by the trainer. The dog takes a sniff at her leg, nudges its nose into the mound of her belly, and she presses herself into Tatyana, the envelope against her baby bulge as if to protect it. The dog's face is huge, and its golden eyes skip all over her as though searching for a sonar bleep somewhere beneath her dress. Tatyana is much more relaxed when the dog scans her. She offers her open palms and turns so it can smell her back as well. Then the trainer calls it over to their bags, which prove to be much less interesting than their bodies, and with a general wave of its nose, the dog moves on to the next cubical — the violation of their privacy over.

Antonina gets busy, replacing the items inside her bag — the paintbrush she holds onto, as well as the unopened envelope. Their two glasses sit uninterrupted on the table, and when they take their seats they automatically take a sip, then grimace at the cold tea. Tatyana signals with a wave that she wants the brush.

Where'd you get that? she asks and runs her thumb

through the fine red hair. I only use bristle. This is the real thing.

Belonged to Makar, Antonina says. Siberian weasel.

Russian weasel more like, says Tatyana. It's so soft. Must have been taken from right up near the arse. Just like Makar. Except he is the arsehole. Did he give it to you?

No, is all Antonina needs to say for Tatyana to give her an all-knowing nod.

By the time the glasses are refilled with hot water and fresh teabags, the guards have moved on to the next carriage. Antonina presses her thumb into the edge of the unopened envelope and hack-saws along the top until it's half-open and she realises what's inside is not a letter, but money. Tatyana has seen it too.

Bloody typical, says Tatyana. It's Kostya, isn't it?

I don't know, Antonina says. She draws the envelope into her lap and digs around the front and back of the notes for a message. There is none. She takes the corner of one of the two notes and lifts it enough that she can see what it is. Two American one hundred dollar bills — more money than she's ever owned in her life.

Tatyana leans in close. He bloody did take the ransom money, she says.

He wouldn't hurt her, Antonina says, not wanting to mention Polina's name in public. He's not that sort.

No, of course not. But he took the money.

One hundred thousand American dollars? Antonina mouths with a scrunch of her nose. She shakes her head. No, I don't think so. He must have skimmed a few notes from the five thousand. Either that or it could have been Makar. She flips the envelope over again, but there is no clue.

Pass it here, Tatyana waves for the flimsy lemon paper of the envelope. Antonina follows her through to the bunk side of their booth. Would Makar have had access to your bag? Tatyana asks, holding the notes up to the sunlight.

Antonina gives it some thought. Probably not, she says. He would have taken the paintbrush if he'd been in my things. He was furious when it went missing, accused the caretakers of selling it on the black market. Anyway, I doubt he'd give me any more than he already has.

Well, they look real enough, says Tatyana, handing the money back. Put them away somewhere safe. Antonina rolls the envelope up and goes to tuck it in her bra when Tatyana stops her. Not there. No one accepts damaged notes. The smallest marks and they'll be rejected.

Tatyana holds the envelope while Antonina unloads her clothes again, and tucks the money and envelope in the middle of her pile of letters inside the Odessa tin. The bag is put away beneath her bed; that's as safe as she can make the money, though not really very safe at all. When she takes her place by the window, she sips her tea as casually as the shake in her fingers will allow.

You think he's all right? Antonina asks.

Weasels can burrow, says Tatyana. Don't worry about that guy.

No, not Makar, says Antonina.

Who? Kostya? Who knows?

You think he's headed back to St Petersburg?

I doubt it. Probably in the Bahamas by now if he's got what I think he does.

You think he'd just leave us like that? The idea of Konstantin gone for good leaves Antonina feeling surprisingly hollow.

Empty of some vital piece of herself. What happened to him in Novosibirsk feels so distant now, as if it happened to someone else. She had almost successfully pushed it outside of her head, and now it's back.

Actually, Tatyana says, I don't think he's gone far at all. He'll probably stay out of sight for a while, but I doubt he's gone for good.

How do you know?

Tatyana sighs into the words. You know he loves you, don't you?

Antonina isn't sure what to do with that. The paintbrush lies on the table beside the saltshaker and she picks it up, thumbs the bristles absently. She brushes her cheek with soft brush strokes, but there is no connection there, no energy. Disappointment has replaced the desire for Makar. When did that happen? Somewhere between The Dvina and the Ghost Train. It has happened quickly. It hasn't happened quickly. Either way, he moved on before she did. She peers out the window to see where the guards are, and spots them near the end of the carriages. Not long now and they'll be free to go. Feels like she's leaving Makar behind now, in Russia, for good. Her hold on him had been vanity anyway, desire at its selfish core. Now she can see him more clearly — how flawed the relationship was, how her nostalgia had glossed over the failures.

You should get rid of it, Tatyana says, drawing Antonina back into the present.

Antonina holds the brush across the table. You want it? she asks.

No, I don't want anything to do with Makar's arse-hair. The thing will jinx my work. Sell it. She looks across at the bag under the seat. Not that you need to, she says. But don't keep it.

Antonina's shoulders half-shrug, giving away the perplexity of her indecision. The brush is valuable. It's beautiful. Get rid of it?

He reminds me of someone I used to know, says Tatyana. A boy in school. Artem was his name. He was one of those guys who would pretend to be nice, but underneath it all he wasn't. A sweet-talker who convinced me to lower my underwear inside the tunnel where the garbage man shovels trash into the furnace. When I heard a skittering I thought it was the garbage man, but Artem assured me it was a rat. Sounded too large for a rat, but my pants were already down, and two other boys ran out of the shadows and burst out laughing. Never told anyone that before.

Makar never had to force me to take my knickers down, says Antonina.

Too much detail, Tatyana says, her face pained at the thought of it. I think I just threw up a bit in my mouth.

Antonina tosses the paintbrush at her, and Tatyana acts like it's a turd and kicks it to the floor. The door at the far end of their carriage is shut with a slam and a jostle of the handle. The new conductor comes through to lock the door at their end, stopping to pick up the paintbrush from the passageway, planting it on their table without a word. Antonina can't help laughing. There seems to be no way of getting rid of it. The air inside the carriage is already starting to become warm and claustrophobic. They remove the extra layers they donned when the doors first opened. The whistle blasts outside, then a moment later the train shunts forward, and that's it — they're through the border that never used to be a border. They are inside the recently independent Kazakhstan.

She wonders what made her cling to Makar for so long. Perhaps it was partly due to the competition of Nataliya. She can have him now, Antonina thinks as she opens the catch at the top of the window and pushes the brush out so fast that she doesn't even see where it lands, whether it bounces or breaks. She should have ditched it on the Russian side of the border, but the Kazakhstan side will do, and Antonina is not sorry it has gone.

Soon the conductor passes through with fresh glasses of black tea, and while she is at their table Tatyana casually asks for permission to have a cigarette.

No smoking, the conductor says, and tightens her curt little mouth.

Tatyana argues that the Russian conductor let her stand in the concertina covering between carriages.

No smoking, the Kazakh conductor insists, and Tatyana pretends to accept the order. She waits until the conductor passes through to the next carriage before she heads in the opposite direction for a smoke.

After disembarking the train at Semipalatinsk, Antonina and Tatyana are both eager to move their legs, and they march straight through the station to the street outside, where the sprinkle of rain feels fresh and welcome. At the bus shelter no one offers up a seat, even though Antonina pushes her stomach out and accentuates a laden walk as they approach. Tatyana is about to say something smart, but Antonina tugs at her sleeve. Leave it, she says. Her trolley bag has other uses, and this time it works just fine as a seat.

Across the road, an old man sits on the concrete-block edging of a raised garden, scattering crumbs near his feet. The pigeons move closer and closer, pecking at the ground. Another man moves like lightning and snatches a pigeon from the sidewalk. He then hands the bird to a woman who tucks it under her coat and twists its neck before dropping it into a sack.

Did you see that? Antonina says.

What?

They're catching the birds and putting them in a sack. Can they do that?

Hey, you, Tatyana yells out. Stop that. Leave those birds alone.

The gypsies swear and move on, settling further away beneath a tree, tossing more crumbs, and the dumb birds follow. Antonina rubs the prickling flesh of her arms. Semipalatinsk is giving her the creeps already.

The sky is darkening and the rumble of a train leaving rolls out from behind the station. Poor Polina. At every stop there has been at least one vendor with a row of flapping coloured flags that reminded Antonina of the fluorescent notes stuck around the streets of St Petersburg. Street girl numbers. Polina and her American. Hope and love dashed to smithereens. It would have been heart-warming to see someone successful in that elusive quest of romance. Knight in shining armour. Do they still exist? Have they ever? Her own father certainly wasn't one.

You think they're together now? Polina and her American? she asks.

Don't be stupid, Tatyana says. That afterlife stuff isn't real. It's just bullshit to trick people into submission — fear of hell turns us passive, hope in heaven makes us hypocrites.

Don't talk like that.

Like what?

Like that, Antonina says. Swearing. It cheapens you. Women shouldn't swear.

It's never bothered you before, Tatyana says, and she moves out from under the shelter to hold her face up to the light rain with abandon.

The smell of dust and diesel makes Antonina cough. She really could do with a drink of water, but the line for the bus is growing. Can't be long now.

It's not until they arrive at the House of Children that Antonina realises they are not going to their hostel first.

We could have done this tomorrow, she says, lugging the old woman trolley bag up the bare concrete steps, so it makes as much noise as possible.

Won't take long, Tatyana assures her, then doubles back to take Antonina's trolley bag. Tatyana shifts the straps of her backpack the moment they pause before the closed door — more with anticipation than complaint, Antonina suspects. The doorbell is the ding-dong variety, which feels comical. When the door opens, there is not the warm face of welcome, though. Tatyana introduces herself to the pant-suited woman with the tired eyes of a funeral director, who stands in the gap of the door so they cannot pass. Tatyana mentions her father's name, and the doctor she has an appointment to see. They are shown into a corridor and told to wait.

You had an appointment? Antonina says quietly.

Tatyana shakes her head and flicks Antonina a secret smug smile, then rubs it out with the side of her hand.

Thought not, Antonina says.

They settle on two green plastic chairs that are sticky to the touch. The woman comes back for Tatyana. This way, she says. Antonina starts to rise, and the woman holds her hand up like a stop sign. Just this one, she says. You can wait here.

While Antonina waits, a door upstairs opens and shuts, the sound of crying babies coming and going carried as if on a gust of wind. Another door opens and closes, this time on the ground floor. A middle-aged woman comes towards her wearing a white pinafore with a flannelette apron that could be made from old sheets, with tiny brown cartoon horses scattered all over it. Her headscarf is of the same fabric, and her short hair flicks out from the sides of the scarf.

Would you like to come have a look? she says and waves for Antonina to follow.

Antonina joins the woman, and together they walk upstairs. On the first floor is another corridor with multiple doors leading away from the centre. The building could be called the house of doors, but when the woman takes Antonina inside one of the rooms, she understands the real name. Only, it's not a house of children so much as babies. Deformed babies. It has the feel of the Kunstkamera Museum, only the curiosities are not pickled inside glass jars, they're alive, crying inside their cots, or sitting on the knees of women at the feeding table being stuffed with mash that goes in their mouths, then comes back out.

What is this place? Antonina asks.

Polygon babies, the woman says with a sigh. Look at this one. She lifts a baby with beautifully expressive brown eyes from a cot and unbundles it to show Antonina the torso with no arms. One of the baby's legs has not developed properly either. Twenty-five years I have worked here, the woman says, and never have I seen them so bad. They're getting worse. First, it was the cleft lips and palate. Now there are no arms and legs.

What about that one? Antonina points to a healthy-looking child with ruddy, full cheeks, who smiles and coos when she comes near his cot. Why is he here?

Look at him, the woman says. How old would you say he is?

Antonina tries to evaluate the age. She has no idea.

He's almost a year old, the woman says. He looks like a three-month-old. He was with his parents at first, then they noticed he wasn't growing and brought him here. This is where they all end up. Abandoned. The woman pats Antonina's belly. Is this a polygon baby too?

No, Antonina says, but the woman squints at her with doubt.

You know you're not allowed to have these babies? It's not too late. The doctors allow late-term abortions here.

But I'm not from here, Antonina says. She steps towards the door, takes hold of the handle.

See all these, the woman says, her hand sweeping across a half dozen babies. They're all monsters, and it's not their fault. It's their parents' fault. They have them, they abandon them. Then it's left to us to care for them.

Antonina covers her belly protectively and opens the door. I'm not having a monster, she says. And I'm not from here. I'm just waiting for a friend.

Well, the woman says. You should have said so at the start.

By the time Antonina has made her way back to the

plastic chair, Tatyana is rounding up her conversation. The door is ajar and Antonina can see them talking. Tatyana has another piece of paper. Instructions and addresses probably, but Antonina's not going anywhere except the hostel after this. She wonders whether the hostel has a bath, hoping it does. It will take a good long soak to remove the tension she can feel across her upper back and neck since seeing those children. Those sad, awful eyes that have made her feel guilty for not doing something to help. Guilty for moving on unapologetically with her own life.

The moment they are out on the footpath and free of the House of Children, Antonina lets her impatience be known. My stomach's burning, she says. I need food and a bath. And I need them now.

Come on then, says Tatyana. The hostel's not far.

Antonina braces herself for a distance. Tatyana knows Antonina doesn't have any issue with walking — they've worn out shoes together over the years, but today her body is fatigued from lack of movement during the past week, travel legs that have become used to not being worked. She'll be right once she gets going, she tells herself.

So, you want to know what I found out? Tatyana says.

What?

My brother was never given up. Tatyana turns around and walks backwards so Antonina can see the stupid smile. That means, she says, he wasn't one of the radiation babies. He must have been safe enough to be adopted. There are records of people with radiation-related illnesses at the Institution of . . . she looks at her piece of paper, then gives up. Anyway, my brother won't be there. That was for civilians. I'll have to get access to military files.

All those deformed babies, Antonina says. You didn't see them. I think I'm going to skip coming with you tomorrow and visit the hospital instead. Get this nugget checked and make sure everything's okay.

You're getting checked? Does that mean you're not selling the nugget?

I guess so, says Antonina. Don't think I was ever really going to give it up.

Tatyana decides they should go straight away to the hospital, and when Antonina agrees, with the proviso of something to eat when they arrive, Tatyana wraps one arm around Antonina's shoulders, and they walk on, Antonina squeezed like a lemon for a few blocks, before they remember to ask for directions.

The bus arrives in a whirl of black diesel stink that is common in the dilapidated Soviet modes of public transport. Antonina moves up and down the aisle, but last on means last on, and people who have queued longer have filled all the seats. A couple of skinny teenage girls have taken an entire seat, so Antonina uses her bag like a bulldozer to shove them towards the window. It's tight, but they manage, with the backpack on Antonina's lap, and Tatyana standing in the aisle holding the back of the seat, trolley bag clenched between her legs. Stop by stop passengers disembark, and the over-crowding subsides. Soon the teenagers go too, and Antonina and Tatyana have a seat to themselves.

Rub my back, will you? Antonina says, turning towards the window and indicating where. Just here.

Tatyana obliges for a minute, then she points out a truck like Konstantin's. There are plenty of ex-military lorries about, though, and it's not until they see his number plate that they get excited. However, as they overtake the truck at the lights, the lift in mood quickly fades.

Who's that driving his truck? Tatyana asks.

He must have sold it, Antonina says, rubbing her own lower back. He's probably halfway to Almaty by now. She doesn't know what her mother will make of him, but she hopes he gets to the mountain. Perhaps there is some safety to be found there after all. Under the watchful care of the snow people. She likes that idea.

You have European ears, the doctor says. She wears a baby blue cotton smock over her clothes, with a matching blue hat that is cylindrical and high and ties at the back like a patient's robe.

What does that mean? Antonina asks.

The inner channel is larger than Asian ones, that's all.

The doctor walks her fingers up the side of Antonina's stomach. Just looking for the top of your uterus, she says, then presses in deeply above the bellybutton. Antonina tries not to wince at the doctor's no-nonsense jabs. You're around twenty-three, twenty-four weeks? The doctor raises her question mark eyebrows.

I guess so, Antonina says.

Just over five months? Is that what your doctor told you?

Antonina feels the pressure of her non-conformance. She has not cared for the child the way she should have from the start. Visiting a doctor at the very least. Now she is stuck inside a room that looks too innocent to deal with emergencies should anything be wrong. Small and narrow, a sink, a desk, a chair. It is no more than a consultation room. And no Tatyana to hold her hand.

Antonina stalls. Where's my friend? Can't she come in?

Don't be silly, the doctor says. I'm not that scary, am I? She places her ear to a cone on Antonina's stomach and ah-has before filling in spaces on a sheet of paper. I take it you have no doctor yet?

No.

Where is the child to be born?

Almaty, I suppose, Antonina says. It's a question she hadn't really thought through. Would it be better to have it in Russia? Probably.

You have a family doctor there?

Yes, says Antonina, then, no, when she realises the doctor wants to send on her files. No secrets in Almaty. Word would spread like wildfire.

Something appears funny to the doctor. Her smile is askew. One front tooth folds over the other like crossed fingers behind the back when telling a lie. She wraps an inflatable belt around Antonina's arm and pumps it up hard. Antonina tries to focus on letting the air in and out of her lungs as naturally as possible while the doctor presses the stethoscope and counts, only it's difficult to breathe normally when you're conscious of it.

The doctor nods then removes her stethoscope. Blood pressure's good, she says. She releases the inflatable belt and asks Antonina to stand on the scales, then hands her a plastic pottle with 'Antonina Sharm' written on it in chunky black felt pen. The doctor clicks her pen a few times and writes more details on the form. I'll make a note to send your details to the maternity ward in Almaty. Let them know your doctor's name when you can, she says. The toilet is down the hall to the right. Leave the urine on the bench then come back, and hop up on the bed and we'll have a look at your cervix. She tucks the pen in her pocket with the thermometer, then collects the heart monitor, winding the tube and hand pump around the cuff.

Tatyana is waiting in the foyer and throws her arms around Antonina when they meet. The embrace is awkward, but Tatyana's body feels like a fortress. A safe place and Antonina lingers there a moment.

You smell like bleach, Tatyana says when she leans away. Is the baby healthy?

Everything's fine, she says, and Tatyana squeezes her again. Won't be if you keep smothering it, Antonina says, and Tatyana lets her go.

The world outside the hospital is saturated with smells that appear foreign after the sanctified confines of the hospital — diesel, pine, cut grass, dust and smoke. The nugget is safely tucked up inside her. All well. All healthy. And, finally, she knows that it won't be handed over to someone else to raise. Tatyana is right. She can do this. How, she's not exactly sure. She's curious, though — the woman who wants to buy the nugget will be at the railway station tomorrow at noon. It wouldn't matter if Antonina stood her up — serve her right, but the gnawing desire to see who she is won't let Antonina alone.

THE SCREAMING BRIDGE

The hostel is a bustle of noise when Tatyana steps inside the door. Pots and plates clatter and clang down the corridor, and the savoury smell of dinner preparation comes to greet them with a homely welcome. To the right, the television competes with the casual conversations of guests sitting around tables, either eating or playing cards. The hostel expected their arrival around one in the afternoon, although their beds were prepaid, so they shouldn't have lost their booking.

Tatyana leans an elbow on the front desk and tings the silver bell while Antonina takes a seat just inside the door and minds the bags. To Tatyana it feels strange to be inside normal daily life after waiting outside the hospital for so long. She hadn't expected the suddenness of their separation — the nurse positioned outside the maternity ward like a guard with clacking knitting needles, refusing entry to the maternity ward to anyone but the pregnant women. Not even a sister? Antonina exclaimed. But rules were rules, as redundant as they seemed, so Tatyana loitered at the front of the building along with expectant fathers who visored their eyes against the sinking sun, waiting for signs from one of the windows for the birth of their babies.

Mine's been in there for two days now, a tall, straight man in blue overalls told her. She should be given the baby for feeding soon, and she knows I've got work at eight. So, keep watch. He points to the end window on the third floor. We should see her soon.

Within half an hour, one of the new mothers came to the window. A boy! she called down through an open wedge, her arms empty of the evidence. The proud papa waved and blew kisses. The old man in the wheelchair beside him waved too, and the blue-overalled man shook everyone's hands. Tatyana took hold of the old man's hand expecting to move on to the proud papa, but the dedushka held her there.

You're shaking the hand of a man who fought in the Great Patriotic War, he said, blinking rapidly.

Papa, the new father said, let him go.

Him. Tatyana couldn't help noticing the male pronoun. The androgynous look is popular amongst her peers, but she has never been called a him before. She said nothing, holding her tongue, enjoying the moment of temporary transition, and while she waits in the foyer of the hostel she allows the pleasure to rise from recapturing the moment.

No one comes to the front desk, so Tatyana lifts her hand and lets it fall heavily on the little bell, which doesn't seem to make much more of a demand than it did the first time. A woman breaks away from a game of cards in the lounge. She is delicate in size. Smart in her white shirt and black tubular skirt. Honey-coloured skin with dark hair.

Kazakh, not Koryo-saram. Tatyana can see the difference Antonina spoke of in the shape of the face. She is friendly but distracted, her attention darting back to the table where her cards wait, face down, her fellow gamers looking on with impatience. She hands over two keys and smiles gratefully when Tatyana declines the offer to show them around the communal areas.

On the second floor, the carpet softens their tread and dulls the voices from the lounge below. The corridor is the same clash of cream damask wallpaper and deep blue and burgundy carpet that flows throughout the lower level. A young woman bursts through a door one room down from their own, face bright and open. Hello, she says with an accent that's hard to pick. Tatyana lifts the corners of her mouth just enough to acknowledge a greeting when the young woman passes. Tatyana watches her head away, moving confidently, all liquid ease, her smooth, thin ankles peeking from beneath rolled-up pyjama pants.

Their dorm is an eight-bunker with the smell of must and resin. Soft pink roses hover on the walls, with scalloped lace curtains finished with pink ribbon bows. A desk of wood veneer and two chairs sit at one end next to a pillar of lockers that could belong in a school. Tatyana opens her locker to find, as she suspected, that it's big enough to hold a towel and a few clothes, but certainly not an entire bag.

Most of the beds are already made up, with the occupier's belongings sitting at the end of pastel duvets of various colours. On the remaining beds, the duvets are still folded, with sheets and a pillow balanced on top. Tatyana chooses the soft green duvet of an upper bunk and climbs up to claim it. The yellow duvet below is for Antonina. Tatyana unhooks her bag from her shoulders and arches her back, slow stretching to the left then to the right, pulling her shoulders back to expand the muscles in her chest.

The day has exhausted her, and the throb of a headache is settling in behind her eyes. Tatyana is not in the mood for company, but her throat feels thick and dry from neglect. You hungry? she asks.

No. Too tired, says Antonina, who is already shuffling with bedding, patting down a pillow, a duvet.

Cup of tea?

No, I'm fine. If you're heading to the kitchen though, bring me a glass of water on your way back. I'll stay here with the bags. Not much security in this place.

There's always the locker, Tatyana points out, but in truth, she wouldn't trust that either. The amount of money Antonina has on her should really be in a bank, but no one believes in banks anymore.

The communal kitchen is a large room on the ground floor, and a cheerful chatter bounces around the hard surfaces. The windows are clouded with condensation, but the outside colours still seep through in the dimming light. Green for grass. Grey for sky. The sharp brown edge of a building next door. Tatyana gulps down a glass of water and thinks about preparing an evening meal with the leftover bits and pieces in her bag. There's enough stale bread for a quick fry-up for two, and possibly a little bit of sausage. But she just can't be bothered.

Potatoes and onions hiss inside a frying pan. A woman rolls sausages over inside another pan. Real food that makes Tatyana's mouth water, and if the roubles in her pocket were worth anything, she'd offer to purchase a serving. She hadn't prepared herself for a new currency. She turns the kettle on. The woman pokes at the pan of potatoes with a spoon, then cocks the lid slightly askew and leaves them to stew. Tatyana ignores the luscious smell of it and prepares her cup with one of their teabags. The kettle starts to bump and roar, and Tatyana picks it up too soon. The hot water still gurgles and spills around the cup as she pours. The cup of tea will do. She takes it through to the lounge to watch a bit of television from a soft chair at the back of the room.

Antonina is asleep when Tatyana returns to the dorm, so she places the glass of water beneath the bed and sits at the end watching her friend breathe. She is ready for sleep too, even though the sun is still setting. Going to bed so early reminds her of her childhood in summer when her mother wanted her out of the way — the hours she would force herself to stay awake, straining to listen to the radio in the lounge, unable to hear anything but the hum of voices.

Sheets she doesn't need, so she tosses them to the end of her bed. The duvet she unfolds and lays flat. Her boots are all she takes off before sliding under the duvet with the hope that being horizontal will rid her of the headache.

It doesn't. The pillow is a pancake, and the pulsing goes on as if the nightclub beneath her studio back in St Petersburg had travelled with her. What she would do for some Valium. Konstantin was good for that at times. Right now, what she needs more than anything is to fall into the deep black hole of sleep before she has to rise in the morning and figure out how to get access to her father's information. The military files are all stored in Moscow, but there must be some way to convince them to tell her over the phone. Konstantin would know what to do. Where is he when she needs him? She imagines him with his skull cracked, buried like the snowdrops that pop up each spring in the thaw — frozen bodies of missing people, killers long gone.

This must be the last thing Tatyana thinks of before she drifts off. When she wakes, the lights are out, and the room feels blessed with the smell of scented soap from fresh-showered bodies. One of the lodgers near the door turns in her sleep and rustles deeper into her blankets. Tatyana's backpack has moved in beside her like a small dog, and she leaves it there, the pressure of it a comfort. She closes her eyes in the hope of a little more sleep. It doesn't come. The lace curtains are tinged with a grey light of early dawn that prompts her to get up. She tries to ignore the stirring. It feels like mere minutes since she first lay down, but the sun is rising, the day spreading out before her with secrets ready to be discovered.

Tatyana moves as gently as she can. She grabs her bag and her boots, leaving the bed for someone else to put away. Downstairs, the light in the kitchen is on, so she helps herself to another cup of tea, and makes her way to the lounge for early morning trash television. She lights a cigarette and sits in front of a rerun of a sitcom on the muted television screen. Moscow is three hours behind. She will have to wait half a day before she can get hold of the military library. She sucks on her cigarette and blows the smoke out with impatience.

Antonina wakes late. Most of the lodgers have left for the day, and they have the kitchen to themselves. From her bag, Tatyana fetches the bread and sausage and breaks them into chunks before frying them with a dollop of dripping, along with a couple of eggs from the fridge with shells branded Ksenia in thick black ink. Tatyana thinks about the woman with the lovely ankles and the bright face who passed her in the corridor. She looked like a Ksenia. The bread fries to a satisfying crisp. Tatyana breaks the runny yolk over it then salts the dish liberally. The culmination of the crisp and the runny is a decadence Tatyana would like to savour, but she encourages Antonina to eat up, just in case Ksenia is around. Before they leave the kitchen, Tatyana places a few useless *kopeks* in the two empty hollows of Ksenia's egg carton, like a tooth fairy.

Some parts of Semipalatinsk have retained centuries-old wooden buildings that would burn down in a minute. They have an almost medieval appeal, and many of the roads are worn so badly that car tyres grind in gravel and stones. There is the odd lovely building, though — refurbished hotels, newer office blocks on the rise amidst the jumble of construction sites. It's into one of the new hotels with its glossy lights that Antonina pulls Tatyana.

What are we doing here? Tatyana whispers.

Antonina points to an exchange booth to the side of the lobby, which is little more than a curtained window where the chest of a woman can be seen, her hands folded, one over the other, her head hidden, like a confessional. Tatyana stands behind Antonina waiting to exchange her roubles. When Antonina is done, she has exchanged the American dollars, as well as her mother's postal notes, and she thrusts enough *tenge* into Tatyana's hand that she doesn't need to change any of her own money.

You sure? Tatyana says.

You've paid for me so far, Antonina says, and she walks to the counter and orders a room for the night, a good room. Tatyana tries to tell her the hostel is prepaid and they won't get the money back, but Antonina won't listen. She pays for this room in advance for one night and takes two keys to the same door, giving one to Tatyana.

Compliments of our favourite black-marketeer, Tatyana says, and there is a moment of bitter-sweetness that ripples between them.

I'm going up to the room, Antonina says. You go do your sleuth work on your brother. I'll be here when you come back for dinner. You've got enough to open some doors if you need to.

She's right. There is enough in Tatyana's wallet now to convince the right person to dig for her information quickly. She hands her bag over to the porter, feeling light enough to fly when it's gone, her feet so eager to get going that her boots tap the marble floor, waiting until the moment the lift shuts and Antonina's face is gone before she wheels around and heads for the door.

———

The railway station is a large block of glass and stucco concrete coloured in soft yellow and teal, finished with a gently scalloped trim. It sits heavy and important in front of a car park with the compulsory statue — this time of a Kazakh on a horse. Mustafa Shokay, another someone they all learned about at school. It feels uncomfortable to lie to Tatyana, but Antonina wants to see what kind of woman would buy a baby, and Tatyana would just complicate things.

The surfaces inside the station are metal, glass and concrete. Utilitarian and functional, with only a hint of ornateness in the repeating patterns of the floor. The central area is cluttered with bags and people that create an obstacle course. Antonina manoeuvres the distance easily since her own bags are stowed at the hotel, her money secure within its safe. She hopes she's done the right thing, leaving it with them.

It's almost midday. The café is full of families, businessmen, and a woman with a clay doll sitting upright on the table — the sight of which jolts Antonina with a small zap of recognition. The doll is not what Antonina notices first, though — it's the winged black eyeliner around the woman's eyes — an older woman, whose grey hair is pulled back into a French knot, her face the crumbling exterior that retains some of its original beauty. A face that Antonina remembers as if it were a door to another place, another time. She draws closer. Her mouth opens slightly at the shock of seeing the woman with the red leather gloves.

It's you. I remember you, Antonina says. She stands opposite the old woman, a table between them. Babulya, she says to herself in disbelief.

Katerina, the woman says. My name is Katerina Mun, or Moon, as you used to say it. How are you, little puppy? It's good to see you again. Please, she waves to the empty seat.

Antonina drags the chair back and sits on a corner of it. She takes hold of the clay doll, her doll, and she looks towards the glass entry doors. She should leave, but there's a disconcerting calmness and mystery about the woman that makes her want to stay. You came to steal another child? she says. My child? Why would you do that?

No, Katerina says. I don't want to steal your child. I don't want to buy it either. I want to pay you to keep it. She hands over a paper bag, rolled at the top like a packed lunch.

Antonina lets the paper bag sit on the table between them. Is this a trick? she asks.

Not at all, Katerina says. Let me explain. But first, I've ordered tea. You like tea, or would you prefer something cold?

Tea's fine.

Katerina wears the same type of red leather gloves that she wore when Antonina was a child. Katerina weaves her fingers together and brings them to rest on the table in front of her, then begins.

You see, she says, my husband Nikolai was taken from me before the deportation of our people. I thought he'd find me. Like the fable. You remember — the crow king, I recited it to you on the train. I thought my rice farmer would come for me the way he did in the story. He hasn't come, but I realise now that Stanislav has stopped him. It's Stanislav who has always haunted me. He was your babushka's first husband. You are not his granddaughter, but if he had lived you would have been, and he would have lived if I hadn't interfered.

What are you talking about?

I don't expect you to understand, but I know they would both want me to help you now — Stanislav and Nikolai. Please, let me help the future in a way that might reach back into the past.

You are looking for forgiveness? Is helping me some kind of penance?

Forgiveness? No, I think I'm well past that now.

A girl in a pinafore delivers a pot of tea, two plates of jam, and two cups. She wipes away some crumbs from the table next to them before fussing over the stacking of dishes, cutlery tinging as it slides from plates and scatters on the plastic tray. Katerina pours the tea while they wait for the girl to be gone.

How did you know where I was?

Katerina laughs. A weak little laugh that turns to a cough that convulses out of her. I listen, and I hear all sorts of things. I put two and two together; it isn't important.

What do you want with me?

A woman should not have to let go of a child she wants to keep. I lost my child once, right here in Semipalatinsk. What I want now is to help you keep your baby. I didn't get to reunite with Nikolai the way I'd hoped, but I have finally understood there is another lost spirit I should have been searching for all this time. Coming here to meet you has made me realise how blind I have been to my responsibility to my own child. I am an old woman now, and I'm dying, the cancer will take me soon. You and your friend Konstantin have led me back here, which is precisely where I should be. I take it he is your rice farmer? This Konstantin?

That's none of your business, she says. And I still don't understand what this has got to do with me.

My Nikolai was your *Ajeossi*. Your babushka was the sister of my Nikolai. I should have been like a sister to Bora. I wasn't. I was too ashamed. I interfered with her family once before and can never put that right. But this time let me interfere in a good way. It won't bring my rice farmer to me, but maybe I will find my own baby when my time comes.

Your husband, Nikolai. Antonina says. You said he was taken from you.

He was shot as a traitor, as they all were, including Stanislav.

They were not traitors, though. We were honourable people. Still are.

And you hoped he would find you even though he was dead?

Katerina reaches across the table and pats the top of Antonina's hand. You don't have to believe what I say. Just trust me. Trust is more important than belief.

I need a minute to think about this, Antonina says and starts to stand, when Katerina grasps her hands as if Antonina were about to go for the militia. I'm just going to the bathroom, she says, annoyed for feeling sorry for the strange woman.

I don't have long, Katerina says. Please, just take it. She offers the paper bag and Antonina takes it with a little attitude, as though it were a packed lunch her mother had pushed into her hands as she shot out the door for school. I'm only going to the bathroom, Antonina says, and walks away from the table to try to settle her thoughts.

What on earth was she going on about? A dead husband coming to find the living wife like the rice farmer — nonsense. *Trust is more important than belief.* Antonina remembers the caretaker using that phrase as well. She checks her phrasing is around the right way as soon as the tinkle of urine starts to fall freely. The toilet door in the next cubicle shuts with an assertive clap, followed by the quick slide of the door bolt. Antonina tries to think about the caretaker. Nikolai — did he say that was his name? He said he knew her family. Could he be her rice farmer? But he was real, not a ghost. Wasn't he? Another woman scuffs across the floor in what sounds like rubber boots.

Sonya, are you in here? she says.

I'm pooping, Sonya replies with a small voice from the next cubical.

Well, poop faster, the woman says. They can all hear the child's effort, the squeeze and the plop. There is the roll of too much toilet paper. Then the grunting effort of pulling clothes back on. The door opens, and it's Sonya's mother who comes to flush the toilet. Wash your hands, she says, and water gushes in the sink before they leave. It's just as impossible to think inside the bathroom of the cafeteria. The heel of her boot shifts the paper bag when she stands, and she sits back down. Inside the bag is an envelope of money. Brand new Kazakhstani *tenge* notes. Twice in a week now she has been given more money than she has survived on in the past four years, and it brings neither the happiness nor the peace of mind she once thought it would. Across the top of the envelope in black ink that is almost calligraphic in style: *Go home, little puppy*, is written, then signed *Katerina Moon*. Gifts for the baby. She doesn't need the old Soviet Union to take care of her the way her mother did. Konstantin is right, the community remains — it's people who take care of people, not systems.

Antonina scrunches the top of the paper bag as tight as she can. She tucks the bag into the pit of her arm while she pulls her underwear up. The bag remains pinned there while she lingers with her hands under the running tap, wondering if it would be right to accept the gift or not. The soapy bubbles slide away, and she shuts the faucet off. After drying her hands, she cups them around her mouth and nose. The smell is not lilac, but strawberry. Nikolai. She must tell Katerina that their Nikolais must be the same person. She never did ask her babubshka about Katerina for the caretaker.

And there's the medal inside the doll she has carried all these years. It's time to give that back.

She rushes back out to the table, but the old woman has gone. On the chair where she sat is the clay doll, weighing down a pair of red leather gloves. Other than that, there is no sign of the woman. Antonina stays for a long time, the information of the old woman's Nikolai growing more and more sure as time passes. But the old woman does not return. She has gone, just like the character in the fable — swept away — and Antonina is left with the deflating disappointment of knowing that she missed her opportunity to reconnect the rice farmer with his wife.

———

Back at the hotel, Tatyana reads aloud:

The Chimerism condition occurs during gestation, when two embryos fuse in the early stage of development, creating one child with the cells from each of the two different genetic combinations. Chimerism is quite common and has little effect on development. However, the fusion of male and female embryos can create a person who has some XX and some XY cells. In some cases, this can lead to the development of intersex characteristics.

What does it mean? Antonina asks.

Tatyana sits next to her on the double bed, in their fancy hotel room that has its own television, its own bathroom too. She balances a chicken and rice dinner on her knee while squaring off the sheets of paper collected during the day, then flops them down on the bed cover.

Antonina has ordered *vareniki*. She should eat some vegetables and meat, but it's not very often she gets such a delicacy as sour cherry dumplings.

It means I have no brother, says Tatyana.

Antonina stops with the fork still in her mouth. No brother, she says through the wall of dough.

Tatyana is chuckling, her body shaking, the laugh threatening to switch to a cry at any moment. Antonina holds onto the food in her mouth, unsure what to make of this news.

Ahhh, Tatyana says, winding herself down. I should have known all along. You remember that boy I told you about? Artem?

Antonina chews without thought of the food in her mouth. She has no idea who Artem is, but she has grown accustomed to allowing space for stories. They all have them.

He's the sweet-talker boy from school, says Tatyana. Persuaded me to pull down my pants in the trash tunnel at school.

Oh, yes. I remember. Reminds you of Makar.

Well here's the rest of the story. When the two other boys ran out of the shadows and burst out laughing, they called me a freak and spat in my face as they left.

I stayed inside the tunnel and listened to that new label as it burst out into the playground like garbage from a chute, spreading all over the place, says Tatyana. It slithered down the concrete walls with beads of moisture, the stink of it taking hold of me. That was the first time I understood my abnormality, Tatyana says. I curled up in the trash and wanted to stay there forever. Never face the world again. I didn't see the garbage man come in. Don't let them worry you, he told me. Easy for him to say. He had this enlarged, pock-red nose that made him look a troll. Clothes so dirty you could smell him before you saw him. And yet I felt even dirtier than him that day. I had teased that old troll for two years straight. I thought he was the freak, but all of a sudden I was one too.

That's nothing to be ashamed of, Antonina says. She reaches across and rubs Tatyana's forearm.

My mother told me the scar above my seedpod was a smile, Tatyana says. A smile I should never have told Artem about. Now that part of me is covered with hair, but the woman parts, they still look strange. I've seen a few vulvas in my adult years to know what normal should look like, and there is no way my seedpod is.

Seedpod, Antonina says. That's kind of cute. Never heard it called that before.

Tatyana taps Antonina's leg with impatience. It wasn't until I passed the time of puberty when my mother explained to me that I had no womb because of the radiation.

Like the polygon babies?

Yes. But in my case, two babies turned into one. A boy. And a girl.

And that means you have no brother?

That means I am my brother. Like the painting in my studio. It all makes sense, doesn't it?

You and your brother are one? Antonina says, the words higher and thinner than before. I didn't expect that.

I know! It's beautiful, don't you think?

It's like the snow people, Antonina says. Like the crow king fable too. Half-animal, half-human beings. But you are not animal; you are brother and sister in one. That is actually pretty fascinating. Will you use it in your work?

Why not? says Tatyana. I am an official chimera. Not the

mythology. I'm the real thing. Want me to show you? Tatyana presses the button of her jeans, but Antonina stops her.

I don't need to see it, she says. So, who chose which sex you'd be?

I guess it was my parents. Only they chose wrong. I should have been a boy.

You have to talk to them about it.

Tatyana places her dish on the side table, then sits up cupping Antonina's ankles gently. I was thinking, she says. We could head back tomorrow. We have enough money to fly. She bounces slightly and makes Antonina rock.

Antonina pushes the last dumpling around the edge of the plate

I thought you'd be excited, says Tatyana.

I have something to tell you too.

What's up? You look like you want to shit. And don't tell me off for swearing again, I'm allowed now that I'm a boy. Might even change my name.

I'm going to go home, Antonina says.

Yes, that's what I'm saying. We'll go back together.

No, says Antonina. Home isn't St Petersburg. It's Alma-Ata. I mean Almaty. I'm going to go home to Almaty. Tomorrow. I've already sent a message to my babushka. She's expecting me.

Tatyana falls back onto her bum from her haunches. Disbelief crowding in. Then, I'll come with you, she says with the grit of determination.

Antonina shakes her head. You need to go speak to your parents, she says. I need to go home to my mother's mountain to wait for my rice farmer.

Your what?

Konstantin — he's my rice farmer.

And there it is, she'd said it out loud. She chooses Konstantin. Over Makar. Over Tatyana. Over the Academy of Art. Over St Petersburg. She chooses Konstantin. She waits for Tatyana to laugh at her, but she doesn't. They finish their meal to the placating ease of a television show, each inside their own thoughts.

Tatyana is not impressed with Antonina's decision. She doesn't say so, but Antonina can feel it in the way Tatyana tosses and turns beside her in the enormous bed. It's all right, she has the night to get used to the idea. She doesn't tell Tatyana about Katerina Moon, or the caretaker. She doesn't tell her that she thinks the dance did work. That it had possibly called up her great-uncle. *Ajeossi*, Katerina called him in the old language. Her uncle and Konstantin — the rice farmers. Both of them unlikely heroes.

Three generations, three countries, three cities, and one train journey into exile — for Antonina, all this has boiled down to the strange woman who stole her from the bedroom window. There is some invisible border Antonina knows she must cross that will give her full insight into who she is, and all that she will encompass as a Kazakh-Korean, a mother, and an artist. What she needs is not just to know the stories of her ancestors, but to become part of that space herself, become part of the story of her people and their resilience, their determination, their trauma, their overcoming. Katerina is right to believe Antonina is the link between the past and the present, as many others of her generation are too. She can see that now.

At the train station, Tatyana hangs around the edges as if expecting Antonina to change her mind. She leans on the counter in a daze while Antonina purchases a first-class ticket for the train to Almaty. Tatyana watches for signs of change, a hoax even, but Antonina is not playing. They move away from the counter, towards the café.

Will you come back to St Petersburg at all? Tatyana says.

Yes, Antonina says. Which is true — she does intend going back to finish her studies, to her art, but right now it's a distant thought, more distant than it has been since she can remember. Katerina's money will help her keep her baby and her art. But for now, there is the baby. And she must go back to her mother's mountain and wait for Konstantin.

Out of the blue, Tatyana says that she should come to Almaty too. That her parents can wait. Only, it can't, Antonina tells her, and it takes some persuasion for Tatyana to see that Antonina wants to head off on her own.

The overhead speaker announces scratchy, indecipherable words, and they rise from their chairs, instinctively knowing it's the boarding of the train to Almaty. The room hollows out quickly as passengers rush through the doors to the platform outside. Antonina reaches for the handle of the trolley bag, but Tatyana interjects, hanging on until the last, and she wheels it out to the platform herself.

This is it, Antonina says. She takes hold of the trolley bag handle for herself. Tatyana massages Antonina's shoulders as if there were an ache there that had encompassed all the misery of their parting, and soon she breaks into a goodbye embrace, and they squeeze each other long and hard to avoid the burn rising in their throats.

This is ridiculous, Tatyana says, her voice tight. I'll be

with you soon enough. After I've seen my parents, I'll come down and stay for a bit.

Yes. That would be great, says Antonina. Come and tell me everything, and don't leave out any details. Deal?

Deal, Tatyana says and pulls away. She stands rigid, arms like planks at her sides, mouth a firm strip, and they both know the stoic mask is a protective lie.

Antonina boards the train without looking back, manoeuvres the trolley bag into the cabin and shuts the door behind her. Tatyana is outside, below the window, on the platform, and they wave bravely at each other through the glass. No tears, Antonina promises herself, and she forces a smile until she can't anymore. Then she has to cover her mouth before the quiver of her chin gives way.

The train tugs until the wheels have momentum and the station begins to slide away, Tatyana with it, her hand held up like an Indian chief. Antonina watches for as long as she can see Tatyana. When the last of her is gone, Antonina leans back into her seat and rests her head against the soft padding, takes a deep breath, and tries to pull her thoughts away from the shrinking image of Tatyana.

Buildings outside the window race towards the train then flicker past until they've all gone. The view opens out into an expanse of motley grey cloud and a landscape that is parched brown in some places and lush green in others. Power-poles that follow the railway track shoot by, and buildings in the distance crawl like brown hunchback snails. First-class is not much different from what she remembers as a child, and here she is again, racing back to her mother, heading towards the screaming bridge.

Thick groves of trees line the riverbanks, and the water

shines like beaten steel. Antonina cannot speak now the bridge is in sight. She opens her mouth and breathes hard and deep. She is not frightened, she tells herself. The river is a snake, sinuous and smooth, rolling side to side, pushing against the banks and streaming straight for the bridge, ready to strike. Antonina shifts to the opposite seat. She doesn't want to see what's coming. The sound of thunder boils in the wheels of the train, and they are up and inside the metal frame of the bridge.

Anxiety churns inside the same way it did the first time she saw Katerina in the café. *Arirang, Arirang*, she expects to hear the words that are orbs of light with a sting. Outside, the forlorn faces of the cursed souls will appear any minute — hundreds of them, thousands of them, each with a hand pressed to the window, desiring to touch the living. She thought she could bear it, but she can't. Wrapping her hands around her belly is not enough to protect the wee blinking soul in her womb, so she moves out into the passageway and paces up and down. There is the sound of wind flying through bars of metal, each rivet like the holes of a flute being played, the mimic of dead souls, the flickering of light and dark as the bars pass by, but no shadows come to pluck the teeth from her mouth. They don't come to sing her songs either, or tell her stories.

BABY OF SILKS

ALMATY, KAZAKHSTAN

When the train arrives in Almaty, Antonina's mother is waiting for her at the station. Her eyes drop to Antonina's belly, then she pulls her across the platform to a space where the crowd doesn't gather.

So, this is why you wouldn't come home, is it? she says. How could you let this happen? After all I've put towards your education. Shame on you.

Antonina forces herself free from her mother's grip when her babushka steps between them.

And you, Antonina's mother aims at Bora, you knew about this?

Of course not, Bora says. But you should be delighted. Look at her, she's glowing, and soon we'll have a little one to play with while she gets back to her studies.

Glowing. Antonina has waited so long to hear that word, but right now she's too angry to revel in it.

Who are you to judge me? she says. You who travelled

to Tashkent and slept with a married man to get pregnant.

That was different. We had no choice back then. You have all the choice in the world. You have all the opportunity in the world too, and this is how you repay me? You are an ungrateful daughter.

I'll leave if you want me to. I have friends in St Petersburg who will help if you won't. They aren't ashamed of this baby.

Don't be stupid. This is your home. The anger is melting from her face. It's just, how could you keep this from me? she says with her palms held out to Antonina, her voice sharp still but also wounded.

I'm sorry, Mama, says Antonina. But what's done is done. She takes her mother's hands and places them either side of her belly. We'll figure it out, she says. I haven't given up on my studies. It will just take a little longer now, that's all.

Who's the father then? Her mother pulls her hands away.

Antonina hesitates. Has anyone been in touch? she asks, hoping Konstantin might be close by.

No. He's not a bloody potato-nose, I hope, her mother says.

The baby stirs, and Antonina replaces her mother's hands on her belly over the top of the tiny tap tap of connection, like a fish nudging the underneath of a lily pad. The delight can't be held back. A small laugh judders from Antonina's mother — a mix of surprise and joy.

You know, Antonina says, I don't think I've ever heard you swear before.

Oh, don't be so surprised, Antonina's mother says. You've been away a long time. Things can change here too. And for the better.

It doesn't take much for the bossy babushka that had laid dormant inside Antonina's mother to come to the surface. The weekly doctor's visits are obsessive, but Antonina likes the way the trips to the city bring the three generations together for tea and cake with a new shift in the territory of naming rights. Bora now promotes herself to great-babushka, with Antonina's mother taking the title of babushka like it's a medal of honour. Antonina is the mama — a term that sits firmly, and naturally. And with every visit, there are new stories to pry from her babushka about their people.

———

Antonina's mother is busy tending the oven of the home-built kiln when Tatyana arrives for the first time. Thankfully, her mother isn't in her underwear, though Antonina would have liked to have seen Tatyana's reaction if she were. Her mother drops the piece of wood back into the pile and shakes Tatyana's hand in welcome.

Another bloody potato-nose, says Antonina, and her mother bats her on the arm.

Any news of Konstantin? Antonina asks Tatyana as soon as she can get her alone.

I was going to ask you the same thing.

What's that sound? Tatyana asks.

It's Antonina's mother's song to the mountain that sounds more like an instrument than a voice. Soon Tatyana is drawn out to the workshop in the same way Antonina was as a child. She can hear her friend's pitiful attempts at the throat chords, and she leaves them to it while she wanders up the mountainside alone. It is hard to climb with such a large belly, but she is determined to reach the spot where she had sat with Viktor when they buried her clay doll and his grandfather's teeth, not long before Viktor exited her life forever. She has also lost Makar for good. She has her mother and grandmother, though, and she has Tatyana, like a sister — or brother — and maybe in her mixed-up way Katerina was trying to get Antonina to see the importance of that. She is not alone. The baby will be more than enough to fill her heart, she tells herself, trying to ignore its ache.

To Antonina's surprise, her mother and Tatyana become quick friends. It's blazing hot inside the workshop, fires adding to the scorch of the tin roof, but Tatyana soon figures out how to dress: Y-fronts and t-shirt under an apron, not so different to the way she paints. They venture off with a new sleigh to cut a collection of clay slabs. Then Tatyana is taken through the process of cleaning and sieving the clay before she's allowed time on the wheel.

In the furthest corner of the workshop is Antonina's bench where her new art is forming, inspired by the clay dolls, only this time, each doll is a metre high. She is slowly collecting the stories of the old people — the survivors of the deportations, and she is even more slowly deciphering the old language, or as much as she needs to translate the stories onto the backs of her dolls. At first, she used to visit the old people and coax their stories out of them. Now they come with cakes and sit in the kitchen with her babushka, who helps write up the words in the old language alongside the new — her very own Rosetta Stone.

One day Bora shows Antonina a photograph she had kept hidden away. Two men are dressed in white from head to toe, another two are in regular clothing, tweed suits, trilby hats.

There, her grandmother says, see. She points out a woman sitting on a chair in front. That's me. I was pretty, wasn't I?

Is that Katerina? Antonina points to a woman sitting on another chair, taller than her babushka, more elegant by far.

Katerina? You've heard about her, have you? She was a beautiful one. She loved too much, lost so much. Cut herself off. Went a bit crazy — some people did. What Stalin did to us was so destructive. The militia thought it was Katerina who stole you away, but no one knows for sure.

Ha! is all Antonina says. As if she didn't connect the strange woman who took her with Katerina.

I don't know if she's still alive, Bora says. Every so often someone would mention seeing her, though that hasn't happened in a while.

Antonina hasn't mentioned her last meeting with Katerina to anyone, and she decides to remain silent about it.

Who are the men in white? she asks.

That's your great-dedushka there, and, I don't remember the other one. Swans we used to call them. All dressed in white. It was the sign of authority. We all respected them, trusted them. That's Stanislav, my first husband, she says pointing at one of the tweeded men.

Antonina leans in, but it's not Stanislav she's looking at, it's the other tweeded man, the one in the trilby hat. Who's that? she asks. But her babushka is reaching for other photographs now, of her second wedding and images of Antonina's mother as a little girl. Antonina has learnt that with the old people it is best not to dwell too long in the past when they don't want to. And anyway, she knows who it is. It's Nikolai — Katerina's rice farmer, Antonina's caretaker. And he is as young in the photograph as he appeared in the great hall when she saw him from the roof of the Academy. At least, he seemed young — all straight and thin, but that may have been an illusion caused by distance and perspective.

Each new doll Antonina creates feels like a restoration of what was lost. They are all a part of the new show in the making that Antonina has decided to call *Ghost Train*. Where it will exhibit, she isn't sure, but she's thinking locally now she has taken the year off from the Academy. When she does present herself again to the art world, it will be as Nina Moon, not Antonina Sharm — this she has decided on for sure.

From her swivel stool, Antonina watches her mother laughing to herself when Tatyana's bowls slip to the side of the wheel or implode and collapse time and time again. Her mother's patience has always been limited with fools in the workshop, but with Tatyana she is gracious, and at one point she even threads her arms through Tatyana's from the back, the two of them guiding the clay together like an Indian goddess with four arms.

See how the mountain loves you, Antonina tells her, and she doesn't mean the clay.

The second time Tatyana visits it's to celebrate the birth of the baby. The Academies have been back for two months when he is born. A boy. Such an honour to the Sharm family line, and when the name is announced, Tatyana is also introduced to the wider community as his godparent. Matvei is the name they choose for the baby. Before they head back to the mountain after the celebration, Antonina insists on a visit to the mural of the dancer and the fan at the railway station. She holds Matvei in her arms.

Look, she says, that's your great-aunt, Katerina Moon. Isn't she beautiful?

Great-great-aunt, Antonina's mother corrects her, but the details hardly matter.

Week by week the dolls suddenly start to arrive. Small, hand-sized clay dolls left over from the *I am not Kazakhstan* apartment show. Each one is wrapped in newsprint and housed inside a box. There is never a note or return address. Antonina's name and address are written in Konstantin's distinctive left-slant text, with a tell-tale stamp that shows her where he is. So far, they have arrived from within Mongolia, China, Kyrgyzstan, Tajikistan, Uzbekistan, Turkmenistan, Georgia, Bulgaria, Romania, and the last one from Odessa in Ukraine. Farther and farther away he roams until Antonina doubts he will ever come for her as he said he would.

Only he does. One day he stands in the frame of the front door introducing himself to her mother as a friend of her daughter. She knows his voice, the echo of his footsteps in the corridor. The familiarity makes her heart skip. The baby sleeps, and Antonina has been lazing about in the kind of nightdress she wore before the St Petersburg days. She doesn't stop to change, or even to cover up, but runs barefoot out into the kitchen, where her mother is already boiling water ready for a round of tea.

What are you wearing? he says when he sees her, and he is right to laugh at the flannelette nightdress with the bow of ribbon tied high around the neck that conceals her entire body. Even the arms are covered with sleeves elasticated to a frill at the wrist.

So, the adventurer returns, she says, suddenly coy.

Look at you all covered in lilac flowers like a babushka, he says.

They stare at each other across the kitchen table, as awkward as teenagers on a first date.

Your face, she says. It has healed well, and she longs to touch it.

He rubs his cheek roughly on the side with the pale scar. He is still handsome — the scar merely adds more drama to his face. His fine hair is short and swept to one side; it has lightened to the colour of weak milky tea. His eyes squint as if deep in concentration, with smile-lines that fan from his temples to resemble white sunbeams against his otherwise tanned skin. He doesn't need to drink the magic water of the fable to fight the crow king for her — he already has the spirit of the dragon within. Always has. Her mother watches. Pours tea, and waits. Antonina can feel her mother's curiosity, and she finally blurts it straight out, thumping the kettle down in resignation.

So, she says. Are you the father or not?

His eyes flick from mother to Antonina, then back to mother.

Then hug already, her mother says, waving them together impatiently. And I expect a wedding, so don't think you're going anywhere soon.

Have they ever hugged before? Antonina doesn't remember. She tucks herself into his chest, trying to make it look natural. He kisses her forehead, then holds her tight. He smells of cigarettes and old leather, burnt wood and soap. He is a bigger man than Makar, broader in the shoulders, yet his arms wrap around her and land in the right way, his crossed wrists press gently into the small of her back. They fit well. Like two sheets of an opened love letter tucked inside each other. They fit.

Antonina's mother lifts the baby from his crib and cradles him as he squawks from the interruption. I raised a child on my own, she says, and I did well. Girls are strong, but boys are different, they need a father. She doesn't wait for Konstantin to ask before handing the baby over, and the moment Matvei is in Konstantin's arms the man's face changes. What was soft and welcoming a moment ago switches to bewildered awe.

In the corner of her eye, Antonina thinks she sees a shadow shift the way they did when she was on board the train with Katerina. It could be her imagination, or wishful thinking, but she feels the warmth of a hand upon her shoulder where there is no hand. Perhaps it's on the inside of her body that she feels the press of Katerina, of Nikolai, of their lost baby. She sends a small prayer into the universe, to whoever is in charge up there — a wish for Katerina. A hope. A desire as well, that the three of them have found each other — the rice farmer, his wife, and their child.

Hey, little monkey, Konstantin says. Can you say 'Papa'? You've got blue eyes just like Papa. Then he leans over and breathes the baby in, like an animal assessing the ownership of a pup, and he comes up beaming.

ACKNOWLEDGEMENTS

Kanaiji oneora — Come, little puppy.

I am not joking when I say the Koryo-saram sabotaged my novel. It's as though Katerina Moon stood at my window in the dark and beckoned me to come. 'Unreliable People', Stalin called the Soviet Koreans, and the story of their exile and threefold loss of identity captured my attention while I was researching a completely different novel. Initially, I tried to combine the two separate strands — one Russian, one Korean. I even handed the book over to my publisher as a two-piece, but the Koryo-saram story seemed determined to be heard, and it was this strand that won out to become *The Unreliable People*.

As always, I would like to acknowledge my husband, James, first of all. You are consistently there to encourage and support me. You have read so many drafts of this novel, each time with extraordinary patience and diligence. I am over-the-moon with the cover you designed for this novel. It's absolutely perfect. I am very proud to call it mine.

Thank you, Harriet Allan, Penguin Random House, for your considered approach to this novel, and the guidance I received that has enabled this story to reflect the beauty and gentle nature of both the Kazakhs and the Koryo-saram people.

I am honoured to have befriended and enlisted the help of Liza Ordinartceva, Anastasia Patsey and Konstantin A. Vasilyev from St Petersburg, Russia; and of Laura Isa and Janibek Issagulov who came to New Zealand from Almaty, Kazakhstan. I would also like to thank Allan Smith, Senior Lecturer at Elam School of Fine Arts; Changzoo Song, Senior Lecturer in Korean and Asian Studies at the University of Auckland; Elena Panaita, my talented and beautiful Russian artist; and my very dear friend John Cochrane; you were always only an email away. When I couldn't find the information I needed, you got to work, found what I needed and wrapped it up inside an anecdote from your own life experience with such wit that you often brightened my day. You are a library of stories needing to be told. To all of my research advisors: your advice and willingness to answer my myriad questions have given me the ability to write with confidence, for which I am genuinely appreciative.

Suji Park — you are one of the most beautiful people I have ever known. Thank you for allowing me into your studio to discuss your work. You have been the muse for my Antonina, and I drew from you unapologetically to create both her character and her artwork. You are always an inspiration. Thank you. (http://www.ivananthony.com/suji-park/)

To Michael Gifkins, I know you still visit. I feel you laughing at me in moments of self-doubt, and I feel the shivers you send through me when you let me know I've done well.

To Martin Poppelwell — the day I spent in my puffer jacket sitting on a stool in the corner of your studio while you formed bowls from clay on the wheel was magical. I have always had a passion for your work, and I am honoured to call you a friend. Thank you, for your advice and encouragement from the beginning. (https://melanieroger-gallery.com/stockroom/martin-poppelwell/)

Thank you to Paula Morris, and the University of Auckland, for accepting me into the Masters of Creative Writing (MCW) programme, and for the honour of being the recipient of a Sir James Wallace Masters of Creative Writing Scholarship. Sir James Wallace, I say this every time we meet, but the contribution you make to scholarships like this makes such a difference to writers like myself. Thank you.

To the University of Auckland MCW Class of 2017 — you have given me such consistent support, and I am so very grateful for the community I am now a part of as one of the Paula Morris MCW alumni. I would especially like to thank Amy McDaid, Heidi North, Meredith Lalande and Meagan France for continuing to read my work long after our classes had ended. Thank you Paula Morris, for your honesty, your intelligence, your constant support, and for the laughter. You are a marvellous person, and I treasure our friendship.

To Katie Marshall, who became a friend and helped me during that first week in St Petersburg when I understood for the first time what it was like to be isolated by language. Thank you for allowing me to draw from your end-of-residency show *WANTED and NEEDED*, which drew inspiration from all the coloured neon flyers plastered around the streets. (https://cargocollective.com/yakatya/Wanted-and-Needed)

I would also like to thank Katie Haworth, for your honesty and direction when I needed to hear the truth.

To my WBBC members, I truly do belong to the World's Best Book Club, and I am grateful for the many times we have unravelled books together. You have opened my eyes to how readers read, and I am always impressed by how deep and wide you see. (https://www.facebook.com/theworldsbestbookclub/)

To Mary Robbins, you are a gem. Your generosity and inclusiveness warms my heart. Thank you for being one of my early readers.

To Barbara Larson, thank you so much for the thorough and thoughtful editing work on this novel, and to Kate Stone and Emma Neale for proofreading.

During the writing of this story I have travelled some miles. Thank you to Anastasia Patsey and Liza Ordinartceva for seeing my artistic passion and giving me the honour of being the first New Zealander to take up the St Petersburg Art Residency. The weeks I spent with you were invaluable.

Thank you to Creative New Zealand for the Arts Grant that allowed me the year to write, and the money needed to travel to Russia to take up the residency. I am honoured that you saw potential in my work.

To the Michael King Writers Centre, I am so grateful for the time I spent in the Signalman's House, for the fantastic ladies I met, and for the continuing support. You are another valuable organisation that encourages and enriches the lives of many writers. Thank you so much.

To Lee Joo-Hye, and Han Byung-Ho — I have tried to make contact with you and your publisher without success. I would like to acknowledge *The Crow King*; a book I adore, and a story I drew from to create my own. Thank you.

Lastly, I would like to thank you, my reader. Once again my book is in your hands, and without that connection my work would remain unheard. Thank you for picking up this novel, and for reading these acknowledgements all the way to the end, to find yourself here, alongside me. Writer and Reader. Together.

DISCLAIMER

For the sake of the story I have changed a few minor details, including, but not exclusively, the following:

I am aware the Petrikirche church does not have bells that ring out to sound the time, and that the main door to Pushkinskaya-10 would have remained unlocked in the 1990s so those without a place to sleep could take shelter — this being the inclusive nature of the Centre of Nonconformist Art during this time. I understand that the Academy of Art would be open on the weekend when the time of final shows are drawing close, and that 1994 is too early for the excavation and gentrification of the buildings in Pushkinskaya Street. I am also aware that the 'Dog-man' performance by Oleg Kulik occurred in November of 1994, not May.

*The song Arirang is a Korean traditional song, often considered the unofficial national anthem of Korea. It is estimated to be more than 600 years old and is included twice on the UNESCO Intangible Cultural Heritage list.